Acclaim fo

'Bridget Jones meets menopause . . . sharp, funny and real'
CECELIA AHERN

'Laugh-out-loud funny with a spiky endearing heroine who runs full tilt at the menopause with a baseball bat in her hands . . . Fast-paced and hilarious' CATHY KELLY

'One of my absolutely favourite authors' SHEILA O'FLANAGAN

'Funny, searingly honest, at times tender and poignant. World, meet Agatha, you're going to love her'
CARMEL HARRINGTON

'I laughed out loud reading this . . . witty, poignant and a complete page-turner' SINEAD MORIARTY

'I love Agatha Doyle. *I know* Agatha Doyle – or rather, I know lots of Agatha Doyles, except that none of them can match this Agatha for sassiness and honesty and humour and plain old likeability. Agatha is a marvellous creation – that voice is so compelling. So snappy, so real – and I'll miss her' ROISIN MEANEY

'Hilarious, perceptive, empathetic. Readers will utterly identify with and adore the superbly drawn Agatha'
PATRICIA SCANLAN

'What a book! Timely, laden with humour . . . it has everything – female friendship and empowerment, family relationships with all their fun and tragedy'
FIONNUALA KEARNEY

QUEEN BEE

Ciara Geraghty is a bestselling Irish novelist. She lives in Dublin and is the proud owner of one husband, two 'technically' grown-up children, a teenager and a handsome but unstable dog called Gary. When she is not writing in her garret, Ciara loves reading, swimming in the sea and playing her violin. She also co-hosts the podcast BookBirds.

Also by Ciara Geraghty

Saving Grace
Becoming Scarlett
Finding Mr Flood
Lifesaving for Beginners
Now That I've Found You
This is Now
Rules of the Road
Make Yourself at Home

CIARA GERAGHTY

Queen Bee

HarperCollins*Publishers*

HarperCollins*Publishers* Ltd
1 London Bridge Street,
London SE1 9GF
www.harpercollins.co.uk

HarperCollins*Publishers*
Macken House,
39/40 Mayor Street Upper,
Dublin 1
D01 C9W8

First published by HarperCollins*Publishers* 2023
This edition published by HarperCollins*Publishers* 2023
1

A catalogue record for this book is available from the British Library

ISBN: 978-0-00-849646-3 (PB b-format)

Set in Berling LT Std by Palimpsest Book Production Ltd, Falkirk, Stirlingshire

Printed and bound in the UK using 100% Renewable Electricity
by CPI Group (UK) Ltd

This story is for you, menopausal woman.

You are not alone; there's an army of us.

22 May, 4 a.m.

Symptoms: Insomnia, rage, resentment, night sweats, resentment

How's that for starters?
  What else?
  Oh yes, resentment. Did I mention that?

23 May, 4 a.m.

Symptoms: Insomnia, boiling (heat and rage)

Brain fog: Does my phone number start with 086 or 087?
Also: Resentment

Everyone else in this house is fast asleep. My sons (like, hadn't you two moved out?). My father, ensconced in the spare room, in the throes of his a-bit-late-in-the-fucking-day midlife crisis. And beside me in the bed, Luke has the gall to smile in his sleep. Like he's dreaming about the hairy bacon and cabbage he's cooking in the café tomorrow.
  He's also snoring.
  He has no idea how close he is to being smothered with a memory-foam pillow.

24 May, 4 a.m.

Symptoms: Insomnia, rage, resentment, hot flush, resentment
Also: Repetitive. Like, I'm supposed to be a writer and I can't
even come up with new words for my symptoms
Also: Frustration. How is this supposed to help? This stupid
symptoms diary? Riddle me that, Dr bloody Lennon

And no, I will NOT call you Susie. You're my GP, not my friend.

Besides, I already find it difficult to take you seriously with your child hands and persistent air of hope.

Fuck you 'Susie'.

25 May, 4 a.m.

Symptoms: Weary, sweaty
Also: Resentful. This is a complete waste of time, I could be
watching *First Dates*. Or *Gogglebox*. Or *Queer Eye*

I could even be writing. Proper writing, I mean. After all, I am contractually obliged to deliver the first draft of my sixteenth novel to my editor in ten weeks' time. Which of course I assured her was no problem during our last conversation:

ANNA: How's the book coming along, Agatha?
ME: So, so, so good, it's literally pouring out of me . . . like . . . I don't know . . . lava! Out of a volcano!
ANNA: Wow! I'd really like to rea . . .
ME: NO! I mean . . . no. Not yet. It's . . . not quite . . . you know . . .

2

ANNA: Is the deadline still working for you?
ME: YES! Definitely. I love the deadline. It's so . . . do-able
   . . . you know?
ANNA: I wish all my writers were as disciplined as you.
ME: Hahahahahahahaha . . .

Pause.

ME: Yeah. That would be . . . nice.
MAM: See? Wasn't I right, Agatha? Oh, what a tangled web
   we weave when first we practise to deceive . . .'

Technically, it's Sir Walter Scott who was right on that score.

Anyway, Anna's been an editor for decades, surely she should be less gullible when it comes to writers and the stories (read: blatant lies) they tell?

26 May, 9.05 a.m.

Symptoms: Impatience

All anyone really needs to know about the new GP – Dr-Lennon-call-me-Susie – is, when I ring the clinic, she answers the phone. And, like, she has people for that. Receptionists and whatnot. She has probably given everyone the day off and a pay rise.

That place has gone to the dogs since Dr Hardiman retired.

Although he didn't retire so much as die of old (read: ancient) age.

I miss Dr Hardiman. He was taciturn. Such an underrated characteristic. Consultations would take five minutes after which he'd shove a prescription for antibiotics across the desk, no matter what ailed you.

Until I caught a dose of menopause. Then he snapped his prescription pad shut with a snap.

DR HARDIMAN: You're just menopausal. It's part of the ageing process. You'll be fine.
ME: When?
DR HARDIMAN (shrugging): Hard to say.
ME: I've heard HRT might help?
DR HARDIMAN: With your family history, you'll most probably get breast cancer and die if you take HRT.

Thanks a bunch, Mam.

'Susie', on the other hand, thinks it's good to talk.

'Good morning, Hearty Healthcare, Susie speaking, how may I help you?'

That's another thing about 'Susie'. She sounds like she really, really wants to help.

ME: The writing down of menopausal symptoms isn't helping.
'SUSIE': Think of it more like a diary.
ME: Do I seem like the kind of woman who keeps a diary?

She wasn't sure what to say to that so she just sort of giggled. I could picture her smiling her angelic smile. The same one she probably uses when she pulls on her latex gloves. Her 'this won't hurt a bit' smile.

This is definitely not a diary. It's actually a *You Can Quit* notebook that Luke bought me a few years ago after the discovery of the nodule. How is anyone supposed to stop smoking when they discover that they might be riddled with cancer? Anyway, it was all benign and dandy in the end so quitting would have been a big waste of time.

'SUSIE': Give it a chance, Agatha, it's only been four days.
ME: Four days is a long time when you're menopausal.
'SUSIE': Give it two weeks.

Fuck sake.

27 May, 11 a.m.

Symptoms: Writer's block

Whenever any aspiring authors ask me for advice about writing, I always say, 'Get in the chair. Look the blank screen square in the eye. Sit there. Stay there. Something will occur.'

So there I was, at my desk in the attic. Usually, I find it a comfortable space to be. Even comforting in its way. I bought it with my second advance from the publishers. The first advance was a paltry affair and meant I had to keep doing my 'proper' job. Giving the Irish history tours around Glasnevin Cemetery hadn't been that bad, really.

In fact, if it hadn't been for the tourists, I might have even liked it.

The second advance was the jackpot.

Jackpot might be overstating it. It facilitated:

- One attic conversion;
- A long weekend in Naples with Luke;
- A telescope for Aidan (birds and stars);

5

- A camera for Colm (early-adaptor selfies in the main);
- Me, no longer having to remind tourists not to walk on the graves. Fine, I roared at them. But come on, who the hell walks on Luke Kelly's grave? Tourists, that's who.

So yeah, pretty life-changing in its way, I suppose. The attic office was my favourite bit. I'd never had a room of my own before. Me and Bart shared a room as kids. I got my nose into the 'spare room' for five minutes when I turned thirteen until Mam started taking in students. They were mostly Spanish, dispatched to Dublin to learn English. We referred to them as 'foreign' and taught them all the swear words we knew.

Then I lived in a grubby flatshare in East Wall with Carol for a few years.

Then me and Luke moved in together. And Carol. Since it didn't seem fair to leave her in that damp, shabby flat.

Then I signed a second contract with my publisher and got a room of my own.

Virginia Woolf was right. A woman really should have cash and a room of her own to write stories.

Although once I got the room of my own, I no longer had money.

But still, I wrote stories.

And now look at me, sitting here, staring at the walls. And they're staring right back at me, with what feels like . . . disappointment.

Which is way worse than anger or disapproval.

It's my own fault for covering the walls so liberally with my 'achievements'.

The covers of all my books, framed and hanging along the walls. Luke insisted. He said, if I was having a bad writing day, I could look at them for comfort and sustenance.

Which, up until now, worked a treat.

Then there's my noticeboard. Mam bought me that.

MAM: Didn't I have to? You were a disaster with your torn-out scraps of paper and whatnots scattered about the floor.

ME: They're flashcards and photographs and snippets of articles actually. And they were strategically and carefully arranged across the floor.

The noticeboard is full to bursting with ideas for the book I'm not writing. I distinctly remember feeling excited about Ellen and Clara, my sixteenth-century protagonists, accused of witchcraft. It was to be a treatise on feminism, religion, patriarchy and, of course, that old chestnut, misogyny, wrapped up in an edge-of-your-seat thriller ride of a story so that men felt okay about reading it too.

It was my favourite part of the process. The first stirring of the idea. Trying to reach for the strands. Convince it to land in my head, stay a while so I could write it down. It's a bit like twirling with your arms outstretched and your face turned towards the sky when you're a kid. It makes you so dizzy, you'll probably puke afterwards. But the sensation when you're doing it. Like everything in the world is yours for the taking. The blank page, giving me those 'come here to me' eyes and me up to my gullet in research, filling up the noticeboard with photographs of who might play my witches, Clara and Ellen, in the movie (Rachel Weisz for Clara and Jessie Buckley for Ellen). Florescent Post-it notes all over it with random words. 'Copenhagen', 'Bridget Cleary', 'Galleon', 'tsukimono-suji'.

12 p.m.

Nothing has occurred.

So far, I have:

1) Eaten half a packet of Raspberry Creams.
2) Made a pot of peppermint tea.
3) Poured the peppermint tea into the – possibly dead? – yucca plant in the corner. Because, you know, you have to keep plants watered, etc. Also, peppermint tea tastes vile.
4) Googled 'Is mint good for plants?'
5) Made a pot of Barry's Tea.
6) Opened the file 'Novel No. 16'.
7) Rearranged Mam's collection of Agatha Christie novels in order of cause of death: bludgeoning, drowning, poisoning, shooting, stabbing, strangulation, etc. It didn't take as long as I would have liked. Also: I seem to have absorbed some of Mam's encyclopaedic knowledge of all things Agatha Christie.
8) Finished the pot of Barry's Tea.
9) Rearranged my fifteen published novels in order of sales. It's just as I suspected. My star is most definitely in the descendent.
10) Googled 'Are the Nolan Sisters still alive?' (Answer: some.) Like, how did they manage to make it so big with those dance moves?

11) Paused for nostalgia: me attending Miss Lyle's Academy For Young Girls. It sounds so quaint now. And a tad groom-y now that I've written it down. Everybody was surprised that I could dance. I was thirteen when I started the class. A broad, tall and awkward thirteen-year-old with a killer glare. These traits are underappreciated but come in handy when you're dancing the paso doble.

12) Googled Miss Lyle to see if she's still alive.

13) Lit a candle for Miss Lyle, RIP.

14) Sentimentality must be catching because after I was done feeling sad about Miss Lyle, I got to thinking about Carol and our Thursday nights samba dancing in Wigwam before she was head-hunted by the Californians. I can't really blame Carol for leaving. Who could have said no to such gloriously sun-kissed, white-toothed creatures?

15) Envy. Such an ugly trait. Left a sour taste in my mouth. But Carol is an easy woman to be envious of. When we were young, she never had a long-term boyfriend. Or girlfriend. Just a series of short ones. Not the boyfriends or girlfriends. They were tall. Or sometimes average height. Always beautiful.

Short-lived is what I mean.

She always said she'd never get bogged down by boys or girls or babies.

When Aidan and Colm were born, I'm ashamed to admit

I felt a bit sorry for Carol. That she would never experience the ferocity of that final push. The unstoppable force of it. How savage it was. And how tiny the baby in my arms afterwards. How protective I felt about those strange creatures curled against my chest.

And it wasn't like I was one of those mothers who closed her eyes and inhaled her baby's head. But I must admit that sentimentality has a way of sneaking into a postpartum mind, cleverly camouflaged by the tide of hormones that flood your body.

I miss hormones.

And I miss Carol. Maybe I'll phone her.

16) Googled 'What time is it in LA?'

It's 4 a.m. there. She'll be asleep, the lucky cow. Even though Carol is a good six months older than me, I'm pretty sure she's not menopausal.

She'd tell me if she was.

The only person I've told is Dr Hardiman and he doesn't count because he's dead.

Of course, 'Susie' knows. Dr Hardiman must have scribbled it in my file and she had to go and read the thing.

She thinks she's so good at her job.

I hate the word 'menopause'. Something battered and forlorn about it, like a pulpy, dog-eared paperback in a charity shop.

It's like saying you have an ingrown toenail. People wince.

Carol's probably sound asleep, wrapped in a warm cocoon of oestrogen and progesterone with a subtle side of testosterone to keep the home fires burning.

Still, maybe it's best that I can't ring her. Because, however depressed I am, my life will seem even bleaker after Carol regales me with her LA tales. Including – but not limited to:

- Yoga at dawn;
- Breakfast meetings with fellow vice-presidents where nobody eats chocolate croissants;
- Lovers (many and varied);
- Another promotion;
- Plans for the weekend (to include convertibles, lobster bisque, fringe theatre, a thrilling and slightly dangerous altercation with an international spy or a jewel thief, a sunrise swim, a discovery of buried treasure).

Like, does she never have any laundry to do?

17) Got a fan letter!! Well, it was a tweet from a history professor who declared the last novel that I actually wrote, *Exile*, to be 'quite a satisfying read' and described my depiction of the soup kitchen as 'not inaccurate'.
    No doubt about it: Reviewers were kinder back when they had to lick the back of a stamp and traipse to a post box.
18) Lay on couch for a brief nap. Woke up an hour later, the witch trials book I'm reading stuck to one side of my face. Pretending not to be meno-pausal while not writing a historical fiction novel is exhausting.

19) Experienced acute spasm of anxiety. Like, I'm supposed to be writing a book, not pretending to write a book. Although it's just as bloody time-consuming. I told Luke not to worry about the roof job that needs doing on the café. 'I'll sort it when I get paid for the manuscript.' I even remember the tone I used. A light breeze of a tone. Like it was nothing. Me, writing a novel. Delivering it. Getting paid and using that advance to replace the café's leaky roof.

Simple.

I made it sound so simple.

And Luke, nodding. Like he thought it was simple too. Just a simple matter of me saying something and then going ahead and doing it.

The way things used to be.

20) Chain-smoked two cigarettes in the back garden to alleviate stress.

Dr-Lennon-call-me-Susie claims cigarettes do not alleviate stress.

I told her about Dr Hardiman who smoked a pack of Benson & Hedges right up until lunchtime on the day of his death.

'SUSIE': I'm pretty sure your stress is related to menopause. Have you considered HRT?

I tell her what Dr Hardiman said.

'SUSIE' (joyful): No, HRT has really improved, Agatha. Your chances of getting breast cancer are much reduced.

ME: So you're saying Dr Hardiman was full of shit.

'SUSIE' (hurt): Of course not!

ME (genuinely contrite because it felt like I'd kicked a puppy): Sorry.

'SUSIE': What I am saying is that the risk of breast cancer amongst people who take HRT is much lower than previously believed. You could do some research into it.

ME: I can't even research Ellen and Clara.

'SUSIE': Who are Ellen and Clara?

ME: Witches.

'SUSIE': Oh.

The two back-to-back cigarettes didn't alleviate as much stress as I'd hoped. I put it down to the rain and the sizeable hole in the golf umbrella I found in the side passage. A Woodie's DIY one. One of the sponsors Colm got for D.I.Guy.

Or at least they used to be one of D.I.Guy's sponsors. To think I joined Instagram just so I could support Colm's 'business'.

I suppose I should stop putting 'business' in inverted commas. Turns out people love that 'Pimp My Toolbox' type of vibe, which was basically Colm on social media in a pair of short-shorts, changing a plug in flattering lighting, with his red hair in a man bun.

One hundred and ten thousand people, to be exact.

Now, all that's left of D.I.Guy is a worn-out Woodie's umbrella with a gaping hole in the canopy and Colm back home in his old bedroom, burrowed under his duvet, trying to sticky-tape his heart back together.

It's for the best really. Not that Colm has figured that out yet. But there was something carefully manufactured about his ex. Like, if Instagram and Snapchat had a kid. Amelia would be it.

I'd repainted his bedroom as soon as Colm moved out. And replaced the bed with a futon that I had taken to sitting on when the sun got around to it.

I miss those afternoons.

The chief suspect in the case of the chewed umbrella observed me from the safety of a monstrosity of a kennel.

LuLaBelle.

Dad bought the kennel when I told him that his girlfriend's dog would, under no circumstances, be allowed into the house while we were minding her.

Since I'd already agreed to let Dad stay with us – just until the work is finished on his place – Dad could hardly argue. Especially given the not insignificant fact of Mam – his wife of billions of years – barely cold in her grave.

LUKE: It's been nearly a year, Agatha. And Leonora's really
    cheered your dad up with the dancing and . . .
ME (gritted teeth): It's been ten months.

Of course, LuLaBelle was asleep in the kennel's 'master bedroom' so my glare was wasted on that ingrate.

21) Returned to attic, damp and stinking of fags.
    Entertained a brief spell of resentment.

Luke promised to go dancing with me when Carol left.

ME: You better not be feeling sorry for me.

LUKE: I wouldn't dare.

ME: Also: You can't dance.

LUKE: I'll learn.

ME: It's not just jumping up and down on the spot. It's serious. It's samba.

LUKE: I'll take lessons.

ME: Now I'm worried you have a brain tumour.

But then the café roof started leaking and the clientele were dying off/moving into nursing homes at an alarming rate and being replaced by ever-hairier hipsters with their Afghan hounds and their oat milk flat whites. And Luke still hasn't found a replacement for Mrs Lynch. Not for the want of looking. But it's hard to find a waiter with her brand of post-war stoicism and world-weary resilience.

All of which means that Luke still hasn't gotten around to taking dance lessons.

Now I'm remembering the weeks leading up to our wedding. Me trying to teach him a rumba for our 'first dance'. My initial mistake was to dance in my bare feet so I could eyeball him. After he'd stood on every toe I owned, he begged me to consider a 'slow dance' instead. As if we were teenagers, dry humping to 'Careless fucking Whisper' at the Grove.

What happened to give and take? I went fishing with him that time, didn't I?

Fishing is even more tedious than it looks.

And Luke throws the fish back in so what is the actual point?

But I sat there, in that precarious little rowing boat, hardly complaining at all and lowering my voice every time Luke suggested we be quiet so we didn't scare off the fish and even eating the egg salad Luke had brought in a Tupperware box, notwithstanding the fact that post-lunch egg breath, especially in the confines of a precarious little rowing boat, is grounds for divorce.

In the end, I was so cold Luke had to give me his jumper. I put it on over my anorak, which put paid to my fishing as I couldn't hold the rod after that. I couldn't really move in any meaningful way. But I did warm up which was pleasant. Until I saw what I thought was a dolphin, breaching the surface of the water, and I stood up and the boat rocked and Luke . . . well he shouldn't have been sitting on the edge like that.

I even offered to go again. Like, that's not just love, that's fucking devotion. He should have been riddled with grati-tude. Instead he said no, he'd go on his own. I said I didn't mind, he said, no, he wouldn't feel good forcing me, I said I'd do it to make him happy (showing him how it's done there) and then he finally just said NO.

Loudly.

28 May, 4 a.m.

Symptoms: Rage

Luke woke me and the annoying thing is, he's still fast asleep. But talking. The only thing I can make out is 'curriculum vitae'. He's not loving the recruitment process. Telling people they're not good enough is not his strong suit. Probably why we've managed to hobble along together thus far . . .

The boys? Yes, yes, technically they're men but have you seen the state they leave the bathroom in? Have you? Anyway, they're asleep.

Dad? Asleep.

Resentful: everyone can sleep except me. Also, why don't men get the menopause? They fucking well deserve it way more than we do.

Boiling: both temperament and body temperature.

Insomnia: the bloody dog, barking. The fact that Leonora calls her spoiled cotton-puff of a dog LuLaBelle is really all anyone needs to know about my father's 'girlfriend'.

Person I'd most like to maim? Dr-Lennon-call-me-Susie. Like, has she even gone through puberty? She doesn't so much as say the word 'menopause' as declare it. Like she's introducing the band everybody has come to see after suffering through the support acts.

She's too young to be anxious about it, I suppose. She doesn't think it will ever happen to her.

The menopause will come for you too, 'Susie'. Mark me.

One day, your neat, pert breasts will slump, as if they've been beaten in a race they've been in training for all their lives.

They too will look like disappointment.

29 May, 4 a.m.

Symptoms: Relief

Colm got through yesterday!

His and Amelia's 'anniversary'.

I can't believe it's been two years since Amelia finally

convinced Colm to meet her IRL (In Real Life) after six months of stalking him online, attracted as she was by his legions of followers on Instagram.

Colm said it was love at first sight.

'Entrapment' is another way of putting it.

Anyway, Colm slept through the day. I'd have preferred him to make a bit of noise. Maybe tear up that framed photograph he insists on keeping. The one where Amelia is pretending not to notice she's being photographed and is gazing out a window, into the middle distance as if she's thinking interesting thoughts instead of ensuring her head is angled at the optimum position for the camera, her skin glowing in the lamplight, like a bowl of peaches and cream you can barely bring yourself to eat because it looks so perfect.

There was none of that. And it's a testament to the kind of restraint I did not know I had that the stupid photograph is intact.

Colm stayed in his room all day. The only reason I know he's still alive is because he eats the food Aidan leaves outside his bedroom door. Even though it's not just vegetarian. It's vegan. Aidan's gone even more codswallopy about the planet since he got back from the Dutch collective farm he worked on last summer.

Which would be all grand and dandy if I wasn't overcome by the fumes of fermenting chickpeas every time I walk through the front door. Which then serves to remind me that Aidan is in the kitchen instead of at a lecture on an obscure eighteenth-century poet in college. When I put it like that, maybe I don't blame him for dropping out. But to give up the free digs on campus he was supposed to move into last September. Some academic award he won.

Like, he doesn't even have to try.

LUKE: You're going to throw away all your opportunities, are you? The ones I never got?
AIDAN: You love working in the café.
LUKE: And you love English!
AIDAN: I still love English! Not going to university to study it doesn't change that.

Aidan's pale face, framed by his thick black hair that always needs to be cut, was heavy with the seriousness that plagues his too-delicate-for-this-world features.

Luke tried to understand.

He couldn't.

He tried not to be disappointed.

But he was.

I was foolish enough to ask Aidan about his 'plans' now that he's a drop-out, so I've no one but myself to blame when he regaled me with talk of bees and hives and growing organic vegetables. All of which is taking place in the back garden.

AIDAN: Just till I get my own place.

Brains to burn. That's what everyone always said about Aidan. But when he smiles like that, even I can't bring myself to say that the chances of him having his own place are as remote as me making the deadline for the book I'm not writing.

And now I'm to be evicted from the back garden to make room for a few fecking carrot sticks and a scrape of honey on my toast, is it? That garden is the only place left on the planet where I can smoke without being upbraided by 'concerned' (read: insufferable) passers-by.

Anyway, in spite of the vegan-centric nature of the meals Aidan leaves outside the door, Colm – a committed carnivore – wolfs the lot.

Handy that his appetite hasn't been affected by his heartache.

Is scepticism a symptom of menopause?

30 May, 4 a.m.

Symptoms: Insomnia, dehydration, annoyance

Dad just scared the living daylights out of me when I went down to get a glass of water. I switched the light on in the kitchen and there he was standing at the counter in his boxer shorts and T-shirt. He used to be a strict plaid pyjamas, belted dressing gown and shuffling slippers kind of man. I'm pretty sure he's dyeing his hair too. It's more of a steely grey now. He claims it's just the gel he's using.

What I hate about sharing the house with these people (fine, my family) is that I, as the matriarch, am not eligible for retirement. Or just plain quitting.

I want to resign.

Or I'll take redundancy. Voluntary or otherwise. I'm not fussy.

I don't understand those women who stress about the 'empty nest'. We're not fucking birds. There were times when I felt like pushing the boys out of the nest myself. The fact I didn't is what made me an adequate mother I thought?

I had it good there for a while. Before the menopause took up residence like a plague of rats gnawing their way through my foundations. When Colm was still in his flat with used-to-be-best-friend, Joe in North Strand. Busy with D.I.Guy. Delirious with love.

And Aidan, working on the farm outside Amsterdam. I knew he was happy because I barely heard from him. He sent photographs – furrows and hoes and mucky potatoes mostly – interspersed with occasional, cryptic WhatsApp messages.

Luke at the café, coming home at a reasonable hour with leftovers so I never had to think about dinner, and me in my attic space, working away on the next book. The fun part. The research. I had the house to myself back then, occasional visits from my father in those first couple of months after the funeral, shuffling up the path in his navy anorak with toast crumbs on one of his many shades-of-brown V-necked jumpers that Mam used to buy him in Guineys.

Now, I can't even go into my own kitchen in the middle of the bloody night without tripping up over Dad in his billowing boxers and one of Colm's D.I.Guy T-shirts. The microwave pinged when I opened the door and out came a bowl of goodie. It's probably the only thing about my father that remains unchanged, since he met 'That Woman'. Which is what my mother would have called Leonora, if she were still alive.

Goodie is like the sun. You shouldn't look directly at it; a lumpen paste of bread and milk and sugar. Sometimes

CIARA GERAGHTY

Dad mixes it up and sprinkles brown sugar over it. Or raisins if he's feeling 'European'.

He threw two teabags into his 'Keep Calm and Salsa' mug and filled it with water from the kettle. I asked him (pointed tone) what he was doing up in the middle of the night but he just responded (airy tone, like he hadn't even registered my pointed tone) that life is too short for sleeping, especially when you're seventy-five.

ME: You're seventy-nine.
DAD: Age is just a number.

He asked me not to divulge the number to Leonora.

This from the man who used to list 'napping' as one of his hobbies. And grocery shopping. He shuffled up and down the aisles behind Mam at the supermarket, eyeing up all the lovely things he wasn't allowed to have on account of his cholesterol/arthritis/blood sugar levels/heart/other random medical considerations.

A new brand of biscuit, say. Or even just a limited-edition biscuit from an old brand. Like when Jacob's put out the blackberry Mikados. Only briefly, mind. Probably for the best. I used to eat them straight out of the packet standing at the kitchen counter with my coat still on.

Where was I?

Oh yes, Dad. Napping and grocery shopping. Shambling after Mam onto the bus. She insisted they sit downstairs because of his knees, neither of which would be able for the stairs.

That's another thing that's come out of cold storage since he met That Woman. His ancient Škoda. He can barely see

22

over the steering wheel. I don't know when he got so small. He used to be able to carry me on one shoulder and Bart on the other. I remember watching an entire Patrick's Day parade like that. And I was always big and tall. Even when I was small.

Dad thinks he's James Bond now, with the leather driving gloves he found in the charity shop. He drives up and down the road. Practising, he says. He tosses the car keys at the hook on the wall when he comes in and says, 'Still got it' to no one in particular.

Mostly, the keys miss the hook and clatter onto the floor.

31 May, 4 a.m.

Symptoms: Nervous

There's a reason you're not supposed to look at your phone in the night. I only picked it up to write in it, since I stashed my *You Can Quit* notebook at the back of the filing cabinet in my office earlier. I have to be careful nobody finds it and discovers I'm not as sweetness and light as they had thought. Besides, even with my ancient one-fingered typing method, it's easier to write on the phone in the dark.

The downside is I can't help noticing the various notifications. Most of them from Samantha-Sorley-Agent-to-the-Stars.

I don't know what I was thinking, rejecting her call yesterday evening. Now I couldn't help noticing that she'd subsequently sent a text, a WhatsApp and an email. Oh, and left a voicemail. I'd say if I looked out the bedroom window, there'd be a homing-pigeon perched on a lamppost with a rolled-up note from Samantha strapped to its leg.

I rejected her call so hard, I nearly broke my finger. I assumed she was ringing to see how the novel I'm not writing is coming along.

Maybe the menopause can incite delusional thoughts?

I just googled it there and yes, it can.

Although you'd have to be seriously fucking delusional to think that you could ignore Samantha Sorley.

SAMANTHA (after I sent her three chapters of my first novel): You can write. That's for sure. But history is so . . . Would you think about writing romance?

ME: No.

SAMANTHA: That sounds like there might be wriggle room . . .

ME: There isn't.

MAM: Aren't you glad now, you stuck to your guns?

ME: It's your fault I was so insistent on writing historical fiction.

MAM: Don't take that tone with me.

ME: Easter Rising project in second year, remember? I got into trouble for taking your advice and writing about Elizabeth O'Farrell.

MAM: Imagine not knowing who Elizabeth Farrell was. After she risked her life, delivering the surrender to the so-called authorities in 1916!

ME: Anyway. What I'm saying is, you piqued my interest in history. You took me to Glasnevin Cemetery to see Elizabeth's grave, remember?

MAM: Well, somebody had to. I don't know why you

wouldn't let me go down to the school and give that so-called history teacher a piece of my mind.

ME: She might have been a terrible teacher and a misogynist but even Ms Reynolds didn't deserve that.

4.05 p.m.

Okay, got my big-girl pants on and opened WhatsApp.

SAMANTHA: Great news darling! I finally managed to persuade the organisers of the Flights of Fancy Festival to include you on one of their panels, 'It's all in the past' (historical fiction 'jokey' reference, obvs). You're welcome!

If I wasn't so menopausal, I might even be pleased. Us historical fiction writers are often overlooked at these literary festivals. At least, that's what I've said to Samantha over the years. In a bit of an Amelia voice, if I'm honest.

It'd be tricky to say no.

Next up is a voice memo in which Samantha mentions the novel in passing, employing an airy presumptive tone in relation to its imminent delivery, before going on to read aloud from the email she received from the festival organiser, Audrey Clarke. Turns out one of the other panellists is the self-aggrandising doseball, George Benjamin Hatch (GBH). Still, when he finally manages to stop bragging about being long-listed for the Booker (twenty years ago) and write, he's not that bad. So it's not like they're putting me at the kids' table.

MAM: You should go. Get yourself out of the house. Doing something productive.

ME: But what if I get brain fog and forget a word, right in the middle of the sentence I'm saying?

MAM: Just use another word.

ME: Yes, but which one?

MAM: I don't know, do I? You're the writer in the family, aren't you?

ME: I'm not sure.

1 June, 4 a.m.

Symptoms: Annoyed (you heard me, 'Susie')

No new messages on WhatsApp.
From anyone.

ME: You awake?

CAROL: What bit of Pacific Time Zone do you not get? Of course I'm awake, it's only dinner time here.

ME: What are you having for dinner?

CAROL: Beets with edamame and arugula.

ME: Now you're just making up words.

CAROL: 😵

ME: Luke's sleeptalking again.

CAROL: Is he doing that adorable thing where he lists the café's specials in his sleep?

ME: I'm afraid so.

CAROL: Hairy bacon and cabbage with parsley sauce?

ME: Yes. And Dubliners' Cockles and Mussels.

CAROL: James Connolly Coddle?

ME: Of course.

CAROL: And don't forget his favourite! Boxty in the henhouse

ME: I mean, it's just a slice of potato bread with a fried egg on top.

CAROL: Stop, my mouth's watering.

ME: Well, certainly better than a plate of beets, that's for sure.

CAROL: At least it's not other women's names he's listing.

ME: I think you're being a bit ambitious on Luke's behalf.

CAROL: It's the quiet ones you have to watch. Especially since you're not putting out.

ME: Shut your stupid foul face.

CAROL: Is there a chance you could be menopausal?

ME: Women can be angry without being menopausal, you know.

I don't know why I'm reluctant to tell her.

Maybe it's because I'm not officially menopausal since I'm still getting rogue periods? Although they're pathetic efforts. If it were a test, I'd write 'Must try harder' in red pen at the top of the page.

My menopause feels like an exercise in failure whereas Carol, being a straight A kind of person, is acing life. Despite being six months older than me.

CAROL: I gotta go.

ME: Is it because I'm a moany bitch?

CAROL: I'm meeting someone . . .

ME: Say more words.

CAROL: Don't want to jinx it . . . later . . . love you.

ME: You'll be telling me to have a nice day next.

CAROL: I know, you love me too.
ME: Fuck you.
CAROL: Get some sleep xxx

Telling an insomniac to get some sleep is unhelpful at best.

And now, as well as not being able to go to sleep, I'm hungry too, thinking about the bloody boxty in the henhouse.

I blow on Luke's face and he stops talking and turns on his side.

He was all, 'You should do it' when I told him about the invitation to the festival yesterday. But he didn't ask me for details, like what other writers had been invited, if I was going to be paid (I think they give you a voucher for a cup of coffee and a fig roll) or if I'd like him to tag along. (No, of course I don't want him there but it would be nice to know that he was willing to accompany me.)

ME: Do you want to come with me?
LUKE: You wouldn't want me there.
ME: How do you know?
LUKE: Because the first time I offered to come with you to one of those things, you said you'd rather stab yourself in the eye with a fork than have me gawk up at you from the audience while you're being all full-of-shit-writerly.
ME: It wouldn't hurt you to ask all the same.

His phone rang then. He inspected the screen, then declined the call. I didn't even know he was capable of such a Machiavellian move.

ME: What the actual?
LUKE: It's Damien again.
ME: It's not like you to dodge calls. Even ones from your
    evil twin.

If you ask Damien what he does for a living, he'll say 'businessman'. And it's true that he has an office in the financial
district like every self-respecting 'businessman' should. But
as to what he does there, I have no idea. I know that he
plays golf and has meetings in restaurants you might read
about in a broadsheet's weekend magazine.

Whatever he does, he must be okay at it because he looks
loaded. And he smells loaded too. You know, that leather
and aniseed type of smell.

He never has pastry dough under his nails and the beds
are pink and shiny.

Some women love that shit. I find it hard to trust a man
with nails that clean.

LUKE: He keeps ringing and offering unsolicited financial
    advice.
ME: He's a mansplainer. That's what they do.
LUKE: Telling me I need to hike my prices.
ME: Can you imagine the auld ones if you dared? I was
    going to say they'd stage a sit-in but that's basically what
    they do on the daily.

He's been so distracted lately with the bloody café, training
in the new waiter. Fernando Something. From . . . I can't
remember . . . did he say Bolivia?

Family businesses are the actual pits. Because of course it's not just about the money, is it? There's all the bloody baggage that goes along with it, ancient family history and whatnot. Not to mention the leaky roof and the dry rot and the fast-disappearing (read: dying) clientele that think Luke is the best thing since batch bread. None of your sourdough for that lot.

Then there's the various vegan-deli-yoga-wholefood types moving into the area. What are they going to do with a plate of rashers and eggs on a slice of white bread fried in real, actual, full-fat butter?

2 June, 4 a.m.

Symptoms: Angry

I can report that the nib of my pen just ripped through this page.

And don't bother looking at me with those pale, Jesus-loves-you eyes, Dr-Lennon-call-me-Susie.

Enough is enough.

I want to kill LuLaBelle.

And I mean proper, limp, lifeless, non-breathing, stench of decay, KILL.

Dr-Lennon-call-me-Susie wondered if I might try some anger management therapy. She said it in a quasi-casual tone without quite looking at me. I said, I'm not angry, I'm menopausal and also a woman who has been persuaded by my born-again father to allow his girlfriend's spoiled brat of a dog to live in my back garden while Leonora is in the hospital getting replacement hips, all the better to salsa dance with my father in Havana next month.

Not even making this shit up.

I mean, there's barely enough room for all the bloody humans in this house, let alone an overexcited mutt with a bad eighties home perm and a penchant for howling at the moon and barking at the DPD man who arrives nearly on the daily since Colm has been filling the void in his world with consumerism. Still, it's a way for me to know that my son is still alive so I suppose I have capitalism to thank for that.

People say you're supposed to feel better if you write things down. I do not feel better. And now, if I do kill Leonora's labrapoodle or -doodle or whatever the hell it is, there is physical evidence to support the case for the prosecution in the form of this stupid menopausal symptoms record.

If there was something wrong with the dog, I'd be more understanding of her incessant barking. But she lives in a bloody dog-mansion. She gets three square meals a day plus all the titbits Aidan and Dad sneak out to her even though Leonora was very particular about LuLaBelle not eating between meals. Apparently her maternal grandfather was diabetic.

LuLaBelle's bark is as sharp as a broken rib. Even Luke admitted the other day that the dog was a little 'highly strung'. And he used to donate fifty per cent of his paper round money to Dogs' Trust when he was a kid.

Dad – who by the way told me and Bart that we couldn't have a dog when we were kids because he was allergic – lets LuLaBelle lick him all over his face when he goes out to the garden to check on her. He says that LuLaBelle is missing Leonora. Maybe if I allowed her inside . . . I crippled him with a glare the last time he suggested it, and he slunk away. He knew he was on shaky ground.

Two weeks, tops. That's how long Dad was supposed to stay with us while his house got a lick of paint. Then the decorator, Frank-with-a-C – although he can fuck right off if he thinks I'm spelling it like that, he's not even French, he's from Cabinteely – told Dad about the rising damp which would necessitate the stripping and treating of walls and floors. But look at those kitchen presses, swollen with humidity. They'd have to go, might as well get a skip. Now the skip is stuffed to the gills, there's a brand-new kitchen getting shipped from Dusseldorf and, while he was waiting for it to arrive, Dad decided he might as well go ahead and do a total overhaul of his bedroom, to include an ensuite wet room, with one of those massive round shower heads that you get in fancy hotels.

This from a man who had the same cabbage rose wallpaper in his bedroom for the entire FIFTY-THREE years of his marriage.

LuLaBelle is still barking and Luke is still asleep, now facing away from me in response to me pushing my big toe into the soft folds of his belly. He'll claim he didn't hear the barking when I ring him at the café later. And then he'll say he's too busy to listen to the recording on my phone. And okay, the barks are a bit muffled but they're still audible if you are in a quiet place and you focus. Luke will say he's not in a quiet place. He's in the café.

ME: I'm not in a quiet place either, you know. This house is crawling with people.
LUKE: Three people.

ME: And a dog.

LUKE: She's in the back garden.

ME: Barking.

LUKE: I'm sorry, Agatha, but I'm going to have to . . .

ME: Go. I know.

LUKE: Talk later?

ME: How much later?

LUKE: I have to wait for a delivery tonight, I'm not sure what time I'll be . . .

ME (curt): Fine.

LUKE: Come on, Agatha. You know I'm trying to focus on my customers while I still have them.

ME (less curt): Fine.

And then he sighed like he was sad or exhausted or a touch of both and said he needed to go and peel the carrots for the stew because it was Monday which is Irish stew day at The Full Shilling.

And then he wonders why the café is doing so badly.

3 June, 4 a.m.

Symptoms: Insomnia

Tonight, the insomnia is served with a side of hot, wet flush necessitating a change of T-shirt and knickers. The heat rushes up my body and I am reminded of that film back in the seventies, *The Towering Inferno*. The sheets are stained with my sweat in a rough outline of my body like a domestic-noir crime scene. Luke is on his back, snoring his head off, and part of me wants to beat him to death with my book.

MAM: Oh, *Endless Night*. That was Agatha Christie's favourite of her novels. Did you know that?

Why couldn't that pesky novelist have been called something else? Phoebe Christie? Or even Julia Christie? I could have put up with Julia.

Now that I'm awake, I notice that LuLaBelle is NOT barking which of course means I have to get up and look out the window to make sure she hasn't been . . . I don't know . . . frightened to death by her own shadow or something.

I had to apologise to the next-door neighbour about the barking last night. Melissa was in her front garden, dead-heading a rose bush, wearing an apron over navy 'slacks' and a pale grey twinset.

Like, she's younger than me!

She swung her head in my direction and smiled, her long, brown ponytail swinging side to side in the brisk breeze, like LuLaBelle's tail.

MELISSA (putting the safety catch on a pair of secateurs): Don't give it another thought, Agatha, it's quite all right and . . .

ME: It's not my fault. Dad got Luke on side about the stupid dog before I knew anything about it and they all ganged up on me and . . .

MELISSA: LuLaBelle, isn't it? What a sweetheart she is . . . but . . . I wonder . . . and do excuse me if I'm overstepping the mark here . . . but . . . I wonder if she likes being in the kennel? I just . . . I'm no expert of course but . . . I just . . . I wasn't sure. . .?

Why the hell wouldn't she like her kennel? It has three 'rooms' for fuck sake. Although one is more of a 'lean-to' made of glass which Leonora calls the 'conservatory' without the remotest trace of irony. She probably thinks a housing crisis is when the view of the Atlantic from your holiday house in west Cork becomes compromised by a tree.

I told Melissa she's welcome to look after the dog herself since she's so concerned. Her entire face wobbled and I was terrified she might cry. Wailing women are such a cliché. Also tedious. She shook her head and breathed deeply, like she was meditating – she's just the type – and bit her lip, which she probably thinks makes her look all damsel-in-distress but in fact just accentuates her teeth which are really long, lending her a sort of tragic Bugs Bunny air. And then she went into a long-winded spiel about 'poor Dermot' being allergic to dogs' fur and how he would come up in welts or boils or blisters or something equally unsightly, if he so much as glanced at one.

Handy.

Melissa – always interested in the fact that I am a 'writer' – wants to know if I've nearly finished the novel about the sixteenth-century witches.

MELISSA: Ellen and Clara, isn't it?
ME: Hmmm.
MELISSA: I cannot WAIT to read it, I loved *Bewitched* when I was a kid.
ME: It's not that kind of witch book.
MELISSA: It'll be brilliant.
ME: Hmmm.
MELISSA: When did you say you'll be finished?

ME: I didn't say.

MELISSA: It must be difficult, the first of your book launches without your dear mother. She never missed one. Even that time the launch was on the same day she was supposed to be going on her annual trip to Lourdes, remember?

ME: She forfeited her deposit.

MELISSA: One hundred and fifty pounds.

ME: She never got over it.

MELISSA: Well, she'll be there in spirit.

I didn't bother telling Melissa the disappointing news about the 'after-life'. Or about the book launch which won't be happening since a book is generally required at these events.

I could see the extent of my stagnation then, like a wide, endless plain with nothing but rocks and dust and scorched earth to show for itself.

Mostly, I managed to avoid thinking about it. This was not one of those times. My breath caught in my chest.

MELISSA: Are you all right, Agatha? You've gone very pale.

ME (clutching at straws): I'm going to be on a panel. 'It's all in the past'. Flights of Fancy. Literary festival.

MELISSA: Oh how exciting! I don't know how you do it. Agatha, I really don't.

ME: Neither do I.

Back in the house, I climbed the narrow staircase to my office and sent Samantha an email, telling her I would attend the Flights of Fancy Festival.

She emailed me back immediately, saying she'd already

accepted on my behalf since she'd taken my silence as consent.

It didn't make me feel good, as such. Having something planned. Something constructive to do with my time that was work-related.

But it did make me feel less bad.

Which I suppose is better than nothing.

5.30 a.m.

Symptoms: Doom

Insomniacs should not be allowed near their phones in the early hours of morning. I've just read a headline in *The Journal* about the high rate of suicide amongst men in their early twenties and, now, here I am in a lather of sweat and anxiety, worrying about Colm.

To distract myself, I came up with the brilliant idea of googling suicide in general, and have now discovered that women between the ages of forty-five to fifty-four are particularly susceptible. Fucking menopause. It's the actual death of some of us.

7.30 a.m.

I waited until the more socially acceptable hour of 7 a.m. before I bustled into Colm's room, all bonhomie and good cheer, armed with a laundry basket. Colm looks much too big for his old single bed, his long, narrow feet hanging over the end of the divan. A stale smell in the room. Not bad exactly. Just a bit . . . defeated.

I stood there until I caught the slight rise and fall of the duvet covering him. My son is defeated but not dead.

Everyone tells him he looks like me, which he does not take as a compliment. He blames me for his hair colour and it's true it is a pretty glaring shade of red and there is a shocking amount of it, spread across his Mr Happy pillowcase.

He used to love the Mister Men books when he was a kid. I cleared my throat.

ME: Good morning!
COLM (sitting bolt upright in bed like someone's just stabbed him with adrenalin): What the actual fuck?
ME: Don't use that foul language in front of your mother.
COLM: Why are you pretending to be cheerful?
ME: Who says I'm pretending?

(I was, it was exhausting, especially at that hour.)

COLM: What do you want?
ME (nodding at my basket): I'm . . . you know . . . collecting laundry.
COLM (suspicious): Why?
ME: How are you feeling?
COLM: What? Fine. Tired.
ME: Tired because it's early? Or tired in general?
COLM: Can you go now?
ME: Answer me.
COLM: Tired because it's 7 a.m.
ME: Okay, fine, that's . . . Oh, and one more thing. Are you suicidal?
COLM: Jesus, Mum.
ME: I'm only asking.

COLM: Why?
ME: Because I'm your mother.
COLM: Well, I'm not. Okay?
ME: You sure?
COLM: Yes. Can I go back to sleep now?
ME: I think you should get some fresh air.
COLM: Now?
ME: Well, no, but in a bit. Later.
COLM: Will you leave if I say yes?
ME: Yes.
COLM: Yes.

That went better than expected.

4 June, 4 a.m.

Symptoms: Weirdly bloated fingers

I can't shift my wedding ring. It's like the patriarchy, fucking with me.

The only good thing about keeping this . . . I'm going to call it a record . . . is that when I tell Anna I'm writing, it's not actually a lie.

The downside is that, in spite of the brain fog, I'm unable to forget about the panel event at the Flights of Fancy Festival, because I wrote it down.

Still, maybe Mam was right. A change is as good as a rest. One of her mantras. Even though she hated change and rarely rested.

In other news, the latest edition of that dance magazine he's subscribed to *Bamboleo* is out!! I know this because

Dad asked me to drive him to his house so he could check the post and see if his copy had arrived.

ME: Why can't you drive yourself?
DAD: My licence is out of date.
ME: How out of date?
DAD: Don't worry, I'm applying for a new one.
ME: How out of date?
DAD: A year or so.
ME: . . .
DAD: Two years maybe.
ME: . . .
DAD: Okay fine, four years. Four years out of date.

Whenever I pull up outside my parents' house, there's still a moment when I expect Mam to appear, reefing back the porch door and glaring at me with her hands on her hips.

'Well?'

Her greeting.

Even her hugs were ferocious. A brief but savage squeeze that would leave you reeling.

Dad was at pains to demonstrate the enhanced security and insulation the new front door offers. He described the colour as 'teal' with not a trace of self-consciousness. 'Frank with a c' said it would be 'stunning' against the red-brick period detail of the terrace. The annoying thing is that the door does look pretty okay.

Mam used to have to ram the old wooden one with her shoulder to get inside. Dad held the door open and said, 'After you, m'lady'. Already I could smell the fresh paint and see the furniture in the sitting room draped in a shroud of sheets, everything the same but unfamiliar at the same time. Like the time I was five, banging on the window to be let in, jumping up and down on the spot and cupping my hands between my legs. I always left it to the last minute to go. And Mrs Roche from two doors up answering our front door as if she lived there. That same sensation as now. Everything familiar yet utterly changed. And the warm wet trickling between my fingers and Mrs Roche marching me inside and telling me that I was much too big to be wetting myself and what would my poor mother say when she came back from the hospital with my new baby brother? Two weeks it took Mam. To come back. And when she did, the whites of her eyes were still yellow with jaundice and Bart never let up with the screeching and Mrs Roche giving me the side of her eye whenever I walked past her house, just because I told her that the semolina she force-fed me for 'dessert' was lumpy.

Which it was.

Dad took my elbow and steered me around the house, pointing out the fresh paintwork – 'dove' white – the newly laid wooden floors and the brand-new kitchen, all soft-close drawers and cupboards in a 'mother-of-pearl grey' with a granite worktop and black and white chequered tiles on the floor, like a crossword grid waiting to be filled in by the 'before' version of my father.

No furniture in the bedrooms yet apart from the camp-bed Dad had slept on when we moved their double bed into the sitting room for those last six months.

MAM: Well? What did you want me to do? Die in an overheated hospital? God knows what diseases I'd have picked up in there.

I opened the back door to the garden where Frank-with-a-c's influence ends abruptly. The grass is waist-high and the few pots and boxes along the path to the clothesline are filled with the withered remains of the annuals that Mam planted two springs ago.

DAD: Aidan's going to sort the garden out. He said the soil is perfect for spuds.

Without the net curtains, the sun spilled into the sitting room which looked so spacious, now that the bed and the table, cluttered with medicine bottles and syringes and sponges and grapes and flowers, were gone.

Why do people bring grapes to dying people? The seedless ones, maybe. But the ones with the pips? As if they think that choking to death is a better look than being eaten alive from the inside out by cancer.

The bareness of the room accentuated the sash windows, the high ceiling with the ornate cornice, the wrought-iron fireplace with the tiled hearth. All the things that are described as 'features' in some estate-agency-blurb to justify the inflated price.

I sounded just like my mother. Maybe it wasn't a bad thing, since there wasn't a trace of her left in her own house. It was like she had never lived there. Never died there.

DAD: Do you . . . think your mother would have liked it?
ME: She would have said there wasn't a thing wrong with the old kitchen.
DAD: She would have said I'd more money than sense.

ME: She would have said a fool and his money are soon parted.
DAD: Daylight robbery, she would have called it.

The truth is, it would never have happened if she'd lived. She would have presented a case for the defence of the old guard. And the case would have been solid. Watertight. Unimpeachable.

The twin-tub had escaped the coup since the skip was too full to accommodate it but its days were numbered all the same. It stood in the middle of the tiny back kitchen, disconnected and useless. It must have been fifty years old. Mam inherited it from her mother as far as I remember. The noise it used to make, shuddering and shaking through the spin cycle. Gone was the corkboard that hung above the machine with an unlikely collection of flyers, bin collection times, bus timetables, the card Dad got from work when he retired, hospital appointments, a photograph of me and Bart dressed up in the pumpkin costumes Mam made for us one Halloween, a novena to St Anthony, her go-to for personal favours and lost items in return for which she would pledge a stipend. She owed him three euros at the end and made me promise to pay him.

MAM: Did you pay him?
ME: Of course I did.

I will. I just haven't gotten around to it yet.

Sticking out from underneath the twin-tub, on a greasy, wrinkled page, her handwritten instructions for the strange and unpredictable workings of the machine, with many cautionary capitals and ominous exclamation marks.

On top of the tub, the hose, coiled and slumped with masking tape wrapped around a section of it. Mam would put a bucket under that section. Just in case.

DAD: You ready? I'm due at Susie's to get my yellow fever jab.
ME: Susie?
DAD: I've switched to your GP. My one's a drug-pushing ageist.
ME: What the hell is yellow fever?
DAD: It's for Cuba. Don't worry, it only kills a small proportion of people and the vaccine is over eighty per cent effective.

I folded Mam's page of washing instructions and shoved it in the pocket of my jeans. The front door closed without as much as a whimper.

DAD: So? What do you think? Tell me the truth now.

The truth is, it would never have dawned on Dad to change so much as a lightbulb when Mam was alive.

The truth is, Mam would have loved it.

5 June, 4 a.m.

Symptoms: Too distracted to note

Aidan has been busy making a beehive to go in the back garden. I asked him if he needed a permit or anything but he just did that annoying Luke-esque smile and nodded and said, 'Everything's under control.'

ME: What about the neighbours? 'Poor Dermot' is probably
    anaphylactic. It'd be just like him.
AIDAN: I've spoken to him. And the rest of the neighbours.
    They're all G.
ME: G as in a-ghast?
AIDAN: G as in good.
ME: Not great then? Just good?

He's using Mam and Dad's old bedside lockers to build the hive. Apparently, Dad was going to throw them out other-wise. Because they don't match the sleigh bed he's ordered from Ikea.

Dad whipped out his phone to show Aidan pictures of his new bed, which is a monstrosity in mahogany. Dad said it was good and sturdy and wouldn't creak no matter what you were at.

In my head, I'm singing, 'The Tide Is High', a habit that has persisted from my youth when distraction is required.

Mam never threw anything out. Not even that warped pot she boiled the ham in every Christmas, with the slivers of aluminium floating on the top of the water.

I can't believe none of us got food poisoning.

MAM: There was nothing wrong with that pot!

Aidan asked me for my wedding veil. He wants to wear it to protect his head when he goes foraging for a swarm of bees.

ME: That sounds dangerous.
AIDAN: The veil will protect me.

Like, do I look like the kind of woman who wore a wedding veil?

I wore a suit on my wedding day. I still have it. A fitted jacket in purple velvet and matching drainpipe trousers. Beneath the jacket, a pale green halterneck, silk and backless. No bra. My nipples were like nails, with the sharp wind whistling through that draughty church. Luke got the taxi driver to stop at our house on the way to the reception in the café. He said he needed to talk to me urgently but it would only take five minutes. I told him it was a little previous to be thinking about an annulment.

In the hallway. Luke got all Hollywood and swept everything off the hall table before he arranged me across it. Mostly wedding cards but also a lamp, which made quite the thrilling crash against the floor tiles. It had been a housewarming gift from a friend of Luke's whose abundance of cash bore little relation to taste.

Luke's boxer shorts, bunched around his ankles along with his new suit trousers. His pink socks with the red lovehearts, pulled taut up his hairy shins. The sharp point of his tan shoes. His hands in my hair and his breath along my neck. I had a red mark across the small of my back from the edge of the table. The phone, which Luke had pitched off the table too, rang and rang.

Like, who the hell rings anyone on their wedding day?

Luke was right.

It did only take five minutes.

I gave Aidan the mantilla I'd unearthed when I cleared out Mam's stuff. It smelled like charity shop. Mam loved a browse in a charity shop. I also found a wide-brimmed straw hat with plastic fruit glued onto the brim. Aidan tried it on, doing his best to get all of his thick, black hair inside. I arranged the mantilla over the hat, pushed the ends of it down the neck of his T-shirt. I'd forgotten how ticklish he is.

Even Colm came out of his room to see what the commotion was. We all pretended not to notice he'd been crying. There was a cardboard box in the porch this morning. Maybe Joe dropped it off? Colm left in a hurry in the end. No time to pack when you find your girlfriend and your flatmate in flagrante on the couch in the middle of the afternoon and not even the excuse of several bottles of wine to shield Joe and Amelia from full responsibility.

No extenuating circumstances. A simple serving of betrayal with a side dish of contempt. Hard to stomach. I used my bossiest voice and told Colm to come down here this instant and help his brother carry the beehives (read: remodelled bedside lockers) out to the garden.

ME (pseudo-casual): You could record it for your Insta followers. People love bees and their carry-on.
AIDAN: They're essential for biodiversity.
ME: I literally just said that.
COLM: I'm not dressed.
ME: Get dressed.
COLM: I'm too tired.
ME: You're twenty-three, you haven't earned the right to be tired.

Colm walked back into his room like he hadn't heard me, which is unlikely since my voice carries quite the way.

AIDAN: Did Granny have mantillas in any other colours? I think black might be a bit intimidating for the bees.

If Aidan wasn't the image of Luke, I could convince myself we adopted him.

6 June, 4 a.m.

Symptoms: Night sweat, also a curious ringing inside my left ear

I googled 'curious ringing inside left ear' along with menopause and yes, of course, it was a menopause-related thing called tinnitus which I've heard of before.

And fucking no. No pun was intended there.

This is what it must be like to be a dog. Or a teenager. Both species can hear noises at a much higher pitch than the rest of us. I have no idea how I know that. It's not even something that will come in handy in a table quiz scenario.

I do love a table quiz. Or any kind of quiz. So long as I win. Which I nearly always do. Probably because of my intimate relationship with Google. But even before that.

I love saying that out loud in front of my offspring. Their faces. Before the internet? They can't conceive of such a phenomenon.

The good thing about the menopause is how distracted I can get. Distraction is good. Distraction is my friend, which is handy since my actual friend has deserted me.

Note to self: acquire more friends.

And now for a brief but intense bout of wallowing: acquiring friends is not as easy as some people (read: Luke, Carol, Colm (old version), Dad (new version)) make it look.

Case in point: schoolyard. I'm ten years old and I break Donal Kelleher's leg in a game of dodgeball in the school hall.

Nobody remembers that it was the winning shot. Just me and Donal left on the court. It was nearly always the two of us left at the end. He was an astute dodger, being small and wiry. I had brute force and a winning streak on my side.

Donal was tired by then. He tossed the ball but it was a flimsy shot and all I had to do was a slight sidestep and it dribbled past my leg. He was maybe ten feet away when I picked up the ball, gripped it between my sweaty hands.

He started to run.

Ha!

Too late!

I swung my arm back, aimed at one of his skinny legs and hurled the ball. It slammed against his shin bone.

Which is the actual aim of the game. It's how you win. Anything below the knee is fair game.

But nobody clapped when I did my usual victory lap of the hall, holding the ball aloft and cheering. It was only when the school nurse rushed in and shouted at the PE teacher to call an ambulance that I stopped running and noticed that Donal was on the floor, clutching his leg and roaring.

Seriously, how brittle must that shin bone have been?

The principal called Mam and hauled the pair of us up to his office.

PRINCIPAL: Agatha is too rough.
MAM: She's strong.
PRINCIPAL: She broke Donal's leg.
MAM: Agatha will make him a get well soon card.
PRINCIPAL: She'll have to apologise.
MAM (standing up): It was an accident.

Outside the school gates, I tearfully declared that nobody would want to play with me any more (which turned out to be pretty prophetic). Mam just said, 'Well, that's their lookout,' and marched me up the road. She stopped at the newsagent and bought me a *Mandy* comic and a choc ice and we never spoke about it again.

7 June, 3 p.m.

Symptoms: Brain fog

Audrey from the Flights of Fancy Festival just rang. Like, an actual phone call. Who the hell even does that any more? You text/WhatsApp/email to say that you are thinking of phoning and wondering when might be a suitable time? A phone call out of the blue from someone who is not in your Contacts is up there with being chloroformed and dragged into the back of a Hiace van.

It is a measure of how shocked I was that I answered the phone and there she was, giving it all, 'Hiiiiiii daarrlliiiing, how ARE you? It's been WAAAAAYYY too long.'

ME: Who is this?
AUDREY from the festival: Why, it's me, darling.

ME: . . .
AUDREY FROM THE FESTIVAL: Audrey?

It's not until she mentions George Benjamin Hatch that my brain sort of jolts awake and shrieks 'AUDREY CLARKE' at me, so loudly I nearly drop the phone.

Audrey Clarke. I've known her for years. Every writer in Ireland knows her. I've met her a hundred times. More. She's involved in every single vaguely-writery event that happens on this island. She organises, promotes, introduces, MCs, blogs, reviews, podcasts . . . I'm exhausted even writing that list. I think I might have shouted 'AUDREY!!!' down the phone, out loud, because there's a bit of a pregnant pause then and, the next time she speaks, her voice has been taken down a notch and she says, 'Are you okay, Agatha?' The shrill edge of her tone has been replaced with a kindly concern and, for a moment, I think I will weep.

Dad would say, 'Jesus H Christ.' I don't know what the H stands for.

MAM: Pull yourself together, quick smart, girleen.

Her accent got very Kerry when she feared an outbreak of emotion. She was also a stickler for people pulling themselves together, as quick as they can if not quicker.

ME: I'm fine, I was . . . just preventing a sneeze.
AUDREY FROM THE FESTIVAL (with great gravitas):
    You should never prevent a sneeze.
ME: What were you saying about George?

AUDREY FROM THE FESTIVAL: Oh, yes, just, you know, we're lucky to get him, before he heads off on tour. He'll really add some gravitas.

ME: . . .

AUDREY: As will you. Of course. But George will draw the male readers.

ME: Men don't tend to come to these events.

AUDREY FROM THE FESTIVAL: Maybe they will now that George has agreed to participate.

I kept saying her name – Audrey – after everything I said. I was terrified of blanking again. But now I'm thinking about the panel discussion. What if I blanked there? I've never been nervous about those events. Until I became the menopausal equivalent of a motorway pile-up.

3.30 p.m.

I rang Dr-Lennon-call-me-Susie.

ME: I'm worried about brain fog.

'SUSIE': Oh yes, yes, brain fog. It's very real.

ME: That's the bit I know. What I don't know is what I'm going to do about it?

'SUSIE': Well, if you're still worried about taking HRT . . .

ME: I inherited my mother's fear and loathing of medication, along with her out-y bellybutton and square fingernails.

'SUSIE': You could try writing things down.

ME: I'm already doing that.

'SUSIE': Yes, but I mean, other things. Like a list of things. Things you don't want to forget.

ME: I don't want to forget anything.

4 p.m.

Blessed distraction arrived in the form of a WhatsApp message from Carol, which was weird because she would have started work by now and she didn't usually take breaks or deviate from the task(s) at hand.

Before I opened it, I tried to guess at its contents.

Scenario 1: Carol had had a really good morning in work. Another promotion, that'd be just like her.

OR:

Scenario 2: She'd been fired and was halfway down a bottle of Californian chardonnay or pinot grigio or both.

That seemed less likely.

The message was long. Which was another oddity. Carol's messages were curt, in the main. To the point, she called them. She's a fan of the bullet point. This WhatsApp was lengthy with full sentences and punctuation and even – horrors – the emoji with the lovehearts for eyes.

It took me ages to read it.

The thing was riddled with happiness.

The cause?

That timeless classic:

She's in love.

There's a lot of detail. Like, what happened to her not wanting to jinx it?

ME (doing best to dredge up some enthusiasm): What's her name?

CAROL: Crystal Kramer.

ME: Her real name, I mean.

CAROL: Funny.

Like, how LA can one woman sound?

While Carol did her best with nonchalance, it was clear to me how much she liked Crystal.

Crystal clear.

ME: Is she a software engineer too?
CAROL: Yes! We have so much in common! And I know, I know, dating someone in work is a hard no for me usually, but it's also sort of hot.
ME: Like, sneaking into the stationery cupboard between meetings kind of hot?
CAROL: Call for you, it's 1993, looking for paperclips and a stapler.

Crystal is also a vice-president although Carol didn't specify whether she's a deputy/corporate/senior one so maybe she's just a lowly vice-president which is probably the equivalent here of an office clerk.

CAROL: I think you'll like her. A lot.

Like, has Carol forgotten who I am? I don't like anyone a lot. Not even people I purport to love.

8 June, 4 a.m.
Symptoms: Nostalgia

List of things I do not want to forget:

1) My secret stash of confectionery (jelly snakes

and fizzy cola bottles in the main) is in the second drawer of the tallboy in the hall, buried underneath woolly hats with their bobbles long gone, fraying scarves and lonely gloves, not a pair between the lot of them. So, while it's a pretty sad place to end up if you're accessories, it's safe as houses when it comes to sweets.

I feel like the first item on this list should be more meaningful.

And now I can't think of anything else to put on the list. If I was a 'good' mother and wife, I'd probably put the birthdays of my children and my wedding anniversary on the list.

I don't think there's any chance of forgetting the birthdays.

2) Colm: 31st December. Quite the entrance. A month early. I was in the café after hours with Luke, having dinner, just the two of us. He'd made moussaka and baked Alaska which remain my favourite dinner/dessert combo – and lit two long-stemmed red candles. The sap. Over coffees, he casually enquired as to his chances of New Year's Eve sex (no such thing as a free moussaka). I said fine, but let him know in no uncertain terms that my positive response had nothing to do with either the moussaka or the baked Alaska. I just happened to want to. My proviso was that there would be no kissing – Luke had eaten mussels – and sex would have to occur in an upright position. No way I was

going to chance those flimsy tables in the café again. Luke had to approach me from behind, so enormous was my bump by then, and no sooner had he manoeuvred himself inside me, my bloody waters broke. He thought he was being genius at sex. 'You're like, UNBELIEVABLY wet.' In fairness, he had spent an admirable period of time before that kneeling between my thighs, and with all the extra blood flooding through my body, my clit was as hard and erect as a pubescent penis. I remember grabbing fistfuls of his hair when I came.

I miss Luke's hair.

My contractions started pretty immediately after Luke's triumphant declaration and Colm burst into the world with a shock of red hair, in the hospital car park of the Rotunda in the back of Luke's delivery van. I made a noise I have never heard before or since in the back of that van. A sort of guttural grunt that seemed to come from some prehistoric place deep inside me. Every so often, a cauliflower rolled across the floor as Luke scorched around corners and shot through intersections. It was the only time I remember him blaring the horn. I bit into the cauliflower whenever the contractions came.

Needless to say, I've never eaten a cauliflower since. Not even cauliflower cheese. I eat broccoli cheese instead which is not as nice but will do, in the circumstances.

I'd better write something about Aidan's birth just in case the feckers ever do find this misery memoir. Sorry to report that there's no sex in Aidan's birth story. Probably because it was two years later and we were the proud owners of a toddler who only slept in cars, buggies, vans and, sometimes, swings.

3) Aidan. Born on his due date. A sensitive Pisces. Labour: a very manageable two hours, from the time I arrived at the hospital till he exited my vagina in his quiet, careful way. All episiotomies declined. No tearing endured. No needlework necessary. Aidan was smaller than Colm. Also quieter. He had the same amount of hair but his was black, like Luke's. He ate every four hours, slept in between, didn't wreck my nipples, delivered teeny-tiny poos at regular intervals, the consistency of which the district nurse declared 'ideal'. I remember swelling with maternal pride. My kid's shits were 'ideal'. I put it down to the postpartum hormonal rampage.

Hormones really have a lot to answer for.

4) Wedding anniversary. Fuck sake, it's in eight weeks' time! And even worse, it's my TWENTY-FIFTH one. I remember my parents' twenty-fifth wedding anniversary and thinking how old they were.

They were MY age.

Luke hasn't mentioned it.

Probably the best tactic. Gloss over it. Ignore it even.

Or maybe he's forgotten all about it.

I'll kill him if he has.

9 June, 4 p.m.

Symptoms: Old before my time

I've just woken up from a nap.

I have officially turned into my father. The 'before Leonora' version. The new version is at his Senior Singles salsa class. He didn't really want to go without Leonora but she insisted. I think she's afraid his hips might seize up if he doesn't keep them moving, which seems reasonable.

Once I got rid of him, I ran upstairs to my office to prep for the panel event at the festival.

I say 'ran' but it was more of a 'brisk walk' if I'm honest. My hips and knees are not the quiet, reliable joints they once were. I'm throwing cod liver oil at the situation but it's repeating on me something rancid.

The cursor on the blank screen blinked at me in its methodical way. I sat down and typed out the name of the festival on the top of the page.

Flights of Fancy.

I changed the font size. Then I changed the typeface. I centred it. Then justified it. Then right-aligned it. Then deleted it.

The cursor was back at the top of the page, blinking.

I closed the lid of my laptop and sprawled across my desk with my face buried in the crook of my elbow.

Afterwards, my Fitbit alerted me to the fact that I'd been asleep for forty minutes.

COLM (bounding up the stairs and skidding across the attic floor in his boxer shorts and socks): Did I hear the landline ringing?

There was such hope in his face and his voice that I could hardly bring myself to tell him that we haven't had a landline for over a year now. And even if we had, Amelia wouldn't know the number and she wouldn't know enough to look in a telephone directory. She's never heard of a telephone directory. Neither has Colm, I'm pretty sure. He was clutching at straws.

I wanted to shake him hard and tell him to cop on to himself. I wanted him to brush his teeth. Even youth can't save him from the sourness of his breath.

I wanted to ask him about work. About his legions of followers on Instagram who hadn't heard from him in a month.

A month is a long time on social media, I wanted to tell him. Those sponsors aren't going to wait patiently while your heart heals.

And it will.

Heal.

I want to tell him that too.

My boy's heart is broken.

I feel the instincts of early motherhood clawing at my innards. That savage protective strain. It could end poverty. Wars. Climate change. It's potent, that stuff.

I can't believe I ever thought that the baby stage was the worst bit. I mean yes, they were demanding, don't get me wrong. Always crying for their next feed, their next nappy change, their next sleep. I remember, when Aidan was an infant and Colm was two, I would have given away one of my kidneys (you only need one anyway) and a good chunk of my liver (it grows back apparently) for six hours' uninterrupted sleep. I struggle to remember those years, it feels like I waded through them, like they were lakes. Vast lakes of milk. Everything smelled like milk. Everything was bathed in a thin film of milk. Milk crusts on the edges of the boys' mouths and milk oozing out of my nipples and my pores when my breasts got too full, it seemed. I couldn't drink milk for years afterwards. Even now, the smell of it can sometimes make me do a neat, mostly unnoticeable, throw-up in my mouth.

But still, give me a baby any day. Anything has got to be easier than looking into Colm's empty face. He's so pale and skinny. Four weeks of no sunlight and enforced veganism will do that to a person. He doesn't even flinch when I storm into his room, gathering cups and roaring about the state of the place. And I can't feed him or change him or wind him or sing 'Major Tom' to him the way I used to when he woke up in the night, crying about Kermit the Frog who he was convinced was hiding from Miss Piggy in his room. I can't swipe under his bed with the sweeping brush. I can't banish frog puppets. Or hum a David Bowie song. Or shove a soother in his gob.

It seems like the easiest bit now. When they were babies. Why the hell did I think it was so hard?

Instead of shaking Colm or asking about work or telling him about the sea and how there's plenty of other fish in it, I tell him about a packet of ham I smuggled into the fridge yesterday. I hid it underneath a punnet of prunes I bought last week. I don't know why I bought them. I don't know anyone who likes them. Mam ate prunes every day. She didn't like them but she ate them. She said they kept her regular. I haven't opened the pack and everyone else gives them a wide and somewhat fearful berth. In fairness, they do look vaguely threatening with their strangled purple colour and their thick, wrinkled skins.

They look angry.

In fact, they look apoplectic.

Genius hiding place for the ham.

I even offered to make Colm the ham sandwich myself. I've a fresh pan of Brennans' batch loaf. The smell of it would force a smile out of 'poor Dermot'. But Colm shook his head and said, 'No thanks' in a voice that had been pillaged of all emotion, interest and animation.

Amelia has cleared him out.

She's like a dose of colonic irrigation.

10 June, 4 a.m.

Symptoms: Loss, rage, witchiness

So, there I was in the shower last night, washing my hair. With hair like mine (read: big, belligerent, demanding), it had to be washed exactly forty-eight hours before the Flights of Fancy Festival to give it a chance to settle down into some semblance of decorum.

It felt strange, preparing for something. Exhausting, yes. But also, productive. My Fitbit agreed, logging the activity as a 'strenuous workout'. Which I felt was spot on even though I'm still mad with Luke for buying me a Fitbit.

LUKE: You said you wanted something to help you get fit.
ME: Everyone says that in January. It doesn't bloody well mean anything.

Anyway, there I was in the shower, working out, minding my own business, when I noticed the water wasn't draining away as usual.

My rule of thumb for DIY is: if you can't fix it, ignore it. Which I did.

Until the shower tray overflowed and I had to turn off the tap before I had properly rinsed my hair and there was shampoo in my eye and even though it's one of those expensive, organic ones with no parabens in it, whatever the hell they are, it still stung like spring nettles. Then, when I got the shampoo out – my eyes looked like a pair of blood clots – I had to get back in the shower to see what was blocking the drain and I removed clumps – CLUMPS – of my hair.

So, that's the latest bit of menopausal news.

I'm going bald.

After all the years – decades – complaining about my hair – the amount of it, the thickness of it, the sheer unmanageability of it – I am now destined to be hairless.

Yet another way the men get away with it. They can be bald as eggs and yet still manage to get a woman to wash their underpants.

Bald women, on the other hand, are witches. Ask Roald Dahl if you don't believe me.

5.37 a.m.

There she goes. Not barking but whining. Which is actually worse.

She usually stops after a few minutes but not this morning so I stormed downstairs and out to the garden.

MAM: That'll be the rock you perish on, girleen.

The dog was sitting at the window of the 'conservatory' when I reached her. Just sitting there, staring out, like she was expecting me.

No.

Waiting for me.

Like she knew I'd arrive.

Sooner or later.

She stood up when she saw me and wagged her tail which, by the way, is a pathetic little stump of a thing.

'What?' I asked her through the glass. She did the thing that dog owners think is so cute, tilting her head to one side and raising her eyebrows in an 'inquisitive' way.

Her home-perm-circa-1985 coat was in its usual tidy state, there was food and water in her pink Ainsley bowls and no sign of a break-in. Or a fox.

And then I saw it. Blood. A few drops, dribbling out of her vulva.

Bloody hell.

LuLaBelle was having her period.

No menopausal, barely-there, pale imitation of a period either.

The blood was starkly red against the bright whiteness of her pelt.

She did one of her little whines which sounded even more pathetic than usual. And then I couldn't help wondering if it was her first one.

Her first period.

Even worse, I couldn't help feeling sorry for her.

I keyed in the code to the 'front door'. It's the date our flights are booked for Cuba, Leonora said, touching my arm in that overfamiliar way she has.

I've just realised something: Dad and Leonora probably expect me to mind the bloody dog when they're in Havana.

For THREE weeks!

And when the pair of them come back, they'll probably need another few joints replaced after all the dancing and LuLaBelle will be dispatched here.

Again.

Jesus H.

LuLaBelle barrelled into my arms as soon as the door opened. As if I was the bearer of everything good in the world.

How can she not sense my animosity?

Even stupid people can, in the main.

I sat on the couch and googled 'dog periods'. I'd already decided that if I had to insert a tampon, I was out.

One site recommended setting aside lots of time during the period for 'cuddles'.

I set the dog on the couch and cleaned the blood off her fur with Cif wipes. LuLaBelle whined and I told her to stop being such a big baby and she stopped. Then, when I was finished cleaning her, she climbed into my lap and laid her head in the crook of my elbow.

Obviously, I wasn't having that so I carried her to the bottom of the garden, set her on the ground in front of her kennel and opened the door to the 'conservatory', all ready to shovel her inside the 'master bedroom'.

But she started doing this pathetic shaky thing, like she was scared. Or cold. She reminded me of ten-year-old me.

The first day of my period. I hadn't a clue what was going on. I cried so hard I was sent home from school. I was positive I was dying. Mam told me to stop the nonsense and gave me one of her sanitary towels that were miles too big and stuck out either end of my knickers.

Then she gave me 'The Talk'.

It's a miracle I ever managed to have a healthy sex life. After 'The Talk'.

But later, when I was going to bed, Mam bustled into my bedroom with a hot water bottle.

MAM: Put that against your belly.
TEN-YEAR-OLD-ME: Why? What's going to happen next?
MAM: Lord above, such a fuss!

She thrust the hot water bottle under the covers, then tucked me in so tight, I could barely breathe.

Eventually I gave in and picked LuLaBelle up, brought her into the kitchen, deposited her on the couch and threw one of Aidan's hoodies over her.

For the record: I'm only letting LuLaBelle stay inside for today.

The first day of a period is the worst bit.

After that, she's on her own.

11 June, 10 a.m.

Symptoms: Mortification

To distract myself from impending baldness and the Flights of Fancy Festival tomorrow, which I felt unprepared for since I was supposed to be talking about the book I haven't written, I agreed to drive Dad to the chemist to fill his prescription. Anyway, I had to get nose plugs for Luke.

LUKE: I don't need nose plugs.
ME: You do need them, you just don't want them. There's a difference.
LUKE: I won't wear them.
ME: I'll just wait till you're asleep, then clip them on.
LUKE: . . .
ME: How do you feel about having sex with a bald person by the way? No reason.

His phone rang and, instead of ignoring it and answering the question, he reefed it out of his jeans pocket, held it at arm's length so he could read the screen, then grinned like he used to when he'd enquire about the chances of sex that night and I'd say, 'Fair to middlin'.'
   Which segued into 'Poor to unlikely.'
   And then, 'Dismal.'
   Now I can't remember the last time he asked me.

LUKE (leaving room at a clip): I have to get this.

11 a.m.

So I happened to be in the chemist with my father when he asked the pharmacist to fill his prescription. In fact, I was standing beside him, having assumed the prescription would be for something ordinary like haemorrhoid cream or bunion plasters.
   Except it wasn't.

It was for Viagra.

I removed myself from the area, mumbling something about, I don't know, dental floss maybe. I stood at the back of the shop. The nose plugs I had picked out for Luke seemed suddenly mean and petty in my sweaty palms. I put them on a shelf and held onto it to steady myself. I was suddenly floored with grief for my lost sex life.

A woman buying tweezers nearby asked if I was okay and her tone of concern pretty much put me back together again. I nodded briskly, then reached for the nose plugs again. The woman nodded sympathetically. 'Snoring?'

'Yes.'

'My husband refused to wear them so I moved him into the boxroom.'

'I don't have a boxroom.'

'Have you a shed?' She winked at me and moved on.

11.45 a.m.

I was quiet in the car on the way home which is where I went wrong. I should have spouted off about any old thing and not permitted a sliver of silence. Because Dad, like nature, abhors a vacuum. The silence intensified when we stopped at the lights and the idling engine was the quietest it's ever been. I even checked to see if the car had cut out.

It hadn't.

Nor were the traffic lights broken in spite of the length of time it took them to change.

Dad cleared his throat. He's had a chest infection recently so the sound was thickened with phlegm. He rolled down the window and spat.

Between the Viagra and the phlegm, my stomach was already queasy. But then Dad took a breath and started up.

DAD: I hope you don't think I'm being disrespectful to the memory of your mother, just because I'm having sex with another woman.

Good Christ, it felt nearly as bad as the time Mam gave me 'The Talk'.

No.

It was worse.

Dad and I have never discussed anything even remotely related to sex. Even now, when we're watching telly at night and there's a sex scene – fuck sake, *Fair City*, I thought I could count on you – I am transported back to my early teenage self, squashed between them on the couch on a Saturday night, watching *Dallas*.

JR has a lot to answer for. No wonder someone shot him. Good riddance!

DAD: The thing is, Aggie . . .
ME (petty): It's Agatha.
DAD: You sound just like your mother.

I couldn't believe he was bringing Mam into this conversation.

DAD: Me and Leonora, we . . .
ME: Please don't talk about your sex life. I'm begging you.
DAD: We're both adults, Agatha.
ME: What does that have to do with anything?

DAD: So you do think I'm being disrespectful to the memory of your mother?

ME: If I say yes, will you stop talking?

DAD: Before I met Leonora, I assumed that that part of my life was behind me. You know, your mother and I, we didn't have . . . well, relations I suppose you might call it, for well over . . .

ME: Green light! (Slamming my foot on the clutch and hauling the car into first gear so that Dad was plastered against the back of his chair as we roared through the junction.)

There was silence then, for a bit. Then:

ME: Look, Dad. I don't mind what you do. As you say, you're an adult. But is it okay if we never talk about it? Ever?

DAD: I want to be open and honest with you, Agatha.

ME: There's no need. We've managed fine up to now, haven't we?

DAD: Leonora says that honesty in relationships, including sexual relati . . .

ME (frantic): Okay, okay. We're open and honest now. Which is obviously brilliant. Excellent. I'm thrilled, I really am. But can we agree that there's no need to talk about sex or Viagra or . . .

DAD: I'm only taking it as a precautionary measure, you know. The doctor says there's no good reason I shouldn't be able to . . .

I burst into song. Dad jerked and braced himself as if we were about to crash. It's true I'm not, strictly speaking, the most tuneful singer. I belted out the first lines of 'The Tide Is High'. Still, my singing must be catchy or something because, after a while, Dad joined in.

12 June, 4 a.m.

Symptoms: Jealousy

Wouldn't you think, if I have to be awake at this unearthly hour, I'd spend the time wisely? Like coming up with pithy, off-the-cuff rejoinders for any questions I might get asked at the literary festival later?

Instead, here's what I'm thinking:

My father is having more sex than me.

When I got back from the pharmacy, I rang Dr-Lennon-call-me-Susie to ask if there is Viagra for women?

She said no, in her apologetic voice.

DR-LENNON-CALL-ME-SUSIE: It's not you, it's the . . .
ME: I know, I know, it's the menopause.

The fucking menopause.

She recommended porn and fishnets.

She didn't use those exact words. She's one of those women who believe that politeness is a virtue.

Now I'm remembering the time I heard Mam and Dad having sex. Only once but once was enough. It was Christmas Eve and they'd waited up for ages. Making sure we were asleep before the annual trip to the attic to get the Santa presents. I was nine and I hadn't believed since I was six. Bloody Yvonne Downey told me. She also told me about sex.

So I knew what they were doing that Christmas Eve. I just couldn't believe they were doing it. They didn't seem the type. Even all these years later, the sounds are scored into my brain, like mine and Carol's initials I carved on our school desk with the point of my compass. The squeal of the bedsprings, low and sporadic at first, then louder and more frequent. At one stage, the thud of the headboard against the wall and the bedsprings still moaning and then a low, desperate grunt (Dad) and then – and this is the worst bit – a sibilant hissing – sssshhhhh – (Mam) and then, after that, silence.

I remember feeling relieved when I heard the more familiar sound of my father's rhythmic snores through the wall. That they weren't unconscious afterwards. Or dead. Yvonne Downey hadn't specified what happened to people afterwards. In my nine-year-old mind, I had imagined it as some gruesome, bloody act of aggression that couples had to engage in if they wanted to have a baby. It was something to be borne.

And in fairness, after hearing the sound of my parents' brief coupling that night, that analysis seemed sound.

12 June, 11.45 p.m.

Symptoms: Addled

The flashbacks to the festival are nearly worse than the event itself.

Which is impressive since the event itself was already pretty horrific.

WHY DID I AGREE TO GO?

In the absence of any rationale, perhaps it might be useful to set out, in clear and concise prose, what occurred. This may help to:

1) Make sure I have it straight in my head.
2) Confirm that what I think happened really happened.
3) Process the event with a view to compartmental-ising/rationalising it. This seems to work for most men.
4) Consider if I need to do some damage limitation with publishing industry/readers/fellow writers.
5) Of course I need to do damage limitation. With all of the above.
6) Work out which bits to tell Luke. He's not on social media so chances are he might never find out?
7) For fuck sake, Agatha, he doesn't live in a CAVE!!
8) Okay. Work out which bits to tell Luke. Is there a way to spin it so I come out smelling of roses?
9) Ha! But good to see I haven't lost my sense of humour.

I had my doubts about this academic approach.
Although maybe it was too soon to tell.
I decided to go for a quick smoke in the garden and then write it all down.

Sequence of Events at Literary Festival (in Clear and Concise Prose):

12 p.m.

The morning actually went okay. Even my hair behaved, having reacted well to the calming serum I had doused it with earlier. I know this because:

LUKE: Your hair . . .
ME: Yes?
LUKE (incredulous): It's like the fight has gone out of it.

The clothes I wanted to wear – my mustard silk shirt tucked into my black leather skirt – were clean and the wrinkles in the shirt had mostly fallen out after a spell in the bathroom during one of Dad's protracted and steamy showers. I didn't even give out to him for using up all the hot water. Again.

The skirt was a bit tighter than I remembered and when I complained to Carol, she sent me a one-word text:
Spanx.
Which sounded like a simple enough solution so I went ahead and bought a pair.

I even decided it would be okay if I wore my favourite shoes which were things of beauty (blood-red velvet with a kitten heel) but also of potential discomfort, given the severity of the point at the toe.

Still, I told myself, I'd only be walking from the car to the hotel so, you know, it wouldn't be an issue. Even the weather was playing ball: stretches of bright blue sky with a scattering of small fluffy clouds that looked like the ones kids draw and a bang of actual heat coming off the sun.

Be grand.
Right?

1 p.m.

Arrived at venue to discover that the car park I was told I could use for free was full so I had to park two streets over and only had enough change for one hour of parking. I fed the machine and walked to the hotel, which is all it took for my feet to swell like feverish glands in my foolish and beautiful blood-red velvet shoes which now felt about a size smaller than they used to be.

And I couldn't take them off because I'd never get them back on again. So I did what women in uncomfortable shoes do the world over. I pushed on through. The pain is not dissimilar to childbirth. If you pushed babies out of your feet instead of your vagina, that is. I decided to run to get it over and done with as quickly as possible. This wasn't as easy as it sounds, mostly because of my skirt – a fabulously tight and short affair – which was a pre-menopausal purchase when bloating wasn't the issue it is today. I did a sort of a hybrid waddle-walk interlaced with groans that seemed to come directly from my feet in my fast-shrinking shoes.

1.15 p.m.

I arrived at the hotel, hyperventilating. By then, my heels were bleeding. I suppose I should have been grateful that the blood was camouflaged by the colour of the shoe.

1.30 p.m.

I found a side entrance into the hotel and hid behind my programme as I made a beeline for the toilets. I barricaded myself into the nearest cubicle, pulled the lid down and sat on it, reefing my shoes off.

The jury is still out on whether it would have been better to ease them off with exquisite gentleness which, yes, would have prolonged the ordeal but lessened the acute agony.

Still, once I got them off and the throbbing subsided, the relief was vast.

I made repairs to my face and feet with powder and Band Aids respectively. There were make-up wipes in my handbag which I used to wipe my armpits. Then I rolled on more deodorant, and sprayed myself liberally with perfume to include my hair since it now looked like defeat after ten rounds in a ring with Katie Taylor.

Getting my feet back inside the shoes was one of the bravest things I've ever done.

And I've pared a corn on my mother's big toe.

1.40 p.m.

I got entangled in a group of 'avid readers' who were thrilled to hear I'm a writer.

RANDOM AVID READER #1: Would we have heard of you?

ME: I don't know.

RANDOM AVID READER #2: What's your name?

ME: Agatha Doyle.

(Pause – pregnant.)

RANDOM AVID READER #1: Do you write under a different name?

ME: No.

RANDOM AVID READER #2: What kind of stuff do you write?

ME: Historical fiction.
RANDOM AVID READER #1: Oh.
(Silence – awkward.)
RANDOM AVID READER #1 and 2: Well . . . this was . . .
    We'd better . . .
(Walk away, backwards, collide with waiter bearing tray of
    ribs in barbecue sauce.)

1.42–2 p.m.

Turned out that Spanx aren't all that. Especially at an event
where food is served. Especially if you eat the food. It was
only finger food but the trays kept being proffered and it
was like a reflex action, taking one, then another and another.
I made a beeline for the meat. In that way, I ate many pigs
in blankets, beef wellington bites, chilli meatballs and pulled
pork pickled sliders. By the time the trays bearing the
too-small-to-matter sausage rolls had been emptied, I had
a severe case of meat sweats.

Or it might have been a hot flush.

Either way, my face was red and damp and my fingernails were shiny with animal fat. I kept my head down
as I made my way to the toilets although it's difficult to
keep a low profile when you're as tall as I am. And I
refuse to stoop. I'll get rounded shoulders. Also, why on
earth should I?

Anyway, I nearly made it to the loos, mostly by walking
very fast and holding my phone to my ear and saying, 'Yes
. . . no . . . oh I know . . . absolutely . . .' but then, right
outside, in front of the doors, there he was. Fecking GBH
with a smile that was greasier than my fingernails. It

matched his lank, black hair and narrow black eyes and pasty, pulled skin.

I picked up my pace, strode towards him, pointing at my phone with an eyeroll so he knew I was on a call with someone I couldn't get rid of.

He stood his ground, his smile spreading across his face like a stain.

And then my treacherous phone took that very moment to ring.

I stabbed at it with several fingers, rejecting the call and pitching the phone into my bag.

GBH (smirking): Darling.

His thin lips puckered up. He's a French kisser. One cold, wet kiss on each cheek. I told him I have a cold. His Achilles heel is germs. I discovered that at the Mountains to Sea Festival two years ago and it's come in handy ever since.

GBH (beating a hasty retreat): I'll see you on the panel, darling.

Turned out that Spanx were hard to pull down over a bellyful of finger food. After I finally managed to get them down and back up again, I was exhausted and had to sit on the lid of the toilet.

I smelled like meat.

Also, shouldn't I have reached a stage, long before now, where the wearing of Spanx became defunct? Not to mention hiding out in a toilet cubicle? Surely I should no

longer care what people thought of my appearance? Wasn't
that the 'upside' of ageing? You gave the two fingers to the
patriarchy and burned your peep-hole bras and your thongs
and – most definitely – your Spanx.

I checked my watch. I was 'on' at 3 p.m. but I needed
to feed the meter before then.

2.17 p.m.

I finally managed to get the grease out from under my
fingernails. I sluiced my face in cold water, which gave me
temporary release from the hot flush, but then I realised
there were no paper towels so I had to dry my face with
toilet paper, bits of which came away and stuck to my skin.
Enter two young women, impossibly dewy and moist and
glowing. I was a husk in comparison.

They eyed me warily and set up their stall at the far end
of the bathroom where they spilled the contents of their
make-up bags and tended to their faces with brushes, pencils,
wands, cotton pads, fingertips. This furious industry was
accompanied by a steady stream of negative self-analysis.
They took it in turns, one dismissing the claims of the other
before presenting her own imagined flaw. There was something almost ritualistic about it. I fished a pair of tweezers
out of my bag and yanked a long, coarse hair out of my
chin. There was a time when I would have winced. The two
young women looked on with a sort of disgusted fascination.

2.40 p.m.

Arrived back at hotel after making a futile and painful
journey to the car to feed the meter, only to discover I'd

left my handbag in the bar where I'd gone to get change for the meter.

It was like a scene from *Apocalypse Now* in my shoes. I hobbled into the bar to reclaim my handbag. The barman looked at me like he'd never seen me before. I pointed to my handbag behind the counter. He was reluctant to give it to me without proof.

YOUTHFULLY PIMPLY BARMAN: Do you remember what's inside the bag?

ME: Of course I remember! There's nothing wrong with my memory, you're the one who should get yourself checked out for early-onset dementia.

YOUTHFULLY PIMPLY BARMAN: Ah here, steady on . . .

ME: You and I engaged in a commercial transaction not fifteen minutes ago in this very place. And yet you have no recollection of the event.

PIMPLY YOUTHFUL BARMAN: There's no need to shout, madam.

Which is what they usually say before they call security so I just told him to give me my handbag in what the boys used to call my 'dangerous' voice. Low and slow, with full stops after each word.

Give. Me. My. Handbag.

He handed it over.

I grabbed the bag and stalked out of the bar as fast as my tragic feet – strapped once more into the cruel shoes – allowed.

Which was not fast.

2.59 p.m.

I made it to the room where the event was happening. The organiser was a woman in a fitted black suit with a bleached buzz cut and a clipboard.

BUZZ CUT: Ticket please.

GBH was man-spreading on a couch on a rostrum at the top of the room.

GBH (smarmy with a hint of smirk): Do you not know who she is?'

Buzz cut glanced at my photograph on the programme.

BUZZ CUT: Sorry, Ms Doyle, I didn't recognise you.

And yes, fine, the photograph was taken over two years ago, in flattering lighting with professional make-up. My hair was in that sharp bob that made me look like one of those elegant, efficient sociopaths.

Also, I was smiling.

I gathered my hair in my hands and tucked it around my jawline in a bob-like way. It's a lot longer than it used to be. Also coarser and threaded with grey. If I were a man, I would be 'distinguished'.

ME (doing my best to smile): Do you see me now?
BUZZ CUT (faint smile with hint of alarm): Of course.
My apologies.

GBH shuffled along the couch, patted it. 'I've warmed a spot for you, Agatha.'

I sat between GBH and an English writer who I've met maybe half a dozen times over the years at events such as these. He offered me his hand and said, 'Ray Black,' with a smile that looked like it had been practised in front of a mirror.

ME: We've met.
RAY BLACK: Are you sure?
ME (pointed): Several times.
RAY BLACK: Oh. Gosh. Sorry. It's just . . . I'm . . . not
    wearing my glasses.

Which was true. But what was also true was the fact that he is myopic so he could see my face perfectly well.

How do I know this? Because he told me, that's how. At our second meeting which was at the Dalkey Book Festival in 2008.

And no, I didn't pay particular attention to this guy because I think he's a brilliant writer or because I wanted to fuck him. He has one of those disproportionately sized heads that makes one worry his neck might snap. And also, there's the small matter of Luke, I suppose. Not that he'd be all 'pistols at dawn' kind of fired up but he might be . . . I'm going to say, annoyed.

Annoyed might be too strong.

Piqued, perhaps.

Anyway, my point is that when people offer me information, I (a) listen and (b) retain the data.

I would appreciate the same courtesy in return, thank you very much.

3.15 p.m.

Event finally kicked off. I cannot understand why events on programmes scheduled to begin at 3 p.m. invariably begin at 3.15 p.m. Why not just write 3.15 p.m. on the programme? But then it would commence at 3.30 p.m. It's infuriating, especially when you're sandwiched on a couch between two man-spreaders, one of whom sort of fancies you in a big-woman fetish kind of a way and the other is doing his best to make me like him again.

Fat chance, Ray Black, you near-sighted little toad.

3.35 p.m.

Introductions done. GBH read from his latest opus. Another one featuring Henry VIII. Men are fascinated by Henry. I suppose it's something to do with his transitory relationship with women and how he gets away with everything.

A simple, 'Off with her head' when the going gets tedious.

3.55 p.m.

Ray Black read something. It was hot in the room, the afternoon sun beating against the windows, not one of which was open. I could feel sweat pooling in the cups of my bra. I leaned against the back of the couch. If it weren't for my ruined feet, I might have dozed off.

I dug my fingernails into the fleshy part of my hand in

an effort to rouse myself but I'd been biting my nails recently and it was a pathetic effort.

MAM: Would you sit up straight. You'll get a hump, slumping like that.

4.10 p.m.

Clapping. Everyone looking at me. I stood up and got myself to the podium somehow, as if my feet were perfectly ordinary feet in sensible, well-fitting shoes with things like 'cushion soles' and maybe a fragrant insole.

4.20 p.m.

I got through the reading! Of course I did! I'm an old pro. I've done this dozens of times. Hundreds! And nobody batted an eyelid when I read from *Exile* instead of from my 'work-in-progress' like Ray and GBH.

4.21 p.m.

Finally! Finally!! Buzz cut opened the discussion to the floor which meant the end was nigh. Most of the questions were directed at GBH and Ray Black. GBH began all his responses with 'Great question!' as if he's never been asked where he gets his ideas from.

Fuck sake.

I was finally asked a question and it was about writer's block and I said that there's no such thing. It's just common-or-garden laziness and the best way to get over it is to write your way through it. The audience – mostly aspiring writers at these events – seethed with a collective resentment.

4.35 p.m.

BUZZ CUT: Time for one last question.

She scanned the room. There were a few hands up. She took her time, then picked a bearded man wearing 'literary' glasses – which is to say Joycean ones – a tweed suit and a beret, tilted at what he probably felt was a rakish angle.

4.40 p.m.

Five minutes it took him! To deliver his monologue, which boiled down to this:

'The only reason I've never been published is because there is a bias against cis white, middle-class men in the publishing industry. Discuss.'

Or no. Not 'Discuss'. But rather, 'I'm right, amn't I?'

No.

Not, 'Amn't I?'

Just, 'I'm right.'

I opened my mouth to respond when he cut in with a public-schoolboy-polite, 'Oh, no, sorry, I'm actually directing that question to Ray. Or George.'

Before he added his adorable little caveat, I was just ordinary angry. Afterwards, I was menopausal angry.

I forgot about my bloodied stumps and leaped to my feet, emitting a guttural roar. Obviously, the roar was a direct descendant of the bloodied stumps but the man and the audience did not know this.

I wrestled my feet out of the shoes.

ME: Does it matter which one?
BEARDY MAN: Sorry?
ME: Ray? Or George?
BEARDY MAN: Eh, well . . . no, I . . .
ME: So just somebody with a dick then?

I emphasised the word 'dick' in case he didn't realise I was angry.

BEARDY MAN: (Nervous, high-pitched giggle.)
BUZZ CUT: I think that's all we have time for, we're way
    over.

She walked up the side of the room, trying to make eye contact with me.

No fucking chance.

ME: Do you know how many writers are cis, white and
    middle-class?
BEARDY MAN: Eh. No, I . . .
ME: The majority of them. And here's a shocker. The women
    in that group earn twenty-five per cent less than men. So
    for every worthy tome a man pens, a woman has to write
    a book and a quarter to earn the same amount, then she
    has to withstand the ire of mainstream reviewers who will
    dismiss her efforts as 'fluff' and 'chick-lit' and 'domestic'.
    What say you to that?

BEARDY MAN: I'm unfamiliar with the exact statis . . .

ME: Well, luckily for you, I'm not. Let's see. Do you know what percentage of writers are Middle Eastern?

BEARDY MAN: . . .

ME: One per cent.

BEARDY MAN: . . .

ME: Do you know what percentage are queer?

BEARDY MAN: Are you supposed to say queer any more?

RANDOM WOMAN IN AUDIENCE: Yes, queer is fine.

BEARDY MAN: Oh . . .

ME: Do you know what percentage are refugees? Migrants? Working-class? Travellers?

My anger scorched the inside of my head and seemed to have frightened my brain fog away. The statistics kept coming.

BEARDY MAN (holding his hands in an 'I surrender' pose): Look, I think you . . .

ME: And to go back to underpaid women writers, do you know how many of us have gone, are going or will go through the menopause?

BEARDY MAN: I don't see what that has to do with . . .

ME: All of them. And do you know how many of those will talk about it, will let you know the challenges it presents and the impact it has on their work?

BEARDY MAN: I really . . .

ME: None of them. Well, actually, no, that's not true. One of them. And that is me.

BEARDY MAN: . . .

ME: I am a menopausal woman, standing here before you all in a lather of sweat, terrified that I might forget a word in the middle of a sentence with the threat of brain fog that looms over me on a daily basis as I sit at my desk and attempt to write to a deadline. I have insomnia, none of my clothes fit me, and there's a chance I'm more irritable than I used to be. Although my husband may have a different view on that.

(Some titters of (nervous) laughter around audience.)

I took the opportunity to collect myself. I was breathing like I'd run up several flights of stairs. It felt like there were broken bits of me lying around the room. When I spoke again, my throat felt dry and my voice sounded hoarse.

I looked at the beardy man.

ME: What was your question again?

13 June, 4 a.m.

Symptoms: Fake migraine

I went to bed when I got home from the event, citing a migraine.

Nobody batted an eye even though I'd never, to my knowledge, complained of a migraine before.

Although in fairness, I don't think Dad heard me. He was on a video call with Leonora, screensharing *Dirty Dancing* again. Leonora saw me walking past Dad and tried to engage me in chat. I have a feeling she sees herself in the role of stepmother. The non-evil variety. She asks me things like, 'How are you?' coupled with one of those sincere head tilts. She says my name after each of her enquiries.

'How are you, Agatha?'

She doesn't call me Aggie like Dad does now. She seems to know how much it drove my mother crazy.

MAM: Well? You were christened Agatha, weren't you?

As for the boys, I'd say they didn't realise I had either left the house or returned. Colm was in his room, blasting his heartsick music, and Aidan was out the back garden, varnishing the beehives, while LuLaBelle sniffed around the outside of the kennel as if she'd never darkened its doors.

Which she hadn't.

Not since periodgate.

MAM: I told you, didn't I?

She did.

Letting LuLaBelle sleep on the couch that night was indeed the rock I perished on.

When she finished her inspection of the kennel, LuLaBelle burrowed into a mound of freshly dug muck, her head on her paws.

Her fleece may not be as white as Leonora remembers.

ME: Where's your father?
AIDAN: At the café. He said he'd be late.

I briefly considered going to The Full Shilling. Surprising Luke. I used to do that sometimes.

But I hadn't done it in ages.

And there was a gnawing worry that Luke mightn't appreciate it. He's been so busy lately.

Anyway, I was bone-tired.

MAM: There's little a hot water bottle and an early night won't help.

So I went to bed.

And now here I am wide awake at 4 a.m. So awake I could do things like:

a) paint the outside of the house, front and back;
b) assemble an IKEA chest of drawers;
c) read *Ulysses*;
d) learn Russian.

Regret has a sour taste. I thought if I ignored the menopause, pretended it wasn't there, like a fart in a lift, I might get through it somehow. Like, there must be a reason it contains the word 'pause'. Normal service will resume presently. I thought I could just wait it out. Wait for normal service to resume.

But no.

I had to go shouting my mouth off at a bloody festival.

MAM: Act first, think later, that's always been the way with you.
ME: Are you ashamed of your life of me?
MAM: Go to sleep now, things will be better in the morning.

13 June, 8.30 a.m.

Symptoms: Shock

Aidan arrived into my bedroom at 8 a.m. with tea. At first, I was grateful but it turned out to be green tea which looked as vile as it tasted. He said I should drink it, it's good for the menopause.

Warning bells.

I'd never said anything to Aidan – or any of them – about being menopausal.

ME: What?
AIDAN: Nothing.

(But he couldn't eyeball me.)

ME: Tell me or you're grounded.
AIDAN: You can't ground me any more.
ME: I'm your mother, I can do whatever the fuck I like.

Aidan closed his eyes and massaged his temples as if HE'S the one faking a migraine. Then, he squared his shoulders like Luke does when he's reached a decision about what the Saturday special at The Full Shilling will be. He took his phone out of his pocket, tapped and swiped and held it in front of my face.

AIDAN: You're on TikTok.

In his quiet voice, it sounded equal parts serious and bad.

I peered at the screen.

There I was, full-frontal at the Flights of Fancy Festival, standing on the stage in my bare feet with my shoes in my hand, held aloft. Behind, GBH and Ray Black stare at me, their eyes out on stalks and their mouths slack with shock. Some smart fucker had edited the footage and dubbed music over me, so, as I'm delivering my diatribe, you can hear X-Ray Spex shriek, 'Oh Bondage! Up Yours!' like a chorus line of vitriol.

ME: What the actual?

AIDAN: Ten thousand views so far.

ME: Ten thousand people have watched this video? Of me? Roaring and screeching?

AIDAN: Yes.

ME: It's little people have to be doing.

AIDAN: You sound like Nana.

ME: I'd definitely be grounded if she were here.

AIDAN: I'll make you tea.

ME: Proper tea?

AIDAN: Fine.

ME: And toast?

AIDAN: All right.

ME: With marmalade? Spread out as far as the crusts?

AIDAN: Are you taking advantage of this situation?

ME: I am.

I picked up my phone when he left and discovered that I was also on Twitter, Facebook, Instagram, Snapchat.

Jesus H! I'm a gif!!

Me, stabbing the air repeatedly with a rigid finger, holding the bloodied shoes in the other hand, like a piece of road-kill. And the caption underneath the image.

Menopause. The Movie.

8.45 a.m.

Ate the toast Aidan made, with the marmalade spread right out to the crusts.

10 a.m.

Symptoms: Achy joints, pins and needles which could be (a) my heart gearing up to have an attack or (b) my body telling me to get out of bed

I asked Aidan what to do about *Menopause: The Movie*. He took my phone and dropped it into his pocket.

AIDAN: The internet's attention span is short.

Which I took to mean 'stay in bed for the day'.

Staying in bed for the day is not as fun as it used to be because (1) Luke's at work so there's no one to play with apart from myself, (2) I can't be bothered masturbating (it takes much longer than it used to, plus could attract a hot flush), and (3) my joints and limbs have seized up, making my frequent pilgrimages to the toilet slow and cumbersome.

Not to mention my feet. They're like a Greek play, they're so tragic.

I suppose I should ring Luke. Better he hears my version of the story than watching me on Mrs Maguire's tablet.

She's never off TikTok since her grandchildren bought her that bloody iPad.

No.

I can't bear it.

I'll tell him tomorrow.

Or the day after.

10.45 a.m.

Luke rang. Coming up to his busiest time! Just after ten mass!

ME: Shouldn't you be making breakfast for Mrs Makem? Her bowels won't move without those figs in her porridge, remember?

LUKE: I already made it.

ME: She's early today.

LUKE: She hasn't come in yet.

ME: Another one bites the dust.

LUKE: Why do you always assume they're dead?

ME: What do you want?

LUKE: Just rang for a chat.

ME: You never ring for a chat, you're always up to your balls in gizzards.

LUKE: Okay, fine. You're in today's *Mirror*.

ME: What are you reading that rag for?

LUKE: Mrs Sheridan showed me the article.

ME: I can't believe she stretched to the price of a news-paper.

LUKE: She lifted it from the wholefoods deli up the road. It's got their stamp on it.

ME: Still got it, Mrs Sheridan.

LUKE: According to the article, you were the highlight of
   the Flights of Fancy Festival.
ME: Finally! A good review.
LUKE: I'm worried about you.

This is exactly why I didn't tell anyone about the menopause.
I'll be treated differently. I'll be othered. I'll be diminished.
   Over the hill. That's what people will say. Over the hill
and far, far away.
   She used to be so vibrant. So full of life.
   Now look at her.
   Washed up like a piece of driftwood on a beach.
   It was a shame the way her writing career just . . . ended
like that.
   Another one bites the dust.

LUKE: Agatha? You still there?

His voice was so familiar; gentle and low and slow. I wished
for one of those sharp, shrill voices that would drill a hole
through my skull and drag me out of the pity party that
was in full swing in my head. Because, for one awful
moment, I felt myself yield to the temptation to bury myself
in his concern. Pull it around me like a warm blanket. At
the back of my throat and nose, I felt the swell of hot,
scalding tears. I was just tired. But Luke of course would
assume it was the good old menopause, stampeding around
my body.
   Not to mention my mind.
   Then he wouldn't just be worried.
   It'd be much worse than that.

He'd feel sorry for me.
I cleared my throat.

ME: Don't mind me, I've just got a slight touch of meno-
    pause. It'll pass.
LUKE: When were you going to tell me?
ME: When you're in the house long enough for me to get
    a word in edgeways.
LUKE: I'm sorry I haven't been around much recently.
ME: It's no big deal.
LUKE: It's just, I'm trying to save the café.
ME: It's not the bloody *Titanic*, Luke.
LUKE: I know. It's just . . .
ME: I know.
LUKE: Do you want me to cancel Damien?
ME: Damien?
LUKE: My brother?
ME: That much, I know.
LUKE: He's coming for dinner tomorrow, remember?
ME: Of course I remember, Luke. I'm menopausal, not senile.

(I do not remember.)

11 a.m.

Aidan offered to go to the newsagents and pick up today's
Mirror.

ME: No . . .
ME: Actually, yes.
ME: No. I mean no. Definitely no.
AIDAN: Are you sure?

ME: . . .
AIDAN: I'll take that as a yes.

The article is pretty much hidden on the bottom of page fourteen: 'A straight flush! Woman writer reveals her battle with menopause at literary festival'.

The word 'menopause' is like a blinking, neon sign beside my name. There's no getting away from it.

Also: woman writer. Fuck sake.

In the photograph, my face is as red as my hair. As red as the bloodstained shoes in my hands. The other hand is curled into a fist and raised in the air, like a masterclass in wrath. Behind me, on the sofa, GHB and Ray Black with their mouths open. Ray's braces have tiny diamanté chips in them. GBH has a grey string of . . . I think it's pulled pork caught between his incisors.

In the caption, they are not described as 'men writers'.

MAM: Tomorrow's fish and chips wrapper.

But you don't get fish and chips wrapped in newspaper any more.

Also: it's the internet.

The internet never forgets.

2 p.m.

I want to be all frail and delicate with a pathetic appetite, but Aidan arrived with an enormous bowl of vegetable stew and a steaming baked potato. He even put a pat of butter on top of the spud and the melting allure of it was too much for my sensibilities. I ended up wolfing the lot.

ME: Did I get any calls?
AIDAN: Well . . .
ME: Why are you looking so furtive?

He handed me my phone.

Jesus H!

I couldn't believe it.

Menopause: The Movie had now been watched 25,498 times.

But that wasn't all.

Videos were popping up on various platforms. Women, filming themselves revolting in various ways, with the heading: *Mad As Hell!*

Then tagging me, with the hashtag, *#menopausethemovie.*

I scrolled through the videos. Aidan sat on the edge of the bed and watched along with me. The last one started out low-key with a shot of a nice, middle-aged lady with sensible brown hair in a manageable bob, comfortable shoes and a wedding, engagement AND eternity ring embedded into the skin of her ring finger, wheeling a shopping trolley into a supermarket. Once inside, a close-up reveals that the woman is clearly having a hot flush and trying to pretend that she isn't. Then, Beyoncé's 'Run the World' starts up, loud, and the woman abandons her trolley in the freezer aisle, climbs into one of the fridges and sprawls across bags of oven chips and boxes of chicken nuggets, holding two frozen garlic baguettes against her hot, flushed cheeks. In a corner of the film, you can just about make out the bottom half of two security guards, bearing down on the woman in the fridge.

The video ends abruptly.

AIDAN: Excellent production values, in the main.

ME: What is happening?

AIDAN: I think you've touched a collective nerve?

ME: I didn't mean to.

AIDAN: It's a good thing.

ME: How is it a good thing?

AIDAN: From the comments, it looks like there's a lot of people out there who are glad you've come out as menopausal.

ME: I want to go back in.

AIDAN: Grandad says it's good to talk.

ME: He also maintains Luke's apple and cinnamon muffins make up two of his five-a-day.

AIDAN: Maybe you should try it?

ME: I've eaten more than my fair share of Luke's apple and . . .

AIDAN: I mean, talking.

ME: I do talk.

AIDAN: About your feelings.

ME: Who wants to listen to me moaning?

AIDAN (nodding towards my phone): Lots of people, it would appear.

He stands up, tells me he's going on one of his 'scouting trips'. Which is basically him walking around the neighbourhood looking for bees to put in his newly built beehive.

COLM: Just buy them, bro.

That boy's a chip off the old block, if the old block was his uncle Damien who is a staunch capitalist.

Of course, Aidan refuses to buy bees on the grounds that they're living things, not commodities, and should therefore not be subject to the slings and arrows of outrageous market forces.

AIDAN: Will you be okay?
ME: Of course. Will you be okay? Bees can swarm, you know.
AIDAN: I come in peace. The bees know that.
ME: . . .

I went through the missed calls, many from random numbers I didn't recognise. Lots of callers had left messages and my mailbox was overflowing. I stopped listening after a while since half of the messages were from people I didn't know and had never heard of.

Unfortunately, some of them I did know.

GBH, for instance.

His voicemail oozed with his unique brand of smug compassion. I could picture the head tilt. I deleted it.

Audrey Clarke I also ignored because, let's face it, she's never going to invite me to anything ever again so, you know, bridge burned there. No point prolonging it.

I had nearly convinced myself that my editor hadn't seen *Menopause: The Movie* at all. Anna is one of those people who says things like, 'The Interweb'. As you'd expect, she doesn't have a massive online presence.

But there she was, near the end of the voice messages.

ANNA: Hi Agatha, it's me. Anna. I'm . . . I'm just checking
    in . . . making sure you're okay. I mean, of course you're

okay, why wouldn't you be okay? I'm just . . . ringing for a chat! Talk soon.

Her voice was so gentle and concerned that any residual hope I had harboured that she hadn't seen *Menopause: The Movie* drained away. However, she never actually requested a call back so I took her at face value and deleted her message.

Of course, the record for the greatest number of phone calls/voice messages had to go to Samantha Sorley. Which she'd be delighted with, given her ruthlessly competitive nature. So far, she had phoned seven times. If I didn't phone her back soon, she'd fly into Dublin and rock up at the front door, all spiky heels and hair. Even if I pretended not to be home, she'd terrorise Melissa next door into letting her in, making her tea and lending her a ladder so she could get into our back garden, maybe pitch a rock at a window.

I don't know why really. I haven't exactly been a cash cow for her. And she's an agent for actual, well-known writers. Like, ones people have heard of, I mean.

Maybe she's a 'look after the pennies and the pounds will take care of themselves' sort of person.

I'm the pennies.

The phone, hot in my hands, juddered and for a moment I thought it was Samantha, ringing for an eighth time, but thankfully it was only a WhatsApp from Carol:

CAROL: OMG, are you off your meds?
ME: I'm not on meds.
CAROL: Why the fuck not?

She really has gone all American since she went to LA, popping pills and going to counselling and having Botox injected into her face and getting 'bangs'.

It's a fucking fringe!

CAROL: I've just seen *Menopause: The Movie*. WTAF?

ME: . . .

CAROL: Say something.

ME: Like what?

CAROL: Like 'Hello Carol, my best friend of gazillions of years, I'm going through the menopause and I feel like a piece of dog shit trapped between the ridges of a smug hillwalker's boot.'

ME: Jesus, it's not that bad.

CAROL: I've watched the movie. Twice. Look what you've done to my face.

She sent me a selfie doing her party trick of rolling her eyes back in her head so the irises disappear and all you can see are the whites.

Despite such contortions, she looks incredible. Even better than before. For starters, the whites of her eyes are really white. And in the time it's taken her to move into her condo (short for condominium, which means really nice digs on the beach), get a Starbucks loyalty card and bleach her butthole, she's been promoted.

Twice.

She started out as a deputy vice-president, then she was promoted to corporate vice-president and now she's a senior vice-president. Or maybe she was a senior and now she's a corporate? Either way, she's doing great.

While I am a raging lunatic on The Interweb.

7 p.m.

I started feeling bad about ignoring every single one of Samantha's – nine in the end – calls, so I rang her office out of hours, thinking my call would go straight to voicemail at that hour.

BORED PA: Samantha Sorley's office, how may I help you?
ME: Is Samantha there?
BORED PA: She's in a meeting and won't be . . .
SAMANTHA (hissing in background): Is that Agatha?
BORED PA: Is this Agatha?
ME: Yes.
(Some grunting, sounds of a tussle in the background.)
SAMANTHA (breathless): Agatha, darling, at long last, I
    was beginning to think you didn't love me any more.

I have never told my agent that I love her.
    Ever.

SAMANTHA: Inspired, Agatha darling. Fucking inspired.
ME: What do you mean?
SAMANTHA: Don't play coy with me, you fucking genius.

She uses fuck and fucking and fucker a lot, which sounds out of place in her posh London accent. I think it's her way of getting her Irish on and demonstrating that she 'gets' me.
    Fuck sake.

But she drives a hard bargain and she's the main reason I was able to make somewhat of a living for the past twenty years, despite my dwindling sales and Ink Press's declining interest in historical fiction that's not about:

1) the Holocaust;
2) WWII;
3) anything to do with the British royal family;
4) or royalty in general;
5) WW1;
6) let's just say War, in general;
7) Also: celebrities (any).

SAMANTHA: I'm talking about your fucking coup, darling.
ME: . . .
SAMANTHA: *Menopause: The Movie?*
ME: Oh.
SAMANTHA: Who knew the world was so interested in menopausal women? But just look at how much traction your little video is getting. Incredible.
ME: I think it's just mainly menopausal women who are interested in menopausal women. Which is, of course, a big part of the stigma. But menopausal women make up around twenty-five million people at any given time so, you know, not insignificant.
SAMANTHA (squealing): Oh Agatha, you're going to be so perfect.
AGATHA: What do you mean?
SAMANTHA: How are you fixed next week? The offers are pouring in for you. Invitations to speak on panels,

radio and TV interviews, articles you've been asked to write. Everybody wants a piece of you, darling.

ME (caustic): I'm the pin-up girl for menopausal women everywhere.

SAMANTHA: Oh my, that's fucking good. I'm going to write that down. No, wait, I'll dictate it to Penelope. PENELOPE!!

I held the phone away from my ear as she blasted Penelope with dictation. Then:

SAMANTHA: This is all working out so well, darling! You're such a clever girl, Agatha. Even I wouldn't have come up with such a scheme.

AGATHA: I didn't plan any of this, in fact I . . .

SAMANTHA: Absolutely, darling. That'll be our story and we'll stick to it.

ME: But . . .

SAMANTHA: Your tagline can be something like, *Menopause needs a new face and here it is.*

ME: Menopause needs a new facelift, more like . . .

SAMANTHA: Oh . . . let me think about that . . . we could get sponsorship from one of those cosmetic surgery clinics. They're everywhere now and they're laden down with cash, I'll just . . .

ME: No!

SAMANTHA: Sounds like there might be some wriggle room?

ME: There isn't.

SAMANTHA: Okay, good, let's discuss it later, shall we? In the meantime, congratulations, darling! You're going to make a wonderful pin-up girl for menopause.

ME: Wait, no . . . I didn't . . .

SAMANTHA: I know, darling, lots to discuss but I really
    must fly. I need to get myself up to speed on all things
    menopausal. I suppose I could ask you! Since you're the
    pin-up girl. Toodle-pip!

I had to sit down after the phone call.

However bad things were before, when I was just menopausal and miserable, they were disastrous now.

Not only was I menopausal and miserable but now, the
world and her mother knew about it.

And if by some miracle they didn't know it, they soon
would, if Samantha Sorley had anything to do with it.

There was no doubt about it, if my agent ever decided
to use her powers for good, wars would end and people
would just have to get along with each other, whether they
liked it or not.

14 June, 12.30 p.m.

Symptoms: Misguided optimism

I felt like I should write something.

Maybe by concentrating on my actual job, I might
persuade Samantha that I don't have time for any other
type of job (e.g. pin-up girl for menopause).

Also: it would be a welcome distraction.

Also: I was contractually obliged to write something.

And not just something.

An actual novel with a beginning, middle AND end.

Like, publishers are so demanding.

There I was sitting at my desk in the attic.
I managed to complete the following tasks:

1) Ate a packet of fig rolls.
2) Drank three pots of tea.
3) Peed six times.
4) Smoked seven cigarettes.
5) Read old reviews of my books in vain bid to boost inspiration and productivity.
6) Typed 'Chapter One' at the top of the screen.
7) Saved the file as 'Novel No. 16'.
8) Closed the file.
9) Checked if Aidan had fed Colm (yes; spinach, chickpea and potato curry).
10) Brought a bowl of spinach, chickpea and potato curry back to my desk (actually not bad for 'good-for-you-and-the-planet' food).
11) Opened 'Novel No. 16'. Renamed it 'Book number sixteen'. Closed the file.
12) Opened my mail with eyes partly shut to avoid seeing any emails from Anna wondering if my witches have been burned at the stake yet. I suppose I'll have to tie them to the stake eventually. There really were no happily-ever-after endings for witches back then.

Nothing from Anna. Relief. Followed immediately by worry. Shouldn't she be badgering me for a couple of chapters by now?

But then, even through my partially sealed eyelids, I noticed that my inbox was bulging with emails.

One hundred and fourteen of them. All from people I'd never heard of.

One hundred and fourteen women.

One hundred and fourteen menopausal women.

I opened the first one:

Dear Agatha,

I hope you don't mind me writing to express my gratitude to you for saying the word 'menopause' out loud – and proud! – at the literary festival. I further commend you for not sounding embarrassed or apologetic when you said it.

This might seem inconsequential for a confident and worldly woman such as yourself but it meant a lot to me. You have given me the courage I had been lacking to say – to myself as well as my colleagues, my family, even my mother – that I am a menopausal woman and that it is not contagious or something to worry or be mortified about.

I'm just menopausal.

My mother actually flinched when I said it.

Menopause.

I keep saying it now. I can't seem to stop.

Menopause. Menopause. Menopause.

Thank you, my dear Agatha!

A grateful – and menopausal – fan,

Breda Collins

I was pretty sure that no one had ever called me worldly before.

I read the second one, then the third and the fourth.

I kept reading.

They said pretty much the same thing. Versions of what Breda said.

I had nearly finished reading all of them when my phone pinged.

CAROL: I have a five-minute window before my next meeting. Tell me things. Keep it brief.

I forwarded a selection of the emails to her.

CAROL: Holy Oestrogel!
ME: ???
CAROL: It's a bio-identical version of oestrogen. How do you not know this?
ME: This is why I can't be the pin-up girl for menopause.
CAROL: It's pretty clear that these women need you.
ME: But I'm none of the things they say I am.
CAROL: Well . . . you seem pretty menopausal in fairness.
ME: Your menopause better be worse than mine.
CAROL: I'll do my best.
ME: It's not like I wanted any of this. It just happened. The menopause burst out of me like the Incredible Hulk out of Bruce Banner.
CAROL: You know, this might be good for you.
ME: How do you make that out?
CAROL: Getting out there. Talking about your feelings.
ME: . . .
CAROL: Have you turned your phone off?
ME: Why can't someone else menopausal talk about their feelings?
CAROL: There doesn't seem to be anyone else.
ME: What'll I do?

CAROL: Being the contrarian you are, you'll just end up doing the opposite of whatever I advise.

ME: Remember when we used to play rounders with the kids on the green and I was the captain and my team always won because I told them failure wasn't an option?

CAROL: I do.

ME: I miss that.

CAROL: Gotta go. Love you.

ME: You never used to say that.

CAROL: I'm leading by example. Talking about my feelings. Try it. The sky mightn't fall down, Chicken-Licken.

ME: Fuck you. That's me feeling angry by the way.

CAROL: See? Easy-peasy.

I tossed my phone on the desk and read the dregs of the emails.

I couldn't seem to stop. I read each line.

And between the lines, I read about pain. And loneliness. And confusion.

Damn it, I always get way too invested in stories.

Except these ones were real.

I'll have to write back to them. I have no idea what to say.

At least I'm writing.

That's something, I suppose.

4.15 p.m.

Doorbell.

Like, do people not know I'm working up here?

It was Melissa McDevitt from next door with her long teeth and simpering ways.

And okay, fine, I was seeing how many grapes I could fit in my mouth at the time – twelve (they're small, in fairness, not those swollen genetically modified ones), but Melissa McDevitt didn't know that, did she? There were grape skins trapped between my teeth because I was forced to eat them so quickly. They're tricky bastards to get at, especially with these bitten nails.

Of course the first thing she did was apologise and, because it was Melissa, she didn't just do it once but many times, over and over again until I had to say, 'STOP.'

And then Dad walked into the hall and wondered if I was going to ask Melissa in. He likes Melissa because she listens when he goes on (and on and on) about his forthcoming trip to Cuba with Leonora. Melissa thinks it's 'refreshing' to see such a . . . mature couple with such purpose.

Melissa smiled at Dad and said, 'Oh thank you' and stepped inside like she owned the place. 'But I won't stay long.'

DAD: Stay as long as you like.
ME: She just said she can't stay long.
DAD: She said she won't. There's a difference.
ME: Shouldn't you be practising the Mambo somewhere?

I headed for the kitchen, stepping over a crate of jars (Aidan may be unrealistic about the quantity of honey two hives can produce), a stack of towels (freshly laundered, no wonder I'm exhausted), a large cardboard box, delivered by the DPD man for Colm this morning, and LuLaBelle who had followed me from the attic and was now lying across the hall floor like a draught excluder.

Melissa picked her way carefully down the hallway. I assume

the state of my house repulses her. She is always cleaning something; I see her at the windows, the brass knocker on her front door, Dermot's jeep. Even the cobble-locking FFS, clutching the power hose like it's a wild boar you're trying to dissuade from eating a handful of junior infants.

And Melissa told me once that she only cleans outside the house when the inside is done.

It was a very matter-of-fact sentence and I could think of nothing to say in response.

5 p.m.

Finally got rid of Melissa by telling her I was expecting dinner guests. Then I remembered that I actually was expecting a dinner guest. Bloody Damien.

Jesus, that woman can talk. You'd think the excess of teeth in her mouth might serve as some kind of impediment.

You'd be wrong.

It turned out she's in a flower-arranging club.

I now know how many members there are, who the treasurer is, the secretary, the health and safety officer.

Wait, a health and safety officer? Like, why? All I could think of was a vase maybe. Getting smashed? It would be an accident of course, ladies who join flower-arranging clubs would not countenance smashing a vase against a wall. Or over another member's head. Even if that member really deserved it.

I'd bet my pension on that. If I had a pension.

MAM: I told you to get a pension, didn't I? There's nothing more unsightly than an old woman with holes in her gusset.

111

I was too old to start a pension now and my tights were threadbare so it was only a matter of time before the gusset gave way.

LUKE: You could just buy new tights.

He thinks he's such a solutions man.

Anyway, the bottom line with Melissa – which I now know because I interrupted her after ten minutes to say, 'What's the bottom line?' – is that she wants me to address the flower-arranging ladies.

That's what Melissa called them. Ladies.

ME: Why?
MELISSA (flushing): It was Dympna's idea, really. She saw *Menopause: The Movie* on Instagram and she sent it into the group chat. The other ladies were very impressed that I knew you personally.
ME: Well, we don't really know each other all th . . .
MELISSA: Do you know how many of us are menopausal?
ME: No.
MELISSA: All of us.
ME: Okay.
MELISSA: And do you know how often we've discussed the menopause?
ME: No.
MELISSA: Never.
ME: People don't have to always be talking about every single thi . . .
MELISSA: It's like you've given us permission to talk about it. We want to thank you.

ME: There's no need.
MELISSA: And we want to listen to what you have to say.
ME: But I don't have anything to say. I'm just . . . a meno-
pausal woman.
MELISSA: Exactly.
ME: . . .
MELISSA: We'll pay, of course.

I'm pretty sure Melissa could tell I was about to say no and maybe lob in an objection on behalf of flowers everywhere, ripped from their roots to be arranged by the clammy hands of menopausal women before dying in an overheated suburban house with excessive exposure to direct sunlight on account of people tearing down good, solid walls and replacing them with windows.

ME: How much?

I know, I know, I shouldn't have sounded so desperate but, the way things were going, it didn't look like I'd ever get my paws on that advance.

Which meant no new roof for the café which meant the insurance company would pull their cover which meant that . . .

MELISSA: Are you all right, Agatha? You look worried.

I'd been thinking about Luke's customers. Mrs O'Brien for instance, seeing a 'For Sale' sign go up outside the café. Her haemorrhoids would swell like balloons, no doubt about it.
I had to start earning something.

Melissa couldn't look at me in my eyeballs when she talked about money. She stuttered and stammered and her whole face flushed and she began sentences, then abandoned them and started again.

'Well, you see . . .'

'The thing is, I . . .'

'I mean, we're obviously . . .'

'What I'm trying to say is . . .'

A nicer person would put her out of her misery, I'd say. Eventually:

MELISSA: Would . . . I . . . two hundred euros be . . . I wish it could be more but . . .?

ME: I'll do it.

TWO HUNDRED QUID. I've been paid less for a sodding short story.

MELISSA (standing up and brushing the dust of my house off her dress): Now, I'd better let you go and get ready.

ME: For what?

MELISSA: Your dinner guests?

ME: Oh . . . yeah.

15 June, 4 a.m.

Symptoms: Irritability

If you didn't know better, you'd refuse to believe that Luke and Damien are twins. You wouldn't even believe they're brothers. Damien is long and thin and pale with salon-fresh luxury hair. Luke is short and stocky and dark and bald.

Mam hated the fact that I was taller than Luke. She wanted me to wear flats on my wedding day. She called them 'ballet pumps' to make them sound more appealing. Luke bought me shoes in the end. Italian ones, soft leather with a high heel, a narrow ankle strap and a slender silver clasp. They even managed to make my size eights look delicate.

Luke had to get up on his toes to reach me. I told him he didn't have to kiss me at the altar. We could tell the priest not to say, 'You may kiss the bride,' at the end.

LUKE (confused): Why would we do that?

Luke arrived with Damien in tow at seven on the dot, looking remarkably fresh and minty for someone who'd been making stew and custard since 7 a.m.

ME: You look lovely!
LUKE: Is that an accusation?
ME: Have you lost weight?
LUKE (shrugging): A few pounds maybe.
ME: We're European. We don't use the imperial system any more.
LUKE: I suppose it could be the yoga.
ME: What?
LUKE: I asked you to come with me, that new studio opposite the café gave me some free passes.
ME: I didn't think you were serious.
LUKE: Why wouldn't I be serious?

ME: We're not yoga people.
LUKE: What does that even mean?
DAMIEN: Is anyone going to ask me in?

Damien has an affected accent. Southside-lite, I'd call it.
Which, for a boy from Cabra, is no mean feat. It must cost
him a lot, in terms of concentration, to maintain it.

You'd nearly feel sorry for the fucker.

He dampened my cheek with his glossy pink lips and
handed me a bottle of wine.

DAMIEN: It's Saint-Emilion Grand Cru. A gift from a
    grateful client.

He went on and on about it (he said things like 'notes of
almond' without any sign of self-awareness as to how much
of a twat he sounded) and he was only dying for one of us
to ask how much it cost but of course I didn't because, well,
it's fun to annoy him. And Luke didn't because it wouldn't
occur to him. In fact, I was pretty sure Luke wasn't listening.
He was at the range, stirring toffee sauce. Apparently it can
stick to the bottom if you don't keep it moving. Also, it
burns the shit out of your tongue if you eat it straight from
the pot.

Yes, Luke was making all the right conversational sounds
– yeah, hmm hmm, really? etc. – but even though he had
his back to me, I got the distinct impression that he wasn't
listening to Damien. That he was off in his head somewhere.
Somewhere lovely. I suspected he was smiling. Although in
fairness, the steam from the toffee sauce would make Carl
Fredricksen from Up smile. Also, his hips were gently swaying

and his bare feet were tapping against the floorboards, as if in time to a piece of music.

Luke doesn't sway to music.

And even if he did – which he doesn't – there was no music to sway to.

Which reminded me to put on music, all the better to drown Damien out.

I put Blondie on the record player. I could still hear Damien but only if I concentrated which, obviously, I didn't.

Dad rocked in then, declaring, 'I love this song' and sashaying across the kitchen floor. He'd want to mind his hips, they crack like a whip when he does that. He declined Luke's offer of dinner – corned beef and roast parsnips – and said he already ate with Leonora at the hospital. They ordered sushi from the Japanese deli on Capel Street.

Six months ago, he probably thought sushi was a tropical disease.

DAD: Leonora showed me *Menopause: The Movie*. She says you're a firebrand.

DAMIEN and LUKE: What movie?

Occasionally, they get their twin on.

Dad looked very pleased with himself. I was pretty sure that's the first time Dad has ever said the word, 'menopause' out loud. He whipped out his new iPhone and swiped at the screen until he got the clip going.

DAMIEN: You'd nearly feel sorry for that guy, haha. . .
DAD: He had it coming.

AIDAN (coming in from garden): 15,439 views so far.
DAD: 15,440 now that I've shown it to Damien.
ME: And Luke.

I looked at Luke's face to see how he was taking it. He looked a bit peaky. He's not a big fan of the public display of . . . well, anything really.

ME: Luke?
LUKE: You're very . . . articulate.

Aidan didn't eat with us because it pains him to see us stuffing our faces with cow. Not that he'd say that out loud but it was there all the same, in the worried line of his shoulders as Damien pumped his hand in that rigorous, businessman way he has.

Like, who shakes their nephew's hand? Aidan's fingers were the colour of a testicle when Damien finally stopped. Aidan answered Damien's quick-fire round of questions.

Girlfriend? (none)

How's college going? (Aidan dodged with a brief, 'Fine,' which nobody contradicted because nobody wanted to give Damien a reason to pontificate on the merits of a university education, even if it is just English Lit.)

Job? (Aidan said he was working on a business idea and Damien winked, gave Aidan a dead arm and said, 'Chip off the old block,' meaning himself. Aidan did not mention scouting for bees or sowing seeds in suburban gardens. Nor did anyone else.)

Aidan plated up a portion of dinner, excused himself and left the kitchen. I could hear his light tread on the stairs, heading for his brother's room, and I knew for a fact that he was holding the plate at arm's length.

Colm is lucky to have a brother like that.

Damien had second helpings of everything, even though he initially smirked at Luke's 'famine-centric' menu.

Like, if they'd had corned beef and parsnips during the famine, a million people wouldn't have starved to death, would they?

The only reason I didn't clip that fucker around the ear and tell him what a twat he is, was because Luke specifically asked me not to physically or verbally abuse his brother during dinner.

He didn't say anything about dessert. Ha!

Then, when Damien had finally finished eating – he practically licked the toffee sauce off his plate – and drinking (he necked most of the poncy wine even though he told us initially that it should be savoured rather than drunk, the better to appreciate its myriad of qualities), he scanned the table to see if there was anything he'd missed.

Myriad.

Fuck sake.

I could have snapped him like a twig right there. Luke impressed one of his fleeting but meaningful looks on me. Which basically meant, 'Don't even think of snapping him like a twig.'

I suppose I get it. Luke was trying to keep Damien onside so he'd agree not to sell the café, which their dad – I still miss Ronnie – left to both of them out of some overinflated sense of fairness which Luke has, unfortunately, inherited. As well as half a dying café.

But before Luke got a chance to talk to Damien about the café, Damien launched into his latest 'business' plan.

DAMIEN: . . . something, something . . . business deal . . . ground floor . . . something . . . venture capital . . . investment opportunity . . . something . . . cash . . . market fluctuation . . . greed is good . . . something else . . . other stuff . . .

I was mostly not listening but that was the general gist.

Bottom line: Luke can either sell the café and give Damien his share. Or Luke can keep the café and give Damien his share.

Either way, Damien wants his share.

I finally persuaded Damien to leave.

ME: I think you should leave now, it's late.

Then I drank the gin and tonic Luke handed me. He even perched a bright pink paper umbrella on the lip of the glass and filled a bowl with black olives in chilli oil.

Then he sat opposite me with his bottle of beer. We sat there like that for ages.

ME: We're one of those couples now.
LUKE: What couples?
ME: The ones you see in pubs who don't have a thing to say to each other.
LUKE: Or we're just comfortable in each other's company. You look nice, by the way.
ME: 'Nice' is up there with 'harmless'.

LUKE: You're definitely not harmless.
ME: Are you sure you're related to Damien?
LUKE: I think it'll be okay.
ME: You always think it'll be okay.
LUKE: Well, it's thanks to you, really. With your advance coming in, we should be able to convince the credit union to lend us the money to pay Damien off. We can fix the roof another time.
ME: . . .
LUKE: I've been reading up. About the menopause.
ME: Can we talk about something else?
LUKE: Sure. You okay? You look a bit . . .
ME: I'm just tired.
LUKE: Me too.

And he did look tired. His eyes, anaemic blue, were shot through with red thread veins, his stubble, grey these days, made a scratchy sound when he pulled his hand along his jaw, his glasses could have done with a Melissa McDevitt style clean and one of the arms was stuck together with Sellotape.

ME: You better not be angling for a sympathy shag.
LUKE: I'm not.
ME: Oh.

18 June, 4 a.m.

Symptoms: Worry

About nothing in particular. Death, I suppose. I can get quite existential at this hour. And the online algorithms either know what I'm worried about or reckon that my day of reckoning is fast approaching because I keep getting ads for gravestones and burial plots.

The price of them!

If ever there was an optimum time for worrying, it's got to be 4 a.m. The conditions are ideal. It's quiet so the worries can come out from under the bed in your head and run amok, uninterrupted by any other distractions. Like how I can't even pretend to be writing the novel I'm supposed to be delivering in a few weeks with all the menopausal stuff that's going on. Keeping up with the correspondence alone is a full-time job. Menopausal women coming at me from all angles, sending me emails and messages on Twitter and Instagram and Facebook. The other day, I got an actual letter. In the post. Handwritten. On Basildon Bond paper. It was addressed to:

Agatha Doyle
Menopausal Writer Lady
Dublin

I'm worried about Dad too. The small matter of him haring off to Havana with Leonora. He hasn't a word of Spanish and his salsa isn't all that, which is probably a hanging offence in Cuba. The last time he was in an airport was for the annual church trip to Lourdes five years ago and Mam organised everything. All Dad had to do was follow her through the airport and remember not to buy the holy water at the grotto.

MAM: Too right! I had it on good authority that it was just common-or-garden tap water with no priestly blessing to speak of.

Good authority meant Fr Finnegan's housekeeper.

Let's see, what else? Oh yes, Bart. Ringing from Canada to complain about Dad squandering 'our' (read: his) inheritance. If Mam heard him at that, she'd tell him he wasn't too old for a clip around the ear even though forty-five really is too old, I'd say.

Although if Mam were around, there'd be no need for Bart to ring from Canada and complain about Dad squandering 'our' (read: his) inheritance because there would be no squandering of inheritance or anything else for that matter. Bart's just pissed off because when he finally relented and went for the IVF, Alice got pregnant a month later with not one, not two, but THREE babies.

Even I felt a bit sorry for him.

BART: I don't know how you and Luke have coped all these years. The triplets are literally draining me of every cent I manage to make. And I'm a senior financial adviser, dammit! I don't understand it. They mostly eat pasta and drink milk. What the actual fuck?

ME (sage): Children are the worst financial decision you'll ever make.

BART: But worth it? Right? In the end?

ME: . . .

Still, I've never seen Dad so animated. He calls the trip 'pursuing his life's dream'. Up until Mam died, his life's dream was to complete the cryptic crossword faster than my mother. He never managed it. In fairness, not many people could. And he certainly wouldn't have referred to it as a life's dream. I'm pretty sure he never had cause to use that combination of words. At least not when Mam was alive. And I never really saw him as someone with a life's dream. He was just a dad. He worked until he retired. Some civil service job, I never really knew what. He watched the telly. Did the cryptic crossword but never as fast as Mam. Fixed things. Like my bicycle. Untangled things. Like the string of Bart's dragon kite. Put oil on things, like the hinge on the back door. Cleared out the shed once a year. Went on holidays to Kerry every summer. Rain. Hail. Shine. Often rain. And hail.

He was like this copy-and-paste dad. He got a fishing rod when he retired. His colleagues thought he liked fishing because he drank out of a 'Gone Fishing' mug which I had given him one year for Father's Day because it was the kind of thing for sale in shops for Father's Day.

When he retired he did the sudoku as well as the crossword. Let his driver's licence lapse. Took the tablets my mother dispensed every morning. I haven't a clue what they were for. Some vague references to iron and blood pressure and, I don't know, bone density maybe? He stopped taking them after he met Leonora at the Senior Singles salsa class. And I have to admit that he looks a lot better than he used to. There's something sort of vital about him.

Luke better be fucking devastated when I die.

19 June, 9.35 a.m.

Symptoms: Dry eyes

Dryness was catching, it seemed. First my skin, then my vagina, my hair and now my eyes. The instructions on the bottle of eye drops said one to two drops per eye but that was like throwing peanuts at an elephant. I was pouring the stuff onto my eyeballs but most of it ran down my face and it looked like I'd been having quite the extended crying jag.

I knew this because Samantha FaceTimed me and wanted to know what I was crying about.

I told her that I was pretty sure my body was incapable of producing tears, should such inconveniences be called for.

SAMANTHA: Save all that raw emotion for the airwaves, darling.

ME: There's no raw emotion. I'm just allergic to eye dro . . .

SAMANTHA: Great, good, fantastic, harness that energy, yes? Now, where was I? Oh, yes, lots still coming in.

ME: Well, the thing is, I . . .

SAMANTHA: I know you're busy so I've taken the liberty of replying on your behalf. No need to thank me.

ME: But . . .

SAMANTHA: People want to meet you, Agatha. They know Agatha the author and now it's time to meet Agatha the Woman. The star of *Menopause: The Movie*. The firebrand who will take on the patriarchy one pair of Y-fronts at a time.

ME: . . .

SAMANTHA: First up is Patti Mason. You're familiar with her radio show, I take it? It's national. Great reach. I got you on that, Thursday afternoon. I know, quite the coup. What else? Oh yes. How would you feel about doing a live *Woman's Hour* type thingy happening in Liverpool

in . . . (SHOUTS) PENELOPE, WHEN'S THAT
WOMAN'S HOUR TYPE THINGY . . . That's right,
end of July, and they want you bad so I told them you'd
do it and . . . there was something else . . . oh yes, have
you thought about podcasting, Agatha?

ME: No.

SAMANTHA: 'Fuck You, Menopause', type of thing? You'd
be marvellous.

ME: Well, I . . .

Samantha barrelled on. A TV interview, another radio show,
a guest appearance on a podcast ('Menopausal Much?') and
an after-dinner speech, the details of which glanced off my
addled brain.

SAMANTHA: So? What do you think? They'll pay you of
course. I realise your last royalty cheque wasn't exactly
inspiring. But don't forget, you're due your advance as
soon as you deliver your new novel. How's it going?
Marvellously, I expect. Well done, Agatha! You just
concentrate on being the best pin-up girl for menopause
that you can be and don't worry your pretty little head
about money, darling.

People with money never think you should worry your
pretty little head about it.

Damn Luke for always supporting my writing, even in
the early years when I made barely a brass farthing.

'Who else will write your stories?' he'd say, when I talked
about going back to my old job that paid actual, real live
money.

And now he was the one who needed my support. Because who else will make sure the customers are getting enough fibre, cleverly disguised as rhubarb, stewed with brown sugar and cloves and ginger, under a thick wedge of his homemade vanilla ice cream?

SAMANTHA: So you'll do it?

It was more of a statement than a question.
   You'll do it.

ME: I'll do it.

After all, it's a paying gig.
   Not many of those around for a menopausal writer with writer's block.

11 a.m.

I rang Dr-Lennon-call-me-Susie who said dehydration is a common symptom of menopause.
   You'd think she'd make something up, just for a bit of variety.
   She advised between eight to twelve glasses of water a day and to cut down on tea and intensive workouts. HA!

11.30 a.m.

Aidan tried to persuade me to drink tea made with the mint he's growing in the garden. He said it's great for irritable bowel syndrome. Which, perversely, is one of the few conditions I do NOT have. I'm just irritable.

2 p.m.

Much needed distraction arrived in the form of a swarm of honey bees.

For a good two weeks Aidan had returned from his scouting trips empty-handed. Today, he actually found one! The swarm was hanging on a branch of the sycamore tree in the car park behind Bank of Ireland. The bank manager offered to pay him to remove it but Aidan said that the honey he would yield from them would be payment enough.

What a dope.

Still, I couldn't help feeling impressed with Aidan when he arrived home with a cardboard box full of bees.

MAM: That boy always had great persistence.

I'm pretty sure she was referring to that time Aidan finally persuaded her to part with a few shillings from her weekly pension to 'adopt a donkey'. To this day, I have no idea how he managed it. I think he went hard on the religious connection, what with Mary arriving in Bethlehem on such a creature.

I could see that Aidan was delighted with the opportunity to finally see if the smoker he'd made worked. He had fashioned it from a couple of empty sweetcorn cans and a foot pedal from an ancient blow-up mattress he'd found in the attic. It looked like a most unlikely contraption but when Aidan lit the pine needles inside it and pushed on the pedal to release the sweet-smelling smoke through the (watering can?) funnel into the cardboard box, the insistent buzzing of the bees quietened and a calmness descended. Like the bees had taken a collective Xanax.

I was reminded of six-year-old Aidan when I saw how gently he shook the box of bees into the hive.

That summer, I had finally caved under the barrage of pleas to get a pet and bought a hamster which Colm insisted on calling Animal, inspired by a brief but intense *Muppet Show* phase.

Hamster wheels are an actual thing! I thought it was just an analogy for the mundanity of life; if you observe a hamster turning and turning on a wheel for long enough, it will drain you of every ounce of vitality you possess.

Colm – who has a similar boredom threshold to me – asked for a basin of cold water, which I provided to him without asking why.

Classic clanger.

Always ask why. Especially when it's an eight-year-old with priors.

Of course Aidan told Colm that he didn't think hamsters could swim. And Colm said that was why he was teaching him. Animal turned out not to be the most receptive pupil, sinking to the bottom of the basin as soon as Colm set him on the surface of the water and staying there, despite Colm's repeated instructions to the contrary. It was Aidan who fished the poor little thing out, patted him dry between two sheets of kitchen paper. I was in the attic, hammering away on my keyboard. I was writing the first draft of what would become my famine novel at the time. I still remember Anna's feedback on the manuscript.

ANNA (nervous): Is it a little . . . political, do you think?

Like, everything's fucking political, Anna.

Anyway, there I was, scribbling away with Patti Smith cranked up on the stereo, but I still managed to hear Colm roaring crying in the garden, shouting for Aidan to save Animal who was dead, dead, dead, shouting it over and over again as if to emphasise just how dead Animal was. And the hamster did look fairly done in when I bolted down the stairs and raced into the garden. It was prostrate on the warm rock Aidan had placed him on. I remember the intense way the kid looked at the hamster, his pale blue eyes tracking up and down Animal's tiny, sodden body, and Colm weeping beside him, jumping up and down and roaring at Aidan to DO something. Aidan picked up the limp creature, lifted it to his face and opened the little fellow's mouth with the tip of his little finger. Breathed into the gap. And of course the mammy in me wanted to tell him to stop it. Immediately. He'd get ringworm or rabies or salmonella doing that. But then the fascination, watching the hamster's small body lift with Aidan's breath. Then fall and lift again.

Just three of Aidan's breaths it took in the end.

And even though the hamster only lasted another four weeks after that – he succumbed to 'wet tail' which is hamster for the trots – whenever Animal comes up in conversation, it is Aidan's careful ministrations I am reminded of.

Even so, I don't mind admitting that I was nervous looking at Aidan, holding the box of bees over the hive. Even in his anti-sting get-up. Even with the smoker all lit and ready to go.

The straw hat with the plastic fruit glued onto the brim

suddenly seemed like a red flag. Although – interesting fact – bees can't see red.

Unlike me.

But the bees might have thought the fruit was real and made a beeline for it (yes, I did search for another word because punning is one of my least favourite forms of humour) and the mantilla seemed way too flimsy to offer much protection against a swarm. Aidan assured me that bees were intelligent creatures and, even if they weren't, they would still never mistake the hunks of plastic for an actual apple, banana and lemon.

Fair point.

The rest of him was safe enough. Baggy track pants tucked into thick socks, rubber gloves and one of Colm's long-sleeved D.I.Guy T-shirts which is enormous on him.

Apparently, baggy clothes are the thing when getting up close and personal with bees.

Or a hazmat suit. That would be a lot safer. But no. Aidan said he wanted to present to the bees in as natural a state as possible so they would get to know him and understand that he meant them no harm.

Jesus H.

He opened the box, slow and steady, then held it over the hive until all the bees were inside. It took ages. Even Colm came down from his bedroom to witness the transfer of the bees into the hive.

COLM: Shake the box, it'll be quicker.
AIDAN: I don't want to scare them.
ME: Can bees feel fear?
AIDAN: All living things can.

I felt a strange prickling sensation behind my eyes and I became convinced that, if there was any moisture in my body, I might cry actual tears.

The bloody menopause.

ME: What's going to happen now?
AIDAN (slotting the wooden frames he made inside the hive and putting the lid on): We wait.
COLM: For how long?
AIDAN: Four weeks.
ME and COLM: FOUR WEEKS???

Aidan distracted us by pointing out the Queen Bee. I'm giving her capitals because she bloody well deserves them, since she spends her entire life reproducing, all while maintaining law and order in the colony using only her wits and her pheromones.

Although she's a tragic sort of creature too. Because as soon as she stops laying her thousands of eggs, the other bees turn on her and either kill her or exile her.

I'd love to give her a dig out when she is confronted with such rude behaviour but Aidan tells me I have to let nature take its course.

Which is basically the same as menopause without HRT.

Which I'm not a massive fan of, to be honest.

20 June, 4 a.m.

Symptoms: Menopausal

And no, Dr-Lennon-call-me-Susie, I cannot be more specific

than that. Sometimes, you just feel 'meh' and that is the menopause fucking with you.

Ergo: menopausal.

Good thing about radio interview: I don't have to worry about what to wear.

Bad thing about radio interview: I'll need to pass as some kind of menopausal guru.

Anna rang yesterday afternoon. I presumed it was about the novel I'm not writing. I let it go to voicemail but, when I listened later, Anna was just wishing me well in my radio interview tomorrow. Also, she wondered where to send the post she's been receiving on my behalf.

ANNA (gently): There are rather a lot of them. I suppose they must be from . . . (lowers voice) menopausal ladies who aren't on The Interweb (tinkly giggle).

Jesus H.

To distract myself, I wandered around Google for a bit.

Interesting fact about sixteenth-century witches: they have a pretty short mortality rate.

If they were any good as witches, surely they could have improved on that.

Interesting fact about bees:

1) All worker bees are female.

Typical.

2) A bee produces a teaspoon of honey (about five grams) in her lifetime.

133

Good luck filling a jar with that rate of production, Aidan.

3) To produce a kilogram of honey, bees fly the equivalent of three times around the world in air miles.

Query: Are air miles the same distance as ordinary miles? Either way that's a lot of flying.

4) Bees communicate with each other using dances.

I miss dancing. And now I'm too old to dance in a club (according to Aidan and Colm), and too young to join Senior Singles salsa (according to me).

5) Male bees are called drones (fitting). The only work they have to do is to mate with the queen. Apart from that, they lounge inside the hive, getting fed and watered by the worker bees, monopolising the remote and putting empty cartons of milk in the bloody fridge.

On the other hand, they have no sting and they die as soon as they've mated.
    Which is nothing less than they deserve.

6) I continue to be impressed with the Queen Bee, all those eggs she lays all day, every day. I don't know how she does it. I've only laid two eggs and I'm exhausted.

Melissa called in again.

MELISSA: Don't worry, I know you're busy, I'm not staying.
ME: Okay.
MELISSA: I just thought you might need some carrot cake
    to keep your strength up.
ME: Oh.
MELISSA: You do like carrot cake?
ME: Of course.
MELISSA: Here you are, I hope it's not too dry in the middle,
    I may have left it in the oven a bit longer than . . .
ME: Do you like tea?
MELISSA: Yes, I do, I . . .
ME: I'll make some.

Which hadn't been my intention at all.

There was a good chance I was nervous about the interview. And it's not like I've never been on the radio before.

I put it down to the subject matter. Menopause. And also, being menopausal. And also, making a show of myself on the internet.

There was a chance that, along with my oestrogen, progesterone and testosterone, my stock of confidence was also running low.

Melissa told me about her latest home-improvement project which is to convert one of the bedrooms into a home office for 'poor Dermot' who often has to send important work emails at the weekend. I was eating the cream cheese icing off my second slice of carrot cake.

MELISSA: I had hoped to fill all of the bedrooms with babies. What's that saying? We plan, God laughs.

ME: That seems like a pretty shitty thing for a god to do.

MELISSA: It wasn't poor Dermot's fault of course. I had cysts on my ovaries and the doctors weren't hopeful.

I knew I should say something here. I picked up the teapot and refilled her cup.

MELISSA: I was hopeful though. I tried IVF. In the end, Dermot said enough. We'd be bankrupt. I got the money for the last one from my dear mum, rest her soul. Dermot never knew. And I didn't have to tell him in the end because it didn't work. So, you know, every cloud.

I cut a second slice of cake for Melissa. It seemed like the least I could do.

MELISSA: My goodness, I didn't mean to bother you with all of that.

ME: You didn't. Bother me.

Then Melissa asked me if I was doing any other talks and I told her about the radio interview and she offered to drive me there. I was about to say I could drive myself thank you very much when she added that she could drop me right outside the door, then go park the car so I wouldn't have to worry about anything other than the interview.

MELISSA: Not that you need to worry, of course.

I was tempted. I still hadn't gotten the blood out of my red velvet shoes.

ME: You don't have to.
MELISSA: I want to. Besides, poor Dermot has to go to a conference in Zürich next week so I won't have to be home to get dinner ready.
ME: Don't you eat dinner?
MELISSA: I'll poach an egg or something.

The next thing you know, I'd invited her for dinner after the radio thing. I think it was the image of a single, solitary egg, poaching in a pan in Melissa's surgically clean kitchen that did it.

I had to tell her to stop thanking me. She hugged me before she left.

Then apologised for being so forward.

Then thanked me for being a good listener.

And for inviting her in.

And making her tea.

Then she hugged me again.

That time, I hugged her back.

There was nothing else to be done with her.

21 June, 4 a.m.

Symptoms: Distracted

I'm trying to remember why I agreed to do the radio interview.

When I remembered – the money – it brought scant comfort.

For starters, it wasn't a lot of money.

I worked out I would have to do about a hundred of them to fix the café roof.

The only other alternative was to write my novel but, in spite of getting in the chair and staying in the chair as per my smug, know-it-all advice to aspiring writers, I had written nothing.

Tonight, the hot flush is in my hair, damp strands of it plastered against my face. I gathered as much as I could in a topknot and got out of bed to change the pillowcase, damp and stained with sweat.

Note to self: buy more pillowcases.

The screen of my phone lit up, highlighting the brown lines of sweat stains on the pillow too.

Note to self: buy more pillows.

CAROL: Hello my little hormonal hellcat.

ME: I could have been asleep!

CAROL: I'm pretty sure you were wide awake, trying to remember why the hell you agreed to talk about the meno-pause on the radio?

ME: How's things with Crystal?

CAROL: Nice pivot.

ME: Well?

CAROL: Early days but . . . cautiously optimistic.

ME: Sex?

CAROL: Obvs.

ME: Good?

CAROL: A woman never kisses and tells.

ME: You always kiss and tell.

CAROL: Okay fine, it's exceptional.

ME: That's nice. I'm gonna try to get some sleep.
CAROL: You okay?
ME: Yeah.
CAROL: Liar.
ME: I'm saving all my moans for the airwaves tomorrow.
CAROL: That's my girl.
ME: Night.
CAROL: Sleep tight.

But I can't. Now I'm thinking about the last time Luke and I attempted sex. Which feels like a hundred years ago. Except the memory of it is as sharp as one of Mam's darning needles.

Sex on a Wednesday night.

A perfectly ordinary Wednesday night.

A nothing-to-see-here Wednesday night.

Luke had brought home the remains of his pear and ginger crumble and we ate it with soup spoons straight from the dish. I can't remember what we talked about. Ordinary things. Our voices sounded echoey in the kitchen. We had the house to ourselves. Everybody was where they were supposed to be.

ME (taking his spoon off him): I suppose I should fuck you now.
LUKE: I suppose you should.

And that should have been that.

Me, reefing off my T-shirt dress, Luke's pupils dilating when he clocked my no-knickers situation, me kicking off my runners, Luke, trying and failing to undo my bra, me undoing my bra, Luke lifting his Full Shilling apron over his head, tossing it on the floor, the pair of us up against the fridge freezer, Luke pulling me against him and sliding his fingers between my legs and kissing me in that way he has. Like he's tasting me and I taste delicious.

I thought it would always be that easy.

Until it wasn't.

Luke was inside me and I had my legs wrapped around his waist when, all of a sudden, my vagina called a halt to proceedings.

It was sandpaper dry.

I kept going. I think I was hoping it was just a temporary glitch.

Normal service will resume shortly.

It was Luke who stopped in the end.

LUKE: I'm sorry, am I . . . hurting you?

ME: No, no, it's fine, it's just . . . a temporary glitch.

LUKE: We could try . . . Vaseline?

ME: I think that may be the unsexiest thing you've ever said to me. And I've heard you listing the ingredients in black pudding.

Normal service did not resume shortly.

Or at all, really. Apart from a few half-hearted attempts. With each of those, my libido, once so high and mighty, shrank and lowered until it was dragging along the floor.

ME: Do you mind? That you're not getting your conjugal rights?

LUKE: Maybe I'll report you to Fr Finnegan.

ME: Ha!

LUKE: Anyway, it's just temporary.
ME: Yeah. It's just temporary.

That was two months ago.

22 June, 3 p.m.

Symptoms: Hard to say. Lowered resistance to flattery maybe . . .

When I arrived at the studio – on time, thanks to Melissa – the producer man told me he liked my 'look'.

I had found my denim shirtdress at the back of the wardrobe.

MAM: Isn't that a bit short for a nearly fifty-year-old woman?

And a pair of cheerful bright orange tights.

MAM: Which will clash with your hair!

I had to make do with my second-best pair of runners.

One of the annoying things about having big feet is that your sons steal your shoes. Of course, Aidan insisted that he got my permission to borrow them but the only reason I agreed was because it was seven o'clock in the morning and I'd only just gotten back to sleep after a savage bout of insomnia.

PRODUCER MAN: I'm Den, by the way.
ME: I'm . . .

PRODUCER MAN/DEN: I know who you are, Agatha. We've all been dying to meet you.

'We all' turned out to be producer man and the anchor – Patti Mason – who was in the studio with a massive pair of earphones clamped on her head, talking feverishly into a microphone. She waved at me through the window and mouthed something indecipherable. I entertained judgemental thoughts about the quality of her diction.

ME: Is Den short for Denis?
PRODUCER MAN/DEN: No.

I couldn't help grinning, which encouraged him to thread his arm through mine and walk me down the corridor, talking all the while. He brought me to the canteen which was a room the size of a stationery cupboard with a kettle and some mugs with initials in capitals painted on the sides in Tippex. He handed me a mug with 'AD' Tippexed on it.

PRODUCER MAN/DEN: That's yours to keep.
ME: My cup overfloweth.
PRODUCER MAN/DEN: I knew you'd be a scream.

Producer man/Den had a lisp which made him seem even younger than he already was. Also, tactile with a lot of eye contact. When he spoke – e.g. 'Patti is ready for you now' – he accompanied it with a wink as if he'd said something outrageous. His tone was confessional and his clothes were hyper-stylish; a mustard military-style jacket over red tartan drainpipe trousers and a pair of vintage Adidas hightops.

Dark hair with the kind of gloss that comes from youth and product. Carefully tousled bed-head on top with shaved sides. Complicated but well-tended facial hair. You could enter it into a topiary competition and it would place. Very smiley, which I told him he would regret when those 'laughter lines' dig in.

Nothing funny about laughter lines once they dig in.

3.30 p.m.

Den led me into the studio and introduced me to Patti who told me I had a great voice for radio.

Which is better than being told I've a great face for radio.

Patti was in the same age bracket as producer man/Den. Mid-thirties or thereabouts. A lovely age, when your roaring twenties are still ringing in your ears. And forty is like an inhospitable island, way out to sea, shrouded in mist and menace but far enough away to give you the – false – impression that you've got ages yet, till you wash up on its rocky shore.

What I wouldn't give for forty now.

3.45 p.m.

PATTI: So, I'll play the audio of *Menopause: The Movie*, then introduce you, okay?

ME: Hmmm.

PATTI: And then you can get into the nitty gritty and tell us all about your menopausal symptoms and the impact it's had on your life.

ME: The thing is, Patti, I'm not quite sure . . . what I mean is, I didn't quite mean to become the, you know, poster girl for menopause.

PATTI (grinning): I know exactly what you mean. I was supposed to be a gynaecologist. Turns out I'm squeamish. My mother's still not over it.

ME: My mother would haul herself out of her grave and drag me home by my hair, if she could.

PATTI (laughing): The listeners are going to love you, Agatha. Okay, here we go.

I was rigid with anxiety as Patti went through her spiel. Any time I went upstairs to my brain to see if it had come up with anything interesting to say, the lights were off and no one was home. The chair I was sitting in was upholstered in fake leather and, between that and the heat of the studio, I worried that Den would have to peel me off the seat, pore by pore.

PATTI: What do you say to that, Agatha?

ME: Oh. Sorry. Could you . . . repeat the question please?

PATTI: Something-somthing-patriarchy-women-something-equal-rights-something.

MAM: Agatha Bernadette Doyle, don't you dare make a show out of me.

ME (sitting up): That's a great question.

And, somehow, I was off.

In the end, it wasn't all that difficult to keep me out of the discussion.

I kept to the facts.

There are over fifty symptoms of menopause at time of speaking. FACT.

The menopause will happen to everyone with a uterus. That's fifty per cent of the world's population. FACT.

I quoted statistics from a survey I had read up on. It was carried out by the Irish Nurses and Midwives Organisation.

Forty-seven per cent of them said that they were not at all prepared for menopause.

Sixteen per cent said they had no education or information at all with regard to menopause.

Ninety per cent said that their symptoms affected them at work.

Sixty-two per cent said they wouldn't talk about menopause to their employer. The reason? Good, old-fashioned stigma.

PATTI: They're pretty scary numbers, Agatha.
ME: And these are nurses and midwives! If they don't have enough education and information about menopause, then what hope is there for the rest of us mere mortals?

Patti seemed pleased with her listeners' response to the item. She turned her monitor around so I could see the tweets and Snapchats pouring in. Then she announced that she was going to open the phone lines.

They saved me, the listeners. One after the other, they revealed themselves, talking about their problems, their symptoms and – of course – their feelings.

So I didn't have to.

RANDOM CALLER #1: I've had to quit my job because of my menopausal symptoms. I love my job. I mean, I loved my job.

RANDOM CALLER #2: I can't tell my mother I'm on HRT because she thinks women who take it are weak and pathetic and vain.

RANDOM CALLER #3: My GP told me I'm depressed. But after listening to Agatha, I know I'm not. I'm just menopausal.

RANDOM CALLER #4: I have vaginal atrophy but my husband still insists on sex.

RANDOM CALLER #5: My GP doesn't believe in HRT, says there's nothing the matter with me that a diet and exercise won't fix.

And on they went.

On and on. So many women. Brave women. So many different symptoms. So much indifference. From everywhere: family, society, employers, the medical profession.

And even though it was radio, I felt the callers' eyes on me. Like these women could see me. And I could see them. Adrenalin raced around my body and I felt the hairs on the back of my neck lift and quiver.

Through the studio window, Den signalled to me, mouthing, 'You okay?'

I nodded.

Weirdly, I was.

I was okay.

4.35 p.m.

The item went way over time and Patti had to cut lots of callers off in the end. She looked at me.

PATTI: You seem to have touched a national nerve there, Agatha.

ME: Keeping menopause taboo and shameful is just another way of the patriarchy fucking with us. Am I allowed to say fucking?

PATTI: Well, you just did so it's a moot question now.

4.40 p.m.

After the ad break, Patti lightened the mood by asking what I was working on at the moment so I had no choice but to launch into my spiel about the sixteenth-century witches. Clara was branded a witch when the ship on which she was sailing to Copenhagen foundered on some treacherous rocks and sank. Clara's husband – a cad – was drowned along with the suitor of Clara's lover, Ellen.

In fact – why not, I was making this up as I went along – everybody drowned apart from our two star-crossed lovers.

Nothing like a storm at sea to drive a narrative.

The pair are arrested on suspicion of witchcraft and are sent to the torture chamber.

Patti wanted to know about the instruments of torture. In fairness, who doesn't love a bit of torture-porn? The pulling off of fingernails always generates a visceral response. Patti's fingernails are small and painted an electric blue. She curled her hands into fists when I regaled her with the ways of the torture chamber.

PATTI: What happens then? To Clara and Ellen?

ME: You'll have to buy the book.

PATTI: I will! When is it out?

ME (airy): Oh, not till next spring, I'm afraid.

The lies! They kept coming. By the end, even I was curious as to what the hell happened to Clara and Ellen. Of course, I know what happened to them – they were burned alive. There were no happy endings for witches back then. Or for women in the main.

5 p.m.

When I was leaving, producer man/Den asked me out.

ME: Like, on a date?
PRODUCER MAN/DEN: Of course.
ME: Why?
DEN: Because I find you attractive and interesting and funny, in no particular order.
ME (curious): What would we be doing? On the date?
PRODUCER MAN/DEN: We could go for iced coffees. Maybe some paintballing. Dancing. A table quiz. Whatever you like.
ME: Can you dance?
DEN: Of course.
ME: What's your favourite type of dance?
PRODUCER MAN/DEN: Disco, obvs.
ME . . .

(Disco is my second favourite after samba but I don't tell him that, men read stuff into that kind of nonsense.)

PRODUCER MAN/DEN: So?
ME: So what?

PRODUCER MAN/DEN: You wanna go out sometime?
ME: No.
PRODUCER MAN/DEN: Can I send you a friend request
    on Snapchat?
ME: Send away.
PRODUCER MAN/DEN: Yes, but will you accept it, is
    what I mean?
ME: Unlikely.

We parted on amiable terms, producer man and me. The
resilience of youth is a powerful thing. I refused to feel
flattered by his attention but it was true to say there was
a – slight – spring in my step as I exited the building. I
know this to be true because:

MELISSA: You've got a spring in your step, Agatha! The
    interview went well, I take it?

Crap. Melissa. I'd forgotten about her and my hasty offer
to cook her something that wasn't a poached egg. I rang
Luke to see if he'd bring some leftovers home from the
café.
    Of course there weren't.
    Bloody liver and onion casserole day at the café. The auld
ones are mad for liver. Luke serves it with mash and peas.
And it was pension day which meant that his Guinness cake
had been demolished too.
    Then he added, like it's an afterthought:

LUKE: Oh, and I'll be late home anyway. I have that thing,
    remember?

ME: No.

LUKE: The appraiser guy. That Damien hired. He's coming around to have a look at the café.

ME: Have you put any serious consideration into telling Damien he's a . . .

LUKE: He's just looking for a valuation.

ME: I'll give him a valuation.

LUKE: Agatha, could you please . . .

ME: In the interests of transparency, I think you should know that a producer-man type called Den finds me attractive and interesting and funny.

LUKE: Oh, the radio interview. How did it go?

ME: Attractive and interesting and funny, in no particular order, were his exact words.

LUKE: Is Den short for Denis?

ME: No.

LUKE: Oh. Look, sorry, I need to go. Did you sign the loan application form I left on your bedside table?

ME: Luke? Hello? Are you there? You're breaking up . . . Can you hear me?

When Aidan got back from the beekeeper conference thingy he was at, he said that three people admired his (read: MY) runners. I said he could pay me back by making dinner but he said he didn't have time to cook, he was going foraging with someone he met at the conference.

ME: Who?

AIDAN: Whom.

ME: You're not too old for a flick of a damp tea towel.

AIDAN: Fine. Her name is Marija.

He blew me a kiss on his way upstairs.

ME: Don't use all the hot water.

6 p.m.

DAD (cha-cha-cha'ing his way through the kitchen): Don't put my name in the pot for dinner, Agatha.

ME: You treat this place like a hotel.

DAD: I'll give it an excellent review on Tripadvisor.

ME: Do you have your keys?

DAD (taking out his keys and rattling them in time to the 'rhythm'): Yes.

ME: Where are you going anyway?

DAD: To visit Leonora. She's just been told she has to spend a week in some recuperation place after they release her from the hospital. I'm going to cheer her up with *Flashdance*.

ME: Tell her I was asking for her.

DAD: Really?

ME (shrugging): That's what people do.

Despite my best efforts to be affronted by Leonora, I couldn't help feeling a soupçon of sympathy for her and her hips. She looked pale beneath her carefully applied pink-powdered face when she FaceTimed Dad the other day. After some grilling – by me, obvs – she eventually admitted that the physio was torturous. I told her about the witches and the fingernails to take her mind off the pain and she agreed that it helped a little.

So I was left with no choice but to make something that wasn't a poached egg for Melissa as Dad cha-cha'd out the front door and down the garden path.

Melissa told me that dinner was delicious. It was basically a tin of tomatoes poured over rice and beans. In fairness I could have served her a carton of Pot Noodles and she would have complimented me. She said she'd never eaten a vegan meal before, since 'poor Dermot' was anaemic and needed his red meat. Aidan shot me a warning glance when she said that. I swear that boy gets more like his father every day.

23 June, 9.45 a.m.

Symptoms: Feelings of inadequacy

Samantha rang. Well, she got Penelope to ring, then say, 'Can you hold for a call from Samantha Sorley please?'

They share the same office, for fuck sake.

A lengthy pause – I'm surprised Samantha doesn't get Penelope to hum bloody 'Greensleeves' – and then Samantha came on the phone and barked, 'Samantha Sorley' so then I had to remind her that she called me.

She had the decency to fangirl me over Patti's interview first ('so brave' . . . 'such authenticity' . . . 'fantastic brand building' . . . etc., etc.) before she got to the real reason for her call.

She'd had a call from the organiser of the *Woman's Hour* event in Liverpool after Samantha sent her the clip of me on the radio.

ME: She's changed her mind.
SAMANTHA: No! Of course not! She adores you!
ME: But?

SAMANTHA: Well, she did mention one thing, I suppose . . .

ME: I'm too menopausal. That's it, isn't it?

SAMANTHA: No! You're perfect! Just the right amount of menopausal in fact. It's just . . .

Of course, I already know what the problem is. The problem is that I'm supposed to have a solution. To the menopause. Before I go on TV or radio or whatever-you're-having-yourself.

Here's how it works:

- The problem (how it started, impact on your life and the lives of Significant Others, yada, yada . . .).
- Denial: doing best to get on with Life on Planet Earth while pretending problem is either (a) not a problem or (b) not happening.
- Realisation: the problem is in fact (a) an actual problem AND (b) happening. To you.
- Anger: you now realise you have a problem and you're mad as hell about it.
- The solution . . .

The thing is, menopause is brand new in terms of evolution. Like, it didn't actually exist for most women until well into the twentieth century, I'd say. Since the average life expectancy was still only fifty in the early 1900s.

Still, a hundred years or so of menopause and the main thing that anyone has come up with so far is HRT – which not every woman feels she can take (at least, not this woman). I'm confused with the conflicting messages about HRT from Dr-Lennon-call-me-Susie and Dr Hardiman.

I'm more inclined to believe 'Susie'. She cited her sources. All Dr Hardiman ever did was make declarations in a smug, know-it-all monotone.

But apart from any of that, there's the small but not insignificant fact that I have inherited Mam's aversion to taking medicine, along with a healthy disregard for the pharmaceutical industry. Then there's the cost of HRT. Sixty quid a month, according to Melissa.

Jesus H.

And even if I do mention HRT in interviews, my testimony in this regard will lack credibility since I've never been on it.

So that bit of my spiel – the last five minutes, which is supposed to have a ring of triumphalism about it – how I 'battled' menopause and brought it to its (now non-achy) knees type of thing – is missing.

SAMANTHA: . . . so have a think, darling. All we need is a pithy soundbite solution for menopause and we're golden. Simples! Oh, and if you could put a bit more of yourself in your content.

ME: What do you mean?

SAMANTHA: The facts and figures are all great but your adoring public want to know how Agatha, the woman, feels. Not Agatha the search engine. They want a map of your emotional landscape as it were. Oh, that's good actually, I'll write that down . . . No, I'll dictate it to Penelope....PENELOPE!!!

ME: . . .

SAMANTHA: Okay, now that's sorted, I'll leave you to get on with your novel. How's it going?

ME: Oh . . . you know . . . a little sluggish with all the . . .
   menopausal stuff.
SAMANTHA: Once you come up with your soundbite,
   it'll be plain sailing, darling.

She hung up before I had a chance to tell her what the
problem is.

The problem is: (1) I don't have a map of my 'emotional
landscape'.

And (2): I'm still at the anger stage.

I don't have a solution.

Nor am I an expert on menopause.

I am just menopausal.

Also, a moany cow who can't keep her thoughts in check
like ordinary people.

24 June, 7 a.m.

**Symptoms: Unslakable thirst. The water I drink seems to go
directly into my bladder, bypassing the Sahara Desert that is
my actual body**

Seven a.m.!! Two hours after I finally managed to fall asleep.
Along came Dad, knocking on my bedroom door, wondering
if I was up. I told him it was seven o'clock in the morning
and he nodded and said, 'Yes!' like that was a good thing.

Bloody hell.

DAD: It's a beautiful day out there.
ME (reefing the duvet over my head): I'll take your word
   for it.

DAD: I could bring you up some breakfast?

ME: No. Thank you.

DAD: It's just . . . the thing is . . .

ME (shoving down the duvet again and sitting up): What?

DAD: I was wondering if you'd give me a lift to the opticians? I've to collect my new glasses. So I can drive. Remember? I told you.

He waited at the door until I remembered. Which I did eventually. He told me all about it in the middle of the night last week when he was making bloody goodie in MY kitchen.

How he had searched high up and low down for his old licence, since he needed it to reapply for his new one

How he eventually found it (in the filing cabinet Mam bought in a fire sale in the local bookies). Filed under L. For Licence. How it was indeed four years out of date.

Then I refused Dad's offer of half his bowl of goodie and went back to bed and forgot all about it and assumed he would too.

Except that now it seems he's applied for a new one. Online.

Leonora showed him how to do it.

Here is the proof, if any were needed, of how drastically my father has changed: he thinks he'll get his new licence in time to pick That Woman and her brand-new hips up from the hospital next week.

ME: What time is your appointment at the optician's?

DAD: Ten o'clock.

Why, why, why do old people arrive much too early for everything?

WHY?

And why are they so interested in the death notices? They read them like they're a Sally Rooney novel; quietly compelling. Mam was no exception. She read the notices every morning. She enjoyed it. Working out the language of them. Reading between the lines. 'Sudden' might be a massive heart attack. Or a blood clot that managed to get all the way to the brain without the heart noticing.

Suicide. She'd whisper that word. Or an accident. If it was in the country, maybe a farm accident. Maybe the poor unfortunate fell into a slurry pit. Or under the wheels of a tractor.

'Peaceful' was cancer, more than likely.

I asked about Parkinson's since that's what Ronnie had. She shook her head. 'I don't know,' she admitted. 'Nothing peaceful or sudden about Parkinson's.'

That's true.

Mam's death notice said 'peaceful'. And 'no flowers'. And 'Donations but only if you can spare it to Breast Cancer Ireland'. She insisted on the 'only if you can spare it' bit. She said she didn't want anyone to feel obligated.

8 a.m.

Dad asked me if I was going to get ready and I told him that I WAS ready. I was wearing a pair of baggy track pants with one of those comfortable elasticated waistbands that allow your waist to expand in direct correlation to your carbohydrate intake, one of Colm's D.I.Guy T-shirts (#*hammerandtongs*) and a fleece jacket. I hadn't brushed my hair but I'd managed to trap it all in a massive scrunchy and place it in a bundle on top of my head.

Dad nodded and said, 'Oh. Right,' and walked quickly into the garden to give LuLaBelle her daily grooming.

Which is what I presume he thinks I need.

8.30 a.m.

There was something wrong with the email notification function on my phone because it wouldn't stop pinging so I went into my inbox to check it out.

It turned out the notification function on my phone wasn't banjaxed after all. My inbox was flooded with emails. I'm talking Noah's Ark flooded. All from menopausal women. I'd been getting a good few on the daily since 'It's all in the past'.

But nothing like this.

This was the mothership.

Hundreds of emails. From women who had heard me on Patti's show.

Samantha wasn't exaggerating when she boasted about Patti's listenership figures.

A lot of thank yous.

Which was nice, I suppose.

But also a lot of questions. I responded to as many as I could with a succinct one-liner, telling them I'm not a doctor and they should ask their GPs, but that only resulted in another onslaught of emails, some of which struggled to conceal their frustration. Doctors had been consulted, it seemed. One email was from an actual doctor who confessed that, over the course of his seven-year medical degree, the menopause was covered in one elective lecture which he missed because he was dog-sitting for his brother's girlfriend's terrier. I felt less hostile towards Dr-Lennon-call-me-Susie who never said she didn't know. If she didn't know, she'd promise to find out.

10.30 a.m.

Dad's appointment was thirty minutes late. Which meant I had to sit in the opticians for forty-five minutes because Dad insisted on arriving early. 'Just in case,' he said, but when I said, 'In case of what?' he had nothing of note to add.

Then, while Dad was in with the optician, I had a hot flush.

A hot flush in public is like being one of those guys walking the streets bowed down with a sandwich board. Passers-by don't pay them any attention but they can't seem to help noticing that you can get an all-you-can-eat buffet for a tenner at Dumplings on Capel Street.

I'm the person that nobody would be able to pick out of a line-up. My sandwich board says: 'MENOPAUSAL WOMAN' with many, many exclamation marks.

The receptionist – a young, blond affair – is appalled but trying not to stare, since she is polite and her mother probably trained her not to stare at amputees in wheelchairs. Or people with tortured walks. Or misshapen heads.

Don't finish sentences for stutterers, her mother probably advised. They'll get there eventually. Be patient.

I'm sure her mother – let's call her Jennifer for now – never specifically said, 'Pretend you don't notice when a woman is being menopausal' but the receptionist has clearly assumed this directive to be the correct – and safest – approach.

Well done, Jennifer!

Hot flush: it started in my head, like my brain sending up a warning flare. Which I suppose is pretty decent of it. But forewarned is not forearmed in this case because, apart from taking off my jacket, there was nothing to be done except wait. The flare quickly became a flame, then a fire. Along came a wind to disperse the fire around my body, the heat building. The familiar rush of blood through my body, the flush of heat along my neck, into my face, my fingers swelling, beads of sweat blooming on my forehead.

DR-LENNON-CALL-ME-SUSIE: Don't forget to breathe, Agatha!

ME: Breathing is an automatic reflex and not subject to forgetfulness.

I took a deep breath in and tried not to notice Jennifer's daughter pretending not to notice me, sitting there brick red and sweating and doing my best not to hyperventilate.

A baby, sitting on her mother's lap, watched me like I was an episode of *Peppa Pig*.

Mummy Pig should have hot flushes. Normalise them so that babies don't stare at menopausal women in waiting rooms. I stuck my tongue out at the baby but that just made her giggle. She planted her pudgy hands over her eyes, then peeked at me through her fingers. Like she thought I was the type of woman who played peekaboo with random babies.

After several rounds of bloody peekaboo, I was exhausted. Kids are so relentless. And my hands were scorched with all the pressing of my palms against the dense heat of my face.

10.45 a.m.

I took my phone out of my bag with a great sense of purpose and the baby seemed to accept that was pretty much end game in terms of peekaboo. True to his word, Den had sent me a friend request on Snapchat.

Which I ignored.

10.50 a.m.

Dad bounced out of the optician's office with a new pair of glasses. Hipster ones with thick black frames.

RECEPTIONIST: Very Elvis Costello!

Like, how does she even know who Elvis Costello is?

Her mother of course! Good old Jennifer. She must be a fan.

11 a.m.

Dad wanted to show Leonora his glasses. He said the number 27 bus would take him all the way to the hospital. He's been taking the bus a lot lately, waiting for his licence to be renewed. It's taking ages. They're making him jump through hoops. I know he's ancient but he's not a bad driver, provided you don't need to get anywhere in a hurry.

I offered him a lift and he said he didn't want to further impose on me while I was working.

At first I thought he was being facetious since I haven't been working but then I remembered I've been sitting in the attic as if I have been working so I can't blame him for his assumption.

I told him I could manage.

I drove past the café on my way to the hospital. It's not that far out of my way. I had a sudden, well, I wouldn't go so far as to call it a longing. Or a need. More of an inclination. To see Luke. It seemed like the longest time since I had seen him upright. Awake. Not tired. Looking at me in that quizzical, vaguely amused way he has. I had a sudden yen to tell him things. Aidan in the garden, sweet-talking the bees, and Melissa's invitation to speak with the menopausal flower arrangers.

He was behind the counter of The Full Shilling as he always is, apron on and a tea towel tossed across his shoulder. Behind him on the wall, the portrait that Luke's mother painted of Ronnie when he was about the age Luke is now. Peas in a pod, the pair of them. The same anaemically pale blue eyes, the same knot of muscles in his arms from all that dough kneading. Carmel was no Frida Kahlo yet she still managed to tell the story of her husband in the painting. The quiet strength of him is there in his gentle smile and rolled-up sleeves, the stained apron struggling to contain his stocky frame.

It was such a familiar scene, through the window of the café. The world's way of saying, 'Don't worry, everything is exactly as it should be,' and I was about to blow the horn and give Luke the fingers and wait for him to come out with oatmeal biscuits the size of our faces. He'd lean in through the window, try and kiss me to annoy me. And I'd swat him away and he'd persist so that it would be easier, in the end, to succumb and then he'd kiss me on my mouth and I'd smell the smell of him. Onions and turnips and that dreadful carbolic soap he favours. And a hint of something warm and sweet like the custard that Mrs Donnelly thinks he makes especially for her.

Then Dad sat up straighter in the passenger seat and said, 'Who's that?'

I cursed his new Elvis Costello glasses. Sashaying through beads strung across the doorway to the kitchen, a creature emerged.

A breathtaking creature. Carrying a tray, loaded with Luke's cherry buns, fresh out of the oven. Her face was flushed from the heat of them. Not menopausal-flushed. No. There was nothing menopausal about this woman. You could take a bite out of her and it would be crisp and sweet and juicy.

She was wearing a Full Shilling apron and had a tea towel draped over her shoulder, just like Luke. She stopped beside him, set the tray on the counter and started talking, not just with her mouth but with her whole face. In fact, her entire body. There was a lot of gesticulation and movement. If her hair hadn't been trapped beneath those hideous hair nets that Luke insists on, it would have been all over the place. An abundance of black curls, so glossy you could probably see your reflection in the strands. Her hair was the biggest thing about her. The rest of her was tiny.

Petite.

Breathtaking.

There is a breathtaking creature behind the counter at The Full Shilling.

The creature stopped talking and Luke started talking, drawing his arms apart, wide as the smile on his treacherous, stinking, lying face, like he's bragging on the size of a fish he caught. I wanted to lean out the car window and shout, 'He puts them back into the water!'

DAD: Are you okay?
ME: Of course I'm okay, why wouldn't I be okay?
DAD: No reason.

I loosened my grip on the wheel and I became aware of my hands. How big they looked. Even bigger than usual. Huge in fact. I could plough a field with them.

Dad leaned over and his hand – which is just an ordinary-sized hand – hovered above my shoulder before he permitted it to land and then he patted me. Not in the effusive way he pats LuLaBelle. This was a single, tentative pat before he withdrew. I drove on.

11.40 a.m.

Dad invited me to join him and Leonora at the café in the hospital.

ME: No.

But then he gushed about the banana and peanut butter muffins they serve and he went into a fair bit of detail; they only ever use crunchy peanut butter. The top is sprinkled with poppy seeds and the size of them! As high as cakes, some of them. But so light and sweet, the texture . . .

At the end of his tribute, he said, 'I'd nearly go so far as to call them . . . divine.'

This was quite the statement since Dad is pretty religious. At least he used to be. He would never have done the dirt on Mam, for example. He had the good grace to wait until she was dead to find the love of his life.

Although now that I'm thinking about it, I don't think he's darkened the door of a church since the funeral.

12.30 p.m.

Leonora is one of those women who is so good-humoured, you're exhausted before you even get a chance to open your mouth. Unlike the other patients in the café, in their jaded dressing gowns and drips on wheels, Leonora was wearing clothes and not just clothes but 'going out' clothes. Dainty pink shoes tied with matching ribbons, like dancers' shoes. A pale pink twinset in tweed. She must have been roasting. You could grow sugar cane along the hospital corridors. Leonora did not look roasting. She wore her pearl-white hair in a sophisticated chignon and, in startling contrast to my own flushed face, hers was pale apart from the dark brows she drew over her eyes, two streaks of bright pink along her cheekbones and the pale pink lipstick (to match the twinset and shoes, I imagine) bordered by a darker pink lip pencil.

She was a hundred shades of pink. And dainty with it. Dad says she is a wonderful dancer and you can see that she might be. There is a delicacy in her movements.

I don't remember Mam ever dancing. Or wearing pink. Nor did she ever dress me in pink. She said it would clash with my hair. She wasn't delicate, Mam. She was robust and capable. Tall and strong. If you needed the bucket refilled from the coal scuttle, Mam would have it done and the fire set and blazing before you'd have the kettle boiled.

You never think of your parents having a 'type'. They're just together and you take it for granted and make assumptions. Looking at Dad, you would think that Leonora is his type. It's in the way he leans towards her when she is talking. Like she's the most fascinating creature in the world.

I didn't open my mouth. Well, apart from eating the banana and peanut butter muffin which, in fairness, did seem to be punching above its weight in terms of both flavour and texture. Dad seemed anxious to distract me. He introduced topics, steered the conversation and insisted on participation. Leonora obliged. I made exaggerated chewing motions and pointed to my mouth. Dad made sure none of the topics he introduced concerned:

1) Luke;
2) The Full Shilling; or
3) Breathtaking creatures.

Or a combination of all three, e.g. how come Luke never mentioned the breathtaking creature who appears to be working behind the counter at The Full Shilling?

Leonora wondered how LuLaBelle was and I said she was annoying and needy. Which Leonora took as an opportunity to talk about LuLaBelle's 'tragic past' and her 'very understandable' separation anxiety.

Mam would have taken to her with a wooden spoon, shouting, 'I'll give you separation anxiety, you dirty-looking eejit.'

We concentrated on our banana and peanut butter muffins for a while after that.

Then, out of the blue:

LEONORA: Me and the girls on the ward watched *Menopause: The Movie*. We all cheered at the end and wished we'd had someone like you back in the day, Agatha.

ME: Oh. Well, thank you. How did you manage? With menopause?

LEONORA: Oh, I drank my way through it mostly. Then I became an alcoholic so I had to stop drinking and that took up a good bit of my time. By the time I came to, my symptoms had gone. So that was nice.

ME (stupid with surprise): But . . . you don't look like an alcoholic.

LEONORA (tinkly laugh): We hide in plain sight, Agatha dear.

Mam's brother, Gerry, looked like an alcoholic although that word was never used about him. He was 'fond of the jar' or 'a great drinker'. He died alone in a bedsit in Manchester. Nobody mentioned cirrhosis and how it leaks onto a face and leaves it as yellow as the nicotine stains on his fingers.

Haven't thought about uncle Gerry in years.

Is that what I've been doing with the menopause? Hiding in plain sight? Hoping it'll give up and move on to some other unfortunate.

ME: I . . . Sorry to hear that. About, you know, you being an alcoholic.

LEONORA: No need to be sorry, dear. It was the making of me.

Dad put his hand over Leonora's and she let it rest there a moment.

I looked at my hands then, for the want of anywhere better to look. I was struck by their resemblance to Mam's hands. The same long, bony fingers, the same square fingernails, the same slight bend near the tips of our index fingers. Mam's hands were often pulpy, plunged so often into buckets of hot, soapy water for washing windows. Washing floors. Washing presses.

I don't remember Dad patting Mam's hands.

She'd have wondered what he was up to, if he had.

3 p.m.

I didn't consciously make a decision to call into The Full Shilling on the way home. When I got out of the car outside the café, there was a smell of scorched rubber.

DAD: Are you not going to park?
ME: I am parked.
DAD: Oh. I'll walk the rest of the way. I could do with the exercise. (Patting his concave belly and scuttling away.)

There were no customers inside. The breathtaking creature was standing on a chair, writing tomorrow's specials on the blackboard. Her barnet, released from the horror of the hairnet, cascaded down her back, the ends brushing against a band of clear sallow skin above the waistband of her tiny jeans.

Everything about her is tiny.

Petite, I suppose.

Her wrists. Her hands. Even her fingernails. Rosebud mouth. Wide amber eyes fringed with such long, dark eyelashes, they should have had the decency to be fake. And her skin. Oh, her skin. It was hard not to covet it. So lush and fecund. You could scatter seeds on skin like that and foliage would sprout up in no time at all.

If possibility had a smell, it would smell like this woman.

Amidst the empty chairs, the fading linoleum, the tired tables, the peeling wallpaper and the persistent smell of boiled cabbage, she is otherworldly. Like finding an orchid in rude health at the bottom of a compost heap.

ME: Who are you and what are you doing here?

Later, Luke wondered why I couldn't have been a bit nicer.

I genuinely don't understand why small talk is deemed 'polite' and asking a direct question is not. Well, two direct questions if you want to be pedantic about it.

The breathtaking creature told me her name. Fernanda. Not Fernando. From Brazil. Not Bolivia. She has replaced Kathleen, she explained.

ME (pointed): Mrs Lynch.
FERNANDA (in annoyingly adorable South American accent): Yes.

Why did Luke have to replace Mrs Lynch with someone so . . . alive? It seemed an affront to Mrs Lynch's untimely death. Well, she might have been old in traditional timeline terms but nobody's ever ready to go. I always felt bad that she never got to finish her last mug of tea.

Fernanda jumped off the chair and told me I must be Agatha. 'You are exactly as Luke described.'

She said 'Luka' instead of Luke. Even her mispronunciation of basic words was adorable.

She didn't go into details.

He'd better have been complimentary about me.

Her voice was low-pitched and moody and she had one of those adorable gaps between her front teeth which made her look both innocent and outrageously sexy; a heady mix. If I had an ounce of oestrogen left, I'm sure I would have felt aroused.

Fernanda told me that Luke had gone to deliver dinner to Mrs Sheridan.

Most of Luke's customers eat their dinner in the middle of the day. I think it's in case they're asleep by actual dinnertime.

Or dead.

Mrs Sheridan usually manages to come into the café. Her rheumatoid arthritis must be at her again.

FERNANDA: I will tell Luke you called.
ME: I'll wait.
FERNANDA: He could be a while.
ME: How long have you been waitressing?
FERNANDA: I am not a waitress, I am a Revitaliser.

I'm putting the capital R in there because that's how she said it. As if it was an actual job, like, I don't know, plumbing. I was about to ask her what the hell that involved when she went, 'I trade in change.' As if that wasn't already dramatic enough, she added: 'Not just change but revolution.'

Which felt like a very South American thing to say.

Then she told me that she has revolutionised other cafés in Dublin. She tapped on the screen of her iPad with her tiny fingernails and showed me a photograph of a sophisticated little eatery, all mirrors and chrome, with two identical smiling waiters in blue and white striped trousers and matching dicky bows and ornate silver trays tucked beneath their arms. They didn't look like they'd ever waited a table in their lives. They looked like models dressed up as waiters while they're waiting on their ship to come in.

I handed her back the iPad.

ME: It looks nice. But it doesn't make my mouth water.
FERNANDA (sweeping a tiny arm around the café): Does this make your mouth water?

The cheek!

I asked her if she was waiting tables as well as revitalising.

Fernanda said she was and went to get an order pad.

I ordered one of Luke's gigantic, misshapen fruit scones and a pot of tea, which made me realise that I'm turning into my mother. Mam only ever ate scones in The Full Shilling. She said they weren't the same anywhere else. Which was her way of saying she adored them.

She adored Luke too. He openly laughed in my face when I told him that at the funeral. Then apologised for laughing at my mother's funeral. I said it was fine, that it was true that Mam wasn't brilliant at . . . you know . . . emotions.

Fernanda only gave me one pat of butter and no clotted cream.

There's a red flag if ever I saw one.

I wished I had a cat in my arms. One of those evil-looking ones. A Siamese. That I could be stroking with menace when Luke came back.

'I've been expecting you.'

But Luke didn't come back. Mrs Sheridan must have waylaid him with her stock of photo albums. She takes them out when she's under the weather and gets maudlin. And Luke's not great at saying no.

He married me when I asked him, didn't he?

I wonder what plans Fernanda will propose for revitalising Luke's meals-on-wheels operation. Waiting for his customers to die of natural causes doesn't seem quite revolutionary enough.

If Ronnie isn't turning in his grave, I'll fecking well dig him up with my bare hands and turn him myself.

4 p.m.

I didn't even have enough energy to maintain a respectable level of anger. By the time I got home from the café, all I wanted to do was find a puddle of sunshine, curl up in it and go to sleep.

I'm a cat!

Or a dog. LuLaBelle does it. Why should she get to do it and not me? Why do I still feel like the smooth running of the house is my job? Maybe smooth is ambitious. Adequate? The adequate running of the house. Melissa would concur with my word choice there, I'd say.

So I threw on a wash, sent emails to five menopausal women, wrote a draft of an article for *Women's Way*, listened to Aidan for half an hour, talking about how bees make honey (I timed the conversation on my Fitbit so at least it's useful for something), took armfuls of glasses/plates/cups/ bowls out of Colm's room (he was buried in his bed but breathing, I waited till I saw the sheet rise and fall) and rated Dad out of ten for his tango (I gave him a 'room for improvement' four out of ten).

He thought 'room for improvement' should be a C minus at the very least, i.e. five or six out of ten.

I told him that nobody says C minus any more and amended it to 'lots of room for improvement'.

I didn't even manage to get to the attic to pretend to write. Like, these people are like limpets, stuck to my rock.

8 p.m.

Meant to spend the evening cutting 'Luka's' clothes into tiny pieces, stuffing them into bin bags and lining them up on the road outside the house. But the kitchen scissors weren't sharp enough and we didn't have enough bin bags. Also, I got distracted by a DMing marathon with Den who wanted to know if he could record my talk at the menopausal flower-arranging club for a documentary on women's health a friend of his was producing.

DEN: Ben needs a menopausal woman and I said I knew where to find a good specimen.

ME: What's in it for me?

DEN: You get to spend time with me.

ME: No, really.

DEN: You get to communicate your message on menopause to more women who need to hear it. And you'll be paid of course. They might even throw in a breakfast roll, if I ask nicely.

ME: I'm in.

DEN: Did you see today's 'Mad As Hell' video on TikTok?

ME: No.

DEN: It's more a collection of photographs than a video really. This woman prancing around a field with a load of red heifers.

ME: How is that menopausal?

DEN: I think it's because her face is the same colour as the cows and the caption is something like, 'Flush till the cows get home.' The music is 'Old MacDonald Had a Farm'. It's super cute.

He sent me the link. I don't know if I'd describe it as 'super cute' but only because I hadn't gotten around to replacing the perfectly functional 'very' with the superfluously flamboyant 'super' yet. Still, I had to admit that the video was cute, mostly because of the cows with their shaggy russet fringes hanging over their eyes.

When the music ends, the woman, in great heaving breaths and a thick Scottish accent, explains how she feels an affinity with dairy cows who are slaughtered as soon as their production levels drop.

FLUSH-TILL-THE-COWS-GET-HOME-WOMAN:

Although they don't go to the bother of slaughtering the likes of us. Too expensive. And also still illegal at time of posting. Instead, they sideline us. Ignore us. Look right through us. Make us feel invisible. Well, guess what? I'm not invisible.

I'm right here.

I am mad as hell.

And I will not take it any more.

The responses run into pages and pages of thumbs-up and flexed-muscle emojis. Gifs of Mexican waves and standing ovations and thundering cheers.

I feel . . . yes . . . menopausal but, also, not alone.

There are literally herds of us.

The video has been liked and shared by 15,032 people so far.

I rap smartly on the screen of my phone.

15,033 people now.

10 p.m.

Before I knew it, there was Luke's key in the door, leaving me no time to take his clothes out of the wardrobe, never mind cut them up into tiny pieces.

I had to make do with standing in the kitchen with my arms tightly folded across my chest, glaring at him when he opened the door. He had the gall to try to kiss me but I performed a smart sidestep.

LUKE: You okay, love?

ME: Fernando from Bolivia, eh?

LUKE: What?

ME: Is really Fernanda from Brazil.

LUKE: Oh yes, she said you popped in. Sorry I missed you.

ME: Did you think I'd never find out?

LUKE: Find out what?

ME: The waiter. That you said you'd hired. Fernando.

LUKE: I said Fernanda. From Brazil. You should maybe think about going for a hearing test.

ME: I suppose you think I'm falling apart.

LUKE: I'm just saying you might need to have your ears
    syrin . . .

ME: And you never mentioned how tiny she is.

LUKE: Who?

ME: Fernanda from bloody Brazil. Stop making me say it
    over and over.

LUKE: Why on earth would I men . . .

ME: Or how beautiful.

LUKE: She's my employee. Anyway, I thought we weren't
    supposed to be objectifying women any more?

ME: You know Fernanda scrimps on the clotted cream? Tell
    me how you're going to save the café with that brand
    of meanness.

HIM: We've actually had a few new customers since she
    arrived.

ME: Hmmm.

LUKE: Are you okay?

ME: I'm too tired to fight about Fernando.

LUKE: Why would we be fighting about Fernando? I mean,
    Fernanda?

ME: We haven't fought in ages.

LUKE: That's a good thing! Isn't it?

ME: Or maybe we just can't summon up the wherewithal
    any more?

25 June, 4 a.m.

Symptoms: Woken by night sweat

I changed my knickers and T-shirt, flung open the bedroom
window and sluiced my face with cold water.

Despite the bathroom door slamming shut in the draught from the window and me yelping when I stubbed my big toe off the leg of the bed, Luke didn't stir.

I felt like I hadn't told him anything recently. Like Dad holding Leonora's hand at the hospital. Or my hands and how like Mam's they are now. Or about the flush-till-the-cows-get-home woman. In my quite impressive Scottish accent. He'd find that funny. Or at the very least, he'd smile. It takes you by surprise, Luke's smile. There's no beginning to it. It happens all at once.

I'm not even sure he's listened to any of the interviews I've done recently. Does he even know about Den recording my talk with the menopausal flower arrangers for a documentary? Or how a hive of bees is not just billions of bees living together but a collective. Where the bees work together for the benefit of the hive.

A bit like a family except good.

I decided not to wake him. He's to be up in two hours. I'll ring him in the morning. After the post-mass rush.

I felt a bit foolish now, being honest. About the whole Fernando/Fernanda thing.

Also, I really hoped I didn't need my ears syringed.

26 June, 7 a.m.

Symptoms: Morning sickness! For. Fuck. Sake

Not actual vomiting the way I spent the first three months of both of my pregnancies. More of a vague nausea. Like I might vomit, if cajoled. If I pictured a bowl of goodie say, I could really go for it.

Or drains.

Or the word, 'mucus'.

Emailed Dr-Lennon-call-me-Susie just there and:

1) It's a thing!! Nausea: a symptom of menopause.
2) I have to hand it to Dr-Lennon-call-me-Susie when it comes to responding to correspondence. Impressive!
3) She's probably terrified I'll barge into her surgery if she doesn't email me back immediately.
4) Which I wouldn't do. She's a busy woman and her job is important.
5) Although she mightn't know that I think that.

7.30 a.m.

I found calculations that Luke had written on the back of an envelope on my bedside locker, under a cup of tea.

How can we apply for a loan when I can't even cobble a sentence together, let alone an entire novel? And it's not like Luke will understand since he doesn't know I can't cobble a sentence together.

Jesus.

Might I have to get an actual job?

Actual jobs:

1) Work in a bookshop? No. Because:
   a) Customers.
2) Work in The Full Shilling? Not a terrible prospect because:

a) Even though there're customers, I know most of them and they know me so expectations would be manageable.
b) Adios Fernanda!

But:

c) On my pins all day. Even in my Docs, my feet would kill me.
d) I'd end up eating a hefty portion of the profits. Which would be on Luke for being a good cook but, at the end of the day, we'd probably be worse off than we are now.
e) If Luke is keen on Fernanda, he'd be all heartsick and sore over her departure, standards would slip, customers would leave and/or die and there we'd be – broke.

1 p.m.

I met Dad in the kitchen and asked him, in a 'hypothetical' kind of way, how I'd go about becoming a civil servant.

DAD: Is it for your book? Research?
ME: Eh . . . yes.
DAD: Well . . . it depends what grade your character is going for.
ME: A couple of notches down from the top.

(I probably need to be realistic about it.)

DAD: You just have to do an exam and not be averse to tedium.

I haven't done an exam since 1990.

3) Dog-walker? I could have LuLaBelle as my referee. She might vouch for me. But then, I wouldn't say the money is great. Look at the pittance childcare professionals earn. And I'd say dogs are down the pecking order from kids.
4) Write my sixteenth-century witch book instead of sitting in my attic, pretending to write it.

2 p.m.

I made a strong pot of coffee and forced myself to sit at my desk in the attic.

Nothing happened.

I turned on the radio and idly turned the dial, looking for an upbeat song that could rouse me to action.

Which is how I happened on the type of phone-in show I am usually at pains to avoid. Just because I like to whinge doesn't mean I enjoy listening to other people doing it on the national airwaves.

The broadcaster – Gerry Bolton – was playing an audio clip of *Menopause: The Movie*.

Jesus H.

I stabbed at the off button and sat at my desk awhile, gathering myself.

I tried to write a page of my novel but I couldn't even manage a paragraph because:

5) menopause;
6) don't care enough about sixteenth-century witches;
7) tired and cranky (read: menopause).
8) distracted by hearing my rantings on the whingey phone-in show.

It was too early to message Carol.

Instead, I googled Fernanda Sanchez.

She was on all the platforms, particularly TikTok which was an excellent way of reminding me how young and fit she is. Her videos were all well-lit and angled and her make-up was flawless. Then there was her hair. The rudeness of its health gave me actual indigestion. I was downing Gaviscon like it was gin and tonic. Her 'thing' on TikTok is dance. Samba dance. With an imaginary partner. Probably because any actual, real-time dance partner would combust as soon as she inserts herself into the circle of their arms.

She's an okay dancer, I suppose.

Okay fine, she's a good dancer. There!

If Fernando/Fernanda ever decided to google me, she'd be treated to the video of me ranting and raving and looking like I might actually burst into flames with the rage and the heat.

It's like, being menopausal has usurped everything else about me. Including being a writer.

A good writer.

At least, I used to be. Didn't I? I suppose, if I'm being all therapist-couch about it, my self-esteem has taken a bit of a battering lately. I don't ever remember a time when I didn't write stories. All I cared about at school was writing stories and history. And I know, boo-bloody-hoo, poor me, etc., etc. But I've never had a battered self-esteem before. And no, Mam, I can't just give it a hot water bottle, tell it to have an early night and everything will be grand in the morning.

To be honest, I don't know what to bloody well do with it. If I ask Dr-Lennon-call-me-Susie, she'll whip out her prescription pad. If I ask Carol, she'll insist I go to counselling. I am NOT going to counselling.

I may be broke and menopausal and talentless. But draped across a leather couch telling a stranger that I'm broke and menopausal and talentless for the princely sum of (no idea) an hour will not help matters.

Jesus H! I've just googled the cost of counselling.

Plan B:

1) Tell Luke about my inability to write any longer.

Or:

2) Hot water bottle and early night. Without the hot water bottle obviously. I'd burst into flames.

ME: I'm having an early night.
AIDAN: It's seven o'clock.
ME: I know, that's why it's called an early night.

10 p.m.

My phone screen lit up.

CAROL: Did you hear the Gerry Bolton show today?

182

ME: Is that not one of the reasons you emigrated? So you don't have to suffer through a Gerry Bolton show ever again?

CAROL: It's the accents. Sometimes I miss them.

ME: You could come home? For a visit?

CAROL: Work's too busy atm. But listen, Gerry said he's never had such a response to an item. He's going to be talking about menopause again tomorrow. You should listen to it, it'll cheer you up.

ME: What makes you think I need cheering up?

CAROL: I know you. Whether you like it or not.

ME: Are you still having great sex?

CAROL: Yeah.

ME: There's a new waitress at The Full Shilling. 'Fernanda'.

CAROL: Why are we putting 'Fernanda' in inverted commas?

ME: She's replaced Mrs Lynch.

CAROL: Nobody could replace Mrs Lynch.

ME: 'Fernanda' did.

CAROL: Sounds like you could do with a break. Come to LA!

ME: I can't. Not right now.

CAROL: Now is all we have.

ME: Fuck sake.

CAROL: Love you.

ME: Fuck off.

I tried to go to sleep then but couldn't stop thinking about Gerry bloody Bolton. Eventually I succumbed and listened to a recording of the show online.

I fast-forwarded through the audio clip, then braced myself for vitriol, the show's main currency.

WOMAN-ON-RADIO: The thing is, Gerry, I've never talked about the menopause. I had a vague idea of what it was all about but I was completely unprepared for it so, when I got it, it hit me like a truck. And then I was on the back foot, trying to keep up with all the symptoms while looking after the kids, holding down my job, arranging care for my mother who hasn't been right since her fall last year.

GERRY BOLTON: You've a lot on your plate there.

WOMAN-ON-RADIO: Yes, but since I saw *Menopause: The Movie*, I feel . . . well, the same really but also, I'm going to say . . . comforted. I'm not alone. It's incredible how much that means.

WOMAN #2: Before I heard Agatha, I was just menopausal. Now, I'm fuming. I mean, where are the services? Where's the help? This is happening to lots of us and there are no supports.

WOMAN #3: I'm on a waiting list for one of those menopausal clinics. Three months I've to wait and then pay the guts of €200 for the initial consultation, €90 for the follow-up, €35 for blood tests and, if I get HRT, that's at least another €50 a month after that.

WOMAN #4: I'm not entitled to a medical card because I earn too much money. I earn €28,000 a year. You try living on that, Gerry!

WOMAN #5: I'm just so relieved that we're finally talking about menopause. There's nothing like stigma to make people feel ashamed of themselves. But we've done nothing wrong. We're just menopausal. Give us a bit of support and we'll surprise you all with what we'll do next. We're not done here. Not by a long shot.

And on they went. The programme ran over its sixty-minute slot. The three o'clock news got delayed.

And Gerry never got a word in.

27 June, 4 a.m.

Symptoms: Bee-curious

Since Aidan won't let us open the lid of the hive to gawk at the bees, I have taken to pressing my ear against the hive. The wood is smooth. And then there's the sound of it. A low and constant hum. They'd put you to shame with their industry.

ME: Why do bees buzz?
AIDAN: It's the sound of the air vibrating against their wings. Which, by the way, they can beat two hundred and thirty times a second.
ME: That seems excessive.
COLM (annoyed tone): I suppose you'll be wanting to know why the sky is blue next.

In spite of Colm's open hostility at pretty much everything recently, he cannot seem to say anything mean about the bees.

He has even been making brief visits downstairs, albeit still in his pyjamas. He asks about the bees in a gruff, resentful way, as if he doesn't want to ask about them but he can't help himself. Aidan fills him in while making him towering triple-decker sandwiches with the sourdough bread he has been learning to bake. He stuffs the sandwiches with the tomatoes and lettuce and scallions he's been growing on one side of the garden, the other side filled with burgeoning shoots of 'bee-friendly' flowers.

Fun fact: bees' favourite colour is purple.

So, Aidan is planting lots of lavender, catmint and hyacinth.

Colm complains about the lack of protein in his sandwich and Aidan tells him that he will have all the protein he can digest, once the rescue chickens arrive.

ME: Vegans don't eat eggs.
AIDAN: No, but you lot do. And these chickens will be respected and loved.
ME: There will be NO chickens.
AIDAN: You said that about the bees.
ME: I mean it about the chickens.

The thing is, Luke is afraid of chickens. I suppose you might call it a phobia since it's a pretty irrational fear. I mean, what threat does a chicken pose? Even in a group – a flock, I suppose – they're a pretty pathetic bunch, just pecking around in the dirt with their pointy beaks and random squawks.

For some reason, I've never made fun of Luke's chicken fear. And really, I could have had a field day with that. I suppose it's because Luke isn't afraid of things in general. I mean normal things like lifts and hairdressers.

Which makes his chicken phobia all the weirder. He only told me the night before we took the kids to that petting farm in Kerry, which was the only day that week it didn't rain. We had finally gotten the boys to sleep and were lying in the long grass behind the cottage we'd rented, at the bottom of the garden, gathering ourselves.

LUKE: I need to tell you something.
ME: Are you dying?
LUKE: No.
ME: Are you fucking someone? Apart from me, I mean.
LUKE: No.
ME: What then?
LUKE: I can't go into the chicken bit of the farm tomorrow.
ME: Fowl Forest?
LUKE: I'll wait for you outside, okay? Or just meet you at
    the next bit. Where the sheep are.
ME: Lamb Lane. They're mad for alliteration.
LUKE: I'll meet you at Lamb Lane, okay?
ME: Okay.
LUKE: Don't you want to know why?
ME: No.

I had pretty much guessed by then. It was in the way his
nostrils flared when he said 'chicken'. Everybody's got something they're afraid of, I suppose. When me and the boys
emerged from Fowl Forest with the eggs we had collected,
Luke was waiting for us at Lamb Lane with honeycomb ice
cream.

   Aidan wanted to know what I have against chickens and
I told him he can have as many chickens as he likes when
he has his own place.

COLM: He's never going to have his own place.
AIDAN: Why not?
COLM: You need money which, let's face it, you're never
    going to have.

And even though this has distracted them from the chickens, the truth of what Colm said hits me like a shovel to the back of the head.

Even if Aidan had stayed in college and gotten a job that bank algorithms like, Aidan – or any young person – would be hard-pressed to secure a mortgage these days.

Impossible if they're not coupled up. And Aidan's chances of attracting a mate are slim too, what with the muck that's always under his nails now and his hair, which hasn't been cut – or brushed – since January, I'd say. Also, he shows scant interest in acquiring a mate. I know because:

ME: Are you interested in acquiring a mate?
AIDAN: I don't have time, with the new business and everything.

Seriously, he said 'business'.

Still, it does take up an inordinate amount of his time, what with all the weeding, planting and watering. And then the bees of course. Although they seem pretty self-sufficient, in the main. The queen is busy laying eggs in the brood chamber. The workers are flying in and out of the tiny entrance in the hive, off to collect nectar and pollen. I could think of worse jobs. It's easy to think of worse jobs when you've cleaned a toilet after two boys who, for years, regarded the bowl as optional.

Yesterday, Colm borrowed Aidan's mantilla and straw hat with the plastic fruit and took a video of the worker bees emerging from the hive. They do this dance at the entrance, a bit like a conga. Which, Aidan reliably informs us, is their way of programming their GPS so they can find their way back home. Colm uploaded the picture to D.I.Guy (#*danceof-thehoneybees*) and, while it's nothing to do with DIY or short-shorts or flattering lighting, it got ten thousand likes in twenty minutes, according to Aidan. And even though Colm only shrugged at the news and returned to his bedroom shortly afterwards, his tread on the stairs was not as heavy as before.

Aidan said the bees can fly three miles away from the hive and will visit up to a hundred flowers in a trip which seems impressive for such precarious little creatures. I don't tell Aidan about the summer me and Bart decided to catch a bee and keep it as a pet.

I suppose I could blame Mam for not allowing us to have a more conventional pet after Mr Chips died. Why not? Us mothers get blamed for most things after all.

We kept the bee in an empty beetroot jar which we had filled with daisies and dandelions and muck. We neglected to pierce the lid with airholes. We wondered why the bee was so lethargic, pulling herself up and over the crest of the dandelions. We shook the jar, turned it upside down, rolled it down a hill. It took hours for the bee to die. We thought she was just having a rest.

Best not to mention it.

28 June, 4 a.m.

Symptoms: Achy knees and hips

I do not know how Luke can sleep through the smell of Deep Heat. It's actually singeing my nostril hair.

Update on hair:

The loss of hair on my head continues unabated if the

quantity of strands caught in the teeth of my hairbrush is anything to go by. While hair growth is still happening, it now seems to be confined to the area above my mouth, along my jaw and on my chin. The hair under my arms – which I decided to grow as a belated 'fuck you' to the patriarchy – is sporadic, wispy and fair. The ones on my chin, on the other hand, are sturdy and belligerent with long roots. Easy to trap between a pair of tweezers and the pain of the yank is satisfying; you can be sure you've left no stragglers behind.

After trying the breathing exercise that Aidan promised would send me off to sleep in no time, I checked my phone. Another email from Samantha. One of those 'wellness' companies has been onto her. They want me to be their 'Menopause Guru' on Instagram.

Samantha didn't even have the decency to put 'menopause guru' in inverted commas. Plus she capitalised the m of menopause and the g of guru.

Fuck sake.

No way am I going to become all Zen and bendy on Instagram, talking about 'anti-oxidants' and 'superfoods' in the flickering light of a million candles.

Things are bad enough without inflicting that on the world.

29 June, 2 p.m.

Symptoms: Excessive sneezing, probably from close proximity to pollen-riddled flower arrangers

The flower-arranging club meeting started bang on time which didn't surprise me. What did surprise me was that it wasn't as awful as I'd expected.

That is one of the few good things about being a pessimist; things are sometimes not quite as horrific as anticipated.

Aside: I'm actually a realist but am often branded a pessimist by the growing population of 'touchy-feeleys' in today's 'mindful' world.

I knocked on Melissa's front door at ten to two and Den answered.

ME: Why are you looking so cheerful?
DEN: Nice to see you too.
MELISSA (swatting at Den from behind in a most familiar way): Let her in, Den.
ME: Do you two know each other?
MELISSA: No, I only met him twenty minutes ago. Which is weird because I feel like I've known him much longer than that.
DEN: I get that a lot.

They paused to smile at each other.

DEN: Melissa's been helping me set up the recording equipment.

Melissa McDevitt's house in general – and conservatory in particular – were as squeaky clean and savagely tidy as I'd expected. The Hoover had been on for most of yesterday, the noise drilling a hole through the attic wall, spoiling my attempts to curate a list of my Top Forty foods. It was either that or write something about my star-crossed witches, Ellen and Clara, and I had already tried that and produced exactly nothing.

I went for forty (as opposed to the more numerically friendly fifty or ten or even a hundred) as a sentimental nod to *Top of the Pops* on a Thursday night, me and Bart jostling for position on the floor inches from the telly, Mam yelling at us to move back or our eyes would go square in our heads.

Even the glass roof of the conservatory was gleaming with elbow grease. Melissa clocked me looking at it so I suppose I had no one but myself to blame for the monologue that ensued accompanied by a demonstration of the squeegee, attached to an extendable pole, all the better to reach the furthest corners of the glass ceiling and effective enough to clean even the most stubborn of stains, e.g. bird poop. She mouthed the word 'poop'.

Den approached me with a tiny microphone which he clipped onto the lapel of my denim jacket.

ME: I should have worn more make-up. For the camera.
DEN: Are you fishing for a compliment?
ME: No.
DEN: . . .
ME: Okay fine, I am.
DEN: You look perfect just the way you are.

The menopausal flower arrangers arrived together in a bunch. When Melissa introduced me to them, she made me sound way better than I actually am.

Then she arranged them in two rows of five down the centre of the conservatory.

MELISSA: So, without further ado, I give you . . . Agatha Doyle.

She settled herself in a chair beside Den while the menopausal flower arrangers clapped politely.

When they stopped, Den said: 'And . . . action!'

ME: I just want to start by saying that reports of my expertise in the area of menopause have been greatly exaggerated. I am no expert on menopause. I am merely menopausal. I do, however, have a collection of facts and figures about how government, society, employers and the medical profession are failing menopausal women. These facts and figures are not particularly helpful and will doubtless leave you angry or sad or frustrated.

However, what I have found helpful these past few days is other menopausal women.

If we have to feel angry or sad or frustrated, there is comfort in knowing we are not alone.

MENOPAUSAL FLOWER ARRANGERS: Hear, hear!

Afterwards, I gave the flower arrangers a chance to ask a question or air a grievance.

At first, they were disinclined to talk about the menopause. Or even say the word out loud. As if they were worried that it might hear them and be insulted at the allegations and come at them with greater intensity than before.

But once they got over their initial reluctance and Melissa had served the tea ('Decaf or herbal?' she asked, like Barry's Classic Blend didn't even exist), they shuffled out of their stalls, took a few breaths and they were off.

Like everyone I have come across so far since *Menopause: The Movie* day, the women just seemed to need permission to talk about menopause. Almost as if they thought it was somehow their fault. Something to be ashamed of. That, without the male gaze looking them up and down, they deserved nothing less than to wither and die in a corner in a timely and dignified manner, having served their purpose.

Den and his camera were forgotten at the back of the room as the women realised they had things to say.

Lots of things.

I had to admit it was invigorating to observe the change in them, like they'd just realised girl power was an actual thing. Something they'd had all along. I couldn't help smiling at each of them in turn, when they spoke up.

Towards the end, even Melissa spoke. Up to then she had been busy being her usual accommodating, polite and helpful self: refilling cups, pouring water (sparkling or still), opening windows (Sadie and Eileen had a pair of hot flushes), pulling blinds (Monica was just over laser surgery and her irises were still a little photosensitive), closing windows (once the hot flushes abated, Sadie and Eileen were feeling the cold), getting more cushions (Tracy was having a sciatica flare-up) and replenishing the goodies: scones, brownies (gluten-free ones because Sylvia was coeliac), apple tart, berry crumble and – weirdly – Rich Tea biscuits. Nobody ate them obviously. Except Melissa and even then, she could only get one down.

DEN: Tell them what you told me earlier, Melissa. About the whales.

It was clear from the way the flower arrangers whipped their heads around to look at the back of the room that they'd completely forgotten about Den and his recording equipment.

MELISSA: Oh . . . okay . . . it was nothing really . . . just . . .

When Melissa spoke, you had to strain to hear her. As if she didn't want to intrude on the world. As if what she was saying was of no consequence and she was apologising in advance with her subdued tones.

MELISSA: There are whales that go through the menopause, just like us.

The flower arrangers oohed and aahed at this revelation and I found myself straining forward in my seat, the better to hear about the menopausal whales.

MELISSA: Well, the thing is, these whales, the females that is, they . . . well, as far as I know anyway, but feel free to google it of course . . . I think that they, the lady whales, can live up to fifty years old. And they stop being, well, you know, fertile when they're around forty but they don't die then.
TRACEY (through a gobful of brownie): What happens to them?

In fairness we all wanted to know.

DEN (gently): Could you speak up a little, Melissa? Just so the monitor picks up your voice?
MELISSA: Yes, of course, sorry . . . I . . . Well, my understanding is . . . and again, you should fact-check this . . . but as far as I can gather, the elderly females become grandmothers and they remain in the pod – I think that's

what it's called – until they die of natural causes. Up until then, the female belugas – that's the type of whale they are – are much sought after for, you know, tips on good places to eat, for example. What areas to avoid, say if there are fishing ships or, I don't know, hunters who might kill them for their . . . meat, I suppose.

SYLVIA: They're basically Tripadvisor.

Everybody laughed. Even me.

MELISSA: Wise counsel. That's what they called it in the article I read. As far as I remember. I think that was the phrase.

Everybody absorbed the information.

Wise counsel. That sounded good. It had a nice ring to it.

There was a smart rapping on the glass and, when we looked towards the sound, there, by the door, was 'poor Dermot' freshly arrived from work with a pained smile across his fleshy face.

MELISSA (leaping up, flushing): Oh. Dermot. I didn't see you there.

'POOR DERMOT': It's minke whales, silly. They're the ones you're thinking of.

MELISSA: Minke? Oh . . . I . . .

'POOR DERMOT' (making a beeline for Den): That's a Leica M6, unless I'm very much mistaken and I rarely am, hahaha. I've a bit of an interest in film, did Melissa tell you?

DEN: It is beluga whales actually. Melissa is right.

'POOR DERMOT': Really? Oh. Well . . . I'm clearly not needed, I see. I'll leave you and the girls to natter, shall I?

He left behind a solid wall of man perfume. You know the type that gets lodged in your throat and makes your eyes water.

SADIE: I never knew that. About the whales, Melissa.
TRACY (pointed): Beluga whales.
DEN (peering into his monitor): The camera adores you, Melissa. You're a natural.

He started to clap and everybody joined in. The noise cancelled out 'poor Dermot's' attempts to make his presence heard in the kitchen where he appeared to be opening and closing all the cupboard doors and rattling the cutlery drawers.

Melissa resumed her seat beside Den with a smile on her face and two pink circles blooming in her cheeks. There was something childlike about her. A wary child who expected the worst but still maintained the capacity to hope for the best.

I helped Den carry his equipment to his car.

DEN: You don't have to do that.
ME: Don't get used to it.
DEN: You were great. Ben's going to be delighted with the segment.
ME: Actually . . . you were great.
DEN (punching the air): Yes! I knew the way to your heart would be to emasculate a mansplainer.

8 p.m.

Den rang.

ME: What do you want?
DEN: I want to take you out for dinner.
ME: No.
DEN: It's business.
ME: What kind of business?
DEN: Radio and telly business.
ME: Be more specific.
DEN: Okay fine, I just want to have dinner with you.
ME: No.
DEN: I'll keep asking till you say yes.
ME: What on earth for? I'm married, menopausal and miserable.
DEN: You forgot to say magnificent.
ME: I'm not going out to dinner with you.
DEN: So you'll think about it? Great! Talk soon.

He hung up before I could say no again.

Flattery was such a vapid thing. I knew this for a fact.

I did.

And yet.

I suppose it was the extravagance of it. It made what passed for exchanges between Luke and me these days seem a little . . . well, more meagre than magnificent.

It all seemed so long ago now. Me and Luke. We met in The Full Shilling. The autumn I turned eighteen. Luke had left school that year and Ronnie was teaching him how to cook.

I told Mam when I got home that day that I'd met the poor fucker I was going to spend the rest of my life with.

I didn't say, 'poor fucker'. Mam would have washed my mouth out with soap and water again.

And it wasn't as if the conversation between us that day had been particularly scintillating. It went something like:

ME: A chocolate eclair, please.
LUKE: We've none left.
ME: That's not very good customer service.
LUKE: Could I interest you in a slice of coffee cake?
ME: I don't like coffee.
LUKE: You do. You just don't like instant coffee.

I don't remember even being annoyed at the presumption. I think it was his voice: low and matter of fact.

Also – and I know this is corny but . . . fine then, his eyes. I'd never seen such a pale shade of blue in an iris. It was a bit . . . well, off-putting, I suppose.

So I didn't kick up the stink I was more than entitled to when he ushered me to a seat and said, in his solemn voice, 'Wait here.'

How many times had me and Carol walked past The Full Shilling, never even glancing in through the steamed-up windows? Even back then, it was for auld ones.

But that day, Carol's mother had poked her head into Carol's bedroom and made pointed remarks about the Leaving Cert and how it wasn't going to 'study itself'. It was raining when I got outside and I knew for a fact that if I went home at that hour on a Saturday, Mam would hand me a mop and a bucket.

MAM: Well? Why wouldn't I? The devil makes work for
    idle hands.

So I went into The Full Shilling instead. There I was, drinking
my first ever cup of real coffee. In a sturdy mug from Hector
Grey's.

I still remember the smell of it. Ronnie had ground the
beans that morning. And the taste. Spicy and exotic, like a
far-flung land I'd seen on a page of an atlas once.

LUKE: So?
ME: Fine. I like coffee. No need to rub it in.
LUKE: And the coffee cake?
ME: Bloody hell, okay, it's lovely, what do you want, a medal?

He grinned then and a shock of his glossy, black hair fell
across his anaemic blue eyes.

LUKE: I'm off at five.
ME: Good for you.
LUKE: *A Fish Called Wanda* is on in the Adelphi.

I had no intention of falling in love.
    That was just something that happened that day.

30 June, 4 a.m.

Symptoms: Night sweat

Who knew that a body could sweat this much? I'm leaking
from every pore. It feels like every drop of liquid inside my

body is oozing out. The very essence of me. Like I am being drained of my womanhood. Seeping onto the Egyptian cotton sheets that Mam got me for my fortieth birthday. She never scrimped on bed linen, being a great believer in the benefits of a good night's sleep. She made her bed every morning like an army cadet and you'd be hard-pressed to get into it, so severely would she tuck the sheets and blankets under the mattress.

It's hard to say which I hate most, a hot flush or a night sweat. If a gun was held to my head and I HAD to choose, I'd say night sweat by a narrow margin. What gives it the edge is the way it leaves you shivering as the sweat cools on your body. So then a shower is called for but of course there's no hot water left because:

1) Aidan
2) Colm
3) Dad
4) Luke
5) LuLaBelle (Aidan washes her in the shower)

I put on the pyjamas I bought for Luke that time he had to go to hospital to have his appendix removed. The surgeon also removed twenty feet of his colon since the appendix had ruptured and spewed its slop across Luke's factory floor. Then he got an infection and ended up in hospital for two weeks. When he saw me coming with the new pyjamas, he got all dramatic and became convinced he was dying. He took my hand and pulled me towards his face, pushed his fingers through my hair as best he could.

LUKE: Do you know how much I love you?

ME: Jesus, your breath stinks.

LUKE: Listen. This is important. I couldn't imagine my life without you. And you're such a great mother to the boys. And . . .

ME: You're definitely delirious.

LUKE: The green bin is every second Wednesday. And . . .

ME: Shut your face. You're not going to die.

LUKE: How do you know?

ME: I won't allow it.

The consultant confirmed the delirium and, while it wasn't quite the touch-and-go situation Luke imagined when he saw the quality of the pyjamas, it took them three days to get his temperature under control and, well, a lot of things go through your head in three days.

Suffice to say I was glad he didn't shuffle off his mortal coil. Also, the green bin is every second Tuesday, not Wednesday.

5 a.m.

Symptoms: Humiliation

Maybe it was because I was thinking about that time, Luke being so delirious and lovesick and the consultant saying how relieved he was when the fever finally broke and me being so grateful that he didn't die.

Or maybe I was feeling a bit guilty for allowing Den's flattery to get under my skin.

Anyway, for whatever reason, I decided to remove the pyjamas and take the lubrication I ordered online out of its packaging and smear it between my legs. There was a pong of lavender off it and I made a note-to-self never to wear it in the garden or I'd be inundated with bloody bees.

I pulled down the duvet and straddled Luke and let the ends of my hair tickle his face.

ME: Eh, hello? I'm ravishing you. Wake the fuck up!

LUKE: Wha . . .?

ME (bouncing up and down on his – still flaccid – penis): Crank that yoke up, would you? There's work to be done.

LUKE (brushing my hair away from his face and scratching at his stubble): What time is it?

ME: It's sex time. You're welcome.

LUKE: Do you mind if we don't? I've to be up in two hours.

ME: I've just smeared myself with lube and that stuff's not cheap.

LUKE: We've got the health inspectors coming today for one of their audits.

ME (dismounting): We?

LUKE: How about we postpone it? Till, you know, a more suitable time?

ME: Who is we?

LUKE: I meant I.

ME: You said we.

LUKE: Can we please discuss this later?

ME (injurious tone): I think I've heard enough.

And then I pulled the pyjamas back on which is when I noticed the price tag was still on them.

I couldn't believe I'd spent that amount of money on such an ingrate.

Also, I must have applied too much of the lube. I could feel it dripping down my leg, cold and slimy.

ME: I'm going downstairs.
LUKE: . . .

He'd fallen back asleep.

And there was me, all set to flounce out the door.

1 July, 10 a.m.

Symptoms: Spots!

I was like a teenager without the plump skin and non-shed hair. I was at the clinic having my bloods done when Dr-Lennon-call-me-Susie clocked the spots and declared them the work of the menopause. When she'd finished stabbing me with a needle, she sat back in her chair and asked me if there was anything else worrying me.

I thought doctors were supposed to be too harassed and overworked to give a shit about their patients? 'Susie' seemed to have all the time in the world with her neat little bun of black hair symmetrically positioned at the back of her head and her stethoscope framing her long, narrow neck and not a speck – of blood or even just pasta sauce – down the front of her buttercup-yellow cotton dress. She also seemed to genuinely give a shit about her patients.

Anyway, I couldn't bring myself to admit that Luke no longer wanted to fuck me so I just mumbled 'writer's block' as if it was an actual, bona-fide condition but Dr-Lennon-call-me-Susie got all supportive then, tilting her small-but-perfectly-proportioned head to the side and smiling with her whole face and not just going through the motions with her rose-pink bee-stung lips. She made sympathetic sort of clucking noises with her tongue while discreetly edging a box of Kleenex towards me.

I'm ashamed to admit that I did not mind the attention. Then I wrecked it all by blowing my nose and Dr-Lennon-call-me-Susie jumped in alarm and banged her elbow off the edge of the filing cabinet and the pain made her eyes smart so I ended up shoving the tissues right back at her and giving out yards about the hazardous ergonomic set-up of her office. There was a pile of books teetering on the edge of the filing cabinet that could brain her if they toppled, given her diminutive size and tendency to jump when startled.

She handed me a prescription for a face cream that will probably cost me five of Luke's steak-and-kidney pies and come in a tiny tube with directions for use so minuscule that I'll still have difficulty reading them even after I've taken a photograph of the tube and zoomed in.

Then I'll apply the cream for a couple of days before I forget all about it. Months later, I'll find the congealed tube at the bottom of my handbag by which time it will be out of date but what won't be out of date is the guilt I will feel at having spent the monetary equivalent of five steak-and-kidney pies when I could just have eaten the pies, washed my face in good old-fashioned tap water and dabbed a bit of Sudocrem on the spots.

MAM: You can't beat a dab of Sudocrem.

Sudocrem was Mam's go-to for skin blemishes. Anything else was doused with two spoons of milk of magnesia.

Tablespoons.

Bart and I kept our mouths shut if we weren't feeling well. I got through nearly a week of chickenpox by wearing long sleeves before she spotted the spots and I had to yield to her ministrations.

Anyway, I took the prescription from Dr-Lennon-call-me-Susie without voicing any of the above because (a) she never says, 'Shut up, you moany cow' and (b) the hard bone of her elbow was still a vigorous shade of purple.

'SUSIE': Are you still worried about taking HRT?

ME: I'm more confused than anything.

'SUSIE': There are alternatives, you know.

ME: Please don't say meditation.

'SUSIE': Well, you could do worse. Or yoga? Mindfulness? Also, I've been looking up herbal remedies for you. There's evening primrose oil, black cohosh, angelica, ginseng, Saint John's wort.

ME: Two minutes out the door and I won't remember a single one of those.

'SUSIE' (pecking away on her keyboard): I've just sent you an email. And don't forget your vitamins. Especially D and all the Bs. Vital.

ME: You're a . . . helpful sort of a doctor, aren't you?

'Susie' looked like she might fall out of her chair. I felt I needed to explain my lavish outburst.

ME: It's just . . . I've been listening to a lot of menopausal women recently and their GPs are pure pants.

'SUSIE': Women's health is my priority. My mother died of cervical cancer. She was one of the women who received a false-negative on her smear test from Cervical Check.

ME: The pricks. Keeping information from those women. I'm very sorry for your loss.

'SUSIE': You know what it's like, losing your mother.

ME: I still go to pick up the phone. Tell her something funny that happened.

'SUSIE': Same. How's the sleeping?

ME: Same.

'SUSIE': You should get back to dancing. I think that would help.

ME: My dance partner ran away to LA. Luke's promised to come to Wigwam with me. Just as soon as he's taken a few lessons.

'SUSIE' (fond smile): Ah Luke, give him my best, won't you?

And like, he hasn't been to the clinic since last year when he had that mole on his back.

Women like Luke.

Maybe it's the bang of food off him? I suppose that can be comforting.

4 a.m.

I didn't end up giving Luke her best because he texted before dinner to say he'd be late getting home.

A yoga class.

He didn't even add a jeery sticky-out-tongue emoji at the end of the text.

Just said he'd be late because he was going to a yoga class. Full stop.

As if we'd always been yoga people.

So I was asleep by the time he got home and now he's asleep and here I am, wide awake. In the olden, pre-menopausal days, I'd just roar into his ear or pour cold water on his head and then, when he jerked awake, tell him that Dr-Lennon-call-me-Susie fancies him and then slag the shit out of him and maybe offer to play a quick game of doctors-and-nurses.

But after last night, I felt a bit . . . well . . . self-conscious.

I suppose all couples at some stage or other simply . . . stop. Date nights are replaced with medical appointments. Conversations once teeming with talk of bands and telly and books and cities are replaced with, 'Type 2 diabetes: Is it nothing less than you deserve?' or 'Blood pressure: Compare and contrast' or a game of 'Spot the blood in your stool', type of thing.

I just assumed that it wouldn't happen to us. For ages. Or at all.

I should have been mad with him. But I seemed to have gone all 'female' about it, wondering if it was . . . MY fault.

Which of course it wasn't. That was just the menopause, fucking with my confidence.

Menopause is like teenagers: take, take, take: fertility, oestrogen, buoyant breasts, firm thighs, bloody HAIR! I refuse to give it my confidence. That stuff is hard to come by.

Even so, I didn't wake Luke.

But I needed to talk to him. Come clean about the advance before he went any further on the credit union loan application.

I decided to tell him tomorrow. Maybe I'd go to the café. See how 'Fernanda' is getting on.

I don't know why I insist on putting her name in inverted commas. Syntactically, there's no need but it gives it a bit of a sneery tone which feels pleasant.

Obviously, I have taken against 'Fernanda' in a massive way.

2 July, 12.30 p.m.

Symptoms: Gnawing suspicion

I went all out!

I wore a dress that Luke used to love. Maybe he still does? I just haven't worn it in a while. An oversized T-shirt dress in tiger print that I wear with a thick leather belt around my waist.

MAM: Would it kill you to pull a brush through that mop of yours?
ME: I literally just did.
MAM: And do you not have a decent pair of shoes, instead of those clod-hoppery boots?

I treated the Docs to an overdue clean. Twenty years old and they're good as new after a spit and polish.

MAM: They're durable. I'll give them that.

I put make-up on! I needed concealer since the spots were still a feature on my face. The tube I finally found – in the cupboard under the bathroom sink – was as lumpy as it was ineffective.

Still, with the clean clothes and brushed hair, I thought even Mam might have agreed that the overall effect was one of some – small – effort on my part.

MAM: Hmmmm.

So there I was, applying yet another layer of lipstick (my lips were so parched these days that they absorbed the lipstick as soon as I'd lashed it on), when in came Aidan, with Luke's glasses in his hand.

ME: You'd better get over to the café and give those to your
    father. He won't be able to tell his parsley from his sage
    without them.
AIDAN: I'm just back. He wasn't there.
ME: What?

And I normally hate when people say, 'What?' when they've clearly heard what you've said but just can't believe/fathom/ stomach it.

But Luke is never not there. Except on his day off which is Wednesday. And Sundays obviously, when there's no point in the café opening, what with the auld ones going to mass and maybe getting invited by their offspring for a Sunday roast which probably won't be a roast at all but a vegetable stir-fry with tofu which the auld ones will pretend to love, all the while dreaming of Luke's Monday special at The Full Shilling.

I checked the calendar to be certain.
Today is Tuesday.
Roast chicken day at The Full Shilling.
Luke should be up to his neck in giblets right about now.

ME: Where is he?
AIDAN: Mrs Daly said he'd be back in an hour.
ME: What was Mrs Daly doing there?

She only helped out in emergencies, given her tendency to interrogate people as to why they hadn't eaten all their carrots or the stalks of their cauliflower.

AIDAN: Working.
ME: Where was Fernanda?
AIDAN: She wasn't there either.

It was my stomach that reacted to the news. A dense heave. Like I'd eaten too many chocolate-covered Brazil nuts.

I always suspected that Luke sees himself as the captain of a ship. He would never abandon his post. He would make sure everyone gets out first.

He'd be the last man standing.
And yet, there he was.
Gone.

3 p.m.

Instead of going to the café, I gave the glass in LuLaBelle's 'conservatory' a good seeing-to. Not because it needed it – or at least not just because it needed it – but also, to distract myself from Luke not being at the café on a day other than a Sunday or a Wednesday. And Fernanda not being at the café either. At the exact same time that Luke wasn't at the café.

Where were they?

Both of them?

And what about the regulars? The clientele of The Full Shilling are set in their ways. They know what they like and what they like is Luke.

Take Mrs Smithers, for instance. She won't eat a morsel unless Luke makes it and she needs all the calories she can get these days with the cancer eating away at her liver.

I kept checking my phone every five minutes but Luke didn't ring to let me know what was going on. I imagined that one of his customers had died and that's why he had to leave the café so suddenly. But why would he take Fernanda with him?

4.30 p.m.

Melissa stuck her head over the garden wall to give me one of LuLaBelle's many 'toys' that the stupid mutt is supposed to fetch after we throw them. Sometimes I throw too hard.

Melissa wanted to know where I was off to.

MELISSA: I'm only asking because you look lovely!
ME: I'm going nowhere.

(I didn't add: 'Fast.')

MELISSA: I've made tea.
ME: Good for you.
MELISSA: And ginger snaps.

ME: Right.

MELISSA: Would you like to join me in the conservatory? You can bring LuLaBelle. I hear her fretting when you leave the house. And poor Dermot's hard at work, so . . .

I went.

The truth was, I was too tired to come up with an excuse. Also, the biscuits would be homemade. I pitched the chamois in the basin, hitched LuLaBelle to her lead and joined Melissa in the conservatory with the ginger snaps.

I was right.

They were homemade.

And delicious.

MELISSA: They're only fifty-six calories apiece.

ME: I should probably have more then. Don't want to fade away.

MELISSA: Help yourself, Agatha.

Melissa and I demolished the biscuits, washed down with Barry's Classic Blend (for me) and ginger and lemon tea (for her). It had a pale pallor and put me in mind of cats' piss which made me think about Mr Chips. We'd had him for years, me and Bart. Took him for granted, I supposed. And really, he managed to live to a good old age in the end. But the shock of finding him at the side of the road that morning on the way to school. I could still taste the bile that filled my mouth when I saw him lying there, his stomach ripped open and entrails oozing out and Mam telling us to stop the nonsense, he was just a cat and a pretty stupid one at that. Didn't even know how to cross the road safely. She put him in a black bin liner and drove away with him in the boot. We never mentioned him again after that.

MELISSA: Are you all right, Agatha?
ME: I'm. . . Yes.

Haven't thought about that cat in years. Getting maudlin. Probably the menopause. Isn't everything?

MELISSA: Would you . . .?
ME: Please don't ask me if I want to talk about it because I don't.
MELISSA: I was going to ask if you would like another ginger snap.
ME: Oh. Sorry.
MELISSA: Well?
ME: Yes. Please.

She thanked me – again – for giving the talk to her flower-arranging club and said that, since then, two of the women had gone on HRT, one had left her husband and one had dyed her hair titian, like mine.

ME: Have you dyed your hair too? It's darker than before.
MELISSA (flushing): Oh, it's just a temporary thing, one of those wash-in-wash-out shampoos.
ME: It's the first time I've ever seen it out of the ponytail too. Suits you.
MELISSA (jumping up to open a window): Anyway, Sadie wants to know if she can interview you.

ME: Which one is Sadie?

MELISSA: The one who left her husband. She's a journalist for *Women Be Well*. It's a health, lifestyle mag. I told her you're probably too busy?

ME: Is there a fee?

MELISSA: Of course! You can't be expected to work for nothing.

ME: I'll do it.

Best to keep myself busy. Less time to think.

Melissa went on to wonder if I knew that Shakespeare's Portia also had titian hair and that Shakespeare said she was the most perfect woman he ever created.

I did know that as a matter of fact. Mam made sure I was equipped with that particular piece of information before the mouthy kids at school had their say.

MELISSA: Den was wondering why you haven't responded to his friend request on Snapchat.

ME: When were you speaking to him?

MELISSA: I wasn't. We mostly send each other cute kitten reels on Insta. He DM'd me.

ME: I don't know why he's so keen to be friends on Snapchat.

MELISSA: I think he has a bit of a thing for you.

ME: He has no idea what a fax machine does.

MELISSA: Besides, there's Luke. The dote. I haven't seen much of him lately.

ME: Me neither.

5.15 p.m.

'Poor Dermot' appeared at the door of the conservatory.

'POOR DERMOT': Isn't it well for you ladies, nothing to
   do all day but sit around and drink tea and eat biscuits.

I stood up and he took a step back and placed his foot in
the bowl of water Melissa had filled for LuLaBelle, which
tipped over and soaked his argyle socks.

ME: That's karma fucking with you, Dermot.
'POOR DERMOT' (red and fake laughing): What do you
   mean?
ME: You could eat the boeuf bourguignon Melissa's prepared
   for you off the floor in that clinically clean kitchen of
   yours.
'POOR DERMOT': Hahaha. I suppose you're one of those
   women's libbers.
MELISSA (putting LuLaBelle's lead on and hurrying
   towards the door): I'll see you out, Agatha.

8.30 p.m.

So by the time Luke arrived home, I'd mostly forgiven him
for everything. I even went so far as to arrive at the conclu-
sion that he hadn't really done anything wrong and he was,
in the main, a fairly decent individual.

   It was late and he was tired and he flopped down on the
rocking chair in the kitchen, accepted the bottle of cold
beer I handed him and only commented on my get-up when
I said, 'Do you like my get-up?'

LUKE: It's nice.

And I didn't even mind that because Luke used 'nice' for all manner of things that he genuinely enjoyed and appreciated. He just had a limited vocabulary when it came to adjectives.

But when I asked him if anything interesting happened at the café today, he just shrugged and said, 'No' and took a long draught of beer. Then I asked him why the café had been closed for an hour and he spluttered and coughed and said the beer had gone down the wrong way so I whacked him on the back and he said, 'Jesus, go easy!' and I said I thought he was choking and he reminded me of the time I did the Heimlich manoeuvre on Mrs Hart in the café and broke one of her ribs.

ME: Better a broken rib than choking to death on one of your Friday Fish specials.
LUKE (still coughing): Yes, it's just, you're very strong.
ME: When you say strong, do you mean rough?
LUKE: No.
ME: Have you stopped choking?
LUKE: Yes.
ME: So?
LUKE: What?
ME: 'Back in an hour'?
LUKE: Oh. That. Well . . .

And then he came up with this unlikely tale which involved the running out of wholemeal flour necessitating an emergency dash to the cash-and-carry and bringing Fernanda with him because he wanted to familiarise her with the process so she could do the run on her own, if Luke happened to be otherwise engaged.

Like, he'd never said 'otherwise engaged' before in his life. That's how I knew it was a cock and bull story. But I didn't pull him up on it because:

a) I was pretty sure he's never lied to me before, making this an unprecedented event for which I had no points of reference;

but also:

b) I was afraid.

3 July, 4 a.m.

Symptoms: Paranoia

At least, if I have to be awake in the middle of the night, there were emails to read.

Dear Agatha,
I knew your mother! She'd be so proud of you.

MAM (tutting): Pride is one of the seven deadly sins.

I went through the menopause decades ago. Awful it was. And nobody said a word about it. It was a dirty secret like everything else back then. I remember the priest coming in after Noreen (my eldest) was born, to 'church' me. I asked him what it meant and he said it was to clean away my 'impurities' after childbirth.

I should have smacked him.

Or at the very least, squirted some breast milk on his face!

Anyway, sorry, I'm getting sidetracked.

I only wanted to let you know how much I enjoyed *Menopause: The Movie*. It makes me feel good every time I watch it. I sent it to my Evelyn (my youngest) in America. She's in the thick of the menopause, raising twins on her own after that dose of a husband left her for an estate agent. They call them 'realtors' in America.

I know what I'd call him!!

Anyway, I'm hoping Evelyn will get some comfort from it.

Fond regards,

Eileen O'Dwyer

PS I can't believe it'll soon be your dear mother's first anniversary. She was a formidable woman, Mrs Doyle. And she arranged the church flowers with such care. May the Lord have mercy on her soul.

MAM: I suppose she wasn't the worst, Mrs O'Dwyer.

Oh, and an email from Samantha. The *Guardian* want me to write an article.

Downside: It's about menopause.

Upside: They'll pay!

Another little bit to add to the misery menopause fund.

It'll involve research which – let's face it – I haven't been good at recently.

I need to research, then write about, menopause policies in the workplace.

I'll take a wild guess and say there aren't many of those.

Maybe I'll be pleasantly surprised.

Ha!

Still, something meaty to get stuck into. Already I can feel the rusty cogs in my brain start to turn. Perhaps the B vitamins are helping after all?

Unlike the magnesium the pharmacist promised would help me sleep.

I thought I should do something, since there's no sign of Luke making good on his promise to learn to samba.

Although I've only taken one tablet so far. Maybe I should give it a minute.

I sent Carol a voice memo about the 'cash-and-carry-cover-up'. It was too long to type.

4.02 a.m.

Carol responded with a voice memo of her own which she didn't usually send, preferring the clarity of the written word.

She's such a contracts lawyer.

It was strange to hear her voice. She was nonplussed and said – in an LA-lite accent, fuck sake, she'd only been there five minutes – that I was being paranoid.

I googled paranoia and learned that it's a symptom of schizophrenia. A jaunty women's health website cheerfully announced:

Menopausal schizophrenia is more common than you think!!

As if that statement wasn't bad enough on its own without the in-your-face exclamation marks.

4.03 a.m.

Another voice note from Carol. She said it was completely normal for café owners to visit cash-and-carrys.

ME: Should that be, '-carries'?

4.06 a.m.

Carol added that it was perfectly acceptable for a manager to demonstrate the ways of the cash-and-carry to a new member of staff in the hope that they (the new member of staff) will be able to carry out the job by themselves, going forward.

And she knows how allergic I am to corporate gobbledygook.

4.10 a.m.

Carol switched to text. She probably realised I was judging her harshly with the LA-lite accent.

CAROL: Sorry about the 'going forward'. It just slipped out.
ME (magnanimous): Don't let it happen again.
CAROL: Luke's crazy about you.
ME: Mad.
CAROL: What?
ME: We say mad. Here, in Ireland. He's mad about you. Not crazy.
CAROL: He won't be for much longer with that level of narky.
ME: Fair.
CAROL: OMG, I nearly forgot to tell you about the menopausal women me and Crystal met at our tai chi class on Venice Beach.

ME: How do you know they were menopausal? It's not like we go around with bells around our necks.

CAROL: It was a flash mob. Although they weren't great dancers, to be fair.

ME: If you're suggesting that menopausal women aren't great dancers, then can I remind you . . .?

CAROL: Steady on, I'm getting to the good bit. They were all wearing T-shirts with #menopausethemovie written across them. And they were dancing to 'Oh Bondage! Up Yours!'

ME: That's not an easy song to dance to. Especially for a flash mob. Even more especially for a hot flash mob.

CAROL: You made a joke!

ME: I did.

CAROL: I think this menopause guru stuff has been positive for you.

ME: Stop saying positive.

CAROL: Also, you've done what Westlife never could.

ME: What?

CAROL: You broke America.

ME: I'll break your face.

CAROL: You'd never think this was the same woman I saw on Melissa's Insta, having tea and ginger snaps in the conservatory.

Melissa's gone feral on social media, since she met Den.

CAROL: Are you best friends with Melissa now?

ME: Yeah.

CAROL: Hard to compete with conservatories and baked goods.

ME: Tell me something awful about LA.

CAROL: You're not here.

ME: Sappy bitch.

CAROL: Stupid cunt.

ME: I miss you.

CAROL: I keep telling you to come over!

ME: Luke's talking about getting a loan from the credit union
to buy Damien out of the café and . . .

CAROL: I'll pay. It can be for your birthday.

ME: I'm not one of those telly orphans you're always sponsoring.

CAROL: You're definitely not as cute as them.

4 July, 12.30 p.m.
Symptoms: Jealousy

It was all Carol's fault. She made me think, in her psycho-
babble-LA way, that I should give Luke the benefit of the
doubt. So I decided to actually go to the café for real this
time. This time, I wore my best Ramones T-shirt and my
loosest boyfriend jeans and away I went to the café. I had
to bring LuLaBelle who has taken to weeping openly whenever I so much as glance at the front door. I refused to put
on her 'raincoat' even though – according to Dad who
mainlines weather forecasts – it was supposed to lash later.

Of course, LuLaBelle's 'raincoat' is pink. Dad says there's
a matching hat but Leonora didn't dare pack that in
LuLaBelle's 'weekend bag'.

On the way to the café, LuLaBelle was at pains to demonstrate the vigorous lead-training that Leonora has subjected
her to. She stopped when I stopped – to light a cigarette,
retie the laces on my Docs and give directions to Glasnevin

223

Cemetery to an elderly man clutching a bunch of garage flowers.

When LuLaBelle suspected that the stop might be protracted – the elderly man was hard of hearing so I ended up drawing him a map on the back of a SuperValu receipt – she sat down to wait, her anxious eyes trained on my face for the signal to go.

The signal was me saying, 'Move it.'

She didn't complain about the distance; five kilometres is quite the journey on those dainty paws and I'm no mincer. But she managed to match my long strides and made it look like it was the most fun she'd had since I dropped a marshmallow on the kitchen floor the other day and she got to it before I did.

Her shit was pink that night. I'd say Leonora would get a kick out of that.

So there I was, like an eejit, outside the café, squatting down to pet the dog and tell her how good she was so she didn't notice me tethering her to a lamppost. She licked the inside of my wrist with her warm, pink tongue which was both gross but also strangely pleasant because she looks like she's smiling whenever she does it.

I heard them before I saw them. They were laughing as they ambled along the path towards the café. Well, Luke was.

He laughs with his whole face. His eyes disappear into slits and his mouth opens wide so you can see the gap where his wisdom teeth used to be. It's not a great laugh if you've just eaten spinach.

Fernanda has a sexy smile rather than a laugh. It's so bloody performative. She leaned towards Luke, put her tiny hand on his arm and used the other to demonstrate something and Luke nodded along, taking it all in, lapping it all up, like he'd never heard anything quite so interesting.

He was wearing a pair of green . . . leggings? He never wears leggings. I didn't even know he owned a pair of leggings. He's a strict blue jeans kind of man.

Well, he used to be.

LuLaBelle barked and Luke and Fernanda looked up.

Luke dropped his arm so that Fernanda's tiny hand was suspended in the air. She lowered it slowly as I stepped in front of them.

LUKE: Hiya! I wasn't expecting you!

ME: Are they Lycra?

LUKE: What? Oh . . . these . . . em, I'm not sure really.

ME: I haven't seen them before.

LUKE: They're new.

ME: New what?

LUKE: Yoga pants.

FERNANDA: He was going to wear his jeans to the class, can you imagine? (Display of performative smile, also showcasing the (adorable/sexy) gap between her (white/even) front teeth.)

ME: Actually, that bit I can imagine.

LUKE: The studio keeps giving us free passes.

ME: Susie thinks yoga might be good for me.

LUKE: Susie?

ME: Dr Lennon.

LUKE: Oh yeah. You should totally come with us next time.

ME: Who's looking after the café?

LUKE: I asked Mrs Daly to cover. Come on in and I'll make you my toasted special.

ME: I better get back to work.

Even though I'm a sucker for Luke's toasted special. It's your basic ham and cheese toastie but there's a lot of butter and then there's the way Luke grills the sandwich with the grated vintage cheddar scattered across the top so that it bubbles as it melts in the heat.

I gave LuLaBelle the signal and we marched off towards home.

5 July, 4 a.m.

Symptoms: Hunger pains

Not only did I refuse Luke's toasted special, I also didn't feel like dinner.

Turns out femme fatales put me off my grub.

Temporarily at least.

Now I could eat my way through Aidan's entire vegetable patch in the garden and not even check them for slugs.

But I didn't want to go down to the kitchen because – even at this ungodly hour – there was a chance that Dad or Colm might be in the kitchen doing various things to bread and milk and cereal.

Despite my tossing and turning, Luke never stirred.

Which was a good sign in one way. I mean, if I were sleeping with an enchanting creature like Fernanda behind Luke's back, I wouldn't be able to sleep, would I? Because:

a) sex flashbacks;
b) guilty conscience;
c) sex flashbacks.

But men. They're genius at compartmentalising, aren't they?

I mean. Yoga. Come on.

Although he did have yoga pants on.

Bloody hell. Yoga pants.

And he didn't even look awful in them. In fact, there's a chance he's lost more weight. And not in a 'I ate a tapeworm and it's eating me from the inside out' kind of way.

I'm talking, on actual purpose.

Was that fucker on a diet?

He'd never been on a diet in his life. He claimed he didn't 'believe' in them.

But then I remembered the packet of fig rolls – which I had bought ONE WEEK ago – were still in the press, unopened.

Luke was the only one who ate them. They were his favourite go-to with tea.

Then there was the small (read: tiny) matter of Fernanda. She was like this freshly baked roll of figs, wrapped in a pink satin bow, reclining on a yoga mat with her come-to-bed gap-toothed performative smile.

I'd never really thought about what Luke's type was. I'd just assumed it was me.

I was his type.

Which brought to mind that horror of a boss I had once, before I started writing full time. He used to proclaim, loudly, from behind his desk, 'Assume makes an ASS of You and Me.'

What he really meant was that it made an ass of me.

6 July, 5 a.m.

Symptoms: Industrious insomnia!

I've just spent the last hour looking for my passport because Samantha has firmed up the details of the *Woman's Hour* event in Liverpool. They're willing to pay me an appearance fee plus expenses.

If I must be a pin-up girl for menopause, I feel like I should get a suite. A penthouse suite. With air conditioning that I can actually control. And a view in case I feel like looking out the window. And a mini-bar that gets automatically replenished so I don't feel bad looking at all the empty spaces where pretzels and peanuts and jelly babies used to live.

6 a.m.

I finally found my passport, behind the bookshelf in the downstairs jacks. It's out of date.

I'm struggling to remember the last time me and Luke went away together. Oh yes, Barcelona. Even though Gaudí never finished the Basilica, it's still a fairly decent build. He was knocked down by a tram as he stood in front of it one morning, admiring it. So it's true I suppose. Pride does come before a fall.

It was two years ago. I had delivered a book (back when I was contracted to do such things and did them in a timely and efficient manner) and, while business could never be described as 'booming', The Full Shillings customers were less likely to die in their sleep and gentrification was still up to its tonsils in Stoneybatter to have any designs on the area in and around the café.

What do I remember? The heat of course. Back then, I

loved heat, the dry, dense smell of it. We could eat nothing hot and subsisted on a diet of tomatoes and mozzarella, ice cream and jugs of sangria. The sirocco, blowing in from the Sahara, making a jungle of my hair. The silk of my dress against my bare legs. We developed a habit of speaking filthy to each other over dinner. I thought it would have been too hot to fuck. We'd be slippery with sweat, barely able to gain purchase on each other. A cold shower afterwards. We could only fit into the cubicle in a spooning type arrangement. The shock of the water and the hard length of Luke's cock against my thigh and me shouting, 'One more for the road,' and back to bed and back to the shower and eating everything in the minibar even though we swore we wouldn't touch any of the goodies because they're a rip-off, and then walking down to the end of Las Ramblas at dawn to sit on the sand and watch the sun rise over the Mediterranean.

Jesus. I'm exhausted even writing that down.

I should have just written:

To Do:

– *Renew passport.*

That wouldn't have left me with this . . . I don't know, it's like a virus except, instead of getting a temperature and a headache, it delivers sentimental nostalgia intravenously and leaves you limp with a maudlin yearning for that former version of yourself. Before the menopause infected every cell and bone in your body.

And joints. Let's not forget the achy joints. Not even Dad hobbles like I do when I manage to coax myself out of bed. In fact, he's a spring lamb compared to my mutton.

7 July, 4 a.m.

Symptoms: Wistfulness

To Do: Print out the photos Aidan took of me for my new passport.

There was a time when having my passport photograph taken was an uneventful occurrence. Just another item on my To Do list to tick off.

The last time I had to renew my passport was ten years ago. I was approaching forty and I wasn't all that keen.

Luke, who had turned forty the previous year, told me it wasn't a big deal.

LUKE: You're healthy, you're hearty, you're grand.
ME: I sound like a heifer you're trading at a mart.

I can't believe I ever complained about forty. When I see photographs of myself at that age, I almost don't recognise myself. The woman looking back at me is like a stranger. There is not a trace of awareness on her face. Nothing to suggest she has the remotest clue of what is awaiting her. Like all women about to turn forty, I'd heard of the menopause, but only worried about it in a vague, theoretical way.

Like the way I worry about tsunamis. I know they exist but feel confident they won't have any adverse effect on me, per se.

I cursed my period when it arrived and stained my knickers because of course I never took note of when it was due. I just knew it would arrive, as it always did, stain my knickers, bloat my belly and make my mouth water for Walnut Whips and Wagon Wheels. I'd get an inkling about two days beforehand, when my mood and energy levels would dip and I'd find myself wondering what the point of anything was anyway? Luke would notice too and arrive home with leftover tea brack which he'd spread thick with butter and place on a napkin on the arm of the couch before turning on an episode of *Queer Eye*. Is there anything more comforting than comfort food in front of comfort TV? And the boys would do their bit by giving me a wide berth for those two days and Mam would guess the minute I arrived on her doorstep with my pale face and tragic air.

She was great with periods, Mam. Although she didn't call them, periods. She said, 'women's problems', the volume turned down on her usual bray.

She'd fill a hot water bottle and make tea and tell me, in no uncertain terms, that I wasn't even to think about cleaning the house even though – the Lord knows – it was only crying out for a spring clean.

I don't know what she called menopause because she was already dying by the time my symptoms began and I didn't want to bother her with such trifles as hot flushes when she was struggling to contain the toxic levels of chemo-therapy flooding her circulatory system.

She didn't want the chemo. I made her go through it in the end. If she'd been in the full of her health, she would have said 'No' and that would have been that. But by the time she was diagnosed, the cancer had already taken its toll and she allowed herself to be persuaded by me.

There was nothing left of her in the end. The day we

moved her bed to the sitting room, Luke was able to carry her downstairs in his arms.

I'd say she might have called it 'The Change'.

No, she wouldn't have given it the capitals.

The change.

I don't remember her having it. She never mentioned it. She was a woman who prided herself on her ability to Get On With Things.

She would not have been a fan of *Menopause: The Movie*.

Or my phone pinging at all hours of the night and day with texts and emails from women.

MAM: Why would you be telling your business to a complete stranger?

Except the women write to me like we've known each other for years.

Like this one here:

Dear Agatha,
Menopause: The Movie has knocked *The Apartment* off my #1 favourite film of all time. And I'm a MASSIVE Billy Wilder fan. Except now I'm an even bigger Agatha Doyle fan.

I adore you.

Karen

xxx

PS please don't be freaked out, I'm not a stalker, just a menopausal woman who finally feels seen.

And this one:

Dearest Agatha,

I got a tattoo that says, 'Oh Bondage, Up Yours'. It's only tiny and it's on my upper thigh so chances are no one will ever see it (my husband is pretty short-sighted and refuses to get glasses). Now, when I'm breaking out in a hot flush, I touch my thigh and think of you.

Yours most sincerely,

Felicity Brennan

And this one:

Dear Agatha,

I've never emailed to an 'internet sensation' before. To be honest, I didn't realise one could. But I was moved to express my gratitude to you. Before my daughter watched *Menopause: The Movie*, she was giving serious consideration to giving up her job which she loves. Or at least taking a sabbatical (she's a university professor, her father and I are very proud). Now, her workload has been reduced after a frank discussion with her ordinarily rather boorish superior, she's seeing the campus counsellor and is on a waiting list at one of those menopausal clinics that are sprouting up these days.

She has also taken to using expletives which, of course, I don't condone but it's great to see a bit of vim and vigour about her all the same.

Yours in gratitude,

Pauline McCarthy

If I have to be miserable and menopausal in the middle of the night, there's a certain comfort in knowing that I'm not alone.

To pass the time, I filled in my passport renewal form and stuck it in an envelope with my out-of-date passport for my long-ago forty-year-old self. Fifty seemed properly old. You're expected to have a handle on things. Like tax returns. And pensions. And servicing the gas boiler.

And I look way more than ten years younger in the picture. Although not quite carefree. Ronnie had died that autumn, Aidan kept crying at the dinner table, Colm was addicted to that awful computer game where people are killed in increasingly gruesome and elaborate ways, I was trying to finish a book and Luke was doing his best to persuade Damien not to sell the café, comfort the customers, and clear out Ronnie's belongings.

The reason I got Aidan to take the passport photograph is because, you know, filters. I stood against the wall on the landing, which is a pale grey so I figured it would tone down the more raucous strands of my hair.

AIDAN (click-clicking away): Stop frowning.
ME: This is my passive face.
AIDAN: Can you get it more passive and less aggressive?

Which was unhelpful because that made me frown away good-oh and it's tricky to get from that back to passive. Then, when he finally stopped clicking and showed me the pictures, I was appalled at the result.

ME: Why didn't you put the filters on?
AIDAN: I did.

My mouth looked like a cat's arse, the skin around it puckered with all the effort I've put into smoking. Also, the photographs are black and white so there's no contrast between the red of my hair and the grey of the wall or the green of my eyes. Everything is just various shades of bleak.

ME: Why are they all in black and white?
AIDAN: That's the requirement. There's a list of them on the website.
ME: I know that!

Afterwards, I read the list of requirements. Why are there always so many requirements? I ticked the box for the ten-year passport and tried not to think about my sixty-year-old self applying for the next passport. I'll probably be dead by then anyway, between the smoking and the Walnut Whips. Which are useful for menopausal symptoms as well as PMT.

Useful might be a little strong. Comforting might be better. Also challenging and therefore distracting. You try getting all the mallow out with your tongue extended through the small opening you've created at the top. And even though Walnut Whips are not what they used to be, both in size and quality, it's still a tricky business.

I finished filling in the form and for a moment felt ridiculously pleased with myself. Productive. I used a red pen to put a gigantic tick beside the 'renew passport' item on my To Do list.

8 July, 4 a.m.

Symptoms: Night sweat exacerbated by annoyance

Today I spent two solid hours in my office and I actually worked for part of that time. I did some research for the *Guardian* article and wrote the first draft of a speech for an after-dinner thing that Samantha had accepted on my behalf.

And okay, fine, I did spend some time playing Scramble but it's taken me so long to get to the top of the leaderboard, I can't afford to let things slide now.

When I came downstairs for a coffee and smoke, Luke was in the kitchen, on the phone.

ME: Good morning.

He jerked around like I was the very last person he expected to see.

LUKE (in a preternaturally loud voice): Okay then, that's great, thanks very much, I have to go now, okay, great, goodbye.

He stabbed at the disconnect button.

ME: I hope that person was at least partially deaf.
LUKE: Eh, it was just Mrs Keogh. She was wondering why I wasn't at the café.
ME: Maybe she forgot Wednesday was your day off?
LUKE: I think she might be losing it a bit. The other day, she thought I was Bruce Willis.

ME: The real question is, what would Bruce Willis be doing in The Full Shilling?

Luke's phone rings and he swipes at the screen, cutting off the call.

ME: Who was that? Damien?
LUKE: Eh . . . yeah. I'll ring him back later.
ME: So, I've been thinking about the yoga class. I think maybe I'll give it a go.
LUKE: . . .
ME: Hello? Did you hear me?
LUKE: Sure, of course, I'll . . . check with the instructor and see what's available.
ME (grinning): We could get matching yoga pants!
LUKE: Yeah.
ME: You okay?
LUKE: Yeah, no, sorry, I'm just . . . a bit tired.
ME: I suppose you expect me to drop everything and do something fun with you?
LUKE: No, I know you're working.
ME: I could spare an hour.
LUKE: Fernanda says we need some new crockery for the café so I'm . . .
ME: You're replacing Ronnie's stuff?
LUKE: Dad bought it in Hector Grey's in 1969. I don't think he'll consider it a haunting offence.

There's nothing bloody well wrong with that crockery. Bloody Fernanda and her sultry looks and revolutionising ways.

LUKE (changing the subject, quick smart): So, what are you working on today? Besides your novel, I mean.

ME: I told you already. I'm writing the article for the *Guardian*, remember?

LUKE: Oh, yeah, sorry, I'm distracted at the moment. Fernanda reminded me that we . . .

ME: You smell different.

LUKE: It's a new cologne.

ME: You've never said that word before.

LUKE: What word?

ME: Cologne.

LUKE: Do you like it?

ME: What was wrong with your old smell?

LUKE: Just fancied a change, you know? I'll read your article later. If you want me to.

ME: I wouldn't bother, it's just me banging on about menopause and the patriarchy.

LUKE (swatting at the air around his head): Those bees keep getting into the house. I've been stung five times so far.

ME: The reason they sting you is because they don't like the stress sweat coming out of your pores. Although I'm surprised they can smell it through that wall of 'cologne'.

LUKE: The reason I'm stressed is because . . .

ME: I know, I know, the café . . . I can't believe the estate agent thinks it's worth that much. Why couldn't the bloody hipsters have stayed in Stoneybatter?

LUKE: Once we get Damien off our backs and the loan sorted, things will be better.

ME: And what if we don't?

LUKE: Can you at least pretend to be positive?

ME: That's like asking me to be somebody else.

LUKE: How's the book coming along?

ME: How come you haven't mentioned our anniversary?

LUKE: So it's going well, I take it?

ME: It's twenty-five years. That's silver, you know. A jubilee apparently. Maybe we should go away for that weekend?

LUKE: No!

And it's so loud and curt, the no, I nearly jump. Then he rallies with a, 'I mean, we will go away. Just . . . you know, not that weekend. We can go after that. When I sort out the café and . . .'

ME: Did I tell you that a man in his thirties with impressive hair fancies me?

LUKE (looking at watch): Sorry, I have to go.

And then he leaned in to kiss me on the cheek, missed, didn't notice and headed for the front door at a fair clip, not even slowing to pet LuLaBelle who was waiting at the door with her pathetic stump of a tail blurry with wagging. The front door banged shut and he was gone.

9 July, 10 a.m.

Symptoms: Unfocused

Since 'periodgate' LuLaBelle has been sleeping on the couch in the kitchen, snoring louder than Luke. Once I'm up, she follows me in a pathetic yet dogged manner. Up the three flights of stairs to the attic to watch me pretend-work. Out to the garden where I go for a smoke and to watch Aidan real-work. Apparently the bees had settled in well. So well in fact, that Aidan is working on a process that he calls 'supering up'. In short, 'supering up' is akin to putting an extension on your three-bed semi.

Aidan made the extension with the wood from the old kitchen table in Mam and Dad's house. Frank-with-a-C declared it a blight on the new topography of the interior landscape.

That's a direct quote.

Every so often, Aidan blew at the thick clump of his black fringe to get it out of his eyes.

He could do with a haircut. (I'm growing it, Mum.)

He could do with some meat on his bones. (I'm a vegan, Mum.)

He could do with a job. (I have a job, Mum.)

Jars of honey and a bag of veg won't impress the bank manager when you're looking for a mortgage.

What's going to happen to him?

I worry that he's not able for this world, Aidan. He had to have counselling after Ronnie died. Grief counselling. For an eleven-year-old. But he was inconsolable. And he kept asking why? And where? 'But where is Grandad gone, Mum?' I hadn't a clue what to say to him. I couldn't say 'heaven' with any sort of clear conscience.

For a while, Luke held out some hope that Aidan might take over the café. Colm certainly wasn't going to. 'I want to be rich and famous.' He always seemed to know that he would be neither of these things if he ran the café. Aidan helped out whenever he was asked. Having inherited my innate awkwardness, he broke many plates, got a fair few orders wrong and – once – scorched the ends of his hair when he leaned across the hob. He said he forgot to put on the hair net Luke had given him and, when I was shoving his scorched clothes into the machine after we got back from the hospital, I found it in the back pocket of his jeans.

Still, Luke declared himself delighted with Aidan's assistance.

But then Aidan became vegetarian and started wearing his 'Meat Is Murder' T-shirts and explaining to the customers about cows and pigs and their flatulence and the ozone layer and wondering if perhaps they might consider a fry-up with mushrooms and tomatoes and peppers and leave the rashers and sausages well enough alone?

After a while, Luke stopped asking Aidan to give a dig out in the café where the auld ones couldn't do without his fresh-out-of-the-oven shepherd's pies and bulging-out-of-their-puff-pastry sausage rolls.

And after a while, Aidan stopped asking Luke if he needed a dig out.

When Aidan finished inspecting the hive, he sat on the garden chair beside mine and asked what I'm writing in my *You Can Quit* notebook. I told him I was working on my novel.

He smiled at me. A bright, trusting smile.

Like, how does he not know that I'm lying through my teeth?

How?

10.45 a.m.

There I was, working in my office – putting the finishing touches on the after-dinner speech – when the doorbell rang. And of course I had to answer it because there was no one else. Luke was at the café, Aidan was out the back tending to the bees and conveniently out of earshot of the bell, Colm was in his room listening to maudlin music (Keane, who else?), and Dad was at his Senior Singles salsa class, dancing with Hugo, the only other man in the class (he had undertaken not to dance with a woman unless it was Leonora). Aidan explained about gender being a social construct but Dad didn't want to take any chances.

Anyway, I yanked open the door and there she was.

Amelia.

She was carefully turned out. You know that look some women can achieve, like they've just rolled out of bed and put on the first thing that came to hand but really, when you break it down, the nonchalance has taken up hours of painstaking attention to detail.

She was wearing a tracksuit but not in the same way as I'd wear a tracksuit. This was a Sweaty Betty, the bottoms low on her hips to showcase her tanned belly which set off the glittering stone that plugged her bellybutton (a suspiciously deep 'inny'). A crop top under the tracksuit jacket in baby pink and her small pink toenails barely visible at the end of her sliders. Tons and tons of soft, blond hair piled on her head in a carefully tousled topknot. Her face was made up to look like it was bereft of make-up and, without her usual fake eyelashes and furious eyebrows, she had achieved a vulnerable quality which she accentuated with a faltering tone when she finally got around to speaking.

AMELIA: Uhm . . . is . . . Colm there?
ME: Why?

AMELIA: Oh . . . I . . . I want to . . . I need to talk to him.
ME: Which is it?
AMELIA: Sorry?
ME: Want? Or need?
AMELIA: I . . . well . . . could you just . . . let him know
     I'm here?

I didn't get a chance to say, 'No,' because, from upstairs, the sound of Colm's bedroom door being wrenched open, the handle banging against the wall and then the rampage of his feet down the stairs. He came to a halt just before the saddle board and gazed at Amelia as if she was a smorgasbord of his favourite food and he hadn't eaten in a week. Amelia gazed back at him and her enormous blue eyes filled with tears, right on cue. And then Colm took her by the arm and led her up the stairs, like she was the one who needed care and attention and a grovelling apology and a litany of explanations that would always be insufficient but might go some way towards encouraging people to move on.

That's right, Colm. Move on!

I tried to send him that message telepathically by boring two holes in his back with my eyes as he moved up the stairs but he just kept going.

The bedroom door closed and I don't know what happened after that because I'm not the kind of woman who listens at keyholes.

More's the pity.

But also because I got a text from Den.

DEN: Have proposition. Have lunch with me and I'll tell
     you all about it xxxxx

ME: Stop putting 'xxxxx's on the end of your texts. It's
    unprofessional.
DEN: So you'll come? xxxxx
ME: I need more information.
DEN: Sworn to secrecy, darling xxxx
ME: . . .
DEN: Pretty please with sugar plum fairies on top? xxxxx
ME: . . .
DEN: I'll send details in a mail. See you at lunch xxxxx

10 July, 4 a.m.

Symptoms: Heartburn, palpitations, night sweat

Although the heartburn and palpitations might be less to
do with menopause and more to do with the size of the
slice of lemon meringue pie I polished off earlier with Den.
He said he'd share it with me. Even asked the waiter for
two forks but, since he was doing most of the talking, I did
most (read: all) of the eating and now it's like my entire
body has been taken over by an army of sugar, rampaging
through my bloodstream.

While I waited for the Type 2 diabetes to abate, I decided
to have a little think about Den.

MAM: Horlicks!
ME: What?
MAM: That's what you should be doing. Making a nice cup
    of calming Horlicks instead of filling your head with

nonsense about men with makey-uppy names. What's
Den short for anyway?

ME: Nothing.

MAM: See?

I actually found a tin of Horlicks at the back of the cupboard
and even went so far as to make a cup of it, just to get
Mam off my back while I had a think about Den.

Not about him, exactly. Just, you know, our lunch.

Our meeting, rather. It just happened to take place in a
restaurant at lunchtime with a man who was at pains to let
me know how attractive and interesting and funny he finds
me, in no particular order.

ME (business-face): So? What's this business proposition
you have for me?

DEN: There's oodles of time for all that.

ME: I'm ageing here, in case you hadn't noticed.

DEN: I hadn't, matter of fact.

ME: (Performative eyeroll.)

DEN: I don't know how many times I have to tell you that
I find you attractive, interesting and funny in . . .

ME: In no particular order, yeah, yeah, yeah.

DEN: Even the way you reject my advances is . . . titillating.

ME: Did you just say . . .?

DEN: I know, sorry, I don't think I've ever said titillating
before, I don't know what came over me.

ME: Make sure it doesn't happen again. Now, business
stuff, go!

He had the grace to flush but then went ahead and told me about a new TV show he's producing with Patti as anchor about women's issues. They want me to appear on the first episode to talk about menopause. While he was talking, I was appalled to notice a sort of warm glow spread through me.

And not in a hot flush kind of way.

And I know, I know, it's pathetic. A woman of my age. Allowing myself to be flattered by such an obvious charmer. But he smelled of youth and adventure (think crisp morning pine forest meets smoky green room with a twist of subtitle on the side) and it was obvious from his clothes that he'd made an effort.

Pinstripe black drainpipes with polished brogues and days of the week socks in day-glo yellow. His trousers were held up by braces and I stopped myself in the nick of time from referencing *Mork and Mindy* because, of course, he's too young to remember that programme. His T-shirt was fitted and – I'm ashamed to say – I couldn't help but notice the ripple of muscle beneath the delicate material.

And yes, of course I know that he's the type of person who always makes an effort with his clothes.

And yes, yes, I also know that he's the type of person who is charming to everyone. Even rude waiters. Probably dentists too. And door-to-door evangelists.

I know all that.

And yet . . .

Maybe my defences were down with the hormone-depletion?

The whole system was down, let's face it.

System-fucking-failure.

So when Den looked at me when I was talking, like he was hearing-impaired and had to read my lips, and like he found everything I said fascinating, I couldn't help feeling . . . just a tiny bit, mind . . . well . . . flattered.

MAM: Need I remind you of the marriage vows you took, Agatha Bernadette Doyle?
ME: It's not like I was having impure thoughts!
MAM: I should hope not, young lady!

Bloody hell.

So anyway, there we were, me and Den, Den and me, all cosy in the corner, bonding over the hands-down-best season of *The Wire* (season three, obvs), when along came GBH with a man young enough to be his son (in fairness, Den was only young enough to be my much younger brother or cousin). I'd say the man was one of GBH's students by the way he waited for GBH to utter his next word so he could hang off it.

GHB: Den, my boy! How the devil are you? And Agatha? How do you know this young rascal?

Dublin really pisses me off sometimes. Like, is there nowhere you can go for a private lunch with a man who is not your husband about whom you might be entertaining impure thoughts?

The young man did indeed turn out to be GBH's student. They were having a tutorial over lunch since GBH had skipped breakfast and was starving.

He's one of those people who're always filling you in, whether you like it or not.

GBH (sly): Well. This looks very cosy.
DEN: I'm trying to persuade Agatha to do a weekly slot on a TV programme I'm producing. She'd be incredible on film, wouldn't she?
GBH: Of course she would! But nobody can persuade Agatha to do anything she doesn't want to do. Am I right, Agatha?
ME: Well, you're a cis, middle-aged white man so you must be.

Laughter from Den, GBH, and his adoring protégé.

GBH (turning to adoring protégé): Oscar, excuse my manners. This is Agatha Doyle. My claim to fame is that I had front-row seats at the live show of *Menopause: The Movie*.
ADORING PROTÉGÉ: Oh! I saw your video. It was super awesome. I really admire your fearlessness in the face of ageing.
ME: . . .

I think I agreed to go on the TV programme. I can't remember the name of it now. Blasted brain fog. There was a time when I'd only need to listen to a Leonard Cohen song once and I'd remember all the lyrics.

Now, look at me.

It's got the word 'women' in it, I'm pretty sure.

Good news: the Horlicks went cold before I had a chance to finish it.

Bad news: I set the cup on the counter and that's when I noticed the response from the credit union to the loan application. On top of the microwave. The gist of which was this:

They will grant the request for a loan, subject to the receipt of my advance.

Which would be fine and dandy.

If an advance was forthcoming.

11 July, 8.30 a.m.

Symptoms: Exhaustion

Turns out Horlicks does not help you sleep. I only managed to nod off around 6 a.m. and was rudely awoken by Aidan at 8, noisily performing his 'bee dance' in the garden because he had inspected the new super and it was already half-full (or half-empty if you're that way inclined which, let's face it, I am) with brood and nectar and pollen and honey and all sorts of stuff that basically means:

The bees are in grand form.

There was absolutely no need for Dad to join Aidan in the garden for the bee dance. Which is nothing like the actual dance the bees perform, may I say.

I blame all the stuff Aidan has planted these past few months. Even the vegetables are flowering. Even the spuds! Gentle white petals, delicate as butterfly wings. You'd nearly be tempted to smell them.

So you've got all the flora and fauna going on, and the – frankly – cheerful buzz of the bees in spite of LuLaBelle yapping at them – at a safe distance mind, she knows who's got the upper hand – all against a hazy backdrop of summer sunshine that seems to envelop everything in a sticky, sickly nostalgia and make us look like a particularly saccharine episode of *The Brady Bunch*.

Although I have to admit I loved *The Brady Bunch*.

But I was young and foolish then.

When I went down to the garden to complain about being woken at this ungodly hour, Aidan and Dad grabbed my hands and, before I could get around to objecting, there I was doing the bee dance along with them. Which is a sort of shimmy with a twist.

I have to admit that I got into it. And while I was dancing, I didn't feel nauseous or achy or worried or tired or laden with doom about the future. And the present. And the past.

When I went back inside, I was out of breath and a little dizzy from the shimmying. Luke was pecking away at the keyboard of his laptop and, when he saw me, he shut the lid with a snap and got up.

LUKE: I'm leaving.
ME: For good?
LUKE: What? No. What are you on about?
ME: I was being funny.
LUKE: Sorry, I'm in a hurry, would you mind arranging the NCT for the car? I'm pretty sure it's due soon and I'm up to my eyeballs at work and . . .
ME: Enough with the sweet talk, you old charmer.
LUKE: No, I'm talking ab . . .
ME: I'm going to be on the telly!
LUKE: Really?

ME: Yeah. You know Patti Mason and her producer? The guy with the impressive hair?

LUKE (picking up his laptop and pecking me on the cheek): Oh yes, Dan.

ME: Den.

LUKE: Great! (Checks watch.) I've got to run. I promised I'd pick Mrs Duffy up today, her bunions have swelled in the heat and she doesn't think she's fit to walk to the café.

And just like that, the morning sickness is back. I think it's the word, 'bunion'.

12 July, 4 a.m.
Symptoms: Forgetfulness. Or amnesia? Or full-blown dementia?

I did what insomniacs are specifically told not to do. I picked up my phone and started scrolling. Carol had sent me one of the 'Mad As Hell' videos that were still doing the rounds. An American woman with big hair and a gingham apron lying on a kitchen floor, sweaty, red-faced, crying. Smarties start falling like rain. I think they're supposed to be HRT. The woman revives, then starts dancing around the kitchen, catching the HRT (read: Smarties) in her hands and stuffing them into her mouth.

ME: That's pedestrian.

CAROL: Come on. The special effects are pretty impressive.

ME: It's probably produced by some pharmaceutical company.

CAROL: So cynical for one so middle-aged.

ME: Fuck you.

Carol didn't say, Fuck you back.

A stark example of someone who'd been in LA too long.

CAROL: I've sent you an early birthday present by the way.

ME: My birthday's not till December.

CAROL: I know. That's why it's early. Check your email later.

ME: Just tell me what it is.

CAROL: No.

ME: Tell me.

CAROL: Fine, it's a return flight to LA.

ME: To make sure I go back home again when you're sick of me?

CAROL: Yes.

ME: That's too much, I can't accept.

CAROL: Tough tits.

ME: I can't go now, everything is so . . . up in the air.

CAROL: It's an open ticket. You can come whenever you like.
   I miss you.

ME: Should I take HRT?

CAROL: You miss me too was the correct response.

ME: And you must say Yes or No.

CAROL: Will the tablets make you easier to deal with?

ME: They're not magic fucking beans.

Melissa only started hers two weeks ago and she said the difference is already ah-mazing.

That wasn't me, by the way. Not knowing how to spell amazing.

She said it like that. To emphasise just how ah-mazing her shedload of HRT is.

She was sleeping better, her appetite was back, she could bend without her hips threatening to pop out of their sockets and also without 'passing wind' as she called it.

MELISSA: You should try it, Agatha. Your followers would
    appreciate your opinion on HRT.
ME: I'm not Jesus Christ Superstar.

I'm trying to be happy for her. I'm doing better than 'poor Dermot' who is now complaining about Melissa eating him out of house and home since the return of her appetite. He cloaks this with concern about obesity, which apparently increases the chances of breast cancer for women on HRT.

Like, there's more fat on a butcher's apron for fuck sake.

I wanted something bad to happen to Dermot. Not life-ending. Or even threatening. Just . . . I don't know . . . a rash maybe. On his face. Boils. Nobody can work out how he got them. He's tried everything. All the creams and lotions and potions. Nothing's worked.

Suppurating, festering, weeping, oozing boils.

Probably shouldn't have written all those words in a row, feel a bit nauseous now.

Serves me right, I suppose.

Maybe just one boil. On his chin.

I wondered then about Luke. Calling Den 'Dan'. If it was on purpose, that wouldn't be so bad. At least I could take some comfort from that; Luke trying to undermine a man who found me attractive and interesting and funny in no particular order.

But the fact of the matter is that he wasn't worried about Den.

Conclusions could be drawn from that. And none of them cast me in a flattering light.

But then I got to thinking that I was overreacting. Like, it's me and Luke, right? We're solid. As solid as Mam's coffin. As frugal as she was, she insisted on solid oak. With brass handles.

It didn't come as a shock, her death. I'd had months to get my head around it. I was pretty confident I wouldn't cry. If there was anything that annoyed Mam, it was the whingeing of a chief mourner.

MAM: Don't let Mrs Brogan do the funeral flowers in the church. She cuts the stems short and uses too many of those oversized daisies. Which are really just weeds.
ME: You already said.

Luke said there was no need for me to carry the coffin, he and Dad and Bart and the boys would sort it.

ME: Are you picking the day of my mother's funeral to become a sexist pig?
LUKE: I know you're well able to carry it. I just . . . it'll be hard.

It wasn't the weight of the coffin that undid me. It was the sudden awareness that it was Mam in the coffin. She was a dead weight inside that hollow box and I was carrying her on my shoulder, as surely as she had carried me, when I was a baby.

And there I was, undone.

I couldn't move. I couldn't feel myself in my own body. It was like the world had stopped turning. Had fallen silent. And there was just this intense realisation, this terrible certainty, that Mam was dead.

The finality of it was there in the weight of her on my shoulder.

And then Luke's hand on my arm. His careful, intimate touch. And when I looked at him across the solid oak of the coffin, his face was as familiar to me as my own.

And the way he looked at me. Like he knew how undone I was. Like he was saying, it was okay. To feel like that.

Everything would be okay.

LUKE: Your mother will haunt you if she's late for her own funeral.

I nodded briskly and we all moved into the church.

Afterwards, I told Luke not to worry, I wasn't going to carry the coffin, when his time came.

ME: I wouldn't trust myself.
LUKE: Well, I'd trust you. You're like my own private Amazonian.
ME: You know those women killed their lovers after sex.
LUKE: I'll take my chances.

I cried when I came. And not just because it was the day of my mother's funeral. It wasn't a sad cry. I remember feeling stuffed full of life and it was sort of glorious, the feeling. Like my body could barely contain all the life, there was so much of it inside me. I could feel the beat and the heat of it, stampeding through my veins.

LUKE: Maybe it's because you feel more alive on the day of a funeral than other, ordinary days.
ME (suddenly and without warning): I love you.
LUKE: Now you're starting to worry me.

Anyway, later, I decided to forgive Luke for being too busy these days to play with me any more. I was even going to suggest we go for a drink or a bite when he got home. Or even just a walk since bloody LuLaBelle insisted on being walked every day. So, you know, two birds with one stone there.

And then! Just when I'd resolved to forgive Luke for being so inattentive and vague lately, he ruined it all by going to some coffee-roasting demonstration or something.

With Fernanda.

And the only reason I know is because Aidan went to the café with some potatoes he actually managed to grow in Dad's garden and Mrs Daly told him (a) she couldn't accept the potatoes without Luke's say-so and (b) the coffee-roasting demo thingy.

What a cow.

Aidan said Mrs Daly was just being careful, who's to say he hadn't sprayed the potatoes with all kinds of chemicals. Or pulled them out of a random field somewhere.

Like, we live in Dublin. There ARE no random fields!!

Also, it's Aidan. You only have to look at his dimples to know that he would have no truck with insecticides or thievery.

13 July, 12.30 p.m.

Symptoms: Mortification

Aidan picked out my outfit for my appearance on Patti's new TV show. I wanted to wear black.

AIDAN: No.
ME: It's slimming. And it'll go with whatever backdrop they're using in the studio. I googled it. It's true about the camera adding ten bloody pounds. That's four and a half kilos to you millennials.

Aidan handed me a dress Luke bought me long, long, long, long ago. It's bright green. We're talking John B Keane's Field-green.

The material was soft as marshmallow. With a deep, unapologetic slit up the side.

ME: No.
AIDAN: Yes.
MAM: That slit is ridiculous. Do you want the entire nation to see your gusset?
LUKE (when he gave me the dress): I saw this dress and thought of you.

He'd been in London at a trade show thing. Near Brick Lane. He bought it in a market there.

MAM: What about my good pearl earrings? You could wear them on the telly. Unless you've lost them!
ME: Of course I haven't lost them.

Because I hadn't worn them. Probably because I was afraid I'd lose them if I did. The earrings were Mam's most expensive item of jewellery. From Brown Thomas. Dad swelled with pride when he told her that. Of course, she berated him for wasting his money in that elite, snooty shop that excelled at daylight robbery. But she wore them every Sunday to mass. I found them in their original packaging in the drawer on her dressing table where she kept her passport, travel pass and hair rollers. She had stuck a note on the box:

For Agatha. Don't lose them! They're from Brown Thomas!!

Melissa thought the earrings were perfect with the dress, which made me question everything. Melissa's style had a bit of a 'mother-of-the-bride' bent to it. There was a lot of mauve.

I dressed the outfit down with my Docs which look like they got set upon down a dark alley one night and never quite got over it. And my short sharp grey leather jacket to hide the worst of the withering skin of my décolletage not to mention the tragedy of my upper arms.

And you, down the back. Don't you dare judge me. Nobody thinks they're vain until they're about to go on the telly.

1.45 p.m.

Melissa insisted on driving me to the TV studio.

ME: But it's Thursday.
MELISSA: So?
ME: You wash the windows on a Thursday.
MELISSA: I'll wash them tomorrow. Along with the floors.
ME: Are the floors your Friday chores?

MELISSA: Tuesdays and Fridays.

ME: I don't want to put you out.

MELISSA: You're not. Besides, I like hanging out with you.

ME: Why on earth would you like that?

MELISSA: I'm not making a nuisance of myself, am I?

ME: Actually no.

MELISSA: Besides, you shouldn't have to worry about parking or change for the meter or anything else other than being ah-mazing on the telly.

ME: I think amazing might be a stretch.

2.10 p.m.

Telly make-up artists have a heavy hand with foundation, I find. Like, I'm supposed to be pale and freckly. I'm Irish. And I don't mean 'new Irish'. I'm the strain of sodden, godforsaken Irish, blighted by the ghosts of the famine, tetchy with post-colonialism. My veins are clogged with black pudding and rashers and salty butter. My circulation is sluggish.

In fact, I'm not just pale.

I'm often blue.

The unnaturally cheerful make-up artist coloured me in. My body, parched with menopause, greedily sucked all the moisture out of the make-up, giving it that 'caked' appearance, the powder seeking refuge in the deep lines across my forehead and around my mouth so instead of looking all fresh and sun-kissed and new Irish, my face was like an abandoned leather bag that's been subjected to adverse weather conditions.

Women Matters. That's the name of the show. Which could be a bit of a controversial play on the BLM platform

OR it could just be a simple matter of subjects that matter to women.

Whatever.

3 p.m.

Den arrived with flowers.

ME: They better be for me.

DEN: You look stunning.

ME: I look like Cyndi Lauper's granny.

DEN (laughing like I'd said something funny): What can I get you? Mint tea? A flat white? Champagne? Kombucha?

ME: Champagne?

DEN: I wouldn't if I were you. Budgets are not what they used to be. It'll probably be Tesco sparkling wine.

Den clipped a minuscule microphone onto the lapel of my jacket. This close, I got a whiff of his perfume, which smelled like sophistication and passion had had a dance-off and it was a draw.

DEN: Feeling good?

ME: Good's a bit strong.

MELISSA: Just be yourself, Agatha. Everybody will love you.

MAM: Keep those legs crossed, for the love of God.

3.20 p.m.

The studio, brightly lit with much colourful pop art as backdrop, was a lot smaller than it looks on the telly. Patti blew a kiss at me and directed me to sit down in one of four enormous beanbags, a garish red that was already howling at my hair and my dress.

You know that sensation where you're moving through the world like a normal person? Everyone assumes you're a normal person. Calm. In control.

Meanwhile, in the control centre in your head, there's a full-scale riot going on.

PATTI: How are Clara and Ellen getting on?

ME: Who?

PATTI: Your sixteenth-century witches?

ME: Oh . . . yes . . . of course . . . they're . . . fine.

PATTI (disappointed tone): Really?

ME (gesturing towards beanbags): Are we supposed to sit on those?

PATTI: Don't worry, they're super comfortable. Try one.

MAM (blessing herself): Jesus, Mary and holy St Joseph.

The other two women on the panel were already in/on the beanbags, while managing to give off a graceful and dignified air. Unlike me, they were proper celebs. One was a broadcaster who enjoyed taking chunks out of businessmen and politicians for Sunday brunch. The other was a telly chef who preferred nibbling on the likes of salmon and asparagus frittata.

I approached 'my' beanbag. The two women encouraged me with bright, fresh-faced smiles.

Weren't they supposed to be menopausal? Wasn't that why we were all there? Both of them were wearing power suits with runners and both of them were fit, elegant and tough.

Like 'career-girl Barbies'.

Patti introduced me to them. I tried and failed to remember their names.

My green dress swung madly about me any time I moved. I felt like a carnival at an AGM.

Next: the beanbag.

I lowered myself into the thing, bending my knees further and further until they couldn't take it any more and I sort of collapsed the rest of the way which wasn't that far but felt far. I tried to blow my hair out of my face but, with the heat of the studio, strands of it were stuck fast to my skin. The itch was unbearable. I couldn't scratch for fear of upsetting the make-up.

I kept a vigilant eye on the slit of my dress and tried not to think uncharitable thoughts about my fellow panellists. (Like, have either of these women ever had a hot flush? Or even a warm one?)

PATTI: You okay?

Of course I wasn't okay, my knees were above my face and I had no idea where the slit was at.

ME: I'm fine.

I struggled to rearrange myself in a more conventional posture.

It was no use. I was lopsided. On live, national television. But then I remembered that it's only Ireland. A small pond really. And nobody watches daytime telly any more. They're all watching unlikely friendships between dogs and cats on reels.

The only other thing that kept me going was the fact that

Mrs Byrne never managed to persuade Luke to install a telly in The Full Shilling all those years ago. She lobbied long and hard for it. She hated missing *Murder She Wrote* on a Thursday when she came in for Luke's fresh-out-of-the-oven beef and barley hotpot. In the end, Luke went to Mrs Byrne's house and showed her how to record it on her telly.

3.30 p.m.

The signature tune started up and Patti beamed into the camera and read from the autocue and already the muscles in my face ached from smiling and a strand of my hair was down the back of my dress, itching my skin every time I moved my head which I kept doing, depending on who was speaking since I was in the middle with the proper celebs sitting on either side of me.

Patti started out by playing a clip of *Menopause: The Movie*. The screen was behind me and I couldn't twist myself around enough to see it. I could hear it though.

Loud and clear.

I am a menopausal woman, standing here before you all in a lather of sweat, terrified that I might forget a word in the middle of a sentence with the threat of brain fog that looms over me on a daily basis as I sit at my desk and attempt to write to a deadline. I have insomnia, none of my clothes fit me, and there's a chance I'm more irritable than I used to be. Although my husband may have a different view on that.

Laughter from the audience.

Jesus H. The studio audience. I'd forgotten about them. Melissa was in amongst them somewhere. No doubt she had a bird's eye view of my gusset.

Now they were cheering and clapping. Even some whoops.

The broadcaster woman and the chef were clapping too. Everyone was looking at me expectantly. I shifted in the beanbag in a desperate attempt to sit up straight and look worthy of the applause.

The chef seemed to appreciate my discomfort so she started talking. Mercifully, the enormous camera that had been pointing at me slid across the studio towards her. I pulled damp strands of hair off my face.

CHEF: Until I saw Agatha's video, I hadn't talked about my menopause. When I was really bad and had to take time off work, I said I was having dental work done. Dental work has no stigma. Unlike my brain fog, insomnia and hot flushes. Then I watched *Menopause: The Movie* and everything changed.

BROADCASTER: Hard agree. Agatha's made it okay for menopausal women to come out. Now, when we're recording the show and I start having a hot flush, I just yell, 'Cut,' wait for it to subside, and carry on. At first, my team were a bit . . . unsure of what they should say or do. Now, they don't even bat an eye, it's part of the process. Do I wish I didn't get hot flushes? Yes. They're uncomfortable but they won't kill us. Whereas shame and stigma can. All you have to do is look at the statistics of suicide amongst menopausal women. Agatha's taken the sting of stigma out of the equation. We should have done that a long time ago. In fact, it never should have been stigmatised in the first place.

I had to talk then. I haven't watched the programme back but I think I said things about menopause in the workplace and how employers need to put measures in place to accommodate women who are experiencing symptoms.

I'm pretty sure I mentioned trade unions and how immediate and significant their input needs to be.

CHEF: Oh.

Everyone looked as the camera panned towards her.

CHEF: I'm having a hot flush. Excellent timing!

She was actually smiling.

CHEF: It started in my feet and it's moving north.
PATTI: Are you able to talk us through it?
CHEF: I'm doing my breathing. That's what my GP recommends. Long, slow breaths, in for five, hold for five and out for five.

The flush had reached the chef's chest and was seeping into her neck and her face. Her eyes were closed and you could make out the rise and fall of her breath. There wasn't a sound in the studio.

In my peripheral vision, the audience strained towards the chef, silently willing her through it.

I even forgot about the polyester of the beanbag, sticking to the bare skin of my leg, poking out of the dress through the slit.

Den was right. Budgets were certainly not what they used to be.

The chef – Cecilia – timed the flush. She described it as

mercifully brief but two minutes never felt so long. When it was over, the chef smiled at us. Then, like nothing untoward had happened, the discussion resumed.

A woman had a hot flush on live, national TV.

Nobody died.

The sky didn't fall down.

We just waited it out and then got back to the job at hand.

I made sure the cameras had stopped rolling before attempting to get out of the beanbag. In the end, it took three of them. Patti and the Sunday brunch broadcaster took my hands and hauled while the chef peeled the beanbag off me from behind.

Afterwards, the broadcaster, chef and Patti insisted on a 'group hug'.

It was a hormonal hotbed of heat. But also . . . okay.

4.15 p.m.

MELISSA (driving me home): You were marvellous. You all were. And Cecilia. Having a flush like that on live television.

ME: She was so calm. And informative.

MELISSA: Before I started on the HRT, I always left the room when I felt one coming on. It made poor Dermot uncomfortable. He said I looked like I was about to explode.

I'd explode if I was married to 'poor Dermot'.

ME: Was my gusset on show?

Melissa ignored my question and instead talked about how invaluable the 'real-time' demonstration of a hot flush was.

Biology in action.

Still, I do wish biology was better at its job when it comes to 'Women Matters'.

7 p.m.

After dinner, I googled the ratings for *Women Matters*.

Jesus H.

Have people nothing better to do?

8 p.m.

I made a mammoth effort to catch up with my correspondence. Which was when I noticed a plane ticket to LA in my inbox. Typical Carol. Always following through on threats / promises.

I'd love to see her.

But I can't accept the plane ticket. It's too much.

Also: I'm not the type of woman who just breezes off to LA. I have responsibilities. I have a job! Just because I'm not doing it doesn't mean it doesn't exist.

I filed the ticket away in my 'things to think about later' folder.

The emails from menopausal women showed no sign of abating.

The problem was, I'd get completely lost in their stories which affected the speed at which I could formulate a response.

Like this one. From a woman called Peggy:

My dearest Agatha,

I really enjoyed reading your article in *Women's Way* recently. I've been struggling in silence for so long, too afraid to ask for help because I didn't feel I deserved it. My sister – who raised me – said that menopause was a natural ageing process and us women must get through it as best we can. But I'm only forty-five and I'm not quite ready for false teeth and slippers.

Although I do love a good pair of slipper socks, if I'm honest.

I suppose I could be described as a meek person. The Lord says we shall inherit the earth but I'd settle for a good night's sleep and a boss who doesn't stare at my chest when I bring him his morning coffee.

I googled you. My word, your hair is a glorious colour. I hope you don't mind me saying that. I'm not a gay although sometimes I think my life might have been easier, had I been. I went to my GP today and she signed me off for a week. She has recommended HRT and I'm going to give it a go. Tomorrow, I'm going to order your books from the library. When they arrive I will read in bed and eat a Terry's Chocolate Orange. I've always wanted to do that.

I have written a letter of resignation. I haven't sent it yet. There's an 'assistant wanted' sign in the window of my local florist. It's run by a lovely, jolly lady who always has her nails beautifully manicured. I go in sometimes. I love the smell of the roses. And the feel of the ferns through my fingers. Such a gentle plant, fern. When the shop isn't busy, I chat with the lady who runs the shop. She's called Juliet. A pretty name, don't you think? I'm going to call in tomorrow and bring Juliet a cup of coffee. She sometimes has a cappuccino in one of those reusable coffee cups. You know the ones with the lids? It's got the name of the shop across the middle of it. If I manage to work up the courage, I'll tell her I'm interested in the job. I'm quite good with plants. You wouldn't call me green-fingered or anything but last year I grew herbs from seed.

I will let you know how it all goes.

In the meantime, continued success with your writing and your work on menopause. I think you're doing a great job. You have had a positive effect on my life and to think that I only heard you because my boss wanted me to finish typing the contract and I was late taking my lunch break. There was no one else in the kitchenette so I was able to hear every word you said. Your family must be very proud of you.

Yours very sincerely,

Peggy O'Donnell (née Burke)

PS I have grown-up sons too. But they live in Australia.

Inside my chest, I could feel my heart swell and threaten to break apart.

I sent it to Carol.

CAROL: Are you crying?

ME: No. There's just something in my eye.

CAROL: Peggy ♥

ME: Peggy ♥

CAROL: I really want her to get that job in the flower shop.

ME: I really want her to shit on her boss's desk before she tells him to shove his job up his jacksy.

CAROL: I really want her to go to Australia to see her boys.

ME: I want them to come home and visit her.

CAROL: She didn't mention a husband.

ME: I'd say he's a bollix.

CAROL: Definitely.

ME: I hope she has a spectacular love affair with Juliet.

CAROL: But what about their working relationship? She wouldn't want to jeopardise that.

ME: It's Peggy. She's got this.

CAROL: Yeah. She'll be fine. And the HRT. That'll help.

ME: Yeah.

CAROL: Well done you.

ME: I didn't do anything.

CAROL: Yes you did. You dope.

14 July, 4 a.m.

Symptoms: Night sweat

The night sweat woke me up so a change of clothes was required. But since I wasn't wearing any clothes, I made do with a cold shower which must have woken Dad up because in he waltzed wondering what I'm up to and I had to wrap the shower curtain around my bulk and tell him to get lost.

DAD (from the landing, injurious tone): I thought we were being burgled.

ME: You thought a burglar broke into the house and took a shower?

DAD: You should have locked the door!

Wouldn't you think you could take a cold shower in your own bathroom in the middle of the bloody night without being disturbed.

I found him afterwards in the kitchen, consoling himself
with a bowl of goodie.

ME: Could you not sleep either?
DAD: No.
ME: Sorry for roaring at you.
DAD: I'm sorry for not knocking first.
ME: You were just trying to protect us from burglars, I
    suppose.
DAD: I thought you were your mother, when you walked
    into the kitchen just now.
ME: There's not a daughter in the world who likes being
    told she looks like her mother.
DAD: Your mother was a fine-looking woman.
ME: Finer than Leonora?
DAD: They're very different women.

That's true. Also, a classic sidestep.

ME: Do you miss her?
DAD: Ah, I do. Hugo's not a bad dancer but . . .
ME: I meant Mam.
DAD: Oh . . . well, that goes without saying of course.
ME: Does it?
DAD: We were a long time married.

Dad looked more like himself tonight. In spite of the boxer
shorts and T-shirt. Maybe it was the soft tufts of hair sticking
out of his ears and nostrils. He hasn't been as vigilant about
grooming since Leonora went off to get her new hips.

271

ME: You seem a lot more . . . enthusiastic about things these
    days. Than . . . before.

DAD: I took things for granted when your mother was alive,
    Lord rest her. Now I know that life's too short for that.
    Especially when you're seventy-four.

ME: You're nearly eighty.

DAD: Even more reason to make the most of every moment.
    Which brings me to a delicate subject . . .

ME: Are you dying?

DAD: Hardly, Agatha, I'm only seventy-six.

ME: Seventy-nine and three-quarters.

DAD: As I was trying to say . . . I got a call from Franc
    yesterday. The house is ready. I can move back in.

ME: Why is that delicate?

DAD: Well, the thing is . . .

ME: Leonora's moving in too?

DAD: Well, yes. She's getting out of the rehabilitation place
    tomorrow and she needs to be looked after while she's
    recuperating.

I waited for Mam to say something but she didn't.

DAD: You know the worst thing about your mother dying?

ME: No one to read the obituaries and let you know who
    had made it through the night?

DAD: It was the silence. I could hear every creak and rattle
    and drip in the house. There was a . . . this sounds stupid
    but . . . it made me feel sort of hollow, the silence. Like
    maybe I wasn't there either?

ME: I told you you could come over to ours any time you

liked. Silence hasn't gotten a word in since the turn of the century.

DAD (patting my arm): You're a good girl, Aggie. Sorry, Leonora told me I shouldn't say girl. Anyway, your mother was very proud of you, you know. All your historical knowledge and your writing and how well you looked after Luke and the boys.

This was news to me.

DAD: Please say something.
ME: Like what?
DAD: Like . . . you don't mind? About Leonora?
ME: It's your life, Dad.
DAD: Or . . . that you're happy for me?

He looked so vulnerable, with his remaining wisps of hair lying gently across his freckly scalp and his pale, watery eyes enormous in the lamplight.

ME: (eyeroll)

He hugged me. He was all elbows and ribs and felt as light as a bag of chicken bones in my arms. Luke would recommend marrow to fatten him up. Dad kissed my cheek and bid me a hasty goodnight. He made a beeline for the kitchen door and closed it swiftly behind him, before I could tell him that I was happy.

I was happy for him.

For a while the kitchen was as quiet as it's supposed to

be at this hour of the night. Then, the toast popped and I stood up so quickly, the chair fell back and crashed against the floor and in rushed Aidan from the garden to ask me if I could be quieter, I'm stressing the bees.

Bloody hell, all I wanted was a cold shower, maybe a quick read of my book (the photographs in Nigella's latest are top-notch), pull a few hairs out of Luke's back, check that his mole hasn't made a come-back, maybe even fall asleep.

AIDAN: I'm worried about the Queen Bee. She doesn't seem to be laying as many eggs as before.

ME: It's the middle of the night.

AIDAN: Could you not sleep either? I didn't mean to worry you yesterday.

ME (bewildered): . . .

AIDAN: Remember? I told you about the eggs? You were skulking around upstairs when Amelia was in Colm's room. That's the second time she's called in. Do you think they're getting back together?

ME: I was most certainly not skulking!

AIDAN: I'm sorry, I shouldn't have said anything.

ME: About what?

MAM: That poor child. Nobody ever listens to him.

AIDAN: About the eggs. There being less of them.

ME: Sure, you can see nothing. It's pitch black out there.

AIDAN: I had my night-vision glasses on.

I shooed him to bed with a politician's promise of how everything will seem better in the morning.

Which, obviously, won't be the case. Not if the Queen Bee has stopped laying eggs. I've gone and googled it.

Damn you, Google, you instantaneous harbinger of doom.

I glanced into Colm's room on my way back to bed. Just to make sure he was there.

Not only was he there, but he was fast asleep.

I had a terrible feeling that Aidan was right. Amelia certainly wanted Colm back. And Colm was being all defensive about her.

Exhibit A: Colm refusing to tell me what Amelia wanted when she called to the house again

COLM (testy): What makes you think she wanted something?
ME: No reason.

Of course she wanted something.

Aidan told me that her social media following has nearly halved since the split.

In the meantime, D.I.Guy is falling down with – even more – followers since Colm started documenting the bees.

And now, instead of roaming the house in the middle of the night like he should be doing, there he was, fast asleep in his bed. like a normal, non-heartbroken person.

That'd be just like Amelia. To come around here with her massive doe eyes and her tail between her toned, tanned legs, sweet-talking Colm with one of those celebrity apologies she copied and pasted from the internet.

Some people say, 'Forgive and forget.'

I'm not one of those people.

15 July, 8 a.m.

Symptoms: I don't know . . . a bit . . . unsettled maybe . . .

I got up especially early to catch Luke and maybe have breakfast with him. Nothing shouts 'I have crap news' better than a bowl of my watery, grey porridge.

Luke says I just need to add cream and honey and it will look like his porridge but no amount of sweetness and dairy is going to make that stuff palatable.

It didn't matter anyway because he'd already left.

I really have to tell him about the advance.

Not advancing.

I rang him but it went straight to voicemail. Then the message. But instead of telling me to leave a message, it informed me that the mailbox was full and then disconnected me.

Aidan was still in the garden, pale and dishevelled.

ME: Have you been out there all night?
AIDAN: I can't find her.
ME: Who?
AIDAN: The Queen Bee.
ME: She's probably just gone for a lie-down. She bloody
    well deserves one.

Since I was up, I decided to finish the after-dinner speech for the National Women's Council of Ireland. A fundraiser they're having in Brooks Hotel next week.

I'll be talking about menopause; how it affects your work. Which seems ironic given my lack of enterprise over these past weeks. Poor Clara and Ellen, waiting patiently at the back of my head for the whirring sound of my laptop, warming up. For me to colour in their lives with my trusty keyboard. They've heard about my prowess with a sex scene. They were looking forward to their first clandestine meeting – in a scullery, I was thinking. Leaning against the heavy wooden door so no one barges in. They kiss so hard, Ellen's lip bleeds. Clara licks the blood away.

CLARA: Even your blood is sweet.
ELLEN (pressing her finger against Clara's wet, swollen mouth): Sssh. They'll hear us.

They kiss again, fumbling frantically at each other's petticoats, hauling them up.

Those things were cumbersome.

But then – disaster – the pair of them crash against a shelf and tins and bottles and brushes fall off it and clatter onto the stone floor and they clutch each other and tense clamping their hands over each other's mouths to quieten their breathing and listen.

From the galley, the sharp clip of cook's hobnail boots against the scuffed wooden boards of the ship's narrow corridor, getting louder.

Samantha rang.

SAMANTHA: I hope I'm not interrupting your flow?
ME (surprised): You actually are!
SAMANTHA (breezy): Just seeing how your soundbite solution to the menopause is coming along.

I threw a selection of random, generic words down the phone.

I can't remember them all now. Something-something-mindfulness-something-exercise-plant-based-diet-something-meditation.

And – of course – that old chestnut: ME time.

SAMANTHA: Brilliant darling, something-something-incredible, you've nailed it, something-something-some-thing.

MAM: Are you even listening to that poor woman?

Dad arrived in the kitchen, weighed down with an enormous suitcase in one hand. In the other he held tight to LuLaBelle's lead as she strained towards me.

ME: Oh. You're taking LuLaBelle with you?

DAD: I thought you'd be delighted?

ME (petting the dog under her chin, which happens to be her favourite spot): Delighted's a bit strong.

DAD: You'll have her back again in no time at all. When Leonora and I go to Havana.

ME: Did I agree to that?

DAD: You said, 'I'll see.'

ME: I see.

MAM: That mangy mutt better not be let up on the new couch in the good room.

DAD: Could I bother you for one last lift? My driving licence still hasn't arrived. I can't ring them again. I just can't.

I couldn't blame him. When he rang up to complain last week, he was lowered into a maze of automation, pressing one button, then another, followed by a star, or was it a hashtag?

Then he was put on hold for so long that when a human voice eventually asked how he could help, Dad couldn't say since he'd forgotten why he'd rang in the first place.

In the olden days, men in hazmat suits would wrestle you into a straitjacket, do a bit of a frontal lobotomy on you then stick you into a padded cell and throw away the key. Nowadays, they just get you to ring an 1800 number and let a call centre do the rest.

Dad said he'd put his suitcase and LuLaBelle in my car.

I was getting dressed when my phone rang. I thought maybe Luke had seen my missed call and abandoned his post at the frying pan to call me back.

But no.

It was Damien.

I let it go to voicemail.

DAMIEN: Oh hiiii, Agatha, how are you? I saw you on the telly the other day, you really are . . . just . . . well, you're something else, you know that? All good here, you know, the usual, busy, busy, busy. So . . . just giving you a little tinkle, Luke said you were the person to talk to about timelines for the refinancing stratagem. So . . . whenever you have a moment . . . call me. I'm in a board meeting from now till 3 p.m. and then I have a window till 4.05 p.m. and then I'll be on con. calls all evening once the Nasdaq opens so . . . I know! So busy! But look, try me tomorrow if you can't get me today, I'll keep an eye on my phone. Okay? Okay. Bye for now.

Jesus H.

12.30 p.m.

LuLaBelle sat in the back seat with her head out the window so that her ears, long and droopy, flew behind her like pigtails.

I parked on double yellows outside the hospice.

DAD: It's not a hospice.
ME: Rehab. Whatever.

He checked his teeth (read: dentures) in the wing mirror, worrying at a piece of gristle between his molars. Then he opened wide and spritzed a mist of peppermint spray into his gob, before licking his forefingers and dampening down his – newly threaded? – eyebrows. He got out, did a twirl and stood on the path with his arms outstretched, refusing to leave until I had admired his freshly dry-cleaned black suit with the silver pinstripe, his black and white spats and the fedora that he found on a mannequin's bald head in our local Depaul's the other day.

He nearly sprinted to the front door of the hospice.

Rehab.

Whatever.

1.15 p.m.

Despite Leonora's heavy hand with the panstick, I could see that her face was pale and drawn.

LEONORA: You're very good to pick me up, Agatha. I promise I won't make a habit of asking. I know you're a busy woman.

Even her voice sounded fainter than before. I struggled to hear her over LuLaBelle's frantic yapping. Dad had to stand between them, otherwise the dog would have bowled Leonora over with the power of her adoration.

DAD: Looks like I'm not the only one who missed you.

In the rear-view mirror, I saw them glance at each other as he arranged the seatbelt around her.

The exchange was fleeting but filled with a tenderness that was as tangible as LuLaBelle's soft, fluffy pelt.

1.45 p.m.

I pulled up outside Dad's house.

DAD: Do you want to come inside, Agatha? Franc's done a fantastic job. You can take a look at Aidan's vegetable patch. The boy's worked miracles in the garden.
ME: I'd better get back to work.

Ha!

I found myself thinking about Luke. He would have said yes. Gone inside with Dad and Leonora. Oohed and ahhed over Frank-with-a-C's handiwork. I couldn't help wishing he was there, in the car with me. So I could order him to distract me with one of his new recipes or something.

Like for tapioca, say. He could do things with tapioca that made it taste actually palatable.

Okay fine.

Better than palatable.

But in the absence of Luke and the distraction he might

provide, it was hard to know how to feel. I tried not to look at Leonora, doing her best not to lean on Dad's proffered arm as they walked slowly towards the front door.

Or the gentle way he helped her navigate the step over the threshold.

As for LuLaBelle. She didn't so much as glance back at me once she was released from the car. She bounded into the house in a volley of joyful barks and disappeared into the sitting room. Through the window, I could still see Mam's bed and the table cluttered with medicine bottles and syringes and sponges and grapes and flowers. 'Don't leave me,' she'd said and she reached her hand – skin and bone by then – towards me. I picked it up and held it.

She'd never been afraid of anything in her life.

But this was her death and everything was different.

When her grip slackened, hours later, I knew she was gone.

I blinked and shook my head. I looked through the window again. Now I could see LuLaBelle making a dive for the new couch, walking up and down the cushions before settling down and stretching herself across the length of it.

2.30 p.m.

You'd think I'd love how quiet the house was.

No Dad blasting the Gypsy Kings on the Bose speaker he'd inherited from Colm and dancing an imaginary partner around the kitchen table.

No LuLaBelle getting under my feet and yapping at me for my undivided attention.

That turncoat.

Aidan was out the back garden dressed like an astronaut and blackened with bees.

Okay fine, he wasn't exactly blackened but there were bees crawling on him while he smoked the hive. The process looked mean but, because it was Aidan doing it, I was pretty sure it was all above board.

ME: Any sign of the Queen Bee yet?

Aidan looked at me through the smoke and shook his head slowly.

Then there was Colm, whose bed was unmade as usual.

But also, empty.

His wardrobe door hung open which meant that, not only had he gotten out of bed but he'd managed to get dressed and go out.

I should have felt glad.

I felt worried.

Even though Colm was big enough to take care of himself.

Of course he was.

Still, I couldn't help fearing the worst and the worst was Amelia-shaped.

Another missed call from Damien. This time I didn't listen to his voicemail which, no doubt, would have been more of the same.

MAM: You're going to have to face the music sooner or later, girleen.

I decided on later.

Still no call back from Luke.

And another love-addled WhatsApp from Carol.

I really like Crystal. I even think she could be the one, Agatha.
I'm talking about the you and Luke version. The real deal.
Sorry for being soppy, I know this message has probably
activated your gag reflex.

Great. So now I can never tell her anything about Den.
About him thinking that I'm attractive, interesting and funny
in no particular order. Because she'll just see that as a betrayal
of my top-notch marriage.

MAM: This is what happens when you commit the sin of
    omission.
ME: What is it with you and the sins?

Although I had to concede that there are many things I
have omitted from my correspondence with Carol since
she's been gone. And it wasn't because I didn't want to tell
her stuff, it was just . . . keeping in touch was harder than
I'd imagined. And so, when we did message, I didn't want
to heap all the stuff that was happening between me and
Luke onto her.

Besides, nothing was really happening.

That was it in a nutshell.

Nothing was happening.

That produced an unpleasant sensation in my gut. Like
stomach acid.

My phone ran out of battery then so I didn't have to
come up with an upbeat, pithy response to Carol's deluge
of delight.

8 p.m.

Finally! A call from Luke. I missed it because I was on a video call, being interviewed for another podcast, 'Menopausal Much?' Nelly, the interviewer – a Latvian living in Limerick – declared herself delighted with me.

NELLY: Before your tirade, I had fifty subscribers and four of them were my mother. She's fond of her aliases. Anyway, I felt like I was talking into the abyss. Then along came you, Agatha Doyle. What's your secret?
ME: Eh . . . I don't have one. I'm just . . . menopausal, I suppose. Also a whinger.
NELLY: I don't know what a whinger is but I'm assuming it's something fabulous. Like you, Agatha Doyle.

She kept saying my full name. Maybe it was a Latvian thing? Afterwards, I listened to Luke's message.

LUKE: Damien says he can't get through to you. Everything okay?

In the background, the gush of water into the sink, the banging of pots and someone singing a mournful and off-key fado-esque song in Portuguese.
    Fernanda.

LUKE: Can you call him? I'll try not to wake you when I get in. I've got that thing in the . . .

Then the sound of Fernanda's tuneless dirge, rising and warbling to some manner of crescendo.

LUKE: . . . remember? So I'll be late home.

What thing?

16 July, 4 a.m.

Symptoms: Irritation

Those nose plugs were a big waste of money. Whenever I try clipping them on, Luke thrashes about the bed like your one from *The Exorcist*.

ME: You awake?
LUKE (reefing off the nose plugs): No.

Within minutes, he was snoring again.

I still hadn't responded to Carol's WhatsApp about Crystal being 'the real deal'.

Which, by the way, did activate my gag reflex.

Even so, it was shabby behaviour which I needed to remedy.

But it wasn't easy coming up with an upbeat, delighted response at this hour in the morning.

Hi Carol, lovely to hear your news. Crystal sounds nice. Make
    sure you bring her with you next time you're coming home.
PS when are you coming home?

That was my first attempt, which I deleted. Obviously, for starters, who says, 'Crystal sounds nice'?

Call myself a writer?

Crystal sounds . . . interesting? Fun? Dynamic? I don't

know anything about bloody Crystal except Carol's in love with her and she's a lowly vice-president.

Oh, that IS Great News! Dying to hear more about Crystal! Tell me more things! Am sure I will like her too!! You've always had great taste in friends 😊 !
   Great News!!!

My fingertip smarted from punching the exclamation mark button.

I deleted that one too. Carol would worry.

Hi Carol,
Finally stopped dry-retching 🤢. Obvs need more details about Crystal before I can comment. But it's 'quite' nice to hear you sound so cheerful about something that's not your job or – even worse – your mind/body/soul (remind me never to move to LA). I know, I know, I'm a contrary old sow but you knew that already and there is comfort in the familiar, is there not? Nothing major to report from these grey and sodden parts. Dad's moved back home and taken LuLaBelle with him. You'd think I'd be glad of the peace but I sort of got used to the sound of that mutt's pathetic yaps and Dad's bones clicking any time he did one of his hip rolls. And him and Leonora on FaceTime with their incessant, 'You hang up first, No, YOU hang up first.'
   Mam spent as little time as possible on the phone and always hung up first. Another one of her money-saving initiatives. She would have called Leonora a rip. I never found out what the word meant but I knew it was nothing good.
   Aidan is still fretting about the queen bee. Remember I

told you she'd stopped laying eggs? Anyway, now he can't find her. More as I get it.

As for the rest of us, we're mostly grand-ish.

Agatha 😎

17 July, 8 p.m.

Symptoms: Anxiety on both micro and macro level

Macro: the state of the universe in general (the blight of capitalism, climate change, misogyny, gender-based violence, yada, yada . . .).

Micro: Aidan's beehive.

Dr-Lennon-call-me-Susie said that worrying about things outside of your control causes stress.

So I was doing my best to only worry about the beehive. And the Queen Bee.

ME: Maybe she's still in the hive. You probably just need to look again. No offence, but they all look the same.

AIDAN: The queen looks totally different. Her abdomen is longer than the others. So are her legs. And then there're her wings. They're shorter in relation to her body. I mean, they don't even reach the end of her stomach. Then there's the way she walks across the comb. I've shown you, remember? She walks with this great sense of purpose. And she wears her authority with such ease and the other bees make sure they don't get in her way because, you know, she's so important. And now she's gone.

ME: Do you want me to have a look?

AIDAN: I've gone through the hive loads of times. She's not there.

ME: But where could she have gone? And why?

AIDAN: If she stopped laying eggs, the other bees might have pushed her out. Or killed her.

I should feel outrage on the queen's behalf. Such shabby treatment after all those billions of eggs she's laid.

But it was fear that slithered up from behind and put its long, bony fingers along my neck.

I was afraid that Aidan was going to cry. I'm bad with people crying. Especially males. And I know that's sexist by the way. But the whole 'boys don't cry' thing was a real, actual rule in my formative years so I probably can't be blamed for that.

I sort of patted Aidan on the back like I did to LuLaBelle when she rolled over. Then she'd lick me. In the end, I suppose I got used to the rough warmth of her tongue.

Aidan leaned against me. His hair smelled like apples and I brushed his black fringe out of his eyes.

AIDAN: I should have done what all the books advised and marked the queen from the start. But I didn't want to stress her out and I thought I'd be able to spot her easily.

ME (murmuring a litany of): There, there, don't worry, it'll all be grand. (And other meaningless bits and pieces.)

AIDAN: I don't know what I was thinking. Setting myself up as a beekeeper. I was so arrogant.

ME: I think naive is more accurate. You're pretty crap at being arrogant, in fairness.

Which got a sort of, not quite a laugh from Aidan and I thought I was out the woods in terms of male-crying. Instead of backing up until I'd reached the safety of the kitchen door, I did my usual running-off-at-the-mouth thing.

ME: Anyway, what's the worst that can happen? If she is gone, you can just order a new Queen Bee, right?

And then a sort of cold stillness descended, like one of those thick sea mists in August.

AIDAN: If the Queen Bee is gone, the hive is in grave danger.

Now, there's a hateful word. Grave. It feels so serious. In a hopeless kind of way. Like an actual grave. Six feet under. Pretty much rock bottom.

And Aidan saying it. It sounded even worse in his solemn voice. It sounded true.

The hive is in grave danger.

18 July, 10 a.m.

Symptoms: Many and varied, not in a good way

MELISSA: Coo-ee, it's only me.

Melissa has taken to knocking on the front door, then stepping into the hall and shouting out that it's only her. Thus robbing me of the opportunity to ignore the knocking and go back to pretending to work in my office.

Although this morning, I wasn't pretending to work, I was actually working. Finishing the article for the *Guardian*. Which wasn't as easy as it sounds since I couldn't just make grand, sweeping statements. I had to back them up with facts and other inconveniences.

Which meant a bit of research. Which, oddly, wasn't as tedious as I feared.

Then along came Melissa with her mating call. Although she brought a lemon drizzle cake too.

Damn that woman and her baked goods. I led her into the kitchen.

MELISSA: I thought you might need a bit of cheering up.
ME: Because I'm menopausal and nearly fifty?
MELISSA: Well, no, I thought you'd be missing your dad.
    And LuLaBelle of course.
ME: It's been quieter all right.

Which made me think of the silence Dad spoke of. After Mam died.

I wish he hadn't told me that.

Melissa leaned towards me and squeezed my hand briefly, then unwrapped the cake and cut two gigantic slabs.

ME: I'm not sure I could manage two.
MELISSA: They're not both for you.
ME: You're having a slice?
MELISSA: I most certainly am. I think you're right, Agatha.
    About diets. Being nothing more than a capitalist, mis-
    ogynistic plot to defraud women of money and
    self-esteem.

She blushed and couldn't quite look me in my eyeballs.

ME: How has 'poor Dermot' taken the news?
MELISSA: He'll get over it. Eventually.

And then she started laughing. Proper belly laughing, not her usual ladies-who-lunch effort. And I have to admit it was infectious. Like chickenpox when you're eight. The pair of us fell around the kitchen and it was a good job LuLaBelle wasn't there because group laughing is one of the – many – things that sets her off with that yap she calls a bark.

I didn't want to kill the upbeat buzz so I didn't mention the possible murder of the Queen Bee by her own, actual children.

Instead I casually mentioned the missing/absconded Queen Bee and Melissa asked me what she looked like and promised to keep an eye out for her.

I had to hand it to her, she's pretty neighbourly.

12 p.m.

Dad rang. He'd left his tap shoes under the bed in the boxroom. Would it be convenient for him to come over to collect them?

ME: Since when did you ever ring to see if it was convenient to call over?
DAD: Leonora said it's better to check first.

Since I'd actually managed to finish the speech – fuelled by lemon drizzle cake and Melissa's quiet revolution – I told

Dad I'd meet him at the parish hall before his dance class and give them to him there.

1 p.m.

Colm appeared downstairs smelling like the Lynx factory floor and looking pink and shiny from the lengthy scrub he'd subjected himself to in the shower.

ME: You better not have used up all the hot water.
COLM (cheerful): See ya.
ME (quasi-casual): Meeting anyone?
COLM: Amelia-don't-say-anything.
ME: I wasn't going to!
COLM: I left some stuff behind . . . in the apartment, you know? Amelia boxed it up so I'm going over to her house to pick it up.
ME: Do you want me to come with you?
COLM: Of course not.
ME: No, I mean, I'm going that way anyway.
COLM (suspicious): Really?
ME: I'm dropping tap shoes over to your grandfather.
COLM: Okay then, but you're not to say anything about Amelia in the car.
ME: What would I say?
COLM: I mean it.

I mostly drove in silence. It was easier to keep my word that way. All I said when I dropped him outside Amelia's parents' house was, 'Goodbye now!' in a tremendously cheerful tone.

COLM: Thanks, Mum.
ME: You're welcome. Just . . . you know . . . be careful.

(Of your heart.)
   I didn't add that bit.

COLM (kissing my cheek): Don't worry about me.

That's the thing. I don't want to worry about Colm. Or
Aidan. Either of them. They're adults and entitled to make
as much of a muck of their lives as the rest of us.
   But there's a part of me that can't let go.
   I never thought I'd be that mother.

MAM: We're all that mother in the end.
ME: Information I could have used before I decided to
      become an actual bloody mother.

Not that it was a conscious decision. We didn't sit down
and plan it all out. I suppose we just assumed that it would
happen at some stage, given our unreliable relationship with
contraception.
   I watched Colm walk down the driveway.
   That nonchalant saunter was fooling no one, my boy!
   Amelia answered the door before Colm even had a chance
to ring the bell.
   Not only was she keen but she wanted him to know how
keen she was.
   Colm could do many things but I doubted he was
equipped to battle such a wily foe.

And could she have looked any more angelic with her endless limbs and cherubic curls and her oversized vintage Adidas sweatshirt with just the very ends of her baby pink short-shorts visible beneath it.

Colm gestured in my direction and Amelia's smile widened as she waved at me and Colm turned around so I could do nothing but wave back before I scorched away.

2 p.m.

I know this is going to sound . . . unlike me . . . but there's something a bit . . . I don't know . . . life-affirming about seeing your elderly father salsa around a draughty community centre in the arms of another elderly man.

Hugo does that thing where he mouths the time signature of the music.

One-two-three-four, one-two-three-four.

Bloody hell, my emotions are so close to the surface. They're like the varicose veins in my legs, threatening to break through.

ME: How's Leonora doing?

DAD (out of breath): She insisted I come. I didn't think I should leave her.

ME: Will she be fit for Havana?

DAD: I've pushed the trip back a week. We'll make the competition, just won't have as much practice time. Leonora still reckons we'll place and I . . .

ME: Hang on. So does that mean you're coming back a week later?

DAD: Yeah, we'll have a . . .

ME: But you'll be away for the anniversary.
DAD: Oh yeah, Luke said the other day that you two are
    twenty-five years married this year. It only seems like
    yesterday when . . .
ME: I'm talking about Mam's anniversary.
DAD: Oh. Right.

If I'm giving him the benefit of the doubt – which I'm
not necessarily doing – I could concede that Mam was the
one who remembered all the birthdays and feast days and
holy days and anniversaries of deaths. She kept it all in
an ancient profit and loss ledger. No idea why. It was
probably going cheap in a fire sale in a stationery shop
long ago.

DAD: I'll light a candle. I'll find a church and light a candle
    for your mother.
ME (pointed): Your wife.

4 p.m.

I called into The Full Shilling on my way home. Sometimes
just the smell of the place is enough to sort me out. There's
a lot going on in there, smell-wise. The dense, warm fug of
food edged with mothballs and hairspray and coats hanging
on the backs of chairs, damp from the earlier rain.

  Luke was writing the specials on the blackboard for
tomorrow. His writing is small and careful, more print than
cursive. He was wearing black jeans, his Ramones Rocket
to Russia tour T-shirt and a pair of flip-flops and for a
moment, watching him, the noise of the world faded away
and it sounded like I was underwater but in a good way. In

a *Finding Nemo* kind of way. At the end of the film. When Nemo is found.

Fernanda bustled out from the back and she barked something guttural at him in, I assume, Portuguese, and he smiled at her like she was the exact person he was hoping to see and then responded with something equally guttural in, I assume, Portuguese, which made her beam and clap her hands which made the auld ones – just Mrs Clancy and Mrs Kelly nursing their usual afternoon pot of tea between them – beam and clap too.

ME: Ahem.
LUKE (no longer smiling): Oh. Agatha. I didn't see you there. Is everything okay?
ME: Why wouldn't it be?
FERNANDA: I will make coffee!
ME: I don't want coffee.
LUKE (climbing down ladder): Did Damien reach you?
ME: No.
LUKE: Oh. He said he . . .
ME: Dad's going to be in Havana for the anniversary.
LUKE: What anniversary?
ME: Mam's anniversary. My mother. Remember? The anniversary of her death. My mother died. Have you forgotten too?

Fernanda reappeared, her perky ponytail swinging with youthful optimism and certainty as she bore down on me with a cup and saucer I'd never seen before. Must have been one of the new ones Luke bought to replace Ronnie's perfectly good Hector Grey delf.

FERNANDA: Coffee!
ME: I said I didn't want coffee.
LUKE: Go easy, Agatha, there's no need to be rude.

Afterwards, everything seemed much too quiet. Fernanda stepped back as if I'd shouted at her and Luke gently took the cup and saucer from her hands, like he was worried she might drop them.

I don't think I shouted.

It's hard to remember now.

Mrs Clancy and Mrs Kelly stopped talking and turned to stare at me with their hands wrapped around their mugs of tea.

5 p.m.

So now I'm someone who flounces out of cafés in the middle of an afternoon. I've never done that before. If it's a choice between fright, flight or fight, I used to fall into a 'fight to the death' category which is a subcategory of 'fight'.

I suppose I can blame my newly acquired 'flight' mode on the menopause.

Another little offering.

When I got home from the café, I had the house to myself so I could smoke and be contrary to my heart's content without anyone sticking their oar in.

I decided to roll a cigarette and think bad things about Luke and Fernanda and Mrs Clancy and Mrs Kelly and Dad and Leonora and – no doubt – countless others, that's just for starters.

5.30 p.m.

I finished my smoke and despite thinking bad things about Luke and Fernanda (I hadn't gotten around to Mrs Clancy and Mrs Kelly yet) I was still as . . . unsettled . . . as before, in the café.

Go easy, Agatha, there's no need to be rude.

Fuck sake.

I wasn't being rude, I was being emphatic.

I DID NOT want a coffee.

Thanks all the same.

5.35 p.m.

My phone rang and I was so sure it would be Luke, ringing to smooth things between us after this afternoon, I answered it without checking the screen.

ME (formal tone): Hello?

DAMIEN: Oh, there you are! You're a tricky woman to get a hold of, hahaha.

ME: . . .

DAMIEN: So, well, the thing is . . . Luke said I should speak to you about timelines and such . . .

ME: . . .

DAMIEN: Agatha? Are you there?

ME: Yes.

DAMIEN: Oh good, well, what do you think?

ME: I don't think you should make Luke sell the café.

DAMIEN: What? No, of course not. That's not what I want at all. We're just talking about a simple refinancing package and . . .

299

ME: We're broke. Luke doesn't know.

DAMIEN: I thought you were writing a book? Something about witches?

ME: I'm not.

DAMIEN: . . .

Then he puts on his 'business' voice.

DAMIEN: Whatever you two decide going forward is entirely up to you. I'm going to have to insist on my share by the end of the month.

ME: Luke has poured his heart and guts into The Full Shilling since he was a boy.

DAMIEN: This is business, Agatha. It's not personal. Luke knows that.

ME: What Luke knows is how to make bread rise. And how to cook a cheap cut of beef so that it melts in your mouth. He can make incredible soup out of whatever's left in the bottom of the fridge at the end of the week. He even knows how to make cabbage taste nice. What he does not know, is business. You know that.

DAMIEN: You should probably tell Luke. It'll be better coming from you.

And then he said he had to go or he'd be late for the international video-conference starting in the boardroom and then he hung up.

I didn't throw the phone against the wall because, the last time, it cost me nearly a hundred quid to have it fixed. Instead, I put on Aidan's straw hat and Mam's mantilla and sat beside the hive.

Aidan doesn't always wear the gear but he insists that we do. He said the bees will smell Colm's heartache and my contrariness and they'll sting us.

Turns out bees aren't fans of heartache or contrariness.

Boo fucking hoo.

I put my hand on the wood of the hive which had warmed in the afternoon sun. The sensation was . . . not unpleasant.

6 p.m.

At first, everything was fine. Nothing out of the ordinary. In fact, for a hive that may be without its queen, the bees seem like their usual busy, buzzy selves, flying in and out of the tiny front door Aidan had fashioned for them on one side of the hive. He'd even carved an architrave around the opening, which is silly, obviously, but looks pretty cute if you're into that sort of thing.

6.10 p.m.

Something had changed.

At first, it was difficult to put my finger on it.

Everything looked the same.

Everything sounded the same.

But the sound of the bees, buzzing, was louder now. Like there were more of them all of a sudden. I pulled my hand away and looked at the little doorway. It was teeming with bees.

Flying out of the hive.

Like a fire drill.

Except there was no fire.

Quickly, one entire side of the hive became coated in

bees. Layers and layers of them. The noise was deafening. The bees took to the air and, through the lace of Mam's mantilla, I saw them on all sides of me, circling and circling in a frenzy of movement, the air thick with them.

It was a mass evacuation.

The bees were swarming.

Oddly, I wasn't afraid. For starters, I had Aidan's hat and Mam's mantilla.

But it wasn't just that.

The bees were consumed with their activity. Whatever it was they were hoping to achieve, they were one hundred per cent invested. I was not part of their plan.

I was of no interest whatsoever to the bees.

Which is pretty good to know if and when you ever find yourself in the middle of a swarm.

What was of interest to the bees was the cherry blossom tree in 'poor Dermot's' back garden.

To say that Melissa adores it is an understatement, what with the glut of pale pink petals it produces in the springtime. She likes standing beneath the tree when it's in full bloom and looking up. She says it's like catching a glimpse of heaven.

ME: There's no such thing as heaven.
MAM: Wash your mouth out, my girl!
MELISSA: Well, I believe there is.

It will come as no surprise to anyone that 'poor Dermot' hates the cherry blossom tree because no sooner does it blossom than it sheds. All over his patch of piously maintained fake grass he calls 'the lawn'.

Anyway, the bees obviously feel the same way as Melissa about the cherry blossom because, after a while, they gravitated towards it, more and more of them, forming a solid cloud of bees, hanging off a branch of the tree looking for all the world like a woolly hat that had lost its shape in an inappropriate wash cycle.

Seeing them like that, I really understood what Aidan meant when he said they operate, not as a collection of individual bees but as a collective.

It's basically communism in motion.

The good kind. Not the Stalin strain of it.

The three musketeers version. Except instead of three, there are, I don't know, several thousand, I'd say.

Even so, it's all for one and one for all.

It is a thing of beauty.

But then of course 'poor Dermot' came out and ruined everything.

6.20 p.m.

'POOR DERMOT': What the bloody hell?
ME (poking my head over the fence): The bees are swarming.
'POOR DERMOT': Why do they have to do it in MY garden?

He swung his arms wildly about his head, jumping this way and that, and I could see the beads of sweat blooming across his shiny red forehead.

ME: Stay calm. They can smell your fear.
'POOR DERMOT': I didn't say I was afraid.
ME: Stop moving. Be still.
'POOR DERMOT': They're all over me.

It was an exaggeration to say the bees were all over him but they did seem to be milling around his head in a bit of a cloud.

6.22 p.m.

I grabbed Aidan's smoker and used the green bin to haul myself over the fence.

'POOR DERMOT': Aghhhhhhh.

He was running now, making for the garden hose which was neatly coiled on a hook on the garden wall.

I fumbled in my pocket for my Zippo to light the pine needles inside the smoker. 'Poor Dermot', his breath coming harsh and fast, trained the nozzle of the hose into the air, at the bees.

ME: Dermot, don't! Stop!

Then he turned on the hose. And the bees turned on him. Like it was personal.

ME: Get inside Dermot. RUN!

But hysteria had the upper hand by then.

'POOR DERMOT': Gerroffme.

He dropped the hose, still gushing water, onto his meticulous 'lawn', and ran in circles, waving his arms like helicopter blades around his head.

I'd say if there's a textbook answer on what not to do when you're being attacked by bees, 'poor Dermot' did pretty much the opposite of that.

I finally got the smoker lit and ran towards him. I had to remove him from the situation and the only way I could think of was to stick my foot out and trip him. He went down like one of those giant bags of spuds Luke orders for the café.

MELISSA (running into the garden): Oh my goodness!
ME: Stand back.

I squeezed the bellows, sending great wafts of smoke into the air. The bees didn't stop but they faltered.

ME: Close your eyes and nose and mouth.
'POOR DERMOT': What are you . . .?
MELISSA: Just do what Agatha says!

I trained the smoker on 'Poor Dermot' and squeezed again and this time the bees lifted up and away from him, still close but not close enough to sting.

6.25 p.m.

I grabbed one of 'poor Dermot's' arms, Melissa grabbed the other and together we managed to get him up. We dragged him across the 'lawn' and into the house, eased him into a chair in the kitchen.

In fairness, I couldn't blame him for being angry. He was a sorry sight, glaring into the mirror he insisted Melissa take down from above the hall table.

'POOR DERMOT': My face! It's ruined!

I managed not to make a quip.

MELISSA (coming at him with the tweezers): You'll be fine, I'll just . . .

'POOR DERMOT' (shrieky): Don't touch me!

MELISSA (firm): I need to get the stings out and then we can assess the damage, okay?

'POOR DERMOT': I could go into anaphylactic shock at any minute, you know. I could be allergic to bee stings and . . .

MELISSA (firmer): You're not. You did all those tests, remember? You're not allergic to anything.

'POOR DERMOT' (petulant): Those tests aren't always accurate . . . OUCH!

Melissa plucked out all the stingers with an expert hand. I stood beside her and admired her handiwork.

You have to hand it to women. We really know our way around a pair of tweezers. I suppose we have eyebrows and hairy moles and splinters embedded in the pudgy fingers of small children to thank for that.

'POOR DERMOT': That hurts!

MELISSA: There. All done. You're as good as new.

'POOR DERMOT': I could have DIED!

ME: If you're calm around them, they . . .

'POOR DERMOT': I AM calm. But I should not be subjected to such a vicious attack on my own property.

ME: I know but look, it was a one-off, the bees have been so happy up to now and Aidan . . .

'POOR DERMOT': I don't care! About the happiness or otherwise of those bees, I am . . .

MELISSA: Stop it! You are being obnoxious.

'POOR DERMOT' (shocked): What?

MELISSA: You should care. About the happiness of bees. Our very lives depend on them.

'POOR DERMOT': Did you just call me obnoxious?

MELISSA: And you shouldn't just care about the happiness of bees. There's me too, you know. What about my happiness? I suppose you don't care about that either.

'POOR DERMOT' (glaring at me): I'd rather not discuss our private . . .

MELISSA: Agatha knows you're obnoxious, how could she not? The point is, you have to stop being obnoxious. Immediately. Or I'll swarm right out of here too, I mean it. And then who are you going to get to iron your underpants?

'POOR DERMOT' (dumbfounded): . . .

Out in the garden, the smoker smouldered, releasing faint trails of vapour into the sky. The last of the bees were disappearing over the top of the cherry tree, flying up and over the horse chestnut tree in Mr Dunne's back garden. The swarm became fainter and fainter as it moved further away.

After a while, there was nothing to see.

The bees were gone.

19 July, 5 a.m.

Symptoms: Flatulence

Although I'm not sure if flatulence is a symptom of meno-pause or merely an offshoot of eating two black-bean burritos? Either way, the condition has rudely awakened me.

Colm threw food – his speciality, black-bean burritos – at the situation when he got home from Amelia's yesterday evening and found out what had happened.

COLM (to Aidan): Don't worry, I'm using black beans instead of beef, okay?

AIDAN: . . .

COLM: We'll just . . . buy more bees, okay? Or, you know, find some. Like before. I'll help you.

AIDAN: . . .

COLM: Do you want one burrito or two?

AIDAN: . . .

ME: Aidan, say something.

AIDAN (in small, broken-down voice): It's all my fault.

ME: It's not. Bees swarm.

AIDAN: I'm going to bed.

COLM: I'll bring you up some food, okay, Aidan? I owe you big, bro.

Aidan walked into the hallway, closing the kitchen door quietly behind him.

Colm whistled as he grabbed peppers and mushrooms and garlic from the fridge. There was no need to ask how things went with Amelia because it was as plain as the spring in Colm's step.

The toxic motherland was back, it seemed.

Still, at least dinner was sorted.

Black beans must be a relaxant as well because after dinner I was overcome with exhaustion and fell asleep, first on the couch before dragging myself upstairs to bed.

Now, of course, I'm wide awake.

For someone with a severe case of writer's block, I seem to have written quite a few words recently. Even had to invest in new *You Can Quit* notebooks, even though I made my handwriting as tiny and indecipherable as I could, just in case it fell into the wrong hands (if you are reading this, know that I'm talking about YOU, you sick fuck).

So. What fresh hell?

Well, for starters, Luke never came home last night.

You'd think I'd be delighted with the extra space in the bed. Nobody's arm flung across my waist, becoming a sweaty dead weight in a matter of seconds. And not having to clamp his nostrils shut with my fingers to silence those interminable snores. No way do I miss that.

When he didn't appear for dinner, I didn't pay much attention. He often worked in the kitchen after he closed the café making his various concoctions (soup mostly. And anything to do with yeast since the auld ones aren't fond of the smell of it) for the next day.

Luke used to cook for me there some Saturday nights. Mam came over, minded the boys. I'd go all out – wash my hair and apply lipstick AND mascara, put on a clean pair of knickers and maybe a shirt instead of a T-shirt over my jeans. Catch the bus over. The bus driver might flirt with me and ask when I was going to get rid of Luke and get myself a real man.

Getting out at the corner and walking the rest of the way so I could have a cigarette. Eating gum afterwards so Luke could kiss me with abandon and not think awful things about the taste of my mouth. Thinking about Luke. Thinking about him kissing me with abandon and pitching my cigarette away and hurrying up the road, the quicker to get there.

Fuck sake.

I am literally being eaten alive from the insides of my guts by nostalgia.

Last night, after I'd eaten the bean burritos and before I fell asleep on the couch, I rang Luke. Mostly to get in ahead of Damien. Also, to let him know that I'd be prepared to accept his apology for snapping at me about Fernanda's offer of coffee. He'd tell me that he had nothing to apologise for and I'd say, 'Apology accepted, we'll say no more about it,' and then he'd grin and, even though it's a phone conversation, I'd feel him grinning down the phone, that's the type of sap he is.

None of that happened because he didn't answer his phone. And I couldn't leave a message because his mailbox is still full even though I told him that he should empty it because how else am I supposed to leave curt, annoyed messages?

When he finally rang back, it was nearly half ten and I jerked awake, whacking my hand off the standard lamp beside the couch which teetered and, before I could grab at the edge of the lampshade, the whole thing collapsed onto the floor.

ME: Fuck.
LUKE: What?
ME: Are you in a bar?

LUKE: Hang on, I'll go outside.

ME: What are you doing in a bar?

LUKE: I told you, I'm at that thingy, the restaurant association whatsitsface thing . . .

ME: You didn't tell me.

(Did he?)

LUKE: I did.

ME: You didn't.

LUKE: I did.

ME: Why are you there?

LUKE: I come every year.

ME: Do partners go?

LUKE: Some do.

ME: So why amn't I there?

LUKE: You said if I ever asked you to go, you'd divorce me or have me killed, whichever was cheaper.

ME: Hiring someone is cheaper. I read an article.

LUKE: See?

There was silence for a bit. I could hear Luke taking a drink of his pint. I knew it was Guinness and that it would leave a frothy moustache on his upper lip which he'd lick with the edge of his tongue but not until he had replaced the glass on the table, preferably on top of a beer mat.

He's fond of a beer mat.

LUKE: So. Were you ringing me for something in particular?

ME: Eh, you rang me.

LUKE: I'm ringing you back. You rang me.

ME: Well, why didn't you ring me?

LUKE: Agatha, I don't have much time, I'm supposed to . . .

ME: I need to tell you things.

LUKE: Okay then, go ahead.

ME: Many things.

LUKE: Well, I don't really . . . Can you tell me tomorrow night?

ME: Aren't you coming home tonight?

LUKE: I'm in Tipperary.

ME: I'm giving that after-dinner speech thing tomorrow night. For the National Women's Council.

LUKE: The night after then.

In the background, I heard someone calling his name.

L-uuuuuuu-ka.

I detected Brazilian.

LUKE: I'd better go.

ME: Is Fernanda with you?

LUKE: What? Oh, yeah. She thought it would be a good opportunity to make a few contacts.

ME: You never brought Mrs Lynch to the restaurant association whatsitsface thing.

LUKE: She would have flattened me with her frying pan if I'd suggested it.

I hated feeling jealous. It wasn't a feeling I equated with myself. It felt like a foreign country but not in a tourist destination kind of way. This one felt barren and inhospitable with vast, impassable mountain ranges and parched riverbeds. Also,

I felt like I was too old to be jealous. To really carry it off, I should either be a teenage girl or a toxically masculine man.

LUKE: Listen, the head cheese is about to do his speech so I need to get a spot near the bar. He goes on quite a bit and I don't want to run out of alcohol.

And then he said goodbye and hung up and I headed upstairs and managed to fall asleep but now I'm wide awake and imagining all sorts.

20 July, 10 a.m.

Symptoms: Confusion

I was somewhat mollified by the competing attentions of Melissa and Den, both of whom rang me this morning, offering to drive me to Brooks Hotel where the National Women's Council of Ireland fundraiser is taking place.

ME: Den already said he'd bring me.
MELISSA: Oh.
ME: It'll be nice for you not to have to cart me around for a change.
MELISSA: I don't mind carting you around. It's for a good cause.
ME: Come with us.
MELISSA: Den would prefer to have you all to himself, I'm sure. Did you know that he thinks you're attractive, interesting and funny in no particular order?
ME: I'm contrary and curmudgeonly.

MELISSA: Yes but also the other stuff.

ME: I thought I could always count on your overt politeness.

MELISSA: Sorry. I think you may have rubbed off on me. How's Aidan?

ME: He's taken to the bed. Now, Colm is up and down the stairs, feeding him. Well, first he takes photographs of the food and posts it on D.I.Guy.

MELISSA: Such lovely boys.

ME: They're pathetic. And I can't even blame the mother because, you know, it's me.

MELISSA: None of this is your fault.

ME: According to Aidan, it's all his fault, he's useless at everything, he couldn't even stay in college and the potatoes he's growing aren't as fluffy as they should be.

MELISSA: Well, the ones he sent in to me were really fluffy. The fluffiest potatoes I've ever tasted, actually. I'll DM him and let him know.

I felt obliged to enquire about 'poor Dermot' then.

ME: How is . . . Dermot?

MELISSA: He'll live.

I was stunned at her tone which was riddled with scepticism. I nearly felt sorry for him.

11 a.m.

I decided to smoke in the front garden this morning. The downside is that neighbours felt entitled to stop at the gate to tell me why it's a good idea to quit. They thought I was greeting them when I was just waving them on.

The upside is not having to look at the abandoned hives at the end of the garden.

It's so quiet out there now.

Without the buzzing.

You don't realise how lovely something sounds until it's gone.

Who knew that I'd turn out to be someone who misses bees. And dogs. LuLaBelle's kennel might as well be boarded up, it looks so deserted.

I checked my phone. Nothing from Luke. He knows I worry about him driving the morning after a few pints.

He is the world's worst Irishman when it comes to 'holding his drink'.

He could at least have texted to let me know what time he'd be back at. I imagined Fernanda in the passenger seat, all big hair and gap-toothed grin and zesty pheromones oozing out of her pores.

So there I was, stress-smoking in the front garden when the postman – Pete – propped his bicycle at the front gate and sauntered down the garden path, whistling 'Willie McBride' in a passably melodious fashion.

PETE: Agatha! Ravishing as always.

His greeting has remained unchanged despite the passage of years and the post-MeToo climate. Still, he's gotten away with it mostly because I find it difficult to take umbrage at a middle-aged man wearing shorts and knee socks held up with suspenders.

ME: What news from Pemberley?

He took a brown padded envelope out of his satchel, held it towards the sun, then poked at it with his fingers.

PETE: Feels like a passport. Where are you going without me?

ME: Hand it over, you great bulging boil on the backside of humanity.

PETE: All that sweet talk will rot your teeth, Agatha my angel.

Pete was right. It was my passport.

Liverpool here I come.

My original plan had been to whisk Luke away to Liverpool with me. A surprise. Don't ask questions, pack your bags, you've pulled, type of thing.

Now . . . well, if I'm honest, I'm just not sure he'd say yes any more.

12 p.m.

I rang Luke. No answer.

I sent him a text: Are you in a pile-up on the M8?

12.15 p.m.

Luke has read my text.

Still no response from him.

12.20 p.m.

In a vain attempt to stop thinking about Luke, I washed my hair. Afterwards my arms were shaking and I couldn't raise them above shoulder level.

1 p.m.

I did a dry run of the speech in front of Melissa. The general gist was, 'Menopause Is Crap', but Melissa – high on HRT – insisted I stick in some positives. So I added a 'hilarious' (read: humiliating) pre-menopausal anecdote, featuring a rogue period which arrived at a meeting I attended with Anna and her publishing team. A spurt of warm wet between my legs alerted me to the fact that the Super Tampon I'd inserted along with the Always Ultra Secure, Extra Long sanitary towel I'd pasted inside the gusset of my knickers less than an hour earlier had not given me a yen to don a pair of rollerblades and find a boardwalk to skate on. Nor had it bestowed on me the 'peace-of-mind-protection' promised in their TV ad.

I knew that, when I stood up, there'd be a bright red slick on the fabric of the chair I was sitting on. At the end of the meeting, everyone headed for the canteen except me. I told Anna I'd be with her shortly, I had to make a phone call, then rolled myself to the ladies on the chair. I met the CEO on the way down the corridor.

And the receptionist.

And Richard from sales.

And the HR manager.

And the guy who waters the plants.

When I finally reached the ladies, Anna and her publishing team were there, reapplying lipstick.

Anna lent me a pair of navy trousers which were too short and too tight and didn't go with my Viv Albertine T-shirt.

The stain on the chair never came out.

MELISSA: Not having periods anymore is definitely a plus alright. But don't forget to mention HRT and how it's done me the world of good.

ME: You sure you don't have a slight dose of breast cancer?

MELISSA: I've more chance of getting breast cancer by being obese or drinking more than I should.

I would definitely drink more than I should if I was married to 'poor Dermot'.

2 p.m.

Dad rang – again – to remind me that their flight to Havana is nine o'clock tomorrow and they want to be in the airport at six o'clock in the morning.

ME: You already reminded me. And I already told you that six o'clock is too early.

DAD: It's not.

ME: It is.

DAD: It's not.

ME: It is.

DAD: We could always take a taxi.

MAM: Don't you dare let him take a taxi. The last time, he tipped the driver nearly TWENTY-FIVE PER CENT.

ME: Fine. I'll pick you and Leonora up at six. And the mutt too, I suppose.

DAD: No, Leonora says it's too early for LuLaBelle to get up. Colm said he'd collect her from mine around ten. She should be awake by then.

It's a low ebb when you find yourself coveting the life of a dog.

DAD: LuLaBelle's really looking forward to seeing you again.
ME: How the hell can you tell?
DAD: Well, I can't to be honest. But Leonora can. Something about LuLaBelle's ears and the way they twitch when your name is mentioned.
ME: That's ridiculous.

It's also ridiculous that the comment gives me a warm sort of glow inside my chest.

The dog's not the worst, I suppose.

6 p.m.

Den arrived early even though I told him how I feel about people arriving early.

He looked so . . . out of place in the house. Like finding a pair of brand-new Levi's high-waist jeans in a charity shop in your exact size.

I left him in the kitchen for five minutes while I went to grab my handbag. On my way back down the stairs, I could hear Colm.

COLM: Who are you and what you are you doing here?
DEN (grinning): You must be Agatha's son.
ME: Where are you going all dressed up like Bob the Builder?
COLM: I'm doing a D.I.Guy thing for Woodie's.
DEN: Of course! You're D.I.Guy! I love your work. I mean, I don't do any DIY. Obviously. But I love your posts.

AMELIA (flouncing into the kitchen): Everybody does!

Colm glared at me so I had no choice but to mumble something in Amelia's general direction that could pass for a greeting.

ME: Don't forget to feed your brother before you go out.
COLM: Already did.
AMELIA: Homemade falafel, they were delicious.
COLM: Oh. Did you taste them?
AMELIA: I mean, they smelled delicious.

Amelia's perfume – an overbearing sweet scent, like end-of-summer – lingered in every room after she'd left. I flung open some windows. Den smiled at me.

DEN: So . . . we hatin' on Amelia, yeah?
ME: She broke Colm's heart.
DEN: My mum'd be the same.
ME: And now he's going to let her do it again.
DEN (wisely changing lanes): Do you want to practise your speech on me?
ME: I already practised on Melissa.

Den looked sad which I couldn't bear. It was like seeing a baby bird fall out of a nest. So I hauled the speech out again. He laughed at the intentionally funny bits and some of the unintentional ones.

DEN: You're a natural.

He picked up a framed photograph of me and Luke, taken five years ago. Long before the menopause got a grip on me. We were cycling around Inis Mór. We'd just had a swim on Kilmurvey beach. My hair was wild with Atlantic salt and wind. Luke was wearing a sunhat. He had finally succumbed and shaved the remains of his black hair off that morning. I remember his scalp. How pale it was afterwards.

LUKE: Oh fuck. Your face. You're never going to have sex with me again, are you?

ME: Well, you'll definitely have to buy me dinner first from now on.

DEN (replacing the photograph on the sideboard): If Luke arrives, will he challenge me to a duel?

ME: I think you're safe enough.

I checked my phone again. Battery dead.

8 p.m.

There I was, at Brooks Hotel, waiting for the guests to lick the last of the pavlova out of their bowls. After that, I was on.

DEN: Where are your shoes?

ME: I don't bring them to these things any more.

DEN: Since the *Menopause: The Movie* day?

ME: Yeah.

DEN: Couldn't you just buy a bigger pair?

ME: No. It's sort of my thing now. Barefoot and menopausal in comfortable clothes.

I was wearing a Blondie T-shirt tucked into a pair of gorgeously elasticated high-waisted mom jeans.

DEN: Just when I think I can't love you more.

Carol sent a WhatsApp.

> Hey Queen, sorry for lack of comms. I won't bore you with details but Crystal, etc. . . .
>
> Good luck at the thingy, sorry I can't remember the name, being in a new relationship with someone that I actually like seems to be a bit like being menopausal. I'm hot and sweaty, my appetite is poor, I can't remember important things (like your thingy today) and I find myself smiling at strangers (which is already dodgy in Dublin but absolutely taboo in LA).
>
> PS when I said 'like', I think I meant love.
>
> PPS eek!
>
> PPPS I love you.
>
> PPPPS sorry, I can't help it, happiness is oozing out my pores.
>
> PPPPPS sorry for being happy when you're not.
>
> PPPPPPS oh! You got a mention on a local radio station this morning. 'An Irish menopausal lady'.
>
> Lady!
>
> Ha!
>
> Carol xxx

Samantha sent a meme. A Minion with a baseball bat breaking the leg of another Minion.

She used to send flowers.

Still, at least she remembered.

There was a photograph of Luke, kneading dough on Fernanda's story. The photo was taken earlier today so at least I knew he'd made it back to Dublin in one piece.

Fernanda had a heavy hand with the hashtag:

#homemadebread #fullshilling #ingoodhands

I've always loved Luke's hands. Solid hands. Gentle hands. They could push a boulder up a hill. They could brush a stray strand of hair across a face.

DEN: Are you going to be all right without me?
ME: Sorry?
DEN: I've to go back to the radio station.
ME: Well, I've managed up till now so . . .
DEN: I'll be back later. I know you'll be magnificent.
ME: Magnificent may be a little de trop.
DEN: De what?
ME: Go.

Still, it was a bit dull once he'd left. Fine, I'll admit it, I liked having my ego massaged.

And let's face it, Den was like my ego's own private masseur.

It was probably the menopause.

Defences weren't what they used to be.

9 p.m.

MAM: That wasn't as awful as I thought it would be.
ME: Watch out, Mother, you'll give me a big head.
MAM: Although why you have to talk about menopause at all is beyond me. And in public too. With a microphone.

ME: Go back to the bit where you were saying my speech wasn't as awful as you thought.

The organiser – Aisling-something-double-barrelly – hugged me afterwards and insisted on buying me a drink. She said that donations were rolling in from all over the place since I took to the podium.

Turned out the speech was live-streamed. Which meant I was out there again, in the ether, badmouthing the menopause.

Still, the cash was going to fund education programmes for disadvantaged women and my feet weren't bleeding this time so I could live with it.

Aisling excused herself to go to the toilet (she called it the 'powder room') and I rang Luke again. This time he answered, albeit not till the fifth ring and all out of breath.

LUKE: Agatha? Is everything okay?

ME: Yes, why wouldn't it be?

LUKE: It's just . . . it's late for you to be ringing.

ME: I thought you would have rung me actually.

LUKE: I didn't want to disturb you. How did your speech go by the way?

ME: Where are you?

LUKE: I'm at the café. Stocktaking, remember? I told . . .

ME: Oh. I thought the stocktake was last week, I must have misunderstood.

LUKE: Where are you?

ME: It doesn't matter. I'll tell you later. Or tomorrow. Whenever I see you.

10 p.m.

When Den came back to pick me up, Aisling-something-double-barrelly thought he was my boyfriend.

Ego well and truly massaged. Egged on by the two large gin and tonics Aisling bought me.

DEN (opening the passenger door for me): That's, like, a sign, isn't it? Aisling thinking I'm your boyfriend.

ME: I told her I was just using you.

DEN (hopeful): For sex?

ME: For lifts and ego-massaging.

DEN: Do you want to come back to mine for some ego-massaging?

ME: Is that a euphemism for sex?

DEN: Does euphemism mean another word for something?

ME: Yes.

DEN: Then no.

ME: Then yes.

Which is how I found myself sitting at a breakfast bar in Den's kitchen drinking a cold beer and eating an enormous slice of lasagne. It was smothered in cheese which I really shouldn't have eaten at that hour. Not unless I wanted to have dreams involving my mother and Tom Jones again.

Den's house wasn't what I was expecting.

What was I expecting?

A loft-at-the-docks type of vibe. Or something communal maybe. An old printing press, retrofitted of course, with paddleboards for furniture and wind-powered smoothie-makers.

Certainly something a little less domesticated than the three-bed semi in Marino we ended up in. The house was disappointingly ordinary. It even smelled ordinary. Like shepherd's pie. And one of those awful plug-in air-fresheners.

ME: I think I should go.
DEN: Stay and have one drink and then I'll drive you wherever in the city you wish to go.
ME: Okay. If you throw in some food.

Which is how I ended up with the cheesy lasagne.

ME: You're a good cook.
DEN: As good as Luke?
ME: No.
DEN: Oh.
ME: If it makes you feel better, you're way better at clothes than he is.
DEN: Anyone can be good at clothes.
ME: Luke missed that particular memo.
DEN: Memo?
ME: Oh, never mind, I'm going to go.

That was when Den stood up and put his hands on either side of my face and for a moment I was distracted by the strange softness of his hands. They were like baby hands. Those hands had never been up to their wrists in bread dough.

While I was thus distracted, Den leaned in.

The sensation of kissing a mouth that was not Luke's was . . . discombobulating.

I'm pretty sure I've never had cause to use that word

before but, in those circumstances, it was the most fitting word I could think of.

First of all, there was the sheer size of Den's mouth. Like, how had I never noticed how wide it was? How fleshy the lips. I used to admire how they glistened, putting it down to the rude health of youth. But no. It was just good old-fashioned spittle. Turned out that Den had a big, fleshy, wet mouth and he liked a LOT of jaw action when he got going. I could hear my jaw pop and click and creak as his tongue did a continuous 360° round my mouth, like a washing machine on spin. And it wasn't easy to disentangle myself because Den had his two hands clamped around my face so I was sort of held there, in front of his big, fleshy, wet mouth while his tongue rotated around mine, careful not to miss a spot.

Never had I ever missed Luke more.

Not even that time he went to Brighton to that catering conference thingy. He was gone for a week and Aidan was still at the 'crawling up my T-shirt to get a squirt of milk' phase while Colm was going through his 'I'm pretty sure I can fly' phase so it was full on what with my nipples leaking every time Aidan so much as glanced at me and trying to stop Colm diving off various platforms, e.g. windowsills, stepladders, the garden wall, the roof of the shed.

I thought it wasn't possible to miss someone as much as I missed Luke that week.

I was wrong.

The noise. When I managed to wrench myself away from Den's enormous mouth, there was this savage suction sound followed by a sharp pop and then the ordeal was over.

DEN: I knew you'd be a great kisser.

There I was, trying to encourage feeling back into my lips so I could come up with a suitable rejoinder when, all of a sudden, the kitchen door flew open revealing a short, sharp, shock of a woman. Den jumped and stood on my – bare – foot, which left me with little option but to screech like a bat. The woman followed my lead and screeched too. She was probably in her sixties. She had curly grey hair that she'd trapped under a net and the rest of her was wrapped in a leopard-print dressing gown with her feet pushed into a pair of sheepskin slippers.

CRAZED WOMAN: Denis St John Maloney, what exactly do you think you're doing at this hour of the night?

Note: it was barely eleven o'clock.
  Also: St John?
  Also: WTAF?

CRAZED WOMAN: And who exactly is that?

She pointed a short, bright blue varnished nail at me. I stood up and even though, without my shoes, I wasn't as tall as usual, I was still a hell of a lot taller than crazed woman and she backed up.

ME: Don't worry, I'm just a historical fiction writer. I'm not dangerous. Unless you happen to be a fictional sixteenth-century witch and then, you know, you'd do well to be terrified of me, in fairness.

CRAZED WOMAN: What?

She glared at me with eyes the exact same colour and shape as Den's.

His mother.

ME: I should definitely go now.
DEN: I'll see you out.

Outside:

ME: You never said you lived with your mother.
DEN: I was trying to seduce you.
ME: You said Den wasn't short for anything.
DEN: It was the only thing I lied about. Everything else is true. Especially my feelings for you.
ME: You should pick on someone your own age.
DEN: Are you mad with me?
ME: No, but I'm pretty sure your mother is. You're probably grounded.
DEN: That's why I didn't want to tell you I lived with my mum. I wanted you to take me seriously.
MAM: I've heard it all now.
ME: I should go.
DEN: Your husband shouldn't ignore you like he's been doing. He should . . .
ME: He's just been busy.

The truth of it hit me then. The enormity of the task Luke had undertaken. Trying to save the café. The sudden realisation that it wasn't just the café Luke was trying to save.

It was . . . I don't know . . . the old days. The past. A bit of it. The good bit. Or maybe it was Ronnie he was trying to preserve. A piece of him. For posterity.

Time is cruel like that. The way it just keeps on going. People are born, people die but time moves on. It keeps on moving on so that sometimes it feels like the people who died were never there at all.

21 July, 00.05 a.m.

Symptoms: Energetic!

Den's a good egg really. He offered to drive me home. I said I wasn't going home.

DEN: You're going to the café.

It was a statement rather than a question. I nodded. I opened my mouth to speak.

DEN: Don't say that I'll find someone like you. Please don't patronise me like that.

I was only going to say, 'Seeya,' but instead, I just nodded and did a stiff little wave which Den seemed to appreciate.

Once I rounded the corner of his road, I started running. My intention was to flag down a taxi but, once I got into a rhythm, running felt good. Productive.

Like I was achieving something.

Or might achieve something.

Or perhaps I was just kidding myself that I could outrun the last disastrous hour of my life.

Recreate it. Like a spin doctor. So it wouldn't smart. When I told Luke. Not that there's anything to tell but . . . a clean slate. That's what we needed. Cards on the table. A reset button.

Then we could laugh about it.

I took my runners out of my handbag, pushed my feet inside. Running with bare feet inside runners is an uncomfortable sensation, once the sweat starts to run. Even so, I ended up running all the way to the café.

Four point six kilometres.

It was like I was flying, my feet barely touching the ground.

I passed a group of homeless men, gathered around a makeshift fire, drinking beer out of cans and rolling smokes. They cheered me on and I performed a small bow as I streaked past them.

Then there was a couple, strolling along, taking up most of the path with their hand-holding so I just charged towards them and they leaped apart, like scalded cats.

I kept going. The night air was heavy and sweet with the honeysuckle and lavender Aidan's bees adore. I ran past gardens where pots and planters struggled to contain the glut of petunias, geraniums, nasturtiums, and begonias that quivered on narrow stems, their petals wide and reaching. The sturdy London planes lining Griffith Avenue felt like silent sentries, granting me safe passage. I kept running. It was quiet. Only the odd thrum of a passing car. A lone cyclist rang her bell. The high-pitched squeal of tiny bats, cutting through the dark. The rummage of a city fox through the detritus of a fallen bin, spilling its bounty across the path.

Seriously, that was how Zen I felt in that moment. Calling rubbish 'bounty'.

Not that I would ever describe myself as 'Zen' obviously. But I was full of something all the same. Some kind of exhilaration. It's not an exaggeration to call it that. Perhaps it was because of Den. With his big, wet mouth and gymnastic tongue.

But no. Because if he had been a good kisser, I think I'd still be here, racing up Griffith Avenue and noticing nature and whatnot.

I just needed a jolt. A short, sharp shock. A needle full of adrenalin stabbed into my chest.

That was what it felt like.

That was why I could run so fast. And for so long.

I kept running until I got to the café.

00.45 a.m.

Now here I am sitting on the kerb outside the café. It's been a long time since I've seen it at night. I'd forgotten how quaint it looks. Inside, the lights are on, a butter yellow against the worn fabric of the gingham curtains pulled across the two windows on either side of the front door. And the fairy lights around and over the front door.

Were they there before?

I don't remember them being there before.

They must be new.

They look strange, like a scene left over from a Christmas film.

And now I'm thinking about Fernanda because of course the fairy lights are all her idea. Not because they're particularly revolutionary but mostly because it wouldn't occur to Luke to string them up like that. Just like it wouldn't occur to Fernanda to put a pinch of turmeric into the oxtail soup on a winter's day. Not too much so the auld ones will notice it but just enough to warm the cockles of their heart.

That's what Ronnie used to say.

And now it's what Luke says.

That's tradition, I suppose. The old ways. The café is still there, still standing, but it feels like the end of something, the last bastion, squashed as it is between what used to be Maher's drapery (now a yoga 'hub') and what used to be O'Reilly's vegetable shop (now a wholefood deli and juice bar).

That's what they call progress, I suppose. Resistance is futile. No matter how many fairy lights you string around it.

I know, I know. I'm procrastinating. I'm still here, writing in this stupid *You Can Quit* notebook instead of barging in there and wrestling Luke to the ground and demanding that he kiss me and promising never to take his kissing technique for granted ever again.

I should stop slow-cooking in useless nostalgia and senti-mentality. I should put down my pen and close this stupid notebook and just barge in there.

I will in a bit.

Any moment now . . .

Date: Who the fuck knows? Time: Hard to tell???

Symptoms: Nausea, vertigo, loss of appetite, cold sweating, confusion, drowsiness, insomnia, headache

Jesus H.

I think I've run away from home.

I know I'm on an aeroplane.

To LA.

And it's too late for me to get off because they've done the 'arm doors and cross-check' thingy.

Oh.

Sweet.

Baby.

Jesus.

Mam used to say that. Very rarely and only in an honest-to-goodness crisis, since it's technically blasphemous, I'd say.

MAM: Well, if this isn't an honest-to-goodness crisis, I don't what is, I really don't. What were you thinking, Agatha?

I'm on an aeroplane.

To LA.

Taxiing to a runway.

We're still on the ground.

It's not too late.

I could pull the emergency cord or something.

Smash this glass in case of emergency kind of thing.

There's no emergency cord.

Or glass to smash.

Only the idling of the engine as we wait to take off.

Which means we're going to take off.

Any minute now.

Damn that centrifugal force. Now my body is pulled back

against my seat as the plane gathers speed down the runway. Outside, the wing rattles against the rush of air as the nose of the plane points up.

Up.

Up.

And away.

Time: Middle of night-ish?

I must have fallen asleep. I'm pretty sure I fell asleep on the shoulder of the man sitting beside me. One side of my face is hot to the touch and very possibly imprinted with the pattern of his wool jacket. Also, I think I detected a line of what might be spittle along the shoulder of his jacket.

Outside, it's black, nothing to see but the tiny red light at the tip of the wing.

So it's nighttime.

Somewhere over the Atlantic Ocean.

On the way to LAX.

Which is Los Angeles International Airport by the way.

And no, it was not my intention to fly to LAX – or anywhere – when I dropped Dad and Leonora to the airport this morning.

Or was it yesterday morning?

Hard to know for sure.

Hard to know anything for sure any more.

Oh, there's a maudlin sentence if ever I heard one.

MAM: Feeling sorry for yourself won't help matters.

ME: I'm NOT feeling sorry for myself.

WOOL-JACKET MAN: Pardon?

ME: Oh . . . nothing . . . I was . . . talking to my mother actually . . . but . . . never mind.
WOOL-JACKET MAN (looking around): Is your mother on the plane? I'll swap seats with her, if you like?
ME: No. She's not here.
WOOL-JACKET MAN (wary): Okay then.

I didn't add any further explanation. Like how, if Mam was still here, I wouldn't have been at the airport in the first place. Dropping Dad and Leonora at Departures for their flight to Havana.

Because Dad would still be the former version of himself and Leonora would be dancing with someone else at Singles Salsa every Wednesday afternoon.

I shouldn't have gone into the terminal building with the pair of them. Dad said there was no need, just drop them outside Departures and go.

The truth was I had nowhere to go to. I certainly didn't want to go back to the house.

So I parked in spite of the exorbitant cost of parking at Dublin airport. Then I insisted they get a trolley even though their suitcases were equipped with long handles and wheels. I even managed to find a two-euro coin in my pocket to release the trolley. As luck would have it, it had a bockety front wheel so I had to give the pushing of it my undivided attention and much of my brute force and ignore my phone, ringing again in my jeans pocket.

DAD: Are you not going to answer that?
ME: What?

DAD: Your phone?
ME: No.

When we got to the gate, I was too tired to fend off Leonora who took advantage of the situation and hugged me. I think I even bowed my head and let it lean on her shoulder for a moment. The skin of her face was as soft as rose petals and she smelled warm and sweet, like rice pudding.

LEONORA: Don't worry about your dad. I'll mind him.

She whispered that in my ear before she released me. Dad whacked me on the back and said he'd send me a postcard and bring me back a stick of rock. I said he was a cheapskate and told him not to forget to put on his compression socks before takeoff.

DAD: You sound just like your mother.

And then they were gone, linking arms through the Departures gate and, after that, I was on my own.

An airport is a funny place to be on your own. It's so busy and noisy and bright and buzzy and everyone is moving at a fair clip and with a great sense of purpose, intent on getting to wherever they have to go.

I checked my phone. More missed calls from Luke. And one from Den.

I turned it to silent and put it back in my pocket.

Then I pulled it out of my pocket and turned it off. I must have been stabbing at the buttons because a tiny, elderly woman, wafting 4711 and many cardigans, said, 'Go easy, dear, things may look sturdy but you have to be careful with them all the same.'

Instead of telling her to go and fuck right off, I had to work at the muscles in my face to make sure I didn't cry.

I pretended to be engrossed in the flight information board so that I, too, would look like I had some purpose.

Like I had a plan.

The top line of the board gave details of a United Airlines flight to LAX.

Which was taking off in fifty minutes.

I remembered the email from Carol. With the return flight to LAX. For my birthday.

The immaculate woman behind the United Airlines desk shook her head and furrowed her brow and worried at the badge of an aeroplane on the lapel of her jacket.

It was very last minute.

Unorthodox.

She wouldn't hold out much hope, at this eleventh hour.

I showed her the email from Carol with the tickets and she said I should really have them printed out and I said that my printer needed new toner and that my husband was having an affair with a beautiful Brazilian woman who was much younger than me.

IMMACULATE WOMAN (grim): Let me see what I can do.

She tap-tap-tapped away on a keyboard with her coral-green gel nails for what felt like hours. Then, she looked up and a smile broke across her face. There was a seat available and did I have any luggage to check in, and did I have a visa?

I said I had no luggage and showed her the email from Carol again, this time opening the other attachment, which was the visa.

IMMACULATE WOMAN (nodding briskly): If you email me the visa, I'll have it printed out for you before you can declare the Pledge of Allegiance.

IMMACULATE WOMAN (handing me a boarding pass): You have a good day, ma'am.

And then I did have a plan.

The man in the itchy wool jacket beside me seems to have relaxed. His shoulders have descended from his ears, he's ordered a gin and tonic from the air steward and he even glanced in my direction and performed a small – nervous – smile.

I bent my head and continued to write, now with an exaggerated flourish to my penmanship, lest there be any doubt about my availability for idle chat.

If only I'd stayed outside The Full Shilling, scribbling away in this quitter's notebook.

But that's not what happened.

The café was closed.

Of course it was. It was 10 p.m. on a Thursday night.

But I knew Luke was inside.

For starters, the lights were on. The actual lights, not just the fairy lights.

Also, Luke had said something about working late.

Stocktaking.

I could hear something. Coming from inside the café.

It was music.

Not Luke's usual diet of trad with a bit of folk thrown in when he was in the mood for a story.

No, this was good music. Dance-y music. Sexy music. Not a hint of box accordion about it.

Did I suspect something then?

No, I don't think so.

Because I went right ahead and rooted around in my bag for the key, slotted it into the lock and instead of having to jiggle it around and variously pull and push at the door handle like I usually did, it turned like the lock had ingested an entire bottle of WD-40 and the door swung open and there they were.

Luke.

And Fernanda.

In a clinch.

A fucking clinch.

But that wasn't all.

It wasn't even the first thing I noticed.

The first thing I noticed were the get-ups. Luke in some class of a tuxedo. A short bolero-style jacket over a white shirt tucked into a pair of high-waisted black trousers. His hand in the small (read: tiny) of Fernanda's back, pulling her against him, the glossy curls of her hair against her dress, a vibrant splash of red silk, and her skinny arms wound around his neck like he was a lifebelt in a stormy sea.

If they'd been kissing, it wouldn't have been as bad. Sure hadn't I been at the same crack myself, earlier. And it had meant nothing.

No.

That's not true.

It had meant something.

It had reminded me of something. Of Luke. And what a great kisser he is. And why I liked him so much.

But they weren't kissing.

It was worse than that.

They were dancing.

21 July (still???), afternoonish

Symptoms: Sunburn, heat rash, constricted pupils from over-exposure to sunlight

The light in LA was so bright when I stumbled out of the airport, it rendered me technically blind for a good thirty seconds.

It's like artificial light, it's so bright.

And the people. They look artificial too. Like they've been manufactured, they're so beautiful. And healthy-looking. A lot of them passed me on wheels, skating by in a blur of LA colour which so far seems to be variations on yellow in the main. Although that could be the sun, fucking with me.

I didn't want to ring Carol at work because . . . well, I couldn't come up with a plausible response to one of her first questions, which would have gone something like this:

'What the fuck are you doing here?'

Although, no, she doesn't curse as much since she moved to LA.

'What the hell are you doing here?'

That sounds more American all right.

I got a cab from LAX.

I'm at it now.

Cab.

Fuck sake.

The cab driver asked me where my luggage was, how long was I staying in LA and if my hair colour was for real, to which I answered:

- I don't have any;
- I don't know; and
- Yes.

After that, he stopped asking me things.

So that's one of the first differences I noticed.

Irish taxi drivers would have kept going.

Carol's neighbours are a nosy lot. So far, three of them have approached me. With caution.

Can I help you, ma'am?

Do you need some assistance, ma'am?

Would you like me to call somebody for you, ma'am?

Is that your for real hair colour, ma'am?

ME: No, no, no and bloody hell, yes.

I didn't say bloody hell. That could be an arresting offence over here.

I mostly didn't think about anything awful during the two hours I waited for Carol. That's the great thing about LA. It's so different from what I'm used to, my brain had to work overtime, trying to process it all.

Distraction.

What every cuckold needs.

But then every so often, when my brain took a moment to recalibrate, there it was.

Luke and Fernanda.

Dancing.

Not just dancing.

Samba dancing.

Which was my thing. After Carol left, Luke said it would be his thing too. We were slow dancing in the kitchen. He said he would take lessons. He said he would dance me to the end of love. I didn't even slag him off for being a sap. Instead I lifted my hair so he could kiss my neck.

Turns out, he could dance all along.

He just didn't want to dance with me.

I can now confirm that heartache is not a thing. It was my stomach that was in bits. It was all over the place, cramping and clenching and heaving. It churned every time my brain eased up on the LA-processing and I saw the pair of them again.

Red silk halterneck.

Black tuxedo.

I felt like throwing up every time I saw them. I could taste bile at the back of my throat.

Like I'd eaten something well past its best before date.

I suppose I knew.

Did I know?

I must have known?

But no.

I don't think I did.

I wouldn't have thought Luke had it in him. It seems crueller than he's able for.

I didn't think he was cruel.

I thought I could depend on him. Right to the end. I assumed I'd go first. Which didn't bother me because I also assumed he'd be there when I went.

He'd see me out.

We agreed not to put each other in nursing homes. We'd do away with each other instead. We'd smother each other with kindness.

And pillows.

We said we'd do it when we're so ancient, we don't bother putting in our false teeth and subsist on a diet of semolina and porridge.

Or – Jesus H – goodie!

We agreed. It was a joint decision.

You never imagine you'll be that woman. The woman who didn't think her husband had it in him.

That's for other people.

Other women.

Stupid women.

Because, let's face it, how could they not know? That's what people think. That's what people will think about me.

Lucky for me I don't care what other people think about me.

Except.

They're right.

How could I not have known?

7 p.m. (Pacific Standard Time)

Carol eventually arrived at four in the afternoon. At first I didn't think it was her because of the scooter. And the hair which is long and blond now. Also, she was wearing what appeared to be a playsuit and there was sinew where her arms and legs used to be.

I'd say one of the neighbours must have phoned her and told her about the wretch stretched out on her doorstep. Because I don't imagine that four o'clock in the afternoon is anywhere near clocking-off time in LA.

What gave her away in the end was her birthmark – in the shape of the starry Plough – on the inside of her right arm.

It was Carol.

And even though almost every single thing about her had changed – her body shape, her hair, her clothes – the relief I felt at seeing this exotic stranger on a scooter with only the occasional flash of the starry Plough as reassurance was like a soothing glass of flat 7UP along the bile-coated tubes of my battered digestive system.

ME: Carol!
CAROL: Agatha? It really is you!

She leaped off her scooter, let it lie where it fell and wrapped me for a glorious minute in her arms and, even though they were hard with muscle and she no longer smelled like the Irish version of herself and even though there was every chance that she had changed, changed utterly, for a moment, it was like old times when meno-pause was something auld ones got because they probably deserved it and there was nothing more pressing to worry about except copying each other's homework before *Top of the Pops* on a Thursday night.

I leaned in. I think I even closed my eyes. I managed to stop myself from saying, 'I missed you so much' although Carol pulled back and looked at me as if I did say that.

She looked worried.

Who could blame her?

I struggled to allay her fears.

ME: Well? Are you going to just maul me out here all day or ask me in?

CAROL: Are you okay?

ME: I could murder a cup of tea and a rasher buttie.

CAROL (shifty): Fine . . . but . . . just so you know, I've only got herbal tea and the rashers are . . . well, they're plant-based.

ME: You promised you wouldn't change.

CAROL: Are you going to tell me what's going on or do I have to beat it out of you?

ME: That's more like it.

22 July, middle of the night-ish?

Symptoms: Jet lag

Carol's gone more LA than I'd feared because, when I told her that Luke was a lying, philandering fucker, she asked me if I 'wanted to talk about it'.

ME: I thought I just had?

Then she made me a smoothie made of many berries, grains and – I think – an egg, tucked me into the futon in the spare room, told me things would be better in the morning and kissed my forehead like I was a six-year-old with mumps.

Jet lag is a powerful thing. Instead of producing any kind of normal reaction to that brand of babying, I fell asleep.

And dreamed of Luke.

Who was dancing.

With a woman.

But in the dream, the woman was me. We were dancing on air, the way you do in dreams, floating and spinning and twisting and turning. But somehow we weren't touching and every time I reached for him, he disappeared and then reappeared and we'd start dancing again until I reached for him and then he'd disappear again. At the end, he didn't come back and I was on a stage now, dancing on my own. Leonard Cohen was in the wings, singing 'Dance me to the end of love' and strumming a guitar and, for a while, it was fine. Me dancing and him singing. But then the music stopped and, instead of dancing, I was falling.

I jerked awake, tensed for impact.

Fairly pedestrian dream sequence for someone in my sorry predicament.

The worst thing?

In the dream, Luke was a better dancer than me.

Carol's condo smelled different to home. There were no cooking smells for example. The inside of her fridge was gleaming and mostly empty apart from a couple of bottles of Californian chardonnay, a jar of stuffed olives, a carton of pretendy-milk and one lone head of lettuce that had seen better days, rolling like tumbleweed when I pulled open the vegetable compartment.

Don't you dare judge me. Who doesn't like a nosy through other people's fridges?

And their bathroom shelves and cupboards? But I didn't go in there because it was right beside Carol's bedroom and I didn't want to wake her. Carol's all sweetness and light until it's time to get out of her pit and then the gloves are off.

So here I am, sitting in the semi-dark of an LA early morning, not wanting to wake Carol but, also, wanting to wake her very much.

What I really wanted was tea and toast. What I ended up having was a glass of 'almond' milk and some out-of-date crackers I found in a press.

Both my phone and my Fitbit were out of charge. My recharger plug didn't fit into Carol's two-pronged sockets. And a – fairly lacklustre – search of a drawer where such things as adaptors might live yielded nothing of any use.

There I was, sitting on the balcony of a condo and looking out at the Pacific. Like a proper holidaymaker.

Except I wasn't a holidaymaker.

I didn't know what to call this . . . hiatus.

The neon lights of a pharmacy – a drugstore, Carol probably calls them now – claimed that it was 69 degrees. And even though that's Fahrenheit instead of Celsius, that was still bloody hot for middle-of-the-night o'clock. I could hear crickets. Or maybe they were cicadas? There was a hint of a breeze and it was that breeze that made me realise just how far away from home I was. It was warm and gentle and had a sweet smell, like, I don't know, the hot cross buns Luke makes for the auld ones on Good Friday.

And then I started thinking about the fact that I'll probably never smell that smell again because I'll never darken the door of The Full Shilling again and my stomach heaved so I had to run to the bathroom, lean over the toilet bowl and retch. The vomit was mostly the 'almond' milk.

I had to really concentrate to work out what day it was.

Bloody jet lag, it's worse than menopause. Or maybe it's a combination of both. Probably.

8 a.m.

I must have fallen asleep on the balcony. When I woke up, I had a thick red line down the left side of my face where it was embedded into the frame of the deckchair.

Carol sashayed out of her bedroom in a cloud of pink silk that looked like an outfit you might wear to the Oscars but was in fact her pyjamas.

CAROL: Sorry I'm so late getting up.
ME: It's eight o'clock in the morning.
CAROL: I know, I can't believe I slept in so late but it's
    Saturday so my alarm wasn't set.

Everything felt weird. The frittatas that Carol ordered from her local deli for breakfast. The tap water I drank before Carol hurled herself towards me, roaring that I am to never, ever, EVER drink the water from the tap because of . . . oh, I can't remember exactly, lots of reasons and none of them good.

The fact that it was Saturday when it felt like a Tuesday, at best.

After breakfast, Carol draped herself across some class of beanbag and said, 'What the fuck, Agatha?' and it was so familiar, this question from her. It smacked of old times and the way things used to be and I was infected, all of a sudden, with a noxious strain of sentimentality – is there any other kind? – and I had to concentrate, hard, on not crying.

If you cried in LA, I'd say they'd call it a breakdown and cart you off to the nearest institution. They'd call it a 'facility' and throw away the key.

ME: I guarantee, whatever happens, I won't stay longer than three days.

CAROL: Why not?

ME: Guests are like corpses. We stink after three days.

CAROL: You stayed with me when I worked in Ibiza that summer. Remember?

ME: The pair of us were off our heads for the entire week so that doesn't count.

CAROL: What are you going to do after three days?

ME: I don't know yet.

CAROL: I can't believe you've left Luke.

ME: Don't say that.

CAROL: Isn't that what you've done?

ME: I don't want to think about it.

CAROL: I'm going to hug you now and I don't want you to argue, okay?

ME: Do you have one of those adaptor plugs? I need to recharge my phone.

CAROL: Yes. But I'm going to hug you first and I don't want you to argue, okay?

Carol smelled different in LA. Not better or worse. Just . . . different. Like Californian sunshine was oozing out of her pores.

When she released me, she put on her 'LA' face and said something horrific about how I'm going to have to 'process the pain' and 'be present in my journey' and 'engage with the feelings' and other horrendous things like that. Like, why on earth would I want to do any of that?

I told her that she had to distract me. Anything else would be tantamount to abuse.

I wanted proper, hardcore, LA distraction.

CAROL: Fine. But you won't like it.
ME: Why not?
CAROL: You'll see.

10 a.m.

I allowed her to strap me into a pair of boot skates but drew the line at wearing the knee and elbow pads she proffered.

Like, what am I, six?

12.30 p.m.

Back at her apartment, she handed me cotton wool and antiseptic cream and didn't call me a dope or say, I told you so.

12.45 p.m.

CAROL: Do you want your phone back?
ME: Is it recharged?
CAROL: Yes.
ME: Okay. I mean no. I don't know. Actually, yes.
CAROL: You sure?

As soon as I started checking my phone, my stomach started up again with the heaving and the churning.

I had missed calls.

A lot of them.

Several from Luke. Along with voice messages. The thought of hearing Luke's voice tied my stomach into tight little knots. Then it performed a shaky sort of heave like it was thinking about a replay of its earlier performance. But I'd already thrown up everything, including all the bile I possess.

One from Anna. Probably ringing me to gently remind me that I was contractually obliged to deliver a novel at the end of the week.

One from Samantha, probably ringing with another meno-pause event she'd accepted on my behalf.

I deleted the messages. Without listening to them. I was struck by the fact that I'd never done that before. And that, from now on, there would be lots of moments like this one.

First times.

And none of them would be good first times. They would just be things I haven't done before because I haven't thought about it or needed to. Like going to the cinema on my own. And I know, there's no need to take that tone with me, I'm not some damsel in distress who can't eat an entire bucket of popcorn on her own, I KNOW I can go to the cinema by myself.

That's not the point.

The point is . . . well, it's a stupid thing really. It's that bloody game me and Luke play. We've played it pretty much since we started going to the cinema together.

And no, I can't remember how it started. The logo for the production company appears on the screen and the first person to name the company wins.

MAM: Wins what?
ME: It doesn't matter.
MAM: Wins what?
ME: Nothing, okay? Except, you know, kudos for recognising the logo and being the first to say the name of the company out loud.

We're both pretty good at it now. Decades of playing the same game will do that to a couple.

MAM: How is that a game, I ask you?
ME: I said it was stupid.
MAM: I can work that much out on my own.

So. Yeah. The first time I go to the cinema and either (a) not play the game, or (b) forget that Luke's not there and play the game. Either way, I'll end up on my own in the dark.

The first time that happens won't be my favourite time. Or the second or third.

I suppose people get used to things after a while.

Also calls from Aidan and Colm which I didn't respond to since I'd left a perfectly self-explanatory note on their bedside lockers ('Gone away. Research.').

I briefly toyed with the idea of doing something mean to Luke. I could out him on social media except he's not on social media so what would be the point?

I could send a really bad review of The Full Shilling to the local paper.

That would actually kill him.

He's so proud of the fact that the café has never had a bad review.

Well, pride comes before a fall, Luke.

But I couldn't persuade myself to do it and it took me a while to work out why and when I did, it was worse than I feared.

It's because I'm more sad than angry. Which made me angry but still not enough to tip the balance.

1 p.m.

Carol and I ate sushi for lunch, then left the condo to attend a flying trapeze class.

3 p.m.

I told the beautiful boy in charge that I was too ungainly and old to be a trapeze artist and the beautiful boy (maybe he was officially an adult but he looked like he'd never had occasion to shave his face) told me that he didn't know what ungainly meant and that his granny (he said 'grandma') did it twice a week and she was even older than me. Then, he strapped me in.

I didn't hang upside down like Carol. The beautiful boy said I would be able to do that next time.

I didn't tell him that there wouldn't be a next time. He seemed like the type who would take a declaration like that personally.

But I had to admit to some small sense of exhilaration

all the same. Carol even put her hand out for a high five as she flew past me and, if I hadn't been afraid for my actual life, I might have released my hand from its death grip on the bar and high-fived her right back.

Although my arse is absolutely killing me.

Those bars are as hard and unforgiving as you'd imagine.

23 July, 1 a.m.

Symptoms: Reality bites

Jet lag is the weirdest thing. For starters, it makes you forget things. Like, I was reaching for my phone just now to tell Luke all about the flying trapeze lesson and how maybe I should have run away with the circus after all, which had been my plan when I was ten and the Big Top was put up in the car park of Super Crazy Prices that Halloween.

I remembered just in time and threw my phone back into my bag.

I didn't think menopausal brain fog would make you forget leaving your husband.

It must be the jet lag.

I've left my husband.

Of nearly twenty-five years.

Or, I suppose, he's left me really.

Then, before the self-pity got a chance to bed in, I fell asleep.

Just like that.

After I ran away with the circus.

When we got back to the 'condo'.

At four o'clock in the afternoon.

Just after I refused to go to the samba-dancing club with Carol at Laguna Beach later.

CAROL: Ah come on. It'll be like old times, you and me, dancing on samba nights at Wigwam.

ME: I haven't danced since you left. Unlike Luke.

CAROL: You told me to punch you in the face if you started in with the self-pity. Remember?

And now I'm awake again and it's middle-of-the-night o'clock again and Carol is fast asleep. The positive thing is . . . look at me, all LA already . . . it's not menopausal insomnia. It's just jet lag which is NOT a symptom of menopause – I googled it just to be sure.

LA is very quiet. At nighttime anyway. When I'm awake in the night at home, I can hear things. Traffic, for example. Rush hour appears to be an outdated concept. Now. there's just traffic, night and day.

Alarms too. House alarms. Car alarms. The regularity and insistence with which they ring is directly related to how little attention anyone pays them.

Dogs barking.

Reminding me of LuLaBelle barking when she first arrived. That seems like a long time ago now.

And then snoring, after periodgate when she managed to worm her way inside my house.

MAM: And your heart, be honest. Although I suppose, as dogs go, she's not the worst.

ME: You do know she's Leonora's dog?

MAM: So?

ME: You never say anything awful about Leonora.

MAM: Why would I?

ME: Since she . . . you know . . . and Dad . . .

MAM (prim): Your father was a faithful man. He respected
his wedding vows. He and . . . they're friends. We all
need those.

I wonder if Aidan's remembered to give LuLaBelle the tin
of tuna she's supposed to get on Fridays?

Leonora says it gives LuLaBelle's coat a lovely sheen and,
while I obviously eyerolled when she made that particular
declaration, you'd be hard-pressed to find a shinier pelt.

I imagine LA pets are of a more manageable variety. Those
tiny little dogs you can fit inside a handbag, their collars
studded with jewels, answering to names like Princess and
Tawanda.

When I strained to hear any noise at all, I could just about
make out the sound of the sea.

They call it the 'ocean' here.

And yes, smartypants at the back, technically it is an
ocean. It certainly doesn't sound like an ocean. More murmur
than roar.

It was so quiet in the LA nighttime that, when my phone
rang, it sounded like a shriek in the silence and I was that
startled I bit my tongue and, as I stabbed at the phone to
get it to shut the fuck up, blood dripped onto the screen
as well as tears from my smarting eyes.

When I wiped myself and the phone down, I saw the
missed call was from Aidan. I rang back.

AIDAN: Where are you?

ME: In our culture, it is traditional to greet people in a less antagonistic manner, at least at first, before they get a chance to annoy you.

AIDAN: Sorry, I've just been . . . worried.

ME: I left you a note.

AIDAN: You never leave notes.

ME: How's Colm?

AIDAN: He's fine. He's in the garden, helping me dismantle the hives.

ME: Sorry it didn't work out. With the bees.

AIDAN: Me too. I was going to ask Dad when he gets back about his customer Mrs Jacob. Her daughter has the farm in Donabate? Maybe she'd let me keep a hive up there? When I find more bees.

ME: When he gets back from where?

AIDAN: Oh. I thought he was with you?

ME: Why would you think that?

AIDAN: I don't know. I just presumed.

ME: Haven't you seen him?

AIDAN: No.

ME: What do you mean? What about last night?

AIDAN: He didn't come home.

Why is the hand of fear so cold and clammy? Why can't it be soft and warm? Is it not bad enough that you're fearful? You have to be clutched by a cold and clammy hand too?

AIDAN: Where are you anyway?

All good things come to an end.

That's what Mam always said. She identified as a realist. She called a spade a spade.

MAM: Well? Why would you call a spade anything else?

And it had been good. Me and Luke. And that wasn't rose-tinted-glasses good. That was just a fact.

A rub-in-your-face sort of fact.

We had it good.

Until we didn't.

And now, here we were.

No.

Here I was.

7 a.m.

I was woken by the sound of vigorous sex. They probably call it 'lovemaking' in LA.

My first thought was not a particularly charitable one and went something like this:

Carol is having sex and I'm not.

Crystal must have come over after I fell asleep. Even though she said she wasn't seeing Crystal this weekend.

She mustn't have been able to stay away.

That sounded serious.

So did the sex.

I tried not to hear anything but even clamping my hands against my ears couldn't prevent me from hearing a set of detailed instructions, barked in a sort of furious monotone:

- Put your hand there.
- No, there.
- Keep it there.
- No, there.
- Don't stop doing that thing with your fingers.
- I said, don't stop!
- Yes, that's it, just there, don't move from there.
- Your hair is tickling my face.
- Why did you stop doing that?
- No, a circular motion.
- That's it. Now keep doing that until I tell you to stop or I have an orgasm, whichever comes first.

I am now in a position to reveal that the orgasm came first.
  Loud and clear.
  Very loud.
  And there was me complaining about the quietness of the nights in LA.

7.30 a.m.

A tanned, toned and presumably post-coital woman with a steel grey flattop haircut barrelled out of Carol's bedroom in an underwire bra and a thong and glared at me.

CRYSTAL (I assumed?): Who the fuck are you?

Which sounded way more NYC than LA.

ME: I'm Agatha Doyle. Who the fuck are you?
CRYSTAL: Are you the woman who was married for twenty-five years?

ME: Didn't quite make it to twenty-five.

CRYSTAL: I didn't even know that could be a thing. I suppose you want a decaf iced tea?

ME: Why would you suppose that?

Carol appeared behind Crystal, planted a kiss on her shoulder and kneaded her – bulging – biceps with the tips of her fingers.

She grinned at me.

CAROL: You've met Crystal.

CRYSTAL: Of course she has. I'm ordering brunch.

ME: Isn't it too early for brunch?

CRYSTAL (withering me with an eyeroll): Who wants a wheatgerm and kale smoothie?

CAROL: Yum!

That's when it hit me. Like, really rampaged through me like gastroenteritis. Luke. And Fernanda. The tired cliché of it all. And how alone I was. And what the hell was I doing all the way out here in bloody LA. And then, strangely, I thought about the thing Luke does with the black pudding and the scallions and the puff pastry.

Now that's breakfast, Crystal!

After she had ordered the 'smoothies' Crystal stalked back into Carol's bedroom.

Even her butt cheeks were toned.

CAROL: Isn't she something?

ME: Uh-huh. (Which is American for non-committal.)

CAROL: You okay?

ME: Just a bit tired.
CAROL: That'll be the heartache.
ME: It's jet lag.
CAROL: You're going to have to deal with it, Agatha.
ME: What?
CAROL: The sadness.
ME: Fuck sake.

Carol and Crystal persuaded me to go with them to 'goat yoga'.
Goat yoga is an actual thing.
It's yoga.
With goats.
Goat yoga.
I couldn't not go.
I wore a pair of Carol's yoga pants (read: leggings) which she promised would stretch to accommodate me, being made of Lycra.
And they did stretch, in fairness. But I'm pretty sure they'll never stay up on Carol's hips again.
The goat yoga class took place in a sandalwood-scented yoga studio with a lot of smugly toned people drinking kombucha out of eco-friendly bottles, with baby goats running about the place, performing jerky little jumps as they went.

MAM: One of the goats is actually . . . doing his business on that lady's back!

Goat 'poop' (which is what they call shit in LA) may look small and inoffensive but you still don't want to step on one of those little black marbles in a bare foot.

Trust me on that.

Soon, the sandalwood was edged with the acidic tang of goat urine. They particularly liked to pee on the cork yoga mats.

Delilah was the yoga instructor. I soon became convinced that she could manipulate her body sufficiently to fit inside the 'conservatory' (read: lean-to) in LuLaBelle's kennel.

One of the baby goats took a shine to me. He was bigger than the others, with startled yellowy-green eyes and coarse ginger fur. He took a run from behind and landed on my back when I was in 'table-top' (read: on all-fours). At first, he nuzzled at my neck – in fairness, not unpleasant – and then settled himself along my spine and fell asleep. Delilah said it was good for my 'core'.

DELILAH: Goats have no boundaries.
ME: . . .
DELILAH: Also, they'll eat anything.
ME: What are you saying?
DELILAH: I'd tie your hair up securely if I were you. By the way, is that your . . .?
ME: Yes, yes, it's my natural colour.

Afterwards, Carol and Crystal parted ways since Crystal had a swimming (with dolphins) class and Carol was rushing to the mindfulness-paddleboarding session she'd booked for us.

ME: Wait. What about lunch?
CAROL: We had brunch, remember?
ME: A goat shat in my hair.

CAROL: Fine, you don't have to come to mindfulness-paddleboarding.

I agreed to meet Carol and Crystal at the restaurant Carol had booked for seven o'clock. It was vegan and she hoped I didn't mind which I didn't. I was just so grateful that dinner was still a thing in LA.

I spent the day on the beach where I:

1) Got sunburned;
2) Cut my foot on a shell;
3) Got windburned;
4) Got chatted up by an octogenarian with pierced nipples and a man bag;
5) Ate what looked like a hotdog;
6) Which wasn't a hot dog. Not even warm.

None of that would have happened to me on Dollymount Strand.

Well, the windburn maybe.

7 p.m.

The restaurant was called Sage and was as earnest as you might expect. The seats were low to the ground and covered in itchy hessian sacks.

Crystal had a kelp noodle stir-fry and a 'warm bread pudding' for dessert that basically looked like one of Dad's bowls of goodie. Carol had salad. For dinner and dessert, as far as I could make out.

Oddly, I wasn't hungry but I knew Carol would do

something mad like call my 'next-of-kin' if I didn't eat so I pointed at something on the menu and force-fed myself with it. I think there was cauliflower in it. Masquerading as a buffalo wing. Which reminded me of Colm's birth, me and the cauliflower rolling around in the back of Luke's van.

Jesus.

Could I be homesick?

Luckily, I didn't have to come up with anything as horrendous as 'dinner table conversation' because Carol and Crystal spent most of the time sniping at each other.

Not sniping, exactly.

Nothing as overt as that.

A sort of under-the-surface passive-aggressive bent to it. Mostly about work. They work together. Some tech giant. Is there any other kind of tech?

Over 'dessert' Crystal insisted on telling me their 'meet-cute', which is LA for how they met.

CAROL (pointed): I don't think Agatha wants to hear all that.

Correct.

Crystal launched in nonetheless. The bottom line of the scenario was thus: Carol thought they were meeting to discuss a work project BUT it was really a date in disguise.

Which sounded a bit predatory to me in fairness.

What's cute about a sexual predator in the workplace?

Carol changed the subject and they went on to not-quite arguing about their new boss who had intimated that Carol might be in line for a promotion.

CRYSTAL: Of course, you're Irish. (Turns to me.) The boss
is just crazy about people from Ireland, you know.
CAROL (forced laugh): And I'm pretty good at my job too,
don't forget. It's not like she wants me to cook her a
pot of spuds and boil a hairy bacon.

Which happened to be the special in The Full Shilling today.

They went on to argue about whose turn it was to pay.
It didn't appear to be mine, I was relieved to hear. The
price!! Of fecking cauliflower!

Outside, it was dark but the air was still and heavy with
a sweet smell, like the coconut oil we used to lather ourselves
with before skin cancer in Ireland was a thing.

Along the coast, bushy fronds of palm trees quivered in
the warm breeze. Carol and Crystal were having what they
believed to be a furtive argument over whose apartment
they should repair to. Crystal wanted to have sex with Carol
in private, I heard her whisper.

I really wanted that too.

I put two fingers into my mouth and whistled. A cab
materialised in front of us, as if by magic. I force-fed the
pair of them into the back seat, assured Carol that I had
keys and wouldn't get lost, told her to take her time, shut
the door and ran away before Carol could object any
further.

9 p.m.

Only nine o'clock! One o'clock at home. The auld ones
would have had their dinner and be horsing into dessert at
The Full Shilling. Rice pudding maybe. Luke laces it with

cream. Crispy with nutmeg at the top. He makes double the quantity so he's ready for them when they form an orderly queue to ask for seconds.

How his customers have any unblocked veins left in their bodies is a mystery to me and to the scientific community at large.

No matter what's going on in Luke's personal life, he won't abandon his post at the café. Especially now, so close to the end.

My hand was in my pocket, fingers tightening around my phone. I pulled it out.

Another two missed calls from Luke.

For a fleeting moment, I thought about stabbing at buttons. Ringing him.

Hello. This is Luke. If you leave a message, I will ring you back.

I used to love getting his voicemail. The calm assurance of it. He will ring you back. You can bet your life on it. Or your bottom dollar, since I've gone all American now.

I put the phone back in my pocket.

If I could have summoned up a good fistful of anger, I'd have rung. Let him have it. Really gone for it. Told him exactly what I thought of him and his underhand, philandering, neglectful, careless ways.

But anger continued to evade me while my levels of useless, pathetic, no-good sadness continued to rise.

I didn't ring.

Even if I did, Luke wouldn't have answered anyway because . . . feeding time at the zoo, etc.

24 July, 10 a.m.

Symptoms: Amnesia

I had no recollection of getting back to Carol's 'condo' but I must have because, the next thing I knew, I was waking up on the futon and it was the next day. Carol had already returned from Crystal's place. She looked fresh as a daisy, as if her drill sergeant of a girlfriend hadn't been barking sex orders at her all night.

Carol told me not to worry about sleeping in. What she actually said was, 'Don't sweat it.' Then she said: 'I'm not sure what the appropriate thing to say is.'

ME: About what?
CAROL: About the . . . you know . . . anniversary.
ME: I couldn't give a damn, as you Yanks say, about our wedding anniversary. In fact, I . . .
CAROL: No, I meant . . . your mother's anniversary.

11 a.m.

Carol found a church. She was pretty sure it was a Catholic one. Once I clocked the statue of St Anthony in an alcove near the altar, I knew it was.

Mam was a fan of St Anthony.

The finder of lost things.

She gave him five pounds once, when she lost her wedding ring. And that was when five pounds meant something. I was only about six or so but I remember it still. Mam in the church, taking the five-pound note out of her purse, folding it in two, then in four, glancing around the pews, only a few parishioners scattered about with heads bowed and rosary beads dangling from clasped hands. She made sure nobody was looking as she slipped the note through the slit of the plinth where St Anthony stood.

Five pounds. Probably more than the ring was worth back then.

Mam, kneeling afterwards, her eyes closed and her head bowed. I asked her if she was making a wish and she said of course she wasn't making a wish, she was praying to St Anthony to find her wedding ring.

I never really understood the difference between a prayer and a wish. Either way, it was a bit miraculous in the end, when the ring turned up in one of the barmbracks Mam had made for the school cake sale. Shauna O'Toole from my class found it in her slice. Her mother got suspicious when Shauna's finger didn't go green after the requisite two days.

It felt strange, wearing it on my finger afterwards. Besides, it's probably safer on the chain around my neck. Sometimes, when I pick up the ring, smell it, I fancy I can still get the faint whiff of nutmeg off it.

I lit a candle and pushed a twenty-dollar bill into the collection box beneath the statue. I took a photograph of the candle and sent it to Dad. I couldn't think of a suitable message. 'Happy anniversary' seemed too jovial.

Carol offered to come in with me but I said no. Crystal had booked her in to have her root chakra unblocked later.

I couldn't help experiencing a brief but intense blast of gratitude that Luke would never make such an appointment for me.

But then I remembered Luke and Fernanda. Dancing. And the gratitude turned to grief and there was no getting away from it. The grief was dense and viscous and it wasn't just for Mam.

It was for me and Luke too. For our relationship that had once been such a source of abundance. Our own private oasis that we could retreat to when the world got too harsh.

We assumed it would always be like that.

I assumed.

And now it was gone.

Squandered.

The grief was for me too. Because what had become of me? Since the invasion of the menopause, I barely recognised myself. Where was the old me? And was she ever coming back? And if not, was I just supposed to live with this new version of myself? This fainter, duller carbon copy of myself.

It felt like loss, this grief.

I had lost myself. Not the kind of lost that St Anthony specialised in, no matter how many wishes or prayers or five-pound notes you threw at it.

MAM: Agatha Bernadette Doyle! Pull yourself together, girleen!

ME: Jesus, Mam, surely I'm allowed to feel sad for five minutes? I don't mean to be indelicate but it is your anniversary.

MAM: You're feeling sorry for yourself. About Luke. That's different altogether. And don't take the Lord's name in vain. In His own house too!

ME: Well, how should I feel then? How would you feel if Dad treated you with disrespect?

MAM: He wouldn't have dared.

ME (sighing): . . .

MAM: You mightn't be aware of this but I wasn't all that fond of Luke at first.

ME (sarcastic): Really?

MAM: Well, he was too short for you for starters. That never changed of course. But I worried. About him providing for you and the boys peeling spuds and frying eggs for the blue rinse brigade.

ME: You always worried. About everything.

MAM: I shouldn't have bothered. Luke is a good father. A good husband.

ME: He's a lying, cheating, philandering . . .

MAM: You need to talk to your husband. Or at least give him a chance to talk to you. Instead of running away.

ME: I didn't run away.

MAM: You went to America without telling anyone and now you're letting goats jump all over you and hanging around with Carol and that . . . friend of hers. What else would you call it?

ME: Well, since you're such an oracle when it comes to relationships, tell me what you would have done?

MAM: I don't care for your tone, Agatha.

ME (standing up): I'm going.

MAM: I didn't raise you to be someone who runs away.

ME: It's literally the first time I've ever done it.

MAM: The slippery slope.

11.30 p.m.

Outside, it seemed impossible that it was still the daytime and not just ordinary daytime but the LA variety, flooded with the whitest, brightest light that ever had the audacity to assault an eyeball.

It's easier to tell when people are giving you a wide berth when they're on wheels. Most of them careered in a wide arc around my person like their off-the-chart optimism and feel-good smugness might be tied to a stake and burned alive if it came into contact with my plain-as-the-nose-on-your-face peevishness, which is really just realism, once you accept that life is, on the whole, disappointing and, in the end, fatal.

12 p.m.

It was that thought, trailed by the steam from a freshly brewed cup of coffee I ordered from the 'Dali-Deli' café down the road from Carol's place, that made me long to hear a familiar voice.

Which is why I picked up my phone when it rang again. It was Samantha. I answered it.

SAMANTHA (breathless): Agatha! Dear girl! There you are! But where are you exactly? I've been trying to get a hold of you.

ME: LA.

SAMANTHA: What? But . . . you're not supposed to be there? Are you? Penelope??? PENELOPE!! Fetch me Agatha's schedule, toot sweet!

ME: I ran away from home.

SAMANTHA: Oh Agatha, you really are a scream. Now listen, I don't mind where you are so long as you get to the Liverpool event on time.

ME: . . .

SAMANTHA: You haven't forgotten, have you?

ME: . . .

SAMANTHA: Agatha?

ME: Of course not.

SAMANTHA: The Woman's Hour people are so delighted to have you. The conference is already trending on Twitter.

ME: Don't worry. I'll be there.

SAMANTHA (tap-tap-tapping on a keyboard): You'll have to go this evening if you're going to make it. I'll get Penelope to organise everything. There's a direct flight from LAX at 6 p.m. tonight. Do you want to stay over in Liverpool tomorrow night?

ME: I need to get back home. There are things I need to do. And say. About the witch novel for instance.

SAMANTHA: Don't worry your pretty little head about any of that until you get back from the conference, okay? Okay! Toodle-pip.

And she hung up.

12.30 p.m.

I told Carol I'd take her and Crystal out for lunch so long as it was someplace cheap. I was hoping she'd say there was no need to invite Crystal. Instead, she said fine so long as we could go sometime after two because Crystal had booked them into a couples counselling session at 1.30. The therapist was supposed to be a miracle worker.

ME: How long have you two been going out?

CAROL: Eight weeks.

I couldn't believe she missed my pointed look. Surely relationships shouldn't be that hard?

But maybe that's where I went wrong with Luke? Just presuming things about us.

Like our happiness.

2.45 p.m.

The restaurant smelled like incense, which is nice when you're in a church but worrying in a place where you're planning on doing a lot of emotional eating. Crystal declared the couples therapy a great success. Carol nodded. They both had red-rimmed eyes. When the waiter arrived, they spent a good ten minutes debating what drinks to order. An Aperol spritz was discussed and seemed to be 'in' at the moment judging by what the other customers were having. But should they have it with or without alcohol? Because yes, while they had both taken the day off, they did have that double-date with Lord and Spence at the skate park tomorrow at 6.

I'd been in LA long enough to know that when they said 6, they meant 6 in the morning.

I ordered a gin and tonic and when the waiter handed me a gin menu, I refused to take it.

ME: Surprise me.
WAITER (blanching): . . .

Carol and Crystal shared a quinoa salad and drank the pitcher of fizzy water they finally settled on. I ordered a hamburger and French fries (read: chips) which of course wasn't really a hamburger because, if it was, there would have been meat in it and meat was murder, etc.

But it looked like a hamburger and afforded me the opportunity to pick it up in both hands and eat it with my elbows planted squarely on the table.

MAM: Did I teach you nothing, Agatha Doyle? Where are your table manners?

I removed my elbows from the table, straightened up and used a napkin to dab at any ketchup that may or may not have collected in the corners of my mouth.

CAROL: What are you smiling at?
ME: I was thinking about Mam.

She lifted her glass of fizzy water and said, 'To Mammy Doyle.' Crystal followed suit, except she said, 'Mom Doyle.'
    We clinked.
    It wasn't quite the anniversary mass that Mam would have wanted in the draughty parish church with Fr Finnegan going to town on the sorrowful mysteries of the rosary afterwards.
    But I suppose it was some kind of marking.

3.30 p.m.

Carol said she'd help me pack but all I really had to do was put my new bamboo toothbrush into my handbag and pick the clothes Carol had lent me off the floor and toss them down her laundry chute. Afterwards, I went to have a last smoke out on the balcony. Carol's neighbour on the floor above and to the right leaned over her balcony to ask if it was a herbal cigarette, if I had sunblock on and if that was my natural hair colour.

ME: No.
ME: No.
ME: Fuck sake, yes!

3.35 p.m.

Carol came out with a mug of tea. Actual Barry's Tea. With the teabag still floating in it, the way I liked.

ME: Where . . . how . . .?
CAROL: It's my emergency one. I broke the glass. You looked like you needed it.
ME: Thanks, by the way.
CAROL: What for?
ME: For . . . everything.

I picked up her hand, squeezed it.

CAROL: Ouch!
ME: Sorry.
CAROL: Don't worry. You just don't realise your own strength.
ME: It doesn't feel like that at the moment.

Carol didn't say anything after that. She just put her arms around me and let me stay there awhile.

4.45 p.m.

I was hard-pressed at the coffee dock at the airport to convince the waitress that I wanted a cappuccino with full-fat milk and two sachets of sugar. She pretended it was because she couldn't hear me over the Tannoy but the truth was she just couldn't believe I was letting myself go so spectacularly.

I checked my phone. Dad had finally responded to the photo of the candle I sent him with a thumbs-up and a smiley face.

Nothing from Luke. He seemed to have stopped phoning me. That produced an unpleasant sensation in my gut, not unlike indigestion.

Aidan responded to my message to him and Colm, telling them I was coming home, with a thumbs-up followed by a screen grab of an article about a possible air traffic controllers' strike at Dublin airport.

Hopefully this won't affect your flight. See you soon xxx

Surely he was too old to be putting kisses at the end of texts to his mother. Still, he sounded in better form and I had to admit that the little 'x's eased the unpleasantness in my gut somewhat.

Melissa had responded immediately to my message about my travel plans. In spite of my annoyance at her excessive use of exclamation marks, smiley faces, flamenco dancers and flexed arms, I couldn't help feeling a surge of . . . I'm pretty sure it was gratitude.

It was definitely time I got the hell out of LA.

MELISSA: All good here apart from poor Dermot having a bad reaction to the roses I bought myself yesterday 😔. He was going to go to bed but I told him I was too busy to play nursemaid 💪 so he went to work instead!!!!!! I am working on a project 🐌😊!!!! Can't wait to see you, it's quiet here without you 🐹.

I responded with a brief but worryingly emotional: Getting on flight now. Looking forward to seeing you too

That was the second time I'd gotten on a flight without phoning Luke and saying goodbye and a begrudging thanks for everything. Just in case my flight went down somewhere over the Atlantic and the black box was never recovered so he couldn't hear me roaring at the pilot to ease up on the bloody clutch or whatever.

A lot of me wanted to phone.

The rest of me was afraid of what he might say.

Time enough to hear it when I got back home.

I turned off my phone and boarded the plane.

25 July, 2 p.m. (GMT)

Symptoms: Early-onset jet lag

Touched down at John Lennon airport in Liverpool. I wondered if Paul McCartney was annoyed that the airport wasn't named after him.

Then again, Paul didn't get murdered so, you know, you win some, you lose some.

Also, what about Ringo and George? They were Beatles too.

Walking through the doors into the arrivals hall shouldn't have been that difficult. I put it down to jet lag. Although it was probably too early for that. Perhaps I hadn't recovered from the original bout?

There were people everywhere and many of them were hugging.

And fine, maybe they hadn't seen each other in a while. Whatever.

But was it necessary to do it for such an inordinate length of time?

And then, there were the children. Really small ones, squealing (with what sounded like delight) and talking in that loud and excited way that children have and then laughing and taking their shoes off so they could run and skid on the tiled floor, against the explicit instructions of their parents who I clearly heard telling them not to do that exact thing.

And then there was me.

There's nothing like the arrivals hall on your own in the airport to give you a dose of the emotional runs. I made sure I didn't look left or right as I came through the sliding doors. Just powered on through the hordes of people hugging and children squealing and sliding and laughing. I set my face into a neutral expression and made a beeline for one of those awful generic cafés and sat down to gather myself, like a piece of lost luggage.

WAITER: What can I get you?
ME: Nothing.
WAITER: Are you waiting for someone?
ME: No.
WAITER: Well, you'll have to move then.

I waited for Mam to make some comment about the paucity of good manners these days.

Oddly, she didn't say anything.

I ordered a chocolate muffin. It was wrapped in layers and layers of plastic, which made me feel bad about the planet, and, if that wasn't enough, when I got over feeling bad about the planet and bit into the damn thing, it was stale.

I never thought I'd miss the 'Dali-Deli'.

2.45 p.m.

LIVERPUDLIAN TAXI DRIVER: Where to, love?

ME (searching for the email with the agenda Samantha 'dictated' to Penelope): The Ritz.

LIVERPUDLIAN TAXI DRIVER: Fancy digs!

He didn't say much after that. I was grateful. There was no way I could have kept a civil tongue in my head if he'd wanted to know where I'd been and why I'd been there and if my luggage had been lost and if I knew that red-haired women were considered a bad omen by fishermen in the olden days.

Luke always sat in front with the driver any time we got a taxi together. A sort of human shield for the unsuspecting taxi driver.

He was right about the hotel. It was one of those grand affairs with a wide facade of red brick and a tiered sweep of tiled steps reaching up to the entrance where a doorman in top hat and tails performed a stiff little bow in my direction.

DOORMAN: Agatha Doyle, it's my great pleasure to welcome you to the Ritz.

ME (suspicious): How do you know my name?

DOORMAN: I saw *Menopause: The Movie* of course.

ME: Really?

DOORMAN: The wife insisted. Said it would do me the world of good.

ME: And did it?

DOORMAN: Did I tell you to smile?

ME: No.

DOORMAN: Did I call you sweetheart or love or pet or chicken?

ME: No.

DOORMAN: There you are then.

He gestured towards the brass and glass revolving doors and offered to carry my 'luggage', which was a plastic bag containing, in the main, Toblerones.

3.05 p.m.

The young woman at reception gave me directions to the function room, told me the event was running over time and I wasn't on till 3.30 p.m. now and reminded me that the organisers had booked a room for me where I could change.

ME: I am changed.

RECEPTIONIST: Oh. Yes. Of course.

3.08 p.m.

Was there anything lonelier than a deluxe bedroom in a fancy hotel for one person? There were chocolates in a basket. Dark chocolates with bits through them. Fancy bits like ginger and raspberries and sea salt and almonds.

Under normal circumstances, I would have tipped the lot into my bag and smuggled them home for Luke.

A silver bucket with a bottle of champagne inside. I liked the idea of champagne more than the reality of it. The fizzy crackle. And the colour of it through a cut-glass. And the glasses themselves. Flutes. The delicacy of them. The bathroom was big enough to have an echo. It had a sunken bath, a tiled, circular affair that could accommodate me and at least one Significant Other.

I made tea and took out my phone, opened the file with the speech I'd written on the plane. I'd done what Samantha suggested and put in a little pithy bit at the end. The sound-bite solution to the menopause. I read through it, then emailed it to the receptionist who said she'd print it out for me.

I whiled away the rest of the time, sitting on the floor in my fancy hotel room, shouting random words into the bathroom and waiting for them to echo back to me.

3.22 p.m.

There I was, at the reception desk collecting my speech, when I heard a familiar voice behind me.

FAMILIAR VOICE BEHIND ME: Agatha? Agatha Doyle! There you are!! I've been looking for you all over.

I turned around and there was Den, all scrubbed and shiny with a buoyant quiff and a bright green suit and black patent shoes as long and narrow as canal barges.

DEN (reaching over to kiss me): You look incredible.

ME (sidestepping): Don't.

DEN: I've been calling and calling.

ME: What are you doing here?

DEN: I'm here with Patti, she's broadcasting from the event. Where've you been? I missed you.

ME: LA.

DEN: Oh. I'm so glad. I thought you were ghosting me.

ME: Is that when you dodge someone's calls?

DEN: Yes.

ME: I was doing that too.

DEN: But why? The other night? It was so special?

ME: Den, it wasn't. I was just mad with Luke and . . . I shouldn't have gone over to your house.

DEN: I don't mind being your rebound guy.

ME: I do.

DEN: It's because I live with my mother, isn't it?

ME: No. I like you, Den, I do . . .

DEN: Here we go.

ME: I've realised something. It's been dawning on me these past few days.

DEN: What is it?

ME: I'm in love with my husband.

DEN: You never said.

ME: I know. That's the problem. I never said.

DEN: But . . .

ME: And even if I wasn't in love with that lying, philandering fucker, I'm too old for you.

DEN: You're not old.

ME: It's fine. I'm okay with it. It's not the end of the world. It's more like the middle. Actually no, it's way past the middle. I keep forgetting about the smokes and the Walnut Whips.

DEN: Walnut whats?

ME: They're these whirl-shaped cones of . . . Look, it doesn't matter, you're a great guy, you'll meet someone fabulous.

DEN: Everyone my own age is so boring.

ME: There's someone for everyone. My mother used to say that.

DEN: Do you really think so?

ME: Yes.

DEN: Nobody kisses like you.

ME: And I can definitely say that nobody kisses like you.

DEN: So . . . that's it then?

ME: Yeah. That's it.

We parted on such amicable terms that, for maybe a full minute, I felt wise and worldly and virtuous and then I remembered that I was in love with my lying, philandering fucker of a husband who deserved to be cuckolded by youth and vigour.

Fuck sake.

3.29 p.m.

I stuffed my speech into my bag and made my way to the function room on the third floor. A woman with a clipboard and an earpiece nodded curtly at me.

CLIPBOARD LADY: Agatha Doyle?

ME: Yes.

CLIPBOARD LADY (touching earpiece): Call off the dogs, I've got her.

ME: I'm not late, am I?
CLIPBOARD LADY: You're cutting it fine.
ME (witty): In my culture, that's early.
CLIPBOARD LADY (unamused): Follow me.

She pushed at a pair of double doors and they opened to reveal a vast room lit by chandeliers and packed to the rafters with rows and rows of women, all clapping as the previous speaker – who I recognised as Magda Novak from Woman's Hour – finished her speech. I clapped as I hurried up the central aisle in the wake of clipboard lady. At the top of the room behind a rostrum on a raised platform was the organiser, Teresa Hadley. She was thanking Magda who had been speaking about gender-based discrimination in the workplace.

TERESA: And now, without further ado, I would like to introduce you to a woman who is in no need of an introduction. We've all seen *Menopause: The Movie* at this stage. And if you haven't, you might want to check your wrist for a pulse, hahaha. Agatha Doyle is an advocate for menopause and menopausal women everywhere. She's made it okay to have a hot flush in public. She's started a global conversation about women's health. Especially menopausal women who all too often are kept out of view for fear of upsetting that delicate little darling, the male gaze.

Teresa gripped my hand with both of hers and shook vigorously, then gestured towards the podium, adjusting the microphone upwards so that it reached my mouth, and sat on a chair to the side of the dais.

3.35 p.m.

When the audience stopped clapping, the silence that fell felt enormous. I cleared my throat and the sound, amplified by the microphone, reached across the room, harsh and phlegmy. I saw some women wince. I stood back a little from the microphone and took my speech out of my bag, unfolded it and laid it on the rostrum, ironing out the creases with the palm of my hand. I glanced up. A sea of faces, all looking at me. There were so many of them, maybe three hundred. Their eyes trained on me, waiting for me to say something coherent, informative, helpful, considered. I picked up the sheaf of papers and tapped them against the wood of the rostrum so they appeared neat and aligned.

I ripped the pages lengthways first. Then widthways. The sound of the paper tearing was even sharper than my croaky cough earlier. There was an audible gasp from the audience.

ME: My husband may have a point when he calls me a drama queen.

AUDIENCE: (A small ripple of nervous, sporadic, muted laughter.)

ME: Took me ages to write that speech. It was riddled with facts and figures and statistics. And all of that's important. We need to arm ourselves with these things so we can fight our corner, get menopause on the map, in our workplaces and homes and government buildings.

I took a slug of water from the bottle on the rostrum.

ME: I never intended being a pin-up girl for menopause. If I was going to be a pin-up girl, I'd want it to be for something good. Like, I don't know, Walnut Whips maybe.

I also never intended to be menopausal. It didn't seem like something I would enjoy. I thought, with the sheer power of my will, I could avoid it. My mother always said I was wilful.

But it seems I'm not wilful enough because along came menopause and floored me.

For a while, I pretended it wasn't happening. All the changes in my body. And my head. And the waistband of my jeans. It was inconvenient. I closed my eyes and put my fingers in my ears and hoped it would stop soon. Which is pretty much how I got through labour. And early motherhood. I did what women are pretty great at doing. Masking. I was hiding in plain sight.

After a while, I realised that menopause was like your kids. They arrive one day and never tell you when they might be thinking of moving out.

The next brilliant plan I came up with was, say nothing. Don't talk about it. Bear up and get on with things and maybe nobody will notice. My GP thought that was a brilliant idea. But then he died and I got shunted onto Dr-Lennon-call-me-Susie's desk and she had other ideas. Ideas about HRT – which I was afraid of – and talking about your feelings – which I was also afraid of.

I swept my glare around the audience but they seemed unperturbed, waiting for me to go on.

ME: My mother called menopause the change. I always thought it was because she didn't want to say the word out loud. Its association with what she called 'women's problems', periods and the like. But I realise now that she was right. Because that's exactly what menopause is.

It's change.

I'm not a big fan of change.

But I'd forgotten another thing my mother always said, which was:

'A change is as good as a rest.'

AUDIENCE: . . .

ME: Up to menopause, our bodies and minds and lives have been colonised. By Church and state. By society. By employers. Our families. Our children. Even our pets. Even other people's pets you happen to be dog-sitting for.

For years, we've been judged purely on our gender. We're too sexy. Or we're not sexy enough. We have too many children. We don't have enough. Or any. We go to work. We stay at home. We breastfeed. We bottlefeed. We get Botox, we're vain. We don't get Botox, we're letting ourselves go. We look too old for our age. We look too young for our age. Our tops are too tight, we're asking for it. Our skirts are too short, we're mutton dressed as lamb. From puberty to menopause, we are subjected to wolf whistles, cat calls, lewd comments, inappropriate touching, mauling, manhandling.

You complain, you're making a fuss about nothing.

You don't complain, you like it really.

We've taken it all because, a lot of the time, it's the easier option.

And then along comes menopause and suddenly everything changes, right?

AUDIENCE: . . .

ME: But I didn't want to change. I didn't want to do anything except pretend it wasn't happening and not talk about it. And then *Menopause: The Movie* happened and there I was, full-frontal, not only being menopausal but talking about being menopausal.

I may look like someone who doesn't scare easy but I was terrified.

I was aware of my hair, heavy and hot against my neck, and I gathered it in my hands and wound the bobbin on my wrist around as much of it as I could manage. My breath was a little ragged and I put my hands on the sides of the rostrum and leaned on them for support.

ME: But then, something happened. Women started contacting me. They told me things. Personal things. Harrowing things. Wonderful things. They thanked me for bringing menopause out into the light but I see now that it was me who should have thanked them. For dragging me out. Kicking and screaming admittedly. Out from under my rock.

I'm not going to tie everything up with a pink bow and say everything's grand, now that I've come out as menopausal.

I'm still afraid. Of standing here. Of being judged. Of getting older. Dying. The usual.

But I can honestly say that I don't feel like I'm standing here on my own. There's a community of women and they have my back.

And I have theirs.

And that feels pretty fucking incredible.

I looked over at Teresa.

ME: Am I allowed to say fucking?

TERESA (smiling): I don't see why not.

RANDOM AUDIENCE MEMBER: Fuck the patriarchy!

AUDIENCE: (Laughter and applause.)

ME: I don't want to be responsible for starting a riot. Well, I kinda do. But I'm not advocating a coup just yet. It's like I told my kids when they were younger. Stick together. We are more than the sum of our parts. Together we are an invincible force. We're like an army but good. We can make things happen. Like free, universal, accessible healthcare. Affordable medication. GPs who know what the hell they're talking about when it comes to women's health. A system that's properly funded and resourced, full of healthcare professionals who actually like women. Who know our bodies. Who understand our physiology. Menopause-friendly workplaces and government policies. That's not too much to ask, is it?

AUDIENCE: (Cheering.)

ME (losing the run of myself now): I said, that's not too much to ask, is it?

AUDIENCE: (Louder cheering, some whooping.) NOOOOOO!!!

TERESA (standing up, waiting for roaring to subside): Thank you, Agatha, that was . . . exhilarating. Thank you for being so frank with us. Now, are there any questions from the audience?

She nodded at clipboard lady, who picked up a microphone and scanned the audience with a pair of steely blue eyes before setting off at a clip towards a lone hand waving at the back of the room.

The lone hand belonged to a woman in tight leather pants who didn't look old enough to be menopausal. Or even peri-menopausal. She glowed as if she'd been poached in oestrogen. I suspected HRT and made up my mind to do a lot more research into it.

Maybe 'Susie' was right and it presented fewer health risks than cigarettes did.

GLOWING WOMAN: Agatha, I think you're a wonderful pin-up girl for menopause. I adore your honesty. These past few weeks, I have felt seen as a menopausal woman. And it's all because of you, Agatha Doyle.
RANDOM WOMEN ACROSS AUDIENCE: Hear, hear!
RANDOM WOMAN #1: Menopause is a rite of passage!
AUDIENCE: Yesssss!!!
RANDOM WOMAN #2: Menopause is one of the very few things that every single woman on the planet will go through. It's something that can unite us all!
AUDIENCE: Yesssss!!!!
RANDOM WOMAN #3: I told my boss to go and fuck himself.

There was a brief delay before another 'Yesssss!!!!' from the audience.

RANDOM WOMAN #4: Girl power!
AUDIENCE: Yesssss!!!!
RANDOM WOMAN #5: Who runs the world?
AUDIENCE: Girls!

RANDOM WOMAN #6 (worried): But, Agatha, it's all very well, all the chanting and cheering but what good's that going to do me when I'm having a hot flush in the middle of a board meeting? And even if I don't have one, I'm still anxious that I might. Everyone tells me to take HRT but I'm somewhat wary of it. Where do you stand?

ME: I'm wary too. I blame my mother for dying of breast cancer mostly. But I can say with conviction that I've seen and heard about the benefits of HRT from lots of different women. For instance, there's a woman who lives next door to me. Actually no, she's not just a woman who lives next door. She's my friend. My very good friend, in fact.

I took a deep drink of water to steady myself.

ME: Anyway, she's been waxing lyrical about HRT ever since she started a few weeks ago. Everything's improved, she says. Her sleep, her hot flushes. And her appetite is back. For everything as far as I can see.

RANDOM WOMAN #7: Agatha for Queen of the World!

ME: No, no, we're a collective, we're all in charge. Every single one of us.

AUDIENCE: Yesssss!!!!

And then they were all on their feet, yelling and whooping and cheering and punching the air with their fists.

For a moment, it felt like I was dancing.

Like we were all dancing.

In time to the beat.

Together.

7.30 p.m.

Symptoms: Creeping dread

Probably no need for the adjective. Is there any other kind of dread?

I'd been so high after the event, I allowed myself to forget about everything. As soon as I came to, the adrenalin and elation dribbled away.

Here I was in Dublin airport, about to get on the bus home when I remembered the car.

Which I'd left in the multi-storey car park.

It took me ages to remember where I'd left it. And then the cost of the parking.

Jesus H!

Still, it was a comfort to be somewhere familiar after everything. The car smelled of wet dog and there was a collection of coffee cups rolling around the footwell, but when I pressed play on the CD player, I knew there was a chance it could be Joni Mitchell and it was.

Maybe it was the hopefulness of the song: 'Sometimes I'm Happy'.

I don't know. But I found myself at the top of the road, driving down towards The Full Shilling, slower and slower, with no idea of what I was going to do when I got there.

Was I going to stop outside it?

Run to the door?

Reef it open?

Drag Fernanda out by her long, luscious locks?

Demand that Luke fulfil his promise of loving me until I was stiff on a slab waiting in line to be boarded up in a wooden box?

The fact that I didn't know the answers to any of those questions became a moot point.

Because The Full Shilling was closed.

Lights off.

Blinds drawn.

Shutters down.

Apart from Sundays, the café never closed. Except now it was.

It looked like a death-in-the-family kind of closed.

6 p.m.

The house was empty when I got home. I had no idea where Colm and Aidan were but I hoped that one of them was walking the dog because of LuLaBelle, there was no sign.

Everything was familiar but also strange, like my absence over the last few days allowed me to see the house as a stranger might. The sound of my runners against the worn and faded floorboards in the hallway. The photographs of us – me and Luke, Aidan and Colm, Mam and Dad, me and Bart, Ronnie and Carmel, Luke and Damien, all of us – in frames along the wall of the stairwell. In the slanting evening sunlight I could see the silky strands of cobwebs reaching from the corners of the frames across the glass.

The jungle of shoes and slides and boots and flip-flops underneath the hall table. Like ten people lived here.

Twenty.

The teapot on the hob, wrapped in the cosy Mam knit last year, with the bobble on top. The cheerfulness of that. Like a statement of intent. Nothing bad would ever happen here.

I could smell the house too. And I was right. LuLaBelle DID stink. A grubby, damp smell. I had convinced myself that she had stopped smelling bad. So now I knew. Nose blindness was an actual thing.

In our bedroom, I couldn't smell anything. Or anyone. The window had been left open and the bed, an ancient and extravagant king-size in solid oak, had been neatly made and no clothes were strewn across the floor or over the back of the rocking chair in the corner.

After all the years of tossing and turning and flossing and fighting and fucking, our bedroom was as bare as a doctor's waiting room and smelled of nothing.

Suddenly, the wardrobe seemed ominous. Like it was taking up more space than it usually did, looming there with its thick clawed feet digging into the floorboards like a standoff. The doors, shut and locked with the long, brass key instead of hanging open on its creaky hinges, like it had something to hide.

Which should have been Mam's chance to pipe up and tell me to cop on to myself and stop acting like a big baby.

Except she didn't.

In fact, now that I thought about it, since I'd left LA, she hadn't said a word.

And yes, yes, I didn't need a psychoanalyst to tell me that she couldn't say a word. That she hadn't said a word for a year (and two days) because she was, in fact, dead.

But that didn't change the fact that she hadn't said a word to me since I left LA.

Maybe she was mad with me.

Or worse: disappointed.

I wouldn't blame her.

Because there I was, standing in front of my ancient, familiar wardrobe, afraid to open it. How fanciful had I become? I could put it down to weariness, I supposed. And Mam not talking to me any more. And the bedroom being so empty and lifeless.

I took a breath like 'Susie's' always banging on about, turned the key in the lock and yanked at the wardrobe doors, the way you do when you're afraid but trying to convince yourself you're not afraid.

Some of Luke's clothes were gone. His favourite threads. His faded blue jeans. His Adidas sweatshirt that Colm called 'vintage' but is really just from the first time around. His black leather jacket. His leather-strapped sandals that he would wear with socks if he were allowed. And his runners that we called his LGBTQ+ runners because of all the colours.

They were all gone.

As was the suitcase on top of the wardrobe.

It was gone.

And so was Luke.

And still not a peep out of Mam even though by rights she should have issued a sternly worded pronouncement on the futility of self-pity.

But she was gone too.

I sank onto the edge of the bed. Like someone had let all my air out, all of a sudden.

I suppose it was the jet lag, draining me of all my energy.

But I also felt empty. A vast emptiness inside my body. And my head.

Was that what people meant when they talked about heartache?

But it wasn't an ache.

It was more of a sinking, sick feeling.

Heartsick.

I felt like I could throw up all over the bedroom floor and it would be nothing but bile.

Heart-bilious.

Time: ??? (Half an hour later?)

MELISSA: Coo-eee, Agatha? It's only me!

I don't think I'd been asleep since I was still sitting on the edge of the bed, staring at the wardrobe.

MELISSA: Welcome home Agatha!
ME: . . .
MELISSA: Agatha? You okay?
ME: No.
MELISSA: Whatever's the matter? Agatha? You're worrying me now. I'm coming up.
ME: Don't.

But it was too late. Or I'd said it in such a pittance of a voice, Melissa hadn't heard me in the first place.

Either way, she started up the stairs and came to a full stop at the bedroom door.

MELISSA: There you are. Oh my goodness, Agatha, what's happened?

I told her in as few words as I could manage. Then I started crying. I really went for it. I was what you might call an 'ugly-crier'. My eyelids swelled, my nose reddened and ran, the whites of my eyes turned blood red and my skin went blotchy. Melissa let me wail away, saying nothing about the sodden shoulder of her silk lilac blouse.

I knew she wanted me to stop when she started saying things like, 'There, there, don't worry, it'll be okay.'

I did my best to stop and she did her best to repair my face with cream she produced from her handbag that had witch hazel in it. But that reminded me of my sixteenth-century witches, Ellen and Clara, whose stories would never be written because I was no longer able to write stories and then I was off again.

MELISSA: Hush, hush, don't upset yourself again.
ME (ugly-crying): . . .
MELISSA (stern): Shut up, Agatha.
ME: . . .
MELISSA: Sorry!
ME: And Mam's gone too, you know. And I know, I know, I'm not going mad but . . . What I mean is, she's . . . gone for good.
MELISSA (wiping my face with two 'man-size' Kleenex she produced from her handbag): Oh, Agatha.
ME: And I never told her that I loved her. Not even when she was dying.
MELISSA: I'm sure she knew.
ME: I miss her.
MELISSA (stroking my hair): I know you do.

After a period of time that Melissa must have deemed appropriate in the circumstances, she extricated herself from me with an almost unbearable tenderness, and stood up.

MELISSA (smoothing her A-line floral skirt): Now, you
should come downstairs. Aidan and I have something to
show you.

It was a measure of how bone-tired and hollowed out I felt
that I didn't ask any questions, just nodded and followed
her meekly down the stairs.

She strode briskly down the hall and through the kitchen,
stepping nimbly around various mounds of detritus without
slowing or even wincing.

She opened the back door and ushered me into the
garden where, impossibly, it was a beautiful evening. A
glorious, summer's evening, everything basking in a soft,
golden light, swaying in a gentle breeze carrying notes of
lavender and honeysuckle, the air full with the sound of
birdsong.

And something else.

Buzzing.

AIDAN: There you are! Oh, are you okay?

MELISSA (hasty): She's fine!

ME: Do you know where your father's gone?

AIDAN: He headed off yesterday with a suitcase. I presumed
he was going to join you?

ME: No.

AIDAN: Oh.

MELISSA (brightly): I told Agatha we'd show her what
we've been working on.

AIDAN: Sure.

He put a straw hat on my head and arranged one of Mam's mantillas around it, tucking the ends into the collar of my dress.

Melissa donned a long plastic raincoat, rubber gloves, a swim hat and an enormous face-mask. She must have been ready to pass out with the heat.

MELISSA: Ready?
ME: . . .

Aidan took one of my hands, Melissa took the other and they led me to the bottom of the garden. The buzzing was coming from LuLaBelle's kennel. Or what had once been LuLaBelle's kennel. It appeared to have been disassembled and reconfigured. Into a beehive. Bees flew in and out of the entrance that Aidan had fashioned – this time with a fanlight over it as well as an architrave.

MELISSA: The fanlight was my idea!
AIDAN: They've settled in really well.
ME: Where did you get them?
AIDAN: I found them in the composter in Grandad's back
    garden.
ME: But what about 'poor Dermot'?
MELISSA: We've reached . . . an understanding.
ME: What do you mean?
MELISSA: He understands that if he doesn't stop behaving
    like a dick, I'll leave him.
ME (stunned): You said dick.
MELISSA (proud): I know.

AIDAN: You've been amazing, Melissa. I can't thank you
    enough.
MELISSA (flushing): Well, we all have to do our bit for
    biodiversity.

We watched the bees coming and going for a while. There
was something so absorbing about them. The way they
appeared at the door, then paused for a bit, like they
were steeling themselves for the big, bad world where
anything could happen and a lot of it mightn't be particularly good.

Then, performing their bumbling, shuffling dance before
flying away on their furious little wings that managed to
beat two hundred and thirty times a second. Melissa and
Aidan cheered. After a while, I joined in. I couldn't help it.

All of a sudden, a volley of barks and there was LuLaBelle,
hurling herself through the back door, a blur of fur as she
pounded down the garden and threw herself against me,
licking my bare legs like they were a pair of Cornettos.
When I bent down to pet her, she leaped into my arms
and buried her head in my neck, her breath hot and furious
on my skin.

She stank.

AMELIA: I think she missed you.

Everybody laughed. Except me, obviously. Amelia looked
her usual stunning self, all gleaming teeth and effortless hair
and obnoxiously rude health.

ME (attempting to be civil): Oh. I didn't see you there.
COLM: We've been out with LuLaBelle.

We.
  Dammit.

AMELIA: Colm took some incredible shots of her for
    D.I.Guy. We had her in a hard hat and a high-vis jacket.

Colm showed us the photographs.

AMELIA: Thirty-six thousand likes already.

Colm shrugged like it was nothing. But there was no doubt
about it. His 'zest for life' levels were on the up. I also had
to concede that he looked better. Like some of Amelia's
rude health had rubbed off on him.

COLM: What's for dinner? I'm famished.
ME: I literally just got back.
COLM: Oh. Were you away?

Jesus H.

AIDAN: I'm afraid I've been too busy with the bees to
    shop. I'll see what I can find in the kitchen.
MELISSA: I'd better go and freshen up. Dermot's making
    paella from scratch using a YouTube tutorial.

I hugged her.
  If she was surprised, she rallied well and hugged me back.

Inside the house, Aidan took to the kitchen and Colm
thundered up the stairs which left me with little-miss-
treachery in the sitting room.

ME: So . . .
AMELIA: Well . . .

It wasn't awkward at all.
   Then:

AMELIA: Colm and me aren't back together by the way.
   If that's what you're worried about.

Colm and I.
   But whatever.

ME: I wasn't worried.
AMELIA: We're just friends now.

Her tone was pure gutted. She looked very young all of a
sudden.

ME: Maybe it's for the best. A clean start for the pair of
   you.
AMELIA: How do you and Luke make it look so effortless?
ME: What?
AMELIA: You know . . . love.

I managed not to laugh.
   Or cry.
   A sweet smell drifted from the kitchen which was Amelia's

cue to leave. She was on one of her crazy diets. She could only eat on Tuesday, Thursdays and every second Saturday.

Something like that.

The 'food' was smoothies in the main. There was talk of kale. Crystal would have approved.

7 p.m.

And then, there were three of us.

We sat around the kitchen table. I presumed that heartache would rob me of my appetite and finally rid me of that bloody menopausal spare tyre that's been hanging around my midriff for the past two months.

Instead, I discovered that I was starving.

AIDAN: The cupboards are pretty bare, I'm afraid. But I managed to find bread, sugar and milk.

He put three bowls of goodie on the table. Nobody said anything about the Luke-shaped space at the end of the table. Why would we? He was often out at mealtimes given the nature of his work.

But today the empty space felt ominous. A harbinger of things to come.

I distracted myself with goodie.

Which was when I discovered that goodie wasn't as awful as I'd imagined.

As long as you don't look directly at it when you're eating it.

Which is what I was doing when the front door opened.

7.30 p.m.

LUKE: Agatha! There you are!

ME: Where else would I be?

He put his suitcase on the floor, dragged a hand down his face. He looked worn out. His clothes were crumpled, like he'd slept in them. If he'd still had hair, I'd say it would have been mussed and tangled. I couldn't help feeling a surge of concern which I quickly turned into scathing disregard.

ME: How come you came back? Forgot to pack your fancy underpants?

COLM: Wait. Dad has fancy underpants?

AIDAN: Are you two fighting?

ME: Your father's been having an affair with Fernanda.

COLM (leaping up): No way!

LUKE: I've been at the airport for the last twenty-four hours waiting for a flight to LA.

ME/COLM/AIDAN: What?

AIDAN: Mum's just back from there.

COLM: Fernanda's WAY too young and beautiful for you, Dad.

ME: Why were you going to LA?

LUKE: Because that's where you were. Or that's what I thought.

COLM (to me): Wait. You've been in LOS ANGELES?

ME (to Luke): How did you know I was there?

LUKE: I phoned your dad. He sent me the photograph you sent him on your mother's anniversary. He didn't know where you were but I was able to make out the name of the church, written over the door. I used Google to work out it was in LA. And Carol's there, so that made sense.

AIDAN: Impressive detective work, Dad.

COLM: There's not a chance in hell Fernanda would have an affair with Dad.

LUKE: I AM NOT HAVING A BLOODY AFFAIR WITH FERNANDA.

There was silence for a good bit after that.

Luke never shouted.

He sat down heavily on the chair beside me. He smelled so familiar and I had a sudden urge to push my face into his neck.

Like the olden days.

AIDAN: I knew you'd fall in love with Fernanda once you met her.

LUKE: I AM NOT IN . . .

COLM: Keep your hair on, he was referring to me. Oh, you don't have hair. Sorry.

ME: You were dancing with her. Dancing, Luke. How could you?

LUKE: I was learning. Fernanda was teaching me how to dance so I could go with you to the samba weekend in Madrid I'd booked for our anniversary.

ME: That seems . . . far-fetched.

LUKE (sighing): Well, it's true all the same. I am not in love with anyone. Apart from you, Agatha Doyle.

COLM (eyerolling): I'm fecking well eating here.

LUKE: Here, I'll prove it.

He took his phone out and swiped urgently at the screen. Suddenly music was pouring out of the Bluetooth speaker on top of the breadbin.

'The Rhythm Is Gonna Get You'.

Only my absolute favourite song to samba dance to.

Luke wrestled himself out of his ancient leather jacket, tossed it towards the back of a chair. It missed and landed on the floor. He looked at me, sheepish, colour flooding his face.

COLM (covering face): Oh Jesus, I can't watch.
AIDAN: Go on, Dad, you can do it.

Luke strode towards me, picked my hand off the table and tugged on it until I was upstanding.

He curled his arm around my waist, pulled me in, lifted my hand in his and we were off.

We were dancing.

Together.

Me and Luke.

Luke and me.

Luke and I.

The two of us.

Dancing.

I'd like to report that we were a sensation. That we danced like a fusion of two bodies, streamlined and smooth and seamless.

That we made it look easy. Effortless.

That it looked like we'd been dancing together for the longest time. For all our lives.

Instead:

Luke stood on my toes.

I elbowed him in the ribs.

Luke missed my hand after he spun me and I stumbled back and narrowly missed tripping over LuLaBelle.

I spun him and I might have done it a bit too vigorously because when I released him, he staggered around the kitchen, only stopping when he hit his hand off one of the knobs on the oven.

The best thing about us was our enthusiasm. And it must have been catching because, after a while, Aidan and Colm started cheering and clapping in time to the music, only stopping to laugh any time we banged bits and pieces of ourselves off various kitchen appliances.

To this day, I don't really know why we kept going, Luke and I. We were pretty terrible, dancing together. Like a pair of baby elephants on a bouncy castle. Heaving and hauling each other around. But still, we kept going, laughing at our attempts to keep in time with the beat and not to hurt ourselves or each other too much.

I think it was a lot to do with the music. Music can lift a mood, no doubt about it. Or maybe it was something to do with hope. Like all was not lost.

Just because you're middle-aged and menopausal, it doesn't mean that it's all over.

There are still things to learn.

Relationships to tend.

Dances to perfect.

So that's what we did.

We danced.

We kept on dancing.

15 September, 11 p.m.

Just back from the launch of *My Life in Bits and Pieces* and, in a rogue fit of sentimentality brought on no doubt by the several glasses of 'champagne' (read: warm white wine) I necked in the bookshop, I decided to dig out my *You Can Quit* notebooks. I can't believe I filled five of them in the end. And that they all got typed out and sticky-taped into a book.

That's what happens when your editor rings on the day of the deadline for your novel about sixteenth-century witches.

ME: The thing is, Anna . . . I haven't written a novel about sixteenth-century witches.

ANNA (admirably composed): Oh. I see. Well, what have you written a novel about?

ME: Um . . .

ANNA: Yes?

ME: It's about . . .

And that's when I spotted the stack of *You Can Quit* notebooks sticking out from under my bed.

ANNA: You still there Agatha?

ME: Oh. Yes. Sorry. It's about this woman and she's menopausal.

ANNA: Go on.

ME: Well, that's it really.

ANNA: I see.

I thought my menopause-misery-memoir might distract Anna for long enough while I came up with a feasible Plan B.

Instead, Anna declared herself delighted with my main character's peevish turn of phrase and declared that she would publish it straight away.

MELISSA: That's the stuff of dreams.
ME: Not if Colm and Aidan ever read it.

Although the chances of Colm reading it while he's back-packing with 'that woman' (read: Fernanda) through south-east Asia are pretty slim.

It turned out Aidan was right. The only reason Colm hadn't been in love with Fernanda was because he hadn't met her yet.

ME: Were you in love with her too?
AIDAN: Only in an abstract sense. Like the way you'd love a Renaissance painting.

Whereas there doesn't appear to be anything abstract about his relationship with Marija the vegan farmer. Marija has sort of adopted us since her own family threw her out, back when she was Tomislav the butcher in Slovakia.

She's fine, I suppose. If a little effusive.

MARIJA: I adore you, Agatha. May I call you Mama?

Still, they're mostly out and about, sowing seeds and harvesting vegetables and making honey and . . .

MARIJA: And making love!

Jesus H.

Still, Marija brought her friends to the launch and lots of them bought the book. I think she told them it was a 'thrilling' book which they may have interpreted as 'thriller'.

MELISSA: I agree with Marija. It is a thrilling book! Well done, Agatha!

'Poor Dermot' was glued to her side, loaded down with several copies of the book.

One for him and the rest for any of his friends at the golf club who have menopausal partners, Melissa explained.

'Poor Dermot' didn't appear to object that much. Or at all, in fact.

I certainly didn't object. The loan we managed to get from the credit union to give Damien his share of the café isn't going to pay itself. Still, it's a much smaller loan than we'd originally feared.

Turns out there's a big demand for misery-menopause-memoir.

Even though I'm blue in the face telling everyone it's not a memoir.

DAD: You're fooling no one, Aggie.
ME/LEONORA: It's Agatha.
LEONORA: Look at your name on the cover. Your dear mother would be very proud of you.

Even Samantha seemed pleased.

SAMANTHA: Misery-menopause-memoir! It's a whole new genre, baby!

I couldn't get over Carol. Surprising me like that. I also couldn't get over Melissa and Crystal. Clicking so immediately.

MELISSA: She's American you! Of course I adored her right from the start.
ME: She liquidises kale and then drinks it.

Dr-Lennon-call-me-Susie came! She said she'd never had a patient who kept a record of their symptoms as diligently as I did.

Damien sent his apologies and dozens of roses. He's still in Thailand with his new girlfriend/business partner.

LUKE: Maybe it's not a great idea to mix business with your personal life?
DAMIEN: It's bitcoin, bro. Solid gold.

He happens to be having dinner in Bangkok with Colm and Fernanda tonight. Colm uploaded a photo of the menu onto The Full Shilling Insta account he set up a while ago. Over ten thousand followers so far. Luke's new customers have quartered the café's age profile in a matter of weeks. So long as there's still hairy bacon and cabbage on the menu, the auld ones don't mind all that much.

Caption: 'This'll have to do until I'm back at The Full Shilling'.

In another photograph, Fernanda has her arms wrapped

around Colm and Damien, the gap between her front teeth curiously endearing from this distance.

Don't get me wrong, she's still annoying as hell. The way she flung her head back and laughed when I told her I thought she and Luke had been . . . carrying on behind my back.

FERNANDA: Luuuuuuke? But he is soooo old?
ME (sniffy): He's not that old. He did a reverse samba roll in class last week.
FERNANDA: Of course he did. I showed him how.

If Mam were still here, she'd tell me that Fernanda wasn't too old for a sideswipe with a damp tea towel.

Still, I'm loving the samba classes we started as soon as we got back from the dance workshop in Madrid. I'm pretty sure Luke is too. Let's just say, the rhythm seems to have gotten us, good and proper, both on and off the dance floor.

I visited Mam before the book launch. My first time since the funeral. The grave was well-tended with a robust hydrangea gaining ground across it.

Mam loved hydrangeas. So long as the blooms were blue.

Dad used to bury copper pennies in the soil beside the hydrangeas in their garden to make sure the blooms would be blue.

The hydrangea bush on the grave has blue flowers.

ME: I suppose you think you've a great excuse not to be at the book launch.
MAM: . . .

ME: Now who's going to march around the bookshop making sure everybody's bought at least one copy of the book? Well?

MAM: . . .

ME: You could have the decency to send me a sign, at least.

MAM: . . .

I rummaged in my bag for Mam's copy of the book. Propped it against the headstone.

ME: Well, there's your copy. The first one you won't insist on paying for.

MAM: . . .

Rain had been forecast so I had wrapped the book in cellophane. But there wasn't a hint of rain. It was one of those glorious early autumn evenings, the warmth of the day lingering around the edges. The nearby beech trees were still full and green with just a hint of gold and bronze across some of the leaves, giving them a regal air. A blackbird sat on a branch, chirruping away to herself like she was singing a song she'd heard this morning and couldn't get out of her head.

In the distance, a church bell rang.

ME (standing up): That's my cue.

Carol was waiting for me at the gates.

CAROL: You okay?

ME: I wish she was here. She'd be wearing that dress she always wore to my book launches.

CAROL: The royal-blue one she got in Arnotts? With the tiny pearl buttons?

ME: Half price in the January sale.

CAROL: Mammy Doyle loved a bargain.

ME: Yeah.

CAROL: And she loved you.

ME: She did.

We linked arms and walked towards Melissa, waiting in her car to drive us to the launch.

Which went well.

But it's good to be home. The house is quiet and familiar. Luke turned off the lights in the kitchen, I checked the doors were locked and we climbed the stairs.

LUKE: I read your book.

ME: And?

LUKE: I liked it. A lot.

ME: I like you.

LUKE: A lot?

ME: Yeah.

LUKE: You never used to be so soppy.

ME: It's the menopause, I can't help it.

LUKE: I like you too.

ME: Next, you'll be wanting to ravish me on the bathroom floor.

LUKE (worried): Well . . .

ME: Actually no, the tiles are freezing.

LUKE (relieved): And hard on the back too.

Now, there he is in bed, trying to remember exactly how many pinches of nutmeg he puts into his parsley sauce since Anna is trying to persuade him to write down all his recipes so she can sticky-tape them into a book for him. He's wearing a faded Phil Lynott T-shirt and is propped up by pillows, with an ancient pair of Ronnie's thick-rimmed reading glasses perched on his nose.

ME: You should get some sleep. You have to be up in six
    hours. Aidan's butternut squashes aren't going to roast
    themselves.

He looks up and smiles his sudden splurge of a smile.

LUKE: I was waiting for you.
ME: I'll be right there.

Read on for an extract from

Rules of the Road

Also by Ciara Geraghty, and
available to buy now.

1

SIGNAL YOUR INTENT.

I ris Armstrong is missing.

That is to say, she is not where she is supposed to be.

I am trying not to worry. After all, Iris is a grown woman and can take care of herself better than most.

It's true to say that I am a worrier. Ask my girls. Ask my husband. They'll tell you that I'd worry if I had nothing to worry about. Which is, of course, an exaggeration, although I suppose it's true to say that, if I had nothing to worry about, I might feel that I had overlooked something.

Iris is the type of woman who tells you what she intends to do and then goes ahead and does it. Today is her birthday. Her fifty-eighth.

'People see birthdays as an opportunity to tell women they look great for their age,' Iris says when I suggested that we celebrate it.

It's true that Iris looks great for her age. I don't say that. Instead, I say, 'We should celebrate nonetheless.'

'I'll celebrate by doing the swan. Or the downward-facing dog. Something animalistic,' said Iris after she told me about the yoga retreat she had booked herself into.

'But you hate yoga,' I said.

'I thought you'd be delighted. You're always telling me how good yoga is for people with MS.'

My plan today was to visit Dad, then ring the yoga retreat in Wicklow to let them know I'm driving down with a birthday cake for Iris. So they'll know it's her birthday. Iris won't want a fuss of course, but everyone should have cake on their birthday.

But when I arrive at Sunnyside Nursing Home, my father is sitting in the reception area with one of the managers. On the floor beside his chair is his old suitcase, perhaps a little shabby around the edges now but functional all the same.

A week, the manager says. That's how long it will take for the exterminators to do what they need to do, apparently. Vermin, he calls them, by which I presume he means rats, because if it was just mice, he'd say mice, wouldn't he?

My father lives in a rat-infested old folk's home where he colours in between the lines and loses at bingo and sings songs and waits for my mother to come back from the shops soon.

'I can transfer your father to one of our other facilities, if you'd prefer,' the manager offers.

'No, I'll take him,' I say. It's the least I can do. I thought I could look after him myself, at home, like my mother did for years. I thought I could cope. Six months I lasted. Before I had to put him into Sunnyside.

I put Dad's suitcase into the boot beside the birthday cake. I've used blue icing for the sea, grey for the rocks where I've perched an icing-stick figure which is supposed to be Iris, who swims at High Rock every day of the year. Even in November. Even in February. She swims like it's

July. Every day. I think she'll get a kick out of the cake. It took me ages to finish it. Much longer than the recipe book suggested. Brendan says it's because I'm too careful. The cake does not look like it's been made by someone who is too careful. There is a precarious slant to it, as if it's been subjected to adverse weather conditions.

I belt Dad into the passenger seat.

'Where is your mother?' he asks.

'She'll be back from the shops soon,' I say. I've stopped telling him that she's dead. He gets too upset, every time. The grief on his face is so fresh, so vivid, it feels like my grief, all over again, and I have to look away, close my eyes, dig my nails into the fleshy part of my hands.

I get into the car, turn over the engine.

'Signal your intent,' Dad says, in that automatic way he does when he recites the rules of the road. He remembers all of them. There must be some cordoned-off areas in your brain where dementia cannot reach.

I indicate as instructed, then ring the yoga retreat before driving off.

But Iris is not there.

She never arrived.

In fact, according to the receptionist who speaks in the calm tones of someone who practises yoga every day, there is no record of a booking for an Iris Armstrong.

Iris told me not to ring her mobile this week. It would be turned off.

I ring her mobile.

It's turned off.

I drive to Iris's cottage in Feltrim. The curtains are drawn across every window. It looks just the way it should; like the house of a woman who has gone away. I pull into the driveway that used to accommodate her ancient Jaguar. Her sight came back almost immediately after the accident, and the only damage was to the lamp post that Iris crashed into, but her consultant couldn't guarantee that it wouldn't happen again. Iris says she doesn't miss the car, but she asked me if I would hand over the keys to the man who bought it off her. She said she had a meeting she couldn't get out of.

'It's just a car,' she said, 'and the local taxi driver looks like Daniel Craig. And he doesn't talk during sex, and knows every rat run in the city.'

'I'll just be a minute, Dad,' I tell him, opening my car door.

'Take your time, love,' he says. He never used to call me love.

The grass in the front garden has benefitted from a recent mow. I stand at the front door, ring the bell. Nobody answers. I cast about the garden. It's May. The cherry blossom, whose branches last week were swollen with buds, is now a riot of pale pink flowers. The delicacy of their beauty is disarming, but also sad, how soon the petals will be discarded, strewn across the grass in a week or so, like wet and muddy confetti in a church courtyard long after the bride and groom have left.

I rap on the door even though I'm almost positive Iris isn't inside.

Where is she?

I ring the Alzheimer's Society, ask to be put through to Iris's office, but the receptionist tells me what I already know. That Iris is away on a week's holiday.

'Is that you, Terry?' she asks and there is confusion in her voice; she is wondering why I don't already know this.

'Eh, yes Rita, sorry, don't mind me, I forgot.'

Suddenly I am flooded with the notion that Iris is inside the house. She has fallen. That must be it. She has fallen and is unconscious at the foot of the stairs. She might have been there for ages. Days maybe. This worry is a galvanising one. Not all worries fall into this category. Some render me speechless. Or stationary. The wooden door at the entrance to the side passage is locked, so I haul the wheelie bin over, grip the sides of it, and hoist myself onto the lid. People think height is an advantage, but I have never found mine – five feet ten inches, or 1.778 metres, I should say – to be so. Imperial or metric, the fact is I am too tall to be kneeling on the lid of a wheelie bin. I am a myriad of arms and elbows and knees. It's difficult to know where to put everything.

I grip the top of the door, sort of haul myself over the top, graze my knee against the wall, and hesitate, but only for a moment, before lowering myself down as far as I can before letting go, landing in a heap in the side passage. I should be fitter than this. The girls are always on at me to take up this or that. Swimming or running or pilates. *Get you out of the house. Get you doing something.*

The shed in Iris's back garden has been treated to a clear-out; inside, garden tools hang on hooks along one wall, the hose coiled neatly in a corner and the half-empty paint tins – sealed shut with rust years ago – are gone. It's true that I advised her to dispose of them – carefully – given the fire hazard they present. Still, I can't believe that she actually went ahead and did it.

Even the small window on the gable wall of the shed is no longer a mesh of web. Through it, I see a square of pale-blue sky.

The spare key is in an upside-down plant pot in the shed, in spite of my concerns about the danger of lax security about the homestead.

I return to the driveway and check on Dad. He is still there, still in the front passenger seat, singing along to the Frank Sinatra CD I put on for him. *Strangers in the Night.*

I unlock the front door. The house feels empty. There is a stillness.

'Iris?' My voice is loud in the quiet, my breath catching the dust motes, so that they lift and swirl in the dead air.

I walk through the hallway, towards the kitchen. The walls are cluttered with black-and-white photographs in wooden frames. A face in each, mostly elderly. All of them have passed through the Alzheimer's Society and when they do, Iris asks if she can take their photograph.

My father's photograph hangs at the end of the hallway. There is a light in his eyes that might be the sunlight glancing through the front door. A trace of his handsomeness still there across the fine bones of his face framed by the neat helmet of his white hair, thicker then.

He looks happy. No, it's more than that. He looks present.

'Iris?'

The kitchen door moans when I open it. A squirt of WD40 on the hinges would remedy that.

A chemical, lemon smell. If I didn't know any better, I would suspect a cleaning product. The surfaces are clear. Bare. So too is the kitchen table, which is where Iris spreads her books, her piles of paperwork, sometimes the contents of her handbag when she is hunting for something. The table is solid oak. I have eaten here many times, and have rarely seen its surface. It would benefit from a sand and varnish.

In the sitting room, the curtains are drawn and the cushions on the couch look as though they've been plumped, a look which would be unremarkable in my house, but is immediately noticeable in Iris's. Iris loves that couch. She sometimes sleeps on it. I know that because I called in once, early in the morning. She wasn't expecting me. Iris is the only person in the world I would call into without ringing first. She put on the kettle when I arrived. Made a pot of strong coffee. It was the end of Dad's first week in the home.

She said she'd fallen asleep on the couch, when she saw me looking at the blankets and pillows strewn across it. She said she'd fallen asleep watching *The Exorcist*.

But I don't think that's why she slept on the couch. I think it's to do with the stairs. Sometimes I see her, at the Alzheimer's offices, negotiating the stairs with her crutches. The sticks, she calls them. She hates waiting for the lift. And she makes it look easy, climbing the stairs. But it can't be easy, can it?

Besides, who falls asleep watching *The Exorcist*?

'Iris?' I hear an edge of panic in my voice. It's not that anything is wrong exactly. Or out of place.

Except that's it. There's nothing out of place. Everything has been put away.